The Dance

*She found her fire,
and he lost his cool.*

KIMBERLY R. VARGAS

Cover design by Gowtham Thangaraj
Interior design and formatting by Jose Pepito Jr.
Edited by Katharine Bost and Raquel Brown
Proofread by Abby Hale

First Edition: October 2025
ISBN (Paperback): 979-8-9995198-0-1
ISBN (eBook): 979-8-9995198-3-2

For content guidance, please see the Sensitive Content note at the front of this book.

Published by Kimberly R. Vargas
www.kimberlyrvargas.com

Printed in the United States of America
10 9 8 7 6 5 4 3 2 1

To Jaime, my—*la, la, la*—cheerleader.

SENSITIVE CONTENT

Reader comfort matters.

The Dance is a story about healing, rediscovery, and second chances, but it also explores sensitive emotional themes. Please take care as you read.

This novel contains references to the following topics, which may be triggering for some readers:

- Emotional/verbal abuse
- Divorce and infidelity
- Body image and weight loss
- Food guilt and binge eating
- Postpartum isolation
- Death of a parent (x2)
- Non-graphic mention of suicide
- Intrusive negative thoughts and internalized shame

While this is a romance with no on-page sex, it includes emotionally vulnerable scenes, romantic tension, and healing-centered themes.

AUTHOR'S NOTE

Thank you so much for reading *The Dance*. This story is deeply personal to me, born out of my own journey through heartbreak, body image struggles, and rediscovery. Like Laura, I had to learn how to love myself again after a season where I felt invisible, uncertain, and disconnected from who I used to be.

This book isn't just about romance. It's about what happens when someone sees you clearly, honors your healing, and reminds you that you are enough, even before the glow-up.

If you've ever looked in the mirror and felt "not enough," this story was written for you. ♥

With all my heart,
Kimberly R. Vargas

1

One glimpse at all the chiseled torsos and long, sculpted legs as I enter the dance studio, and I know—I'm going to kill Yana. This isn't just a workout class. It's a casting call.

And I showed up with the wrong résumé.

I tug at the bottom of my T-shirt and yank up my sweatpants, wishing I could disappear as I inch through the maze of fitness models splayed across the hardwood floor, gossiping as they stretch.

There might be three guys in the room.

"Laura! Get your fabulous behind over here!" My cousin, Jayana Gardner, waves like she's just spotted Beyoncé in a crowd, but in that canary-yellow sports bra and yoga pants, she's the one stealing the spotlight.

I drop my gym bag and water bottle near the pile of others against the back wall, then shuffle forward. "Why are you up here, front and center?"

"To get the best view, of course." Yana beams, already bent in half, golden-bronze fingers wrapped around her ankles like she's training for the Olympics.

Meanwhile, I can barely reach my knees without something cramping.

"I'm going to the back." I turn, but Yana bolts upright, grabbing my arm.

"Naw, girl! You're supposed to be here with me."

I glance at the tall, slender girls to my left and the short, skinny girls to my right, all of whom look like they're preparing for a photo shoot rather than a ten-a.m. workout class. And I am definitely the biggest in the room. "I'm not staying up front." Not when I'm already sweating just from walking in.

"Okay, okay!" Yana grips my arm tighter. "Second row. How about that?"

I cave, grumbling under my breath, and we take a giant step back. We're starting on basic arm stretches when a skinny blonde in a halter top—with biceps bigger than my son's head—steps in front of us.

"I don't know why I let you convince me to do this," I hiss. "I don't belong here."

The words come out too soft. Like if I say them any louder, they might echo in this room full of people who already know.

"Of course you belong here." Yana side-eyes me like I've lost my mind. "All these folks are just trying to be the best version of themselves."

That's easy for her to say. I bet ninety percent of the women at her monthly theater auditions are rail-thin. And despite eating whatever the hell she wants, my cousin is leaner than a Slim Jim.

"Relax, okay?" She slaps my arm. "Last week, the music was hot, the moves were *fire*, and that Roman, honey. *Mmmph!*"

"Gets my panties wet every time," says a sultry-voiced brunette passing by.

That's right. Roman. My cousin's latest target in her mission to snag a man. It's no wonder she's stunting ruby-red lipstick today. The girl has always been a flirt and rarely struggles to pull her fellow cast members out of the friend zone and into her bed.

But when it comes to a serious relationship, the poor thing gets laughed out of the room. With gigs coming more slowly these days, she's looking to settle down.

"Listen, I'm getting older," says Yana, fluffing her big black curls in the mirror. "I can't keep wasting time with these playboys."

"Isn't that what you've been encouraging me to do all summer?"

"Griffin tied you down for a full decade," she says with a pointed look. "Do you know how many tasty treats you could've sampled by now?"

"That's just the problem," I say. "If I hadn't had so many high-calorie treats, he might've hung around."

Between my husband's pizza chain and escorting my kids to all their classmates' birthday parties, I haven't seen my size ten jeans in several holidays.

"Please," says Yana, "one session with this *foine* guru and Griffin will be the furthest thing from your mind."

After her first attendance last week, Yana insisted on me dropping Eli off at childcare and trying "Roman's Cardio Hip-Hop Class." Besides, my Saturday mornings are free while my daughter is here at the rec for ballet.

I've done maybe a handful of workout videos in the last decade, but with the downward spiral my marriage has taken over the past six months, I know it's time to do something.

Ten years, two children, a 6,600-square-foot home at the center of Bloomfield Hills. We were happy. I know we were. But along the way, something got broken. And I think that something was me.

"Just be your beautiful, *amazing* self." Yana's eyes—the same signature gray as my own—sparkle with assurance. "And don't worry about these chicks. We about to outshine all they flat asses. *Okay?*"

If I had an ounce of the confidence she does, I'd be on tour with J.Lo by now.

A hush falls over the room.

All attention centers on the Nubian god that's just darkened the doorway. A perfectly chiseled work of art with thick lips, a mohawk fade, and intense brown eyes.

That must be Roman.

He hasn't got an ounce of fat on him—just lean muscle. More sculpted than Griffin, and that man works out daily.

Yana grips my shirt tight, and I smack her hand away.

Sure, the guy might be cuter than my first celebrity crush, but I'm not here for that. I suck in my stomach and force my feet apart like it'll make me look more like I belong here. One hour. That's all it is. I can sweat through one hour if it means Griffin might see me again. *Really* see me. Not just the tired mom who let herself go.

Some girls are brave enough to wave. "Hi, Roman," calls our sultry-voiced friend from the back.

With an enticing smirk, he jogs up to the platform at the front of the room, where a towel and giant gallon water bottle await him atop a stool. People drool as he flips back the bottle's cap and begins chugging, his oversized Adam's apple pulsing with every gulp.

"Does he do this every class?" I whisper, struggling not to stare.

Yana gnaws at her thumb as she watches intently. "I certainly hope so."

As the man turns to the mirror and begins stretching, I notice everyone still gawking. "Shouldn't we be stretching, too?"

Yana shrugs. "Eh."

He pulls up one ankle in a smooth quad stretch, checking himself out as his copper biceps tense and release, glistening like he oiled them on purpose.

"Is he... checking himself out right now?"

"Girl." Yana sighs, a hand beneath her chin. "If I looked that good, I would too."

Okay. I get it. He's hot.

But I'm not paying hundreds of my monthly allowance to watch *Magic Mike*. I'm here to dance. I cross my arms with an impatient huff. And to my surprise, *that* draws his attention. I'm honestly shocked he'd notice anyone else in the room.

Finally, concluding his unnecessary stretch, he slips on a headset. "I see we've got a few stragglers who didn't make our first class," he says, pulling up a playlist on the laptop beside him. "Fresh meat."

Students giggle as my cousin elbows me, and I push her off.

OutKast's "The Way You Move" booms through the mounted speakers, and the beat has my shoulders bouncing before I realize it. A soft smile tugs at my lips. I haven't heard this song in years.

"Who's ready to get sexy this morning?" the trainer asks, voice gravelly like a Malibu version of Batman. The room erupts with whoops and claps.

Roman turns to the class, pressing the mic to his lips. "I said, who wants Roman to make 'em *sexy* this morning?"

Everyone screams louder, and I suppress a laugh.

This is going to be annoying as hell.

He throws his arms wide like a gameshow host. *"Let's work!"*

Yana whoops beside me like we just won something.

Finally, the bass calls to my hips, and they answer with a gentle sway. Everyone's body seems to be reacting the same, including Roman's. He pops his chest like he's in a music video and runs a hand up his torso mid-move, lifting his tank just enough to show off that V-cut no one asked for. Giggles ripple through the front row as Roman's lips twitch in satisfaction. It's no wonder these people are sweating him so hard. They think he's God's gift and apparently, he knows it.

He plants his feet and beckons us to move with him. "Soak up that rhythm, y'all. Let it flow through your veins. Feel it *deep down* in your soul." He winks at someone in the mirror. "You can do it. Put your back into it."

A chorus of anxious chuckles rises behind me.

It's been ages since I've been around this kind of collective energy. My heart twists as I recall the day I packed away my dance shoes. But like Griffin said, *"Sometimes we've gotta make sacrifices."*

After some basic warm-ups—and Yana craning her neck during a lengthy stretch for a better view of Roman's ass—we're moving into the first combination.

"Fix your eyes on Roman," he says, "and see if you can keep up." And for just a second, his gaze rests on my reflection.

Is that a challenge?

Roman steps in and out, marking each movement as I count along in my head. Seems simple enough.

"Alright, y'all! *Let's work!*"

Sneakers squeak and feet stomp as the music seems to swell. With a breath, I force my legs to keep in time, and somehow, I make it through. Others laugh off their mistakes. I'm too focused on surviving the next eight counts.

We've only done the combination a few times before Roman stops, a shout exploding from his corded throat. *"Whoo!* That's what I'm talking 'bout! We getting *sexy* today!"

I'm going to need some aspirin by the end of this workout, and I doubt it'll be for my muscles.

My curls are already clinging to my forehead, and I can feel my sports bra riding up. But I'm still in it.

As the music switches to Biggie Smalls' "Hypnotize," Roman adds to his combinations, one by one. *Arms up, legs out, swing left and right.* Everyone freezes, mesmerized as the man flawlessly executes every move. Even my eyes get locked on the sway of his ass. It's no wonder the man was hired for this job—his body alone is motivation.

After a few run-throughs, we've built a decent hip-hop routine. I'm winded, and sweat is beading at my brow. It's been ten minutes. My lungs say forty. My thighs say betrayal.

I know it's been a while, and I've gained a good fifty pounds, but I didn't think I was *that* out of shape.

It isn't long before folks are stopping for water breaks, including Yana. But despite my racing pulse and the hot breaths searing my lungs, I don't want to miss a beat. I'm not going to quit on my family. I'm not going to quit on my husband. Besides, it's been forever since I had so much fun.

I avert my gaze from the warped version of myself huffing and puffing in the mirror and focus on Roman instead. Sure, I've received comments on the gleam of my gray eyes or the clear complexion of my caramel skin, but my chubby cheeks and frazzled dark hair certainly aren't doing me any favors. If it weren't for my little girl or my cousin's insistence that this would help me reach my goal, I never would've left the house today.

Look at you.

A raspy laugh echoes in the back of my mind.

You seriously think someone could love that ugly face?

I swallow, trying to block it out. I have to keep going. For Griffin. Griffin would never speak to me that way.

It's impossible to shake the memory of how pathetic I must've looked, falling on my knees as he packed his final bag. Clutching his hand in both of mine, I begged. Pleaded.

"Griffin, please don't go. I can change."

Weeks before, he'd sat me down and calmly explained that we needed to separate. We'd already shared the sad news with the kids.

But I didn't find the will to fight until he was ready to walk out the door.

I needed him. Who else was going to love me?

"Laura, don't do this." He'd pulled from my grasp with tears in his eyes, gathering what was left of his things. *"This isn't healthy anymore. It's toxic."*

He's too much of a sweetheart to say it outright, but I know exactly what he meant. *I'm* not healthy anymore. *I'm* toxic. I use his words to fuel me.

As we wrap up another routine, returning to an upbeat march, Roman's watching me. I don't think he expected me to keep up. But he doesn't know me at all.

Roman turns his attention to the rest of the class. "We're on fire today, fam! Ain't that right?"

Some of the students clap, others catcall.

Yana jogs back to our row with a huff. "Girl, how the hell are you dancing so fast?"

This morning's Cinnamon Dolce Latte may have helped. Besides, I'm not going to let anyone tell me I can't do this. Certainly not this guy.

"Y'all ready to kick it up a notch?" he asks. Folks move back to the floor, hollering in excitement as Usher's "Yeah!" begins to play. "I need you to give it to me," says Roman. "And I need you to give it to me *good.* Can you do that?"

More people scream as Yana calls out, "Yes, baby!"

The enchanting grin that inches up Roman's chestnut-brown face is enough to make a woman take off her top. "Alright, sweetheart. Let's go!"

He introduces a tougher routine for the next round: funky arms, knee bends, a crisscross jump, and spin. I freeze, looking to Yana as my mouth falls open, and she tosses back an apologetic shrug.

I'm forced to return to marching as I study the routine again. It's something straight out of an award-winning music video. The guy might have an ego the size of Russia, but he can dance. *For real*, for real. And people are already catching on.

"Now, if it's too much, if you wanna *quit*," says Roman, his electric eyes linking with mine in the mirror, "there's a nice walk aerobics class next door."

A few students groan and chuckle. But a fire flares in my belly.

As if waiting for me to give up, Roman holds my gaze. But he has no idea who he's dealing with.

He blinks first. "Okay. Don't say I didn't warn you."

He walks us through the combinations, and I mirror each twist, bend, and jump. But when we reach the spin, I stumble.

"Some of you got it. Others? Not so much." His stupid smirk grates on my bones as he starts us over again.

My feet are throbbing, and my breaths are shallow, but I inhale through my nose and out through my mouth, the way I learned decades ago. When we get to the spin, I modify it. I'm not going to kill myself trying to keep up with him.

"Uh-oh!" yells Roman. "Looks like somebody's getting tired!"

What?

Yana throws her hands on her knees with a puff of air. "Girl, that's me. I'm out."

I stare at my cousin as she waves and heads to the back. All around me, girls are dabbing sweat from their brows, panting like overheated puppies.

Up front, Roman nods at me and mouths, *"Need a break?"*

Just because I skipped his stupid spin? What an idiot.

Another moment passes before he shrugs. "Okay. I want you to give it all you got. We're gonna do the full routine again… Three. More. Times." Roman throws out his hands, somehow baffled as students whimper and head to the back. "Y'all gonna leave me hanging?" he asks.

They apologize as they collapse along the wall.

But I've gotta show Griffin I can do this. I can push through, no matter how hard it gets.

"That's alright." Roman nods at the quitters with pursed lips. "We gonna see who the *true* soldiers are today. Y'all ready?"

"Yeah!" I cheer with the remaining handful of girls.

Roman raises a hand to his ear. "I said, *are y'all ready to work?*"

At the top of my lungs, I shout, *"Yeah!"*

Roman nods at that. *"Let's work!"*

As we launch into the routine once more, I do my absolute best, stepping in sync, bending low, jumping with all my might. But when the turn catches me off guard, and I miss, that sly grin creeps to Roman's lips. He won this round. But the man isn't satisfied.

His palms slap together like gunfire. "Again!"

You can do this, Laura.

You've done it before. You can do it now.

I push harder as we continue: heart thrumming, adrenaline racing, muscles aching. The memory of my kids' tear-streaked faces and nights alone in bed flash through my mind.

Come on. Keep going!

One girl drops out, then another. Despite my short breaths, I feel I could dance circles around them all day. *Speaking of circles...* When the spin arrives, I'm a little late, but I get it. I can't help smiling to myself. I can't believe how much I've missed this.

Roman relents with a nod. "That was decent. But I know it wasn't your best." Without allowing for the slightest breather, he shouts, "Again!"

Summoning every ounce of energy, I push myself. And this time, as an exhilarating rush surges through me from head to toe, I nail it. Spin and all!

"*Whoo!*" Roman's shout echoes through the speakers as my heart threatens to explode.

Only a few girls kept up. And I was one of them.

I look to Roman, waiting for that jaw drop. But he's too busy admiring his own reflection, rolling his hips like the stage is his bedroom.

Of course he didn't notice. I don't know why I thought he would.

Roman calls everyone back to the floor to cool down, and despite my pounding heart, the sweat trickling down my neck, and the jerk at the front of the room, I feel better. A *lot* better.

"Girl!" Yana smacks my shoulder. "I told you this was your thing. That was *amazing.*"

Yeah. Just not amazing enough.

2

*W*e haven't taken two steps into the hallway of the rec when Yana declares, "I'm out."

I freeze in the path of sunlight streaming through floor-to-ceiling windows while crowds of gym members mill around me. "What do you mean you're 'out'?"

"The ladies were telling me Roman's got some ridiculous non-fraternization policy in place. Won't even consider dating one of his clients." My cousin lifts a noncommittal shoulder as she digs into her bag. "Them chicks might have time to waste, but I don't."

"So that's it?" I fall in step beside her as she tosses a foiled candy wrapper into a nearby trash can. "Yana, I joined the class for you."

"And I joined the class for *him*." She whips out a Snickers bar and starts munching. "But *you*..." She waves the candy bar my way as she swallows. "...*you* have to stay."

By myself?

"Yana, I don't know—"

"Girl, you *killed it* today. Do you know how long I been waiting to see you dance again?"

The ache rises, thick and bitter. I swallow hard. "I'll think about it."

But after the hell that man put me through today, I honestly don't know.

Passing the clanking weight machines and whirring treadmills of the main gym, we make our way up the hall. The childcare center is packed with rambunctious climbers and wobbly toddlers alike. Of course, my son, Elijah, isn't playing with any of them. He's parked by the bay window, holding up one of his playing cards to a couple staff members.

"Is... this your card?"

The man and woman exchange a glance before slowly shaking their heads.

Eli pulls another. "Is *this* your card?"

Nervous smiles appear on their faces as they wag their heads again.

Everywhere we go, it's the same routine. He's been obsessed with performing magic tricks since his father brought in a magician on his fifth birthday. Swears he's the next David Copperfield. He strolls around in his little argyle vests and suit jackets, claiming his style is *essential to his brand* or whatever. I blame his dad.

Throwing a dramatic hand on her hip, Yana calls, "Is that my little Eli working on his birthday?"

"Yana!" My son scrambles across the room and into my cousin's arms. She lifts him with a laugh, fingers brushing his curls. Despite the two front teeth missing, he's beaming. "Did you bring snacks?"

"*Eli.*" I frown, but he blinks at me innocently, his sparkling brown eyes magnified behind full-rim glasses. The only thing the little boy loves more than magic tricks is food.

Yana tosses me a sly grin as she sets him down and digs into her tote. She promptly passes him a bag of cheese puffs, and he digs in.

I shoot my cousin a look. "That's the only reason he likes you."

"Then I must be doing something right." Yana grabs Eli by the hand, and we thank the childcare workers as we leave. "I can't believe you're six, boy! Where does the time go?"

My stomach knots thinking of the last five years, and once again, I'm grateful to have finally reconnected with my cousin. She's only one of the many things I let go of in hopes of saving my marriage. Thank God she was willing to forgive me this past summer.

My daughter Madison's ballet class is held on the opposite end of the rec, just beyond the basketball court and not too far from the pool. She's been dancing for three years now, but this is her first at the Perry Recreational Center. Griffin and I originally had her in a program much closer to our house—a dance school where she could learn the finest techniques of the Cecchetti method and a little tap. But so far, the girl only seems to care for ballet. Joining this more informal program in Southfield was Yana's idea. The owner, Alyssa Hall—one of the handful of dancers of color to tour with the New York City Ballet—launched the studio, hoping to provide a more diverse experience for the kids back home.

Among other parents and restless siblings, we look on through expansive glass windows as my little girl gracefully bends in the perfect third position plié, then stretches high on her toes. Back straight, chin up, neck stretched tall like a swan. She reminds me so much of my little sister at this age, though I doubt April stuck with dancing nearly as long.

Yana softly shakes her curls as we watch Maddie practice pirouettes with her classmates. "She's just like you," she whispers.

Goodness. I hope not. She deserves better than that.

Even after class has ended, Maddie carries herself like a ballerina, shoulders back, head high, gentle and elegant. Her black leotard and tights are still crisp. Not a single brown hair has strayed from her bun. "Hi, Mom. Hi, Cousin Yana." Tiny diamond studs glisten from her caramel-brown earlobes. The girl's only nine, but I swear she's nearing twenty-two.

Yana wraps Maddie in a hug, swaying gently like she hasn't seen her in years. She's the auntie my daughter never had.

"Maddie, girl!" Yana snaps her fingers over her head. "You were incredible, *okay*? Now, tell me all about it." They turn for the door, leaving me and Eli behind.

"*Look at them calves,*" Yana would say when Maddie was still in diapers. "*She's gonna be just like you. I can feel it!*" Guess this has been just as much Yana's dream as it was mine.

My uncle enrolled Yana in acting classes by the time she was eight, shortly after our parents took us to see *Disney on Ice*. She's been in local productions of *Rent* and *Little Shop of Horrors* and even played an extra in one of Tyler Perry's early plays. In her spare time, she offers virtual coaching sessions for aspiring young actors. I, on the other hand, have devoted the past decade to being a loyal mother and wife, and all I have to show for it is an empty bed and a broken heart.

It seems Yana and Maddie have completely forgotten about Eli and me until we reach my Lincoln in the parking lot.

"So, what's the plan?" asks Yana. "We getting pizza and cake for Eli's birthday? I could grab the balloons when I..."

My throat goes dry as Yana continues. Plans were made weeks ago. I just... didn't tell her.

"Anything but that nasty Blue J's pizza," she says. "The last time I had that, I must've been on the toilet for—"

"Actually... we've got plans," I say.

Yana pauses midsentence, looking at each of us pointedly. "Oh. And what kind of plans are those?"

Maddie taps her elbows, shifting her gaze, as Eli presses his hands into the pockets of his jeans like his dad.

Things were never the best between Yana and Griffin, and matters were only made worse when I took her around his family. It was the beginning of the end. For all of us.

"Griffin's mom is sorta having a thing for Eli this afternoon," I say quickly.

"A *thing?*" Yana's lip curls in disgust. "You mean like a party?"

None of us answer.

And Yana's eyes go full fire and brimstone.

⁘

A lengthy line of luxury cars winds up Daphne's driveway to the top of a hill, where her mansion overlooks the upscale neighborhood, awaiting our arrival. I'm already perspiring by the time we make the hike beyond the manicured grounds and lush trees to her house.

"Phew!" Yana blows a couple curls out of her eyes as she reaches the top of the palatial staircase and leans against a thick pillar. "This food better be bomb. I wasn't trying to get in a second workout today."

Maddie giggles as Eli tosses a penny into a nearby marble fountain. They've always loved this place.

"No red carpet, huh?" says Yana. "It's been a minute since I dropped by, so I forgot to bring my tiara."

Sighing through my nose, I brush a few dark hairs from my face. "Just be cool, okay?"

"Wha—?" Yana stands up straight. "When am I not cool? If it weren't for me, this party would be lame as h—"

"*Shh!*" hisses Maddie, covering Eli's ears. Yana purses her lips as I ring the doorbell.

Of course my cousin insisted on coming along once she realized she hadn't been invited. I wanted to look my absolute best for Griffin this afternoon, so I agreed to have her join us, as long as she did my makeup and put a few curls in my hair. Yana still doesn't love the idea of me chasing after the man who left me, but she knows I love him, and she wants me to be happy, so she agreed.

I'm stunned into silence when Daphne opens the door. I'm sure there are a dozen staff members who would've been more than happy to do the job.

"Laura, dear." The retired Dominican beauty queen with chestnut-brown hair and the figure of a twenty-year-old pulls me in for a hug, pressing a kiss to both of my cheeks. She and Griffin's dad—the handsome black founder and former CEO of Blue J's Pizza—made three of the most beautiful children Michigan has ever seen. Griffin's strong jaw and wavy hair captivated me from day one.

"It's been *so* long." Daphne steps forward, all warmth and high cheekbones. But her smile glitches when she peeps the stiletto boots and minidress—Yana's go-to uniform when she's not trying to impress anyone's momma.

I try to find the words to explain my cousin's last-minute attendance, but Daphne's attention turns to the children before I can. "Oh, my little *princesa*." She kisses Maddie's forehead. "And my handsome *nieto*. If only your *abuelo* could see you now. You're getting so big!" Pressing a kiss to both of Eli's chubby cheeks, she spots his little blazer and hugs him tight.

Griffin's dad may have passed four years ago, but truthfully, as the descendant of a long line of politicians, Daphne's always been queen of this castle. Being from a family of high-class attorneys, Griffin's dad was plenty comfortable with luxurious living himself. Hence, the cobblestone path and Victorian lampposts. Even with six bedrooms and a walkout lower level, my home couldn't hold a candle to this palace.

Quickly, Daphne ushers the kids inside, leaving Yana and me to follow.

"You see how she acted like I wasn't even here, right?"

"Yana, don't start," I whisper.

Servers weave between clusters of unfamiliar parents and over-dressed toddlers, delivering every hors d'oeuvre imaginable beneath a massive diamond chandelier—red, silver, and black balloons tethered to the sweeping staircase overhead. The aroma of sizzling garlic shrimp, spicy empanadas, and, of course, Blue J's Pizza hovers in the air while a mix of top reggaeton beats provides a decent soundtrack throughout the mansion. I used to be so impressed by all this. I'm not even sure where my children have been spirited off to.

Bianca and Gabriela, Griffin's younger, golden-skinned sisters, spot us before we spot them. Champagne glasses in hand, they drift our way in their form-fitting designer dresses—Bianca in pink, Gabriela in blue—as we set our gifts aside.

Breezing past Yana, Bianca is the first to greet me, pressing a kiss to my cheek. Her engagement ring from her fiancé—a former city council president and a mayoral candidate—could put the three carats I still wear to shame. "So glad you could make it," she says.

Gabriela—the older one—leans in next, the ringlets of her slick ponytail brushing my ear. But like their mother, she sails right past Yana without so much as a glance.

"You look good," says Gabriela, giving my simple black dress a once-over.

The girl is two years younger than me, and my heart still leaps at the compliment. But I've only lost seven pounds. "Thanks. And you... always look amazing."

Gabriela and her husband—recent MVP for the Detroit Lions—just had their first child last year, but looking at her hourglass figure, you'd never know it.

I'm sure I must look like a pig in lipstick to them.

Gabriela tosses a hand to her chest, releasing a bubbly chuckle that would rival the classiest princess. "You're too kind." She turns toward her sister, eyes bright. "Bee! Do you remember how adorable Laura was when we first met her?"

"I know, right? She was smaller than me," Bianca adds. "You were carrying Madison by then, weren't you?"

Of course I was. Not that it's something I'd like to brag about around all these strangers.

"But a little meat looks good on you," says Gabriela.

"So good," adds Bianca.

Heat creeps up my neck as they press another kiss to my cheek and invite us to make ourselves at home before gliding off to other guests, leaving Yana scowling like a pissed-off poodle.

"Maybe you shouldn't have come," I whisper.

"I'm not the only one," she says. "Now, where's the champagne?"

Pointing in the direction of the table of towering glasses, I head for the kitchen. I need a breather before someone rich and nosy pops by and starts questioning where I've been.

Adults chat in the downstairs living room while Eli and Maddie join a massive group of children in the sunroom for a magic show. Of course there's a professional magician. I don't know why I thought Daphne would spare any expense. She's been this way since my first visit—back when they side-eyed my Nike tee and twenty-dollar watch during a five-course dinner on fine bone china.

Griffin's family never thought I was right for him. I could see it in their eyes from the beginning. His father called him an idiot for knocking up someone like me before marriage. His mother cried.

But determined to make things right, Griffin insisted on us going to a justice of the peace the next morning. We'd been together less than three months. With a little groveling and his usual charm, Griffin managed to get back into his family's good graces by the time Maddie was born. And despite his dad cutting us off financially, his family learned to tolerate having me around. Not that it didn't take effort on my part—regular trips to the salon, manicures every week. But considering my less-than-ideal upbringing in Detroit, it seemed I came from the wrong stock. Like a puzzle piece that didn't quite fit.

You're a waste of space.

Pushing open the door, I enter the massive industrial-style kitchen with its oversized appliances and polished white floors. Both of our home kitchens are plenty spacious as well, but this house dwarfs anything we own—or, I guess that *I* own. Nothing's official yet.

Where is Griffin anyway? I wouldn't have worn heels if I didn't think he'd be here.

A gorgeous, six-layer birthday cake stands tall in the breakfast nook. It's expertly frosted, adorned with glitter and game cards, a magician's top hat at its peak. It's more incredible than anything I could give Eli, especially now. And I bet it's his favorite at the center: *chocolate.*

No one would notice if I stole a taste. With the briefest glance over my shoulder, I swipe a bit of icing. *Mmmm. Buttercream.*

One of my favorite Shakira songs comes on, and my hips begin to sway as the sweet cream coats my tongue. But the kitchen door creaks behind me.

I turn to find my husband Griffin watching, a soft smile on his lips that he quickly tucks away. "Hey, Laura."

"Hey." My breath stutters as he moves right past me to the fridge and pulls out two bottles of water. The man rarely greets me with a hug anymore.

He's grown out his beard over the past few months, and it suits his sun-kissed bronze complexion, but he still keeps his wavy hair low. It's been two weeks since we've seen each other, and he still makes my heart flutter just as much as the day we met in my college dorm—when I was paying him for a pizza delivery, and he said, *"You have the most gorgeous eyes."*

I dab my mouth for any remnants of frosting. "How's it going?"

He nods as he turns back to me, biceps flexing under his button-down. "It's going. You?" There's a familiar crease in his brow, the kind he has whenever he's stressed.

Could it be work? Or something else?

At the heaviness of his gaze, I drop my head with a bitter laugh. "Honestly? Been better."

He responds with a soft chuckle of his own and steps closer. "No kidding."

Searching his tired brown eyes, I find myself wondering if he feels just as lost as me. "Can you believe our baby is six?"

"I cannot," he says, scratching at his scruffy face. "I think I got my first gray hair this week."

"You're joking."

He tilts back his head to show me his chin, and I gasp. "Wow. I guess running Blue J's is wearing you down."

"You have no idea," he says.

With all the drama between him and his dad, nobody expected Griffin to inherit the whole pizza empire. Not after all those years he spent clawing his way up from the bottom—like he didn't have the same last name as the CEO. But he was the firstborn. The namesake. And I guess, in a family like his, that's what matters most. He's only thirty-three.

I take the opportunity to inhale the familiar spicy scent of his cologne, memorize the sharp angles of his face, and stare into the same warm eyes that gazed at me all those years ago, the first time he whispered, *"I love you."*

I wish I didn't read into his pause. But I do.

It aches to miss him this much.

Clearing his throat, Griffin takes a small step back. The simplest reminder of his choice to move on. He glances toward the door as if trying to decide whether to head back out to the party or not. "How have the kids been? Any problems?"

"They're fine." Then with a small shrug, I add, "Maddie started a new ballet school today."

His brow lifts slightly. "A *new* one?"

"Mmhmm. In Southfield."

He frowns. "That's like half an hour from the house, ain't it?"

"Yeah, but there's a little more... diversity there."

He nods, but it's distant. Like the conversation's already over.

Maybe that's what makes me reach for him. But he goes still.

His gaze drops to where my hand rests on his arm, like he's deciding whether to shake it off. When he finally looks at me, it's not the way he used to. I know I shouldn't. But I've gotta do something. Nothing makes sense without him.

"Griffin, we need to talk."

He doesn't answer right away. Just watches me like I'm the one who broke this.

But I can fix it. I can fix *us.*

Mercifully, with a lengthy sigh, he bobs his head. "Yeah, I guess we should—"

The kitchen door swings open, and I draw back my hand.

"Girl, why is this house so *hot?*"

Griffin clocks Yana over his shoulder, fanning herself like she's allergic to the heat.

And just like that, the warmth leaves his face.

"*Hey*, Griffin. Long time, no see." Yana grins extra wide just to piss him off.

The last time the two were within ten feet of each other was five years ago on the Fourth of July. Griffin's parents were having a pool party at this very house, and against his wishes, I'd brought my cousin along. Things were going okay until Yana started accusing his family of fawning all over the kids while disregarding me. She went off on Griffin for doing nothing about it—right in front of everybody, full-out Detroit-style. Griffin told me he'd never been more humiliated in his life. *She shouldn't be around our kids.*

So, I kept my distance and stopped returning her calls. And before long, Yana put two and two together. Griffin didn't insist that I do it, but I felt it was for the best. Besides, I'd already distanced myself from most of my old high school and college friends. What was one more? My mom did the same for her marriage. Though I suppose it didn't work out for her, either.

Now Griffin's holding my cousin to a staring contest.

"You picking up strays now, Laura?"

Yana throws back her head with a hearty laugh. "That's funny! 'Cause I remember saying the exact same about you." She tosses back what's left of her champagne and slams the glass on the counter like it owes her money.

Griffin is simmering as he turns back to me. And my stomach flips so fast I nearly choke on air.

"Listen, I'm sorry."

"Girl, don't apologize to him!"

"Hey, why don't you mind your own damn business?" shouts Griffin, staring at my cousin with steely eyes.

"I'm sorry, what was that?" Yana cups a hand around her ear. "Oh, that's right, I don't speak *stupid*—"

"Yana!" I throw up my hands, looking at the two of them. "Griffin, she's just here to celebrate Eli's life, just like the rest of us. Can both of you please get along for one day? Or better yet, just... separate."

"Yeah, we know he's good at doing that," mutters Yana. Thankfully, she heads out.

I don't know why I saw this playing out differently.

Griffin's jaw remains tense as we're left alone. "I thought y'all weren't talking anymore."

"We weren't. But with everything going on... I kinda needed a friend, ya know?"

The two of us fall silent as he glowers toward the door, my window quickly closing.

"Listen, like I was saying—"

"Yeah. We need to talk," he says. But the kitchen door swings open again.

A couple of boisterous Pomeranians scramble inside on rhinestone leashes—one sniffing the floor, the other incessantly barking—as their owner struts in behind them in four-inch designer pumps. "Griffin, honey, I thought you said you'd get water—" She pauses at the sight of me.

Full lips and almond-shaped eyes, voluminous black hair cascading across her cocoa-brown shoulders. I've seen this woman before. It's *Michigan's favorite weather girl:* Vicki Washington. She's frozen as I blink at my husband and back at her.

Griffin speaks first. "Laura, you remember Vicki. From the news."

Vicki. From the news. Griffin had a promo segment with her sometime last year. They flirted like it was scripted—right there on live TV—and the orders flooded in.

He told me not to read into it, but... We're not even divorced.

Vicki replaces her wide-eyed stare with a frigid smile. "So, you're Laura." She gives me the briefest once-over, a not-so-subtle evaluation I've grown accustomed to among Griffin's family. "What a pleasant surprise," she says. As if I wasn't invited to my own son's birthday party. Neither of us makes a move to shake hands.

"And this is Penelope," Griffin says, pointing at the one sniffing around the fridge. "And the one that never shuts up is Piper."

My husband meets the mutt's growl with the same grin he gave Eli for babbling *"Dada."*

I think I'm going to be sick.

Vicki grips her leashes tight as the Pomeranians attempt to tug her in opposite directions, her perfectly sculpted legs extending from her halter dress like smooth tree branches. "Eli looks adorable in his little blazer."

She says my son's name as if she's met him before. I look to my husband for an answer, but he won't meet my gaze.

The silence turns suffocating, as it seems neither of us knows whether to stay or go.

Penelope barks, forcing us to decide.

"Griffin, the girls are incredibly thirsty," says Vicki.

The girls? As if she carried the furry balls of energy in her womb for nine months.

Griffin passes her the bottles with the briefest glimpse my way. "I'll call you," he says.

They walk out like a perfect little postcard. Not even a glance back.

And I'm right back where I started.

Forgotten.

"Girl, forget his ass."

Yana pops the final bite of shish kabob in her mouth as we stand on the sprawling lawn. Across the yard, Griffin and Vicki look on as Eli and Maddie take photos with various friends and extended family members.

"At least the kids look happy." I keep my eyes on them, not on him. It's easier that way.

"I say we torch the place and stomp out of here, *Waiting-to-Exhale*-style," says Yana.

"First of all, arson. Secondly, what about the kids?"

Yana squints at me like I've lost what's left of my mind. "We'd take Maddie and Eli with us, of course. What do you think I am? Some kind of lunatic?"

"And the other kids?"

She tilts her head side to side as Griffin squeezes between his sisters for a photo with Eli. He smiles bigger for strangers than he ever did for me. His mother's boisterous laugh echoes across the yard as Bianca playfully swats his arm. A little ways away, Vicki presses a hand to her chest with an affectionate giggle.

"I've got a mind to go wipe that smile off his little side chick's face right now," Yana says, but I yank her back by her belt.

"He never said they were a thing. Maybe she's just a friend." And maybe she's the type of friend who calls everyone *honey*. The cashier at my favorite grocery store does the same.

As I twist my wedding band, Yana turns her venomous glare on me. "Please. A kid with his finger up his nose could've connected the dots. That man knew what he was doing bringing that tramp around you."

"Actually, based on their response, I'm not sure either of them expected to run into me. Maybe the family figured I'd just drop the kids and go."

Yana jerks her head so hard I think she pulled something. "Oh, hell naw!"

She takes a step toward them, but I catch her arm just in time.

"Relax," I mutter.

She whirls around like I just said something wild.

"If your momma and April were still around, they'd never ice him out like this."

"Even if they'd met him, it still wouldn't have bought us a seat at the table."

She shoots me a look, lips pursed.

"The point is, the way these people treated you today ain't any different from how they treated you all them years ago. Now, I know you've been through... a lot. But you still deserve to be around people who see your light."

I wave her off, maintaining the grin I've mastered over the years. "Everything's fine."

"Then tell me why they're inviting his *little friend* into the photo-shoot and not you?"

My heart plummets as Vicki struts over, her designer dogs trotting behind like backup dancers, and claims the spot beside my husband like it's hers by right.

A woman like that would be the perfect plus one to his red-carpet events. A woman like that looks flawless in any photo. With a woman like that by his side, Griffin stands a little taller, smiles a little wider.

And if I don't do something fast, any space that was held for me could be erased forever.

3

*E*ven with Yana out, Roman's cardio hip-hop class is more packed than last Saturday. Of course it is. Because today, I'm alone. No backup. No buffer.

With the spot Yana and I had last week being filled by a couple of girls in matching side-striped tracksuits and the back row overflowing with gym bag handles bound to twist an ankle or two, I head up front.

If I want my family whole again, I need to become a woman my husband can be proud of. Even if it means putting up with a talented jerk once in a while.

Roman struts into class in a loose tank, a fresh towel draped over his shoulder to catch every smug drop of sweat. A soft smirk spreads across his lips when he sees me.

Is my being here really that offensive to him?

After another dramatic hydration and warm-up of his own, Roman finally straps on his headset. "I see that some of you are gluttons for punishment."

Oh. It is on.

The speakers thump with Nelly's "Hot in Herre," and Roman launches straight into it—barely a warm-up before the twists, squats, and turns come flying at us.

It's chaos, sweat, and rhythm. And I'm eating it up. It hurts, but it's wild. Who knew I could still love this?

Every count brings Griffin's smile back to me. His touch, his warmth, his promises. And with every pulse, I dig a little deeper, thighs turning to jelly as my skin flushes hot.

"That's right! Give Roman all you got," the trainer shouts.

Just stop, whispers the raspy voice I can't seem to shake. *You're nothing but a joke.*

Despite my burning feet and aching back, I push on, a hypnotic rhythm pulsing through my bones with every breath.

I'm going to do this. I *have* to do this.

Because right now? I'm too much. Too heavy. Too loud when I laugh. Too quiet when I cry. But if I can just… fix myself, maybe that'll be enough. Maybe he'll finally want me again.

We wrap up another routine, returning to a march, and a surge of joy flows through my body. It might not be easy, but I'm doing it.

One of the girls nearby tosses me a high-five, and—*man,* it hits something in me I thought was gone. It reminds me of when I was twelve, making up routines with my friends after school, trying to copy the moves we saw on *106 & Park*. Back when moving my body felt like magic. And now that I've found it, I don't want to let it go.

"I got one more tough one for y'all," Roman calls out, his voice laced with challenge as the beat shifts. "Not gonna lie, it's a beast. Might be fun… if you can hang."

He waits, letting the music do the talking, then shrugs like it's no sweat off his back.

"If not? No shame in tapping out now." His gaze locks with mine in a dare.

My lips curve in a silent invitation. *Bless his heart. He still thinks I'll fold.*

At first, it looks simple enough—some swaying, a slow roll of the arms, almost a Caribbean vibe. But then his feet launch into overdrive: crisscrossing, twisting, gliding across the floor like he's got four legs instead of two.

Wow. I knew he was good, but not *that* good. His knees go one way while his arms go another. He ends it with this complicated jump, twisting his body in the air and falling to his knees in a B-Boy pose. *Whoa.*

"Oh, hell naw," somebody mutters. Others are laughing, too.

"And that's why I call it 'The Suicide,'" says Roman, hopping to his feet with a cocky grin.

Why is this guy trying to make my life hell? I'm just trying to have fun and lose weight.

"Like I said, keep up with Roman…" He zeroes in on me, his sexy voice rumbling with provocation. "If you can."

A fire sparks within me as I nod. *Challenge accepted.*

He breaks it down, slower this time, making it easier to keep up. My feet follow his lead.

Left. Right. Left. Right.

It's clicking now. When he demos the jump again, I pause to watch. But this time? I think I've got it.

"Alright." He rakes his gaze over me in the mirror, and adrenaline kicks like a drumbeat in my chest. "Show me what you got. And five, six, seven—*let's work!*"

From the jump, I'm hitting every beat, shadowing Roman step for step.

Front, back, out, in.

The tempo picks up, and I match it stride for stride. But Roman stops short of the jump.

Groans ripple through the crowd as arms fly up in protest.

He chuckles, shaking his head. "Naw, y'all ain't ready for that. Let's get these feet right. Again!"

And just like Roman commands, we hit it again... and again— feet pounding in unison, energy ricocheting off the mirrored walls. The bass of Sean Paul's "Temperature" pulses through the floor, through our chests, driving us faster, deeper into the rhythm.

Roman's a greedy boy. People are starting to back out. Some have already left. But I promised myself I'd stick with it, and I am. Each round, I'm getting a little sharper, a little quicker. And for the first time in forever, I don't want to stop. I honestly think I could do this all day.

Despite the class size gradually dwindling, Roman doesn't seem to care. It's like he's in a trance, letting the music take control. It's captivating. And I envy it.

As we take it from the top, I shut the doors of my mind to everything else: my thoughts about Griffin, what others might think, even concerns for my kids. I just let loose, going for the ride.

I'm weightless. Untouchable. A silent shadow following Roman's every twist and turn. With each step, the beat pounds through me, the melody lifting me higher, until I'm soaring.

Oh! It's been so long.

And this time, when Roman goes for the jump, so do I. I fall to my knees with him.

The room erupts in applause, yanking me back to earth. Everyone's clapping and nodding... at me.

I figured all of us were going for it, but apparently, I was alone in that assumption. Tucking a loose strand of hair behind my ear, I stand. But Roman doesn't flinch. No reaction or praise. Just that same arched brow and a stare I can't quite place.

"Good work today, fam," he says, voice flat and distant. Without another glance, he strips off his headset and steps down, heading straight for one of the instructors at the door.

That's it? No wink? No air kiss?

Somebody's got his gym shorts in a bunch. With a huff, I head back for some water.

"Girl, you did your thang, honey," says a chick with a curly ponytail.

I thank her as she passes, still feeling a little thrown. It's too bad Yana dropped the class. She would've been hyping me up right now, telling me I crushed it... reminding me I'm not invisible.

Who cares if the trainer's an idiot? Today was so much fun.

Then Roman jogs back up to the platform and retrieves his headset. "Ladies and gents, I've got great news. Pilates is being held up the hall today. So, anyone who wants to head out can go ahead. And anyone who thinks they can keep up with Roman"—he looks directly at me—"can stay."

Now who's a glutton for punishment?

I glance up at the clock. I've got some time to kill.

Most of the class apologizes as they head out, but a handful of girls stay behind, prepared to go to battle.

A remix of Junior Senior's "Move Your Feet" thumps through the speakers. I lock in, hitting every beat as we dive back into Roman's Suicide routine. Just like before, I'm right there with him, moving like the rhythm was made for me.

Can't stop. Won't stop.

I have to prove I can do this. To Griffin, to this instructor, to myself. No more quitting.

If I give up now, I'm not just walking away from a workout. I'm admitting that Griffin was right. That I wasn't worth fighting for. That I never deserved our happy family in the first place.

And maybe… I never did.

The shame sits heavy on my chest. I move anyway.

Pretty soon, Roman abandons the Suicide routine and goes full rogue, freestyling like he's one of Janet's backup dancers on tour. I blink hard, breath catching in my throat.

Am I supposed to keep up… or just survive?

My body answers before I can. *Try me.*

The rest of the group scrambles to keep pace, and Roman barely looks their way. His focus stays locked on me, footwork wild and deliberate.

Mid-step, his eyes dare me. *You like that, don't you? How about this?*

I respond with every twist and thrust of my hips: *Yes, please. Can I have another?*

One by one, the others drop off.

The final two hang on a little longer—but eventually, even they retreat, breathless and spent.

I stay right where I am. Still moving. Still standing. And yeah… grinning.

Roman stops, hands on his waist, panting like he chased a train and almost caught it. He stares at my reflection as I blink away salty beads of sweat, my chest heaving in defiance.

Are we done now? Can we finally acknowledge that I belong here?

He dabs his brow with the edge of his shirt, flashing the barest strip of toned brown abs, then switches the track to Missy Elliot's "Lose Control."

The other girls whoop and holler as Roman steps off the platform and moves beside me.

No mic. No instructions. Just a look.

His body speaks first. A slow grind of his hips. A roll of his shoulders. Feet gliding to the beat like sin wrapped in sweat.

I answer without hesitation. A sway. A pivot. A flick of my wrist that dares him to keep going.

But he's not saying anything. Or maybe he is.

You got my attention, baby. Show me what you can do.

No problem, I respond. *I'll do this and a whole lot more.*

I devour the rhythm. Let it crawl over my skin, slip into my hips. Take up space in every inch of me, luring him closer.

He spins. I match. He drops low, and I follow, teasing him with every move. Like I was made to mirror him. The space between us vibrates, charged and thin, every beat drawing us together.

We don't speak. We don't have to. The music pulses through me like breathless pleasure, something wild building in my chest. And the way Roman watches? I know he feels it too.

But I'm not dancing for him. I'm dancing like I remember who the hell I am.

And maybe that's what undoes him.

By the time he plants his hands on his knees, breath pleading for mercy, I'm still moving.

He cuts the music with a flick.

"Damn, girl." His voice is hoarse. Wrecked. "You wore me out!"

Poor thing. He thought I came here to play.

The words echo in my mind like they came from someone else. Someone braver. Freer. Definitely not me.

All the ladies scream and applaud as I slap a hand over my mouth, heart hammering like I just landed a Broadway callback. The man's still catching his breath when they swarm me, offering high-fives and cheers.

I can't believe I actually did it. Thoroughly satisfied, I head to the back and dry off, cheeks growing warm as the last of the girls commends me and heads out. *Wow. That felt good.*

Roman's staring me down from the far corner of the otherwise empty room, gulping water like it's holy. I stare right back. *You see me now, don't you?*

I'm preparing to grab my things and go when he asks, "What's your name?"

I throw my towel over my shoulder, honestly surprised that he'd care. "Laura Phillips."

He crosses the room and offers a hand slick with sweat and swagger. His grip is firm but tender. Electric. It climbs my arm, curls beneath my ribs, and I jerk away fast. Like I touched something I wasn't supposed to.

"Where'd you learn to dance?" he asks.

"Detroit School of Arts."

That jogs his brow. "Where Aaliyah studied?"

I nod. Only one of the best schools in the state. And I bet he knows that, too. "I was on the dance squad at U of M for a minute."

That maddeningly sexy grin stays in place, but I know he's eating crow. He prejudged me, like everyone else.

Seeing the time and recalling I have to pick up Maddie, I head for the door. "Have a good one."

"You know," he says, "I could help you."

I turn back, brows drawn tight. "Help me?"

He sizes me up with a tilt of his head. "You wanna get in shape, right?"

My breath hitches as if he punched me. I fold my arms, speechless. But his piercing eyes meet mine as he steps closer.

"You looked about ready to pass out today, and you clearly love to move. So, I could help you with your... problem."

I looked about ready to pass out? "Thanks. But no thanks."

Like anyone asked his opinion anyway. A pat on the back would've been plenty.

I turn for the door, but he moves in front of me. *"No thanks?* Wha—what do you mean, *no thanks?"* His face twists tight as if he's never heard a woman speak to him in plain English.

I adjust my bag on my shoulder, looking him dead in the eye. "I mean, no, thank you."

An affronted, high-pitched laugh escapes him. "Do you even *know* who I am?"

"I know a jerk when I see one."

The man's jaw is on the floor as I move past him. But before I can savor it, his hand grips mine and yanks me back. The move is so quick, my body collides with his, chest to chest, breath to breath. I freeze, caught beneath the weight of his gaze. Dark. Focused. Dangerous.

His warmth settles over me, slow and possessive, like his body already knows mine. For one breathless second, something deep inside answers, arching closer.

Then I remember who he is.

He releases my hand, thank God, and I stumble back a step, pulse thundering like I just climbed five flights of stairs.

"Look, I didn't mean to—" He clears his throat. "What I meant was, you've got potential. And I could help you succeed."

"And you think I couldn't succeed without you?"

"Look, mama!" He throws up his arms, glancing down at his perfectly sculpted body. "I am offering you a *major* gift here. And I promise, you stick with Roman, and I'll completely transform your life by Christmas." His gravelly voice gets me sweating again, his grin as seductive as a serpent.

I've gotta admit, I've had more fun in the past two weeks than I've had in a long time. And the guy's got some moves. "How much do you charge?"

He looks me over once more, folding a fist in his hand. "Three hundred a week."

"Bye."

"Okay. Okay." He strokes his stubbled chin like he's negotiating a hostage release. "Look, someone with my expertise wouldn't usually do this, but I *really* wanna help you out. So, I'm willing to do it for... two-fifteen. But that's my final offer."

The hopeful flicker in his eyes almost makes me laugh. "I'll think about it."

———————— ✦✦✦✦✦ ————————

"Mom, I can't wait," says Maddie as she and Eli buckle into the backseat a little while later. "The Christmas recital's gonna be *so* awesome."

"That's great, honey." I'm listening as I start the SUV. But not really. Not with everything bouncing around in my head. Between this morning's proposition and waiting to hear from her dad, I've got a lot on my mind. I check the side mirrors as I put my Lincoln in gear and head out of the gym parking lot. The first time I heard the hum of this beauty I yelped with delight.

"*You like it?*" Griffin had grinned. This beast of a car was his first gift to me after he took over his father's company. An anniversary present. A celebration on wheels. I must've kissed him forever as we sat in the parking lot of our old one-bedroom apartment. "*I'm gonna take care of you, babe,*" he'd said. "*Always.*"

We were hanging on by threads back then. Collection calls. Closed credit cards. Eviction notices. And the chump change I made as an assistant dance instructor was barely enough to cover diapers.

It was a struggle sharing our ancient, beat-up Mercedes every day, especially when we were low on gas.

Then, one day, his dad suffered a massive heart attack out of the blue, and... he left everything to Griffin. It was a shock and, in its own twisted way, a blessing. Overnight, we went from borderline poverty to this super-wealthy life. Just like that, everything flipped.

If I'd known it all would lead to cold nights and polite texts, I'd have taken back that old, busted Mercedes in a heartbeat. But despite his surprise guest, the resolve of Griffin's gaze at Eli's party gave me hope.

Speaking of which, he never did call me. I have the car shoot him a casual text as we pull up to a red light: *Still picking up the kids at two?*

I already know he'll keep his commitment. I just want to hear from him. But he's yet to respond as the light turns green. With a sigh, I hit the gas.

"And Ms. Alyssa says my *grand jetés* and *relevés* are brilliant, Mommy," Maddie gushes as she reemphasizes her point. "*Brilliant!*"

I expect to catch Eli frowning at his sister going on, but he's busy teaching himself to shuffle cards. Plenty must be on the floor by now.

"I'm sure they are brilliant, honey," I say, flashing my best smile. At least she never has to worry about someone recognizing her abilities while insulting her at the same time.

What does that trainer even mean, "my problem"? Maybe I like being on the thicker side. I mean, I don't, but he doesn't know that. And who the hell does he think he is, tugging on me and making my heart beat all crazy like some groupie? I seethe with irritation as I turn the corner.

"And I'm only one of *ten* kids picked to audition for the solo in this year's recital."

I glance at Maddie in the rearview mirror. "Really?"

She nods with pride. "It's for the role of Susan. We're doing *Miracle on 34th Street*."

I blink away the fog in my head and smile. "That's amazing, sweetheart." And I mean it. "Maybe we could work on your audition with Cousin Yana." But the notification of an incoming text pulls my attention as we reach another red light.

Emergency meeting, the car responds, reading Griffin's message. *Let's do four.*

Just like that. A calendar alert instead of a conversation. From the man who used to whisper promises against my skin in parking lots like he'd never leave.

That's so like him these days.

All business. Not even a *how are you?*

I'm contemplating how to reply when a car horn blares behind me. Light's green. With a heavy breath, I step on it.

I doubt Griffin is even working. He probably plans to keep his little weather girl sprawled out somewhere that he can make sweet love to her until late afternoon. I gnaw my tongue in frustration, refusing to let myself believe he could do such a thing. Though, I can't remember the last time he even attempted touching me. It's been at least a good two years. And if I ever want to change that, I know I'm going to need help.

I've looked into the shots, the pills, the magic fixes everyone swears by. Insurance won't cover it, and I've got mouths to feed.

But the trainer? Could he really get me to my goal in less than four months?

Even if I pass on the man's pricey fees, between the cost of this new dance school and the gear Maddie will need if she gets this role, my budget could take a serious hit. I could text Griffin about raising my allowance, but I'd rather have that conversation in person.

I jump when I receive an incoming call. But it's only Yana.

"Hey, girl, hey," she says, and the kids sing back hello. She's smacking loud enough for the entire city block to hear.

"What are you munching on?" I ask.

"I'm at the bakery. I was craving donuts, so I said, why not? Ya know?"

Only she could snack on a 500-calorie donut whenever she feels the notion and maintain her slim figure.

"I didn't get that callback I was hoping for, so I thought I'd drop by later. You free?"

"Sure. Griffin's picking up the kids around four. Just headed home from the rec now."

"Oh *yeah...*" says Yana, suddenly invested. "Did you go back to Roman's class?"

"Yeah." I'm not sure I want to get into what happened, but my cousin is very perceptive, and the lax tone of my voice gives me away.

"Yeah? *And?*"

"And... it was fun," I say. "We sorta had a dance-off, and... I was the last girl standing."

Yana's high-pitched yelp explodes in the car. "*What?*"

"Whoa, Mom! Are you serious?" asks Maddie.

I motion for Maddie to put on her headphones as I round the corner.

There's a fumbling on the other end of the line as Yana mutters a faint apology to someone in the background. "Girl, what did Roman say? What did he do?"

I could tell her about the dramatic back-and-forth between us, but what does it really matter? "He asked me to train with him."

Yana inhales all the air around her. "You're kidding!"

"I'm not. He's willing to do it for two-fifteen a week. But I don't know."

"*You don't know?*" Yana damn near ruptures my eardrum. I scramble to take her off speaker as she shouts, "*What do you mean, you don't know? Girl! Have you lost your mind?*" My cousin goes on and on about *all the sweaty pushups* I can do with that *fine, beefy man,* and *the guy's mile-long waitlist,* and *he doesn't offer his services to just anybody.*

"He's also a jerk," I mutter, praying my little boy can't hear me.

"Wha—? *What?*" Yana scoffs. "No, he's not. Roman's *adorable.*"

It isn't uncommon for Yana to see straight through people. It's one of her superpowers. But when it comes to Roman? The girl's got a serious blind spot.

"Look," says Yana. "This is *Roman* we're talking about. Okay? If he offers you anything—and I mean, *anything*—girl, you better take it."

I shake my head, thinking about his obnoxious comments and taunting smirks. "I don't know, Yana. I feel like he has it out for me."

My cousin lowers her voice, her lips nearly kissing the phone. "Laura, you're my girl, and you know I ain't never asked you for nothing. But I am begging you, *please*, do this… for both of us!"

4

*J*ade's "Don't Walk Away" echoes in the kitchen as I scrub the granite countertops, winding and dropping my hips as I go.

Griffin should be here any minute, and we've got a lot to clear up. I've just gotta stay positive.

So, maybe he got caught up this week. Forgot to call. Forgot to text... Forgot he still has a wife.

But that doesn't negate the fact that we had a moment at Eli's party—the smile he tucked away, the warm chuckles we shared. Him bringing along Little Miss Sunshine was simply an oversight. A blunder I'm sure he regretted the second the party was over. Probably left the poor thing in tears when he dropped her off at home. And as soon as he gets here, we'll straighten this out.

The doorbell rings, and I turn the music down. Running my hands over my sweater and jeans, I cross the foyer with a quick scan. *Floor clean, doors closed.* Smoothing my hair down, I open the door.

"Griffin! Hey."

He stands on the porch, peering up at our three-story house, hands buried in the pockets of his topcoat. We used to laugh at people who wore that sort of thing. He claimed they were reserved for stuffy businessmen like his dad. Now he's wearing money again: Rolex, polished Oxfords, a crisp designer shirt peeking from beneath his coat like it costs more than my weekly grocery run. And I hate how *fine* he looks in all of it.

But he barely bats an eye when he sees me.

"Come in," I say, flashing a pleasant smile as if I haven't been expecting him all afternoon. The sofa cushions have been fluffed, the beds neatly made. I even stocked his favorite beer in the fridge.

"Maybe next time." He glances back at his Lexus sitting at the bottom of the steps in our curved driveway. Piper and Penelope are in the backseat, raising hell. Vicki sits up front, too busy scrolling to notice. Or care.

"Why is she here?" I ask, staring at Griffin in a daze.

He looks me over, then flicks another glance over his shoulder. "Listen, just like you, I needed someone to talk to, and..." He trails off, like finishing the sentence would snap the last string holding me together.

He's serious about this woman? Fury spikes in my chest, and I fold my arms.

"Is this why you wanted to separate? So you could screw the weather girl?"

His gaze drifts to the sweeping staircase that leads upstairs, crushing my heart to pieces. "Where are the kids?"

My tongue begs for blood, but I choke it back. *Not around them.* I call out, and they stumble from the master suite doors behind me. Six bedrooms in this house. Plus, a small theater. And the only place they want to watch TV is my room. Maddie and Eli rush over, extending their arms for hugs, but their father recoils.

"Why aren't you ready? And what is that all over your face, Eli?"

Eli beams at Griffin with a gap-toothed smile, oblivious to his father's grouchy attitude. "We had pizza."

With pursed lips, Griffin tosses another glance at Vicki. The two connect eyes in some sort of silent exchange, and finally, he crosses the threshold.

Avoiding Vicki's hard stare, I gently shut the door behind him. "Kids, your daddy's ready to go. Clean up and grab your things." The kids dutifully run upstairs, but the knife twists in my gut as Griffin checks his watch like he has somewhere better to be.

"You never called," I say, careful to keep my voice at an even tone.

"Yeah, that's my bad." He shoves his hands in his pockets, leaning back on his heels. "Things got kinda busy."

I want to remind him that he's always busy, but this is already going much worse than expected. "Okay. Then you should know that things are tight."

Griffin lifts a skeptical brow. "What do you mean *things are tight*?"

"Things are tight. I mean... financially."

He releases a bitter laugh, scratching at his beard. "Yeah, okay. *Kids! Hurry up!*"

"Okay!" They frantically shuffle around in their rooms.

"Griffin, I'm serious. Food and clothing aren't getting any cheaper, and the fees for Maddie's ballet lessons aren't as low as I thought they'd be." If he'd stayed, things would be a lot less complicated. For the kids. For me.

He runs a hand across his face, throwing back his head. "Come on, Laura. You *said* this was a good amount."

"Well, it's not. And I said a lot of things I shouldn't have when you thought up this whole idea." There's a hint of sadness in his eyes as he stares at me. "Now, I'm trying to make it work, but I've gotta have a life too. Things are expensive."

"Things like what?"

Like a boob job. A tummy tuck... Personal training to mold me into someone you could actually love.

I'd work up the courage to say it all, but I honestly doubt he'd care.

"Laura, I left y'all a wood-paneled library, my exercise room, and two gourmet kitchens." His glare is so sharp it wounds me. "You wanna know what's expensive? Keeping up with private school tuition while paying two mortgages. I've gotta live on a budget. Why don't you?"

The stare-down he gives is the same as when he'd caught me crying in our apartment after learning Eli was on the way. Maddie was finally out of diapers. I'd just started to hit my stride assisting with dance instruction. I was just feeling like myself again. *"Do you know how many people would kill for an opportunity like this?"* he'd asked. *"Eventually, the extra weight is gonna fall off, and you can do the dancing thing again. In the meantime, count your blessings."* Both of us misunderstood the weight of that assumption. And when nothing returned to normal, he eventually walked away.

I blink, trying to refocus. "I can't stick to a budget when I keep receiving new bills."

"Then lower your expenses. Maddie ain't gotta take ballet."

"Griffin, she loves ballet!"

"It's just a hobby," he says. "And an expensive one at that."

"Yeah. Where have I heard that before?"

A lengthy silence stretches between us as our gazes battle one another. Both of us know he never respected what I did. Said it was cute, *admired my skills.* Came to maybe a handful of my performances before I had to quit to have Maddie.

He exhales hard, glaring at the ceiling. "How about an extra grand a month? You good with that?"

Hope swells in my chest as his jaw somehow seems to relax. "That would be perfect."

I ache to reach for him, kiss and make up. But his glance toward the door reminds me that isn't allowed anymore.

Ten years, endless devotion, two precious babies. If I could, I'd give him so much more.

"Look," he says, gazing over my shoulder, "did you get the papers?"

Papers? "Griffin. You filed for divorce?" I stare at him in shock as the kids come bounding down the stairs. The bit of my heart that'd begun to heal fractures all over again.

"Hey, Dad. Look what I can do!" Eli pulls a playing card from his pocket and dangles it by a thread as if it's floating in mid-air. But I'm too afraid that a blink could lead to tears.

"That's great, little man," says Griffin, tousling Eli's curls. But his attention is centered on me much more than our son's new talent.

Why is he doing this to me? I honestly thought I had more time.

"Laura, I'm—" Griffin swallows, looking away. "Let's talk later, alright?"

Later. Always later. With a nod, I bend to hug Eli goodbye, but just like this past week, I know his father won't be calling. I swipe at a tear before it falls and squeeze my little boy tight.

Maddie frowns as I embrace her. "Mom, you okay?"

"I'm fine. I'll see you tomorrow." I turn and collect myself as Griffin ushers the kids out the door. He lingers behind me for the briefest moment before following them outside.

We've overcome so many obstacles together. Never used to argue. Could find a way to laugh in the most desperate of times. And still...

I have to fix this. I have to fix this.

I turn around, prepared to call my husband back, but he's already made his way down the stairs.

Meanwhile, Vicki awaits my children near the Lexus, toned arms stretched wide. "How are my little angels? I missed you!" She embraces them with the warmth of a hundred aunties.

The sun stretches over the sprawling grounds and pine trees in the distance, catching each of my kids' bright, trusting faces as they wave goodbye.

Like this is normal.

Something caves in my chest. And my husband doesn't bother looking back.

5

I've been killing this routine for twenty minutes straight, and Roman hasn't glanced at me once. Whatever. It's finally Saturday again, and I came for a win today.

The divorce papers came Tuesday. I cried so hard I thought I'd never stop. This class is the first thing to pull a real smile out of me all week. Roman keeps throwing us complex turns and ramping up the combos, and I match every move with grit I didn't know I had. Still, not one glance.

After class, I bend to adjust my laces, but my eyes stay on him, thrown by his silence. He's posted by the dumbbells, arms crossed, intently focused on a student's question.

I hope he hasn't changed his mind.

I linger by my gym bag as the class clears, drawing out farewells I don't mean. But one of the chicks is *extra* thirsty today. She coils a perfect blonde curl around her finger like it's bait, lashes fluttering like she's auditioning for a rom-com. Roman's gaze dances with charm, indulging her.

Oh, brother.

Pilates is just about to begin when Miss Thirsty finally heads out, so I stand to make my approach. But without so much as a glance, he walks out the door.

Seriously?

He's headed toward another studio when I call out to him. "Hey!" But he continues down the nearly vacant hall as if he can't hear me through a crowd. "Roman!" I snap.

He stops and squints back like he doesn't recognize me, the shadows of the trees outside the tall windows dancing across his angled face. "Can I help you?"

Okay. I get it. He was insulted when I put him off last time, and he's trying to save face. But I'm at my wit's end here. I've gotta remind my husband of what we had before he rides off into the sunset with the weather girl.

Chin lifted high, I take a few steps toward Roman with a hand on my hip. "I'm going to train with you."

Anticipating some childish form of song and dance, I hold my breath, but he doesn't say a word. Instead, he crosses his arms, examining me as if considering my offer. But I'm still on a high from today's class, and... I'm not going to let him intimidate me. Pushing back my shoulders, I raise my chin a little higher.

"I have some conditions."

A lazy grin spreads across his face. "Care to share?"

Crossing my arms, I mirror his tough exterior. "I'm not a morning person. I'll need afternoon workouts. And I prefer one-on-one sessions. I like my privacy." He blinks, waiting for me to go on, so I continue. "I control what I eat. I want three days off each week. And I don't do calisthenics. They're unnecessary torture." Maintaining my stance, I conceal a self-satisfied grin, but Roman is completely unmoved.

"Are you done?"

I think I've just about covered it, so I nod.

"Good." He uncrosses his arms, taking a giant step toward me. "'Cause I have a few *conditions* of my own."

I also uncross my arms. "What are those?"

Roman studies the ceiling as he moves my way, the muscles of his chest swelling. "I *am* a morning person, and my afternoons are full. We'll work out when I say. Most of my sessions are one-on-one, but if I request that you join us in a class or two, you sure as hell better be there." He closes what's left of the space between us, leaning his face mere inches from mine. His scent hits first. Cool, clean. Like ocean mist and danger. Nothing like a gym locker room. The fine hairs above his lip curve, sparks of light flashing in his eyes. "Any successful client of mine will follow my meal plans—and *my* meal plans alone. You'll get *one* day off, maybe two if I'm in a good mood. And I agree, calisthenics *are* torture, which is exactly why you'll be doing them *every single* time you work with me."

My entire body tenses as he arrests me with a heavy gaze, nothing but the tranquil music of the Pilates class firing up behind us. I know I'm crazy to even consider working with him. But if I want my family whole again, this is my last resort.

The enticing smirk remains on Roman's lips as his eyes bore into mine. "Any questions?"

My lungs pump hard as I take the tiniest step back.

"You take Venmo?"

<hr />

The doorbell rings the next morning, waking me from my slumber, and between yesterday's brutal workout and last night's ice cream binge, I'm a wreck. I've barely rolled out of bed and checked the clock before the doorbell rings a second and third time.

It's seven-thirty a.m. The lunatic's pounding on the door as I throw on my robe and rush into the foyer. *This better not be anyone but the police.*

But it's Roman. "Morning, Sunshine!" His teeth shine brighter than the rising sun as he struts inside, a bag of groceries under his arm. "You still aren't dressed?"

Rubbing sleep from my eyes, I shut the door behind him. "It's Sunday, Roman."

"Yep. And I've been up since 4:30." He takes a look around at my decorated foyer and the spacious great room to his right. "Aha! Kitchen straight ahead."

How can anyone be this chipper when the sun is barely up? I painfully drag my feet behind him.

Roman plunks his bag on the breakfast bar, seeming pleasantly surprised as he studies the arched doorways and two-story ceilings. "At first, I thought I had the wrong address. But apparently"—he checks out the limestone floors—"you've got a lot more coin than I thought, mama. And you *definitely* played me on payment."

I shrug. He should know by now that looks can be deceiving. Wandering to the opposite side of the counter as he starts unloading groceries, I thank God I finally called that cleaning crew to scrub the place down. "What are you doing here, Roman?"

He flashes a smile that could make any of his students faint. "Did I forget to mention I make house calls?"

It's impossible to conceal my wide-eyed stare. What kind of sick torture is this guy into?

"Roman Graham's here to change your life! I gave you my word," he says with another wicked grin. "And I plan to deliver."

I run a hand over my face, praying this is just a weird dream. *Maybe I should ask for my money back now.*

"For the next three months, I own you," he says. "I'm gonna infiltrate *every* inch of your life and ensure you make it to our goal."

"*Our* goal?"

"Our fitness goal—for you."

"Do you even know what my goal is?"

"Do you?" He's wearing another obnoxious smirk as he whips out pints of egg whites and broccoli like they're gold.

The man is much too enthused about this. I thought he had some nonfraternization policy or whatever. "You do this with all your clients?"

"Nah. Roman's a very busy man."

He plucks some grapes from his grocery bag, looking me over.

"But Roman's not above helping one out in the midst of a crisis."

"Anyone ever tell Roman he's a bit of an asshole?"

"Every damn day, sweetheart." His smile is torture as he pops a grape into his mouth.

He proceeds to go through my cabinets as he gives a rundown of his rules: *No carbs after lunch. Two salads a day. At least a gallon of water before ten p.m.*

It sounds like diet boot camp, minus the snacks. And meanwhile, he's tossing things out, left and right. Hundreds of dollars in the trash. If Griffin were here, I'm sure he would've exploded by now. Honestly, I'm starting to wonder if I'm a little in over my head myself.

Roman checks the label on some barbeque sauce and casually tosses it in the trash. "No more than two servings of fruit per day. *No* eating after seven o'clock."

Seven o'clock? I rarely eat my first meal before two. I'm just about to question that one when he turns and looks me dead in the eye.

"Absolutely *no* drinks with calories."

"What about coffee?"

He skims what's left of my practically bare fridge. "Only if it's black."

"Not even the occasional… Cinnamon Dolce Latte?"

He frowns, looking about ready to vomit. "Do you know how fattening those things are?"

I blow out some air as Maddie and Eli come moseying down the stairs in their PJs. They grin at the sight of company but seem much too tired to talk.

Eli snuggles at my side, blinking up at the unexpected visitor digging through the freezer.

"Chicken nuggets? *Fish sticks?*" Roman shakes his head with a snort. "Somebody doesn't give a sh—"

"*Shh!*" I throw my hands over Eli's ears, and Roman tosses me a glare. But he stops when he sees the two small children at my side. Shutting the fridge, he clears his throat.

"Who's this?"

"Roman, these are my kids." I gesture at each of them. "Madison and Elijah."

The trainer gives a slow nod, looking about as thrown as he did when he realized I could actually dance. Stepping around the counter, he shakes Maddie's hand. "Nice to meet you...?"

"Maddie," she says.

"And I'm Eli!" says my little boy, jumping in front of his sister.

"Sup?" As soon as he shakes my son's hand, Roman wipes his palm on his jeans. Then, as if afraid to make any sudden moves, he plants his hands on his waist, blinking at each of my kids.

"You look like a superhero," says Eli.

I nudge my son for being so candid, but I suppose he's got a point. The man's muscles are putting in work under that skintight sweater.

Roman's attention shifts to me. "What is he—like, four?"

"He's six."

"Oh." Roman squints at my son like he's doing mental math. "So small."

"Kids, why don't you go watch TV?"

They groggily follow my orders and head to my room. I can almost see the tension melting from the trainer's brawny shoulders as they distance themselves.

"Where's their dad?" he asks.

"He's not... here right now." I play with my wedding ring, and Roman seems to notice it for the first time.

He clears his throat once more. "What'd you eat for breakfast?"

"I haven't had anything." And I'm met with a horrific death stare. "I mean, I haven't had anything *yet*. I'll get some cereal." Making my way to the pantry, I grab the healthiest choice I can find. But Roman snatches the box, takes a look at the nutrition label, and tosses it in the trash.

"Too much sugar," he says.

I pull out another.

"No fiber."

I pull another.

"Junk." He's about to toss that box, too, when Eli runs up and grabs it.

"That's my favorite!"

Roman looks to me as Eli takes off with the cereal. "Obviously, the little one's just as addicted to this garbage as you are."

My chest rises and falls with a sigh. "Then what do you suggest I eat?"

٠٠◆◆◆◆٠٠

It isn't long before Roman's sliding a plate of scrambled egg whites and grapes across my dining room table.

He pulls a chair up beside me, positively giddy, as I take my first half-hearted bite.

"You forgot the salt," I say, gagging as I swallow.

"Nah," he says. "There's enough natural sodium in the egg whites. You don't need it."

Reluctantly, I return to chewing as my children silently giggle at the opposite end of the table, their much more delicious-looking cereal in their bowls.

Roman leans back, typing on his phone. "Shooting over this week's meal plan right... now."

My phone chimes. The smile I give him is all stretch, no joy. "Can't wait to check it out."

"His voice is funny," says Eli with a mouth-filled chuckle.

Roman leans in and pins Eli with a look like he's about to expose the Easter Bunny. "You know you're losing your teeth because you keep eating all that junk, right?" A wicked smirk inches up Roman's cheek as my little boy gazes at his cereal in horror.

"That's not true, Eli." I smack the man's arm. "Go ahead and eat your cereal." The poor boy chews much more slowly.

Maddie's trying—and failing—to hold in her giggles as she shoves another spoonful into her mouth.

Roman turns to her. "You like eating this junk too?"

Maddie slows her chewing and looks to me, seeming unsure of whether to speak or not.

"Maddie's the healthiest one in our house," I say, tossing her a lifeline. "She dances at the rec."

Roman studies her a beat. "Ballet?"

Maddie nods. "How'd you know?"

"You carry yourself like a ballerina. Who's your teacher? Ms. Alyssa?"

Maddie nods again, seeming just as impressed by his assumptions as I am.

"I teach for the dance studio, too," he says, giving me a wink.

And my heart falls out of rhythm before I can look away.

"That's right..." Maddie's eyes grow big as they link with mine. "You're *Roman*."

The man's grin is two inches wider as he reclines in his seat, his gaze pinging between my daughter and me. "So, you've heard about me?"

A flicker of panic flares in my chest. *Lord, please don't let my daughter repeat anything Yana said. Especially not the part about his "vein game." Or that "Sexiest Man at the Rec" award.*

I stare at my daughter hard, and she returns to her cereal. "Just... a little," she says.

"*A little?*" Roman crosses his arms, looking at me.

"She means she heard you're a good teacher," I rush to say. "And you're at the rec a lot."

"Uh-huh."

Roman's tone is doubtful as he gives me a penetrating stare, and I focus on my dry eggs, wondering if I should turn up the AC.

"Well, between my physical training, aerobics classes, and dance lessons, the rec is kinda my second home," he says.

Eli's little head pops up from his bowl. "Daddy has a second home—"

"Can I please have some salt?" I ask, dropping my fork with a clatter.

Roman gives me a quick side-eye before looking back to Eli. "What do you mean, 'Daddy has a second home'?" he asks.

I cough into my napkin, nerves racing up my veins. "Their dad basically lives at the office," I say before my son can share all the pathetic details of my life. "Travels a lot, too. It can be difficult to keep up with a wife and kids. As busy as you are, I'm sure you'd understand. That's... if you're into women."

Roman drops his head with a rumbly chuckle. "Well, I definitely like women. And as far as marriage and babies, that's for suckers."

I purse my lips as he turns back to Maddie. "So, Ballet Girl, you any good?"

Maddie shrugs, meditating on her sugary cereal. "I got asked to audition for the lead role in the Christmas recital."

Roman jerks back his head. "For real?" She nods, face glowing as Roman looks to me. "That's *huge*."

My pulse slows a little. "You think so?"

"Absolutely." He carefully observes Maddie, visibly impressed. "If Ms. Alyssa is eyeing you for the lead, you must be the real deal." I swear there's a flicker of heat in Roman's gaze as it settles on me. "Wonder where she gets it."

A bubble of pride rises in my chest, and my cheeks burn hot.

"And I do magic," says Eli, his mouth full of cereal. "I'm not that good at it yet, but I'm gonna be *really* good at it one day. The next *Whodunnit*!"

"You mean Houdini, honey," I say before turning to Roman. "Mainly card tricks."

Roman's brow remains creased. "Right."

The table falls silent as the kids wrap up their breakfast, and I try my best not to choke on my disgusting eggs. Meanwhile, Roman sits back, rubbing his chin, the wheels spinning behind his eyes as he watches me eat.

The moment the kids stand to clear the table, he's grilling me.

"You work?"

I shake my head.

"Any hobbies?"

"Not really."

"And what does Mr. Invisible do for a living?"

"That's none of your business."

"When will he be home?"

I spring from my seat as the kids return. "Look, it's been fun, but if I'm going to stick to this meal plan, we're going to need a lot more groceries. In fact, we should head to the store soon."

"Really?" Eli's already dancing a jig.

Great. Now we'll actually have to go. As hungry as I am, I could use a breakfast sandwich anyway. I give Roman my best smile and push in my chair. "Thanks for dropping by."

The trainer glances at his watch as he stands. "I've got some time. I'll go with you."

"We're, uh, not going until after a movie," I say.

"*A movie?*" Both of the kids jump and shout at the news while Roman lifts a skeptical brow.

"Yeah, remember?" I toss the kids a light chuckle. "Cousin Yana bought us tickets to that... sold-out show?" I nod at their little scrunched faces before turning back to Roman. "Jam-packed schedule."

The man crosses his arms, his intense eyes raking over me. "Alright. But *no* movie snacks."

"Got it." *Whatever it takes to get this crazy man out of my house.*

I send the kids upstairs to get ready for our unplanned day out while Roman and I head for the door.

"The girl seems cool," he says. "But the little one's gonna have to grow on me."

"Thanks for the tips. It sounds a little tough, but..." I slow to a stop, following his gaze to the closed double doors.

"This your bedroom?"

"Yeah, but—"

He doesn't wait. Just shoves the door open and walks in like he owns the place.

What the hell?

"Roman!" I rush in behind him, but it's too late. The man's already rifling through my nightstand like he's hunting for buried treasure.

My stomach drops.

"Are you insane?"

He keeps going. "Stay-at-home moms tend to treat themselves in secret," he says, like he's narrating a damn documentary. "Especially at... night."

I can't breathe as he seems to move in slow motion, pulling out a framed photo of Griffin and a much smaller version of me with the kids at Virginia Beach, then the wedding band my husband left behind. He turns to see Griffin's open and mostly empty closet, nothing but a couple of shirts and an old robe hanging inside.

My heart plummets into the pit of my belly.

I storm around the bed, snatch the photo from his hand, and clutch it to my chest.

"Are we done now?"

Seconds stretch into hours as Roman stares at me. He only nods once before setting the ring on the nightstand and heading for the door. Swallowing the lump in my throat, I place my picture face down on the bed and follow him out.

"Meet me at the rec tomorrow," he says. "Nine-thirty sharp. Got it?"

I agree as I open the door, praying he'll never come back. But he hesitates, looking at me like he wants to say something but doesn't know how. As if he might actually feel sorry for me.

Hoping to avoid any more stupid questions, I shift my gaze and study the hills and valleys of my nearly two-acre property outside. Everything my husband was happy to leave behind. This is hard enough as it is.

But without a word, Roman leaves, shutting the door behind him.

oman and his smoldering gaze are waiting in the lobby
when I arrive at the rec on Monday. "You're two minutes late."

"Sorry." I huff. "Terrible traffic at drop-off."

Maddie and Eli's private school is one of the most selective in the
state, and it's still become overcrowded in the past few years. I long
for the days when Griffin and I alternated dropping them off in the
morning.

Roman stands from his perch on a lobby armchair, the rope-like
veins in his arms flexing as he crosses them.

"Drop and give me twenty."

"Twenty what?"

"Ten pushups for every minute you're late."

He cannot be serious. But he doesn't crack a smile as I gape at him.

I slip off my gym bag and plunk it beside me, my glare never leaving his as I slump to the floor with its dusty footprints, loose gravel,
and dirt nestled in its cracks. "I don't have to do the man kind, do I?"

He shrugs.

Fine. I lean on my hands and get started.

"Keep your back straight," he says. "Don't stick your ass out like that."

I hate this guy. My arms are on fire as some rando strolls past with a chuckle like I'm part of the entertainment.

"What's up, Roman? New recruit?"

"You know it!"

This is so humiliating. I can feel the weight of everyone watching me struggle to lift myself on wobbly arms as they pass, the clanking weight machines and news broadcasts on the mounted TVs overhead mere background noise to my embarrassment.

I'm here to dance, not survive bootcamp. I'm probably dehydrated. My shoes aren't even tied tight. And if I throw my back out, who's going to take the kids to school?

"That all you got?" he shouts. "Nah. You on Roman's time now! *Let's work!*"

Sitting back on my knees, I blow out some air. "I *am* a lady, you know. Shouldn't you be nicer to me?"

The man jumps down and does twenty pushups himself—the fancy kind, with his legs spread out, one hand behind his back—his copper, toned muscles drawing the envy of every guy and girl as they pass.

Show off.

Hopping to his feet, he dusts the dirt from his hands. "You got ten to go."

⁘

We start with what Roman likes to call *basic conditioning* in the gym. That means an obnoxious amount of running on the overhead track and plenty of calisthenics. Thirty minutes later, he's got me squatting against a wall, beads of sweat collecting at my brow.

"It's tough, ain't it?" He paces like a drill sergeant in front of me, a stupidly handsome smirk on his face. "It's okay if you wanna quit. People quit all the time."

I hate him. I hate him so much. And I hate *this*. I just want to dance! My thighs sting with heat as my heart hammers in my chest. Maybe I should just go home.

Roman leans in my face, a seductive gleam in his eye. "I get it. Roman's workouts might not be your cup of tea," he says. "Maybe you should try something slower. Like needlepoint."

Ignore him, Laura. You've heard worse.

Roman's voice blurs behind the pounding in my ears. Suddenly, it's not him I hear. It's my stepdad, ripping through my spine with every bitter syllable.

"What's up, fatty? Why don't you get in that kitchen and make us some dinner?"

He saved his favorite for when I was headed to a dance class or audition.

"It ain't never gonna happen. How about you stop wasting everyone's time and have a seat?"

And then there were the insults he hurled at April.

"Why do we even bother to send this idiot to school?"

And Mom.

"What's a man gotta do to get a decent lay once in a while?"

I press my lips together, sweat trickling down my cheeks. *I have to do this... for Maddie, for Eli... for Griffin.*

"Fifteen more seconds," says Roman. "Ten... nine... eight..."

My legs tremble beneath me as a storm gathers in my belly. *"Yahhhh!"*

"And... time."

I collapse on the floor, every limb screaming. "Okay," I pant. "I did it."

I honestly can't believe I made it through.

Roman hovers above me, eyes cool and clinical. "Another jog."

"*What?*"

———— ✦✦✦✦ ————

By the time I collapse into the driver's seat, my legs are as heavy as wet sandbags. We didn't dance once. Just Roman, barking commands like I'm in basic training. Why does that jerk get a kick out of torturing me?

At least he didn't launch into twenty questions today. I'm humiliated enough.

I'm tempted to grab ice cream on the way home, but my phone rings before I can put the SUV in drive. It's Yana. She's supposed to be coaching, but she's got her student on mute while he goes over some lines.

"Girl, I gotta know, how was it?"

I release a stifled puff of air. "I just literally got out."

"I know." Yana's giddy. "I couldn't wait to hear!"

I run a hand over my face, leaning against the headrest. "It was awful."

"*Awful?*" Yana sounds like she's never heard a more ridiculous notion. "You mean, awfully good? 'Cause ain't no way you didn't love working with that *fine,* juicy man."

"You'd be surprised."

Yana lowers her voice, as if her student might somehow overhear our conversation. "He help you... *stretch* or anything?"

"Don't you have work to do?"

"I can take a break. Come on, girl! I bet he's into you."

"Don't be ridiculous. It's strictly business—he made that much clear when he dropped by yesterday to help me in the 'midst' of my 'crisis.' Besides, I hate his guts." But the line goes quiet. "Yana, you there?"

"*Roman was in your house?*" She shrieks so hard the phone slips from my hand.

⁘⁘⁘

Roman's back to looming over me the next day, stroking his chin as I struggle to do crunches.

"Forty-five... forty-six—come on, Laura. You can push harder than that!"

He doesn't know what I can do.

"Forty-nine... fifty. Alright. Take a break."

I fall back on the floor with a hot breath. With Griffin growing more distant by the day and the deadline to sign the papers approaching, I thought working with Roman might be worth a shot. But I was insane to sign up for all this. And I'm *hungry*! My eyes burn hot with sweat as they flutter open.

Roman's shadow stretches over me as the corners of his mouth tug into a smug little grin.

"Tell me what's on your mind."

I purse my lips, annoyed that he'd actually pretend to care. But the softness of his gaze gives me pause. He seems almost... sincere.

"Honestly?" I roll my eyes to keep from crying. "This sucks."

"Being unhealthy *does* suck." He chuckles as I glower at him but extends a hand to me. "Let's dance."

Soon, we're in one of the dance studios, a little up the hall from where Maddie's class is held. It's not all that different from the cardio classrooms on the opposite end of the rec. And there's no platform here to prop up Roman in his full glory.

"Is this where you teach your dance classes?"

Roman nods, pulling something up on the laptop at the front of the room. "A handful of boys and girls. Hip-hop and breakdancing."

"Really?" I study his sculpted shoulders and toned calves, the perfect curve of his ass, simply because I can. "You going to show me some of your moves?"

He doesn't even look my way as he shakes his head.

Rude. It's not like I requested a striptease.

Jason Derulo pulses through the speakers, and I sway with it, the beat slipping down my spine like warm honey. Roman drifts up beside me, catching the rhythm like he was born in it. Maybe now we can have some fun.

The bass thumps low and thick, vibrating through the studio floor and into my chest like a second heartbeat. Velvety chords glide over the rhythm, slick and hypnotic, coaxing movement from my hips before my brain can catch up.

Roman swings his own side to side, every motion a tease.

"Rock with me. Rock with me."

I mirror him, already feeling the beat.

"I'm gonna show you the full routine first," he says. "Then we'll break it down."

Let's see what he's bringing this time.

He steps out, arms flowing like waves on the ocean, then hits me with a spin and balances on his toes like Michael Jackson. Falling back a few steps, he rocks with his knees. Then ends with this too-hot-for-kids body roll.

Not half-bad.

His eyes are aflame as he turns to me. "Think you can do it?"

"I can try."

Before long, we're moving in sync, bodies swaying, falling into rhythm like we've done this a hundred times. I might not be perfect, but I'm keeping up. Adrenaline rushes through me as I raise my arms and rock my hips, a grin pulling at my lips as I catch remnants of her in the mirror. The girl I used to be.

I've missed her more than I ever let myself admit. I can't believe I stayed away from all this for so long.

"Cool. Now let's go over the body roll at the end." Roman repositions his feet, his voice a smooth, quiet command. "You see where we left off, with your left foot in front? You're gonna keep it there."

He's fully in his element, commanding the room without trying. His compression shirt clings to every sculpted line of his chest and arms, veins carved like rivers across his forearms. Below, his black athletic shorts ride just above the knee, revealing thighs that look like they could crack coconuts. The man is a walking thirst trap, and he knows it.

The fire's still lit in his eyes—controlled, but intense—as he steps closer, his eyes skimming me slow.

My skin burns beneath the warmth of his fingertips as he gently tips back my jaw. Goodness. How long has it been since a man was this close to me?

Laura, chill. He's a jerk, and you're married.

"Start at your chin." His voice is all gravel and slow seduction. "Like a raindrop just kissed you, right there. And you don't wanna let it go."

"Got it," I say, though my voice betrays me—thin, shaky—as he retreats just enough for me to try.

"Roll it down your neck. Over your chest. Catch it in your belly... Now drop your hip back. Just like that."

I follow along and hold the pose, breath catching as his gaze drags down my body like a lazy zipper. Every inch of me is on display, and

I suddenly wish I'd worn something looser. Or at least remembered to suck in my stomach.

He steps in close. Too close. Heat rolls off his chest like a second skin.

"Open your legs," he says.

"Huh?"

He doesn't repeat. Just nudges my thighs apart with his knee, adjusting my stance.

It's ballsy. It's *hot*. And borderline inappropriate.

But that doesn't stop the spark in my belly from flaring like a match.

He steps back to assess. Another sweep of his dark eyes.

My pulse pounds like bass under my skin as he lingers—reevaluating, inspecting... surely not imagining. Though, maybe I am.

"Again."

We run the roll a few more times until he finally gives the nod to put it together. And then we go for it. Arms flowing. Spin tight. Pose locked. Knees riding the rhythm like we're dancing for our lives. The music surges, and that addictive high floods my system. I move like I was made for this. And when I glance at Roman, his eyes are lit—focused, alive. He's in it. Just like me.

"*Whoo!* Now roll that raindrop from top to bottom," he shouts. "There you go, mama. And let's reverse!"

And I've gotta admit, I feel damn sexy doing it. I throw in a slow hip roll at the end, grinning as my reflection winks back at me.

But Roman's grin shrinks. "What was that?"

My smile flickers. That was joy, actually. Just a hint of who I used to be. Playful, alive, free. I almost forgot what she felt like.

"I was just getting into it," I say, swallowing a chuckle

His frown deepens as his eyes drop back to my hips. "Don't get into it so much. This ain't your solo."

His jaw ticks as I blink at him, confused. Didn't think it was that deep. His throat works a silent swallow as he takes a measured step back, eyes nowhere near mine.

"Let's take it from the top."

We run it back, syncing like two halves of the same song. The tempo, the movement, the sweat. It all blurs into heat. Every step a spark. I'm not just moving. I'm lit from within.

Man, I've missed this, and I know if I keep showing up, keep eating right, it's only a matter of time before my husband rips up those papers and comes home. Then we can give our kids the life they deserve—one full of laughter, love, and both their parents under one roof.

I watch myself in the mirror, not hating the way I look for once. I honestly can't wait to show Griffin some of these moves.

But Roman stops a second time, a crease deepening his brow. "You just did it again."

"What did I do?"

"*That!* Throwing that extra... *sass* on my routine." His face twists tight as he wags his head. "I ain't ask for all that."

I roll my eyes. "I'm sorry if it's too much for you."

Roman's defined pecs heave in his skintight compression shirt, his heated glare boring into me. "Do it the way I said."

"Yes, sir," I say with a sarcastic salute. *He just wishes he could do it.*

We take it from the top, and I follow his lead. Keep it clean. Keep it sharp. But I still see it. That shift in his jaw, the way his hands flex. Like I got under his skin.

Maybe I hit a nerve.

But this body has carried babies. Buried dreams. Survived silence and shame. If it wants to roll a little? Let it.

So I slip in one last roll, just to remind us both I can.

Roman glares like I burned the place down. And I smile like I did.

"We're done," he says, cutting the music.

"What?" I look at the clock. "We've got at least another half-hour."

"Nah. Since you seem to know so much better than me, I'll leave you to it." He heads for the door as I throw out my arms.

"Roman! I was just having fun!" The words tumble out before I can stop them. But I don't know who I'm trying to convince—him or the part of me I almost let come back to life.

He tosses me the peace sign without looking back. "You hit me up when you're ready to work."

✦✦✦✦✦✦

I thoroughly messed up yesterday, and this morning, Roman's going to make sure I pay for every second I wasted. I sent him a text last night and got him to agree to continue working with me, but he's barely uttered a full sentence since I arrived at the gym. Instead, it's been basic instructions like:

"Jump."

"Squat."

"Run."

And that's all I've been doing since he gave that last direction.

What the hell was I thinking, pissing the man off?

I huff and puff as I trot on the belt, my legs about ready to give out. But Roman's never satisfied. His fierce gaze bounces back and forth, intensely studying my form and the treadmill's clock. I don't know how much longer he wants me to do this or if it's ever going to end, but my lungs are about to explode. I hit the STOP button and jump off.

Roman's eyes ignite with rage. "What do you think you're doing?"

I throw my hands on my knees, my heart threatening to burst out of my chest. "I can't take this, Roman." I wheeze and gasp. "Can't we just dance?"

He flips the machine back on. "You just earned yourself another five minutes. Get back on there." The man is immune to my pout as he focuses on his watch. "For every second you hesitate, I'm gonna add another two minutes."

Despite my legs throbbing, *pleading* for me to stop, I get back on. At this rate, I'll be in a wheelchair for the rest of my life. I'll never dance again.

His sexy smirk elongates as he increases the treadmill's speed.

"Oh, come on, Roman!"

But the man doesn't bother answering as he returns his attention to his watch.

My thighs are burning, each step heavier than the last. Sweat clings to my neck, my back, soaking through my clothes as my lungs claw for air. Every inhale feels like breathing through fire.

I can't do this.

I should've known better. Why did I think I could ever keep up? Ever change?

This man's crazy. And I... I just can't.

I slam the STOP button and stumble off.

Roman chuckles, shaking his head. "I'm gonna have to push back my twelve o'clock 'cause, obviously, you wanna double your time." He has the nerve to reset his watch.

"Roman, *please.*" I swipe heavy beads of sweat from my brow. "You know all I want to do is dance!"

"Yep. And all you seem to care about is what you *want* to do instead of what you *need* to do." There isn't a hint of sympathy in his expression.

"But..." I throw out my arms, struggling to catch my breath. "It's *hard!*"

"Aren't my classes hard?"

I lower my eyes, but he lifts my chin, angling my face toward his like he owns the right to see me.

"What happened to that fire you bring to every dance routine?" he asks.

And something about the feather-light softness of his raspy voice, the concentration of his warm eyes raking over my face, persuades me to get back on with a huff.

"Alright." Roman resets the treadmill. "Let's just adjust this incline a bit more... And since you *clearly* have a problem with following instructions, we're gonna do some sprints."

"Wasn't I sprinting already?"

"Not even close, mama."

So, I do my best—sprinting and jogging whenever Roman tells me to, hot breaths piercing my throat like needles, my vision blurring with every stride. It feels like I might pass out at any moment, but I keep going. Griffin better love every inch of me by the time I'm done with all this.

God, please let this be enough.

"That's right," says Roman. "And three... two... one. That's it."

I double over, gasping for air as he stops the machine. "You... asshole."

"That's my middle name!" His booming voice is loud enough to draw the attention of the entire gym. I'm still glowering at his radiant smile when he says, "I think we're ready to dance."

————— +++++ —————

In the studio, I don't breathe a word as we review yesterday's routine. I do every single move the way Roman asks, not daring to add a hint of my own style—not that I could, as sore as I am.

A wicked smile plays on his lips in the mirror as he approaches the computer podium and turns off the music.

"That's better," he says.

I'd roll my eyes if I weren't terrified he might put me back on that stupid treadmill. But the grin doesn't leave his face as he turns back to me.

"You know what your issue is, Laura?" He strolls behind me and locks his gaze on mine in the mirror. "*You* have a control problem."

I cut my eyes at him standing beside me. "I think *you* are talking to the wrong person."

But he takes my chin in hand and redirects my attention to the chubby girl in the mirror. "Your problem, Laura, is self-control."

My stepdad thought so, too. He let me know every time I'd open the fridge for an afterschool snack: *"Packing on a little more, huh?"*

Maybe that's all I've ever known. Men pointing out what's wrong with me. But Roman's gaze is soft as he studies my reflection.

"You don't just wanna dance," he says. "You wanna drive."

His hands settle firm on my hips. Like they've been there before, like they remember me.

I forget how to exhale as his gaze holds mine, heavy and sure.

"This?" His voice drops lower. "This is a gift. And there's only one way to bring it under control."

He taps my temple, slow and deliberate, his breath grazing my neck like he's marking territory.

And just like that, my legs go soft again. But his dark eyes are still holding mine.

"Don't sell yourself short."

He's got a point. If I'd been patient, I could've had so much more fun today. How many times have I let myself down—have I let *everyone* down—by avoiding the hard things?

I nod, and the tiny quirk at the corner of his lips sends a shiver through my chest.

Roman steps back and slaps his hands. "Alright, firecracker. Run it back."

I smile to myself as I shake out my legs.

7

I collapse into a seat across from Maddie's ballet class like it owes me comfort. With all my one-on-one dance sessions with Roman, I had every intention of dropping his Saturday class, but he insisted I stay enrolled. His students need to be *motivated to keep up*, and a girl like me is the *perfect inspiration*. He probably means a girl *my size*. But whatever, I'm just grateful to be free of the madman for the next forty-six hours.

Eli's settling in with a game on my phone when Maddie rushes out of her class early.

"Mom! Mom! I got the part!" She bounces on her toes, dance bag swinging on her shoulder. My breath catches in surprise.

"That's amazing, sweetheart!" I hug her tight, students and parents congratulating us as they pass.

My little girl's gushing as we head to the car. *Costume fittings. Stage blocking. Extra rehearsals each week.* I was just as excited when I got into DSA.

"All those kids were such good dancers," I told Mom the day I got accepted. *"I can't believe they picked me."*

"You ain't the only one," my stepdad had muttered, pulling open the fridge.

And just like that, disappointment settled on my thirteen-year-old shoulders. Again.

I'd floated through the door that day, heart still spinning from the news. But one look at his face, and I crashed right back to earth. When it came to joy in my family, it always had a ceiling.

It wasn't until he'd suggested I bring in the trash cans to get a head start on my future job that I gathered the courage to talk back. But my mom, who'd been shelling and deveining shrimp at the kitchen sink, had turned to me with a ragged sigh. *"Laura, just do as your father says."*

No matter how worn out she seemed, she always took his side. But deep down, I know she was doing her best to hold things together. For April and me.

No matter what, my little girl will always have the support she needs.

As we buckle into the SUV, it crosses my mind to call Yana right away. I'm sure she'll be anxious to hear every little detail. But first, I've got a little bragging to do. Asking Eli to pass me the phone, I shoot Roman a text before I can think twice: ***Maddie got the lead!!!***

I wait a few moments for him to respond, but when he doesn't, I start the engine. Okay, so maybe that was a little forward. It's not like I care about his opinion or anything. I pass the phone back to Eli—who's anxiously waiting to return to his game—and pull out of the lot. I'll call Yana when we get home.

"I've gotta schedule time to rehearse my lines," says Maddie. "I should practice *at least* twice a day. Oh! And I'm gonna need another pair of ballet slippers, Mom. The ones I have are gonna wear out quick." I swallow a smile as we round the corner. That energy runs in the family. Thinking about the way she practiced all summer, I know she couldn't be more deserving of this moment.

But a flash of Roman's heated gaze at our house last week ignites in my mind.

Wonder where she gets it.

My tummy pirouettes at the thought.

Then there was the soft tone of his voice as he encouraged me, the warmth of his touch as we danced, his gentle hands on the curve of my hips. A cool breath escapes me as goosebumps snake up my thighs.

Uh-uh, Laura. You are a married woman, and you've only got eyes for Griffin. Pull it together!

I straighten my wedding ring as we stop at a red light, wondering why my hormones are raging like some starry-eyed teenager.

The trainer is an asshole. A hot, flirtatious asshole.

"I'll have to practice my dances before and after school *every* day," says Maddie. "Maybe even before the extra rehearsals."

Eli attempts to plug one of his ears as he continues his game with one hand. His tongue curls at the corner of his mouth as he hums some song from *Kidz Bop*.

The girl can get so wound up. April was the same way. "Maddie, you've gotta take it easy, okay?"

"I just wanna do my best, Mom. Everyone's counting on me." She pulls her dance bag into her lap and starts rooting around. "I need some pen and paper for a to-do list. Got any?"

"Sorry. All out." I tuck away my smile as I hit the gas.

Maddie huffs and whips out her phone, then begins feverishly typing. The girl is so much like my sister, it hurts.

<hr />

Hours later, my curls are flawless, and my black dress fits just right as I finish my makeup in the mirror. "Do I need false lashes?"

"Eh. You don't wanna do too much," says Yana from the phone on my dresser. She's in Ohio, waiting to audition for a small role her agent promises will open doors. Despite her reservations, she's not completely against helping me prepare for my husband's visit. With some big event planned for next week, Griffin requested swapping weekends before he goes. But if I have my way, we'll be sharing weekends by the time he gets back.

"I honestly don't understand why you're trying to get back with this loser when you've got a *fine* man working you every day," says Yana, biting into something crunchy.

"Roman's not my man," I say. And my stomach sinks when I pull up my messages and see he still hasn't responded. "We're not even friends. And he's definitely not working me."

"*Pssh*," she says. "Keep swaying that ass, honey. He'll take a bite before long."

"Shut up, Yana."

She's cackling on the other end. "Listen, I should be back a little later tonight. You want me to swing by if your plan falls through?"

My jaw drops in the mirror. "Yana! I thought you had my back."

"I do, girl, but... Listen, according to you, the last time he swung by with his little chick in the car, you were ready to start up some drama of *Love & Hip-Hop* proportions."

"I know, I know. But just because he made a couple of foolish mistakes doesn't mean I'll give up on us. Or our family."

Yana sucks her teeth. "I just don't want you getting your hopes up."

"My hopes are always up, Yana. It's the only choice I have."

"Right," she says with a sigh. "There's no other way you'd have made it this far."

A shard of sadness pierces my chest as I realize we're not necessarily talking about my marriage anymore. Between my history with Griffin's family and my own, I have no interest in continuing this conversation. But before I can rush off the phone, she's asking the million-dollar question.

"You still miss them a lot, don't you?"

Heartache blooms in my chest as I silently pack my makeup away. "Mom and April?" I swallow my emotions for fear of wrecking my makeup with decade-old tears. "Of course I do. But it's not like my feelings could bring 'em back."

"I just..." Yana releases another exhale through her nose and sets aside whatever crinkly-wrapped snack she's working on. "I think things would be different if they were still around, ya know? I mean, sure, things were never perfect, but... at least y'all had each other. And they definitely wouldn't be encouraging you to waste your time chasing after that jerk."

"That *jerk* is the father of my children. And technically, I'm not chasing him. I'm just trying to remind him of what we had."

Snuggling on a rundown sofa, kissing beneath a scratchy old blanket when the heat was out, sharing his bomb concoction, Ramen Noodle Casserole, with our baby girl at the wobbly kitchen table.

That inheritance from his dad was just as much a curse as it was a blessing.

The lightest grunt resounds in Yana's throat, but she drops it. "Okay. Call me."

With a lengthy breath, I hang up. I know my cousin means well, but she doesn't see things the way I do—the long talks Griffin and I have had, the endless hours we've shared. Every couple has their rough patches, and all of us make mistakes. I know I've made mine. And if I'm patient, maybe Griffin will realize he's doing the same.

I tease curls I swear I don't care about in the dresser mirror, already rehearsing my smile for when he notices.

But my gaze falls on the reflection of our king-sized bed behind me, thinking of those frigid winter mornings when Griffin would snuggle by my side, promising to work from home to avoid the snow. How the kids would run in and burrow between us, begging for waffles. I must've cooked all day back then.

Then there are the sweet memories of earlier days. Like the time he'd climbed in beside me in nothing but a bath towel, nuzzling his scratchy, newly sprouted beard into my neck.

I'd pushed him back, screaming bloody murder. *"You need to shave!"*

"You know you love it," he growled, kissing all over my face and making me giggle. We had only been in the house for a couple days, and he was just settling into his new role as CEO. *"Let's take the kids to a beach or something,"* he'd said, eyes gleaming as they searched mine. *"We never do that sorta thing."*

I'd told him no. I'd put on more weight than expected during my pregnancy with Eli, and I didn't exactly love the way I'd been looking in swimsuits. But he'd insisted.

"Come on. You know you wanna take a dip with me."

That was back when he smiled more. When he still had time for fun.

A heavy lump presses at the pit of my throat as I stare at his empty pillow now. I turn my attention to the family photo of us at Virginia Beach that's sitting on the dresser. I decided to keep it out after Roman's discovery—a reminder of why I'm torturing myself at the gym every day.

In the picture, Griffin wears his most handsome grin with an arm around me, his hand on five-year-old Maddie's shoulder. I'm smiling, too, with an anxious-to-toddle Eli in my arms. And despite the twenty pounds I'd yet to lose, I remember I was happy. We were happy.

The doorbell rings, and I nod to myself, resolute. I simply have to remind him.

Griffin's staring out at the rolling landscape when I open the door, no Vicki or Pomeranians in sight. Thank God.

"Hey." Recalling how we got off on the wrong foot last time, I place a hand on my hip and suck in my tummy. With Roman's help, I've dropped another five pounds—not that I'm supposed to be checking the scale, according to his guidelines. But Griffin's gaze drifts over my shoulder the second he turns.

"Sup. They ready?"

"Of course," I say, maintaining my best smile. "Kids! Your dad is here!" Maddie and Eli call back that they're on their way, but thankfully, they're taking their time. Unprompted, Griffin meanders inside, and I shut the door behind him. "How ya been?"

He nods, studying the floor. "Good. You?"

"Staying busy." I figured I'd tell him about my training sessions once he noticed the progress I've made, but he seems content with examining anything but me. "Any plans for the kids this weekend?"

He shrugs at the floor like the limestone's more interesting than I am. "We might check out a football game or something. We'll see."

I bob my head, wishing all this could go as smoothly as I imagined. We've barely spoken at all since I was served the papers, and when he dropped off the kids last week without getting out of the car, I gave up on hoping he'd call.

"Oh!" I raise a finger as if it slipped my mind. "Maddie got the lead role in the Christmas recital."

"Oh yeah?" He pulls out his phone to check a message. "At that new, uh... dance school?"

"Yeah." I clear my throat, waiting for him to look up, but he responds to the text instead. "And I know it's last minute, but there's a talent show at the kids' school on Wednesday."

His weary eyes finally lift to meet mine, but I press on anyway.

"Maddie wants to focus on the recital, but Eli would love for you to see his performance."

And it would be great to spend some time together as a family.

Griffin frowns as he slips his phone back into the pocket of his overcoat. "Let me check my schedule, and I'll get back to you." Both of us know he stays busy, but it was no different when he lived with us. He's always been willing to do anything for his kids. At least until now.

Against my best efforts, frustration shoots through me. "Look, Griffin, I know you've got a lot going on these days, but these things aren't a waste of time—"

"Did I *say* it was a waste of time?"

"What I mean is, it means a lot to him. To both of them." *To me.* "What they want matters, not just what you want *for* them, ya know?" I hold his gaze, wishing I'd said the same from the beginning: not just about the kids, but when it came to me and his family, my dancing, and... so many times before he walked away.

Griffin sniffs as he looks past me. "Like I said, I'll see what I can do."

At this rate, I'll be lucky to see him at all in the next month. "I got the divorce papers."

"Yeah?" His eyebrows lift curiously, as if he's surprised I'm not a weeping puddly mess. But like I told Yana, I've gotta stay positive.

"And I'll be contesting it."

His eyes split wide with rage. "You *what?*"

"We've gotta make sure the kids are set, and I could use spousal support."

Griffin's nostrils flare as he lowers his gaze to meet mine. "Laura, we had an agreement. I get the kids every other weekend, and y'all will never want for anything."

"And just last week, I had to beg for more support." I cross my arms, holding his narrow eyes hostage. "I never agreed to anything, Griffin. And you knew it the day you walked out of here and left me crying on the damn floor."

He's battling me with a glare as the kids come racing down the stairs, but I'm not letting this go. And I'll do anything to keep him from finalizing this thing before he's come to his senses.

Griffin's dark gaze is still locked on me while Maddie and Eli hug him hello and me goodbye. If I didn't know any better, I'd think he was a little hurt.

At least now he sees how it feels.

"I'll have them back early," he says, following them out the door.

The second they're gone, my body sags under the weight of everything I didn't say. It's always like this. Hope cracking into hurt.

I suppose I'll invite Yana over after all. I've been so busy this week that it didn't occur to me I'd be spending the weekend alone. Don't want to treat myself *in secret* or whatever.

But a text is waiting for me on my phone. Roman. He sent a thumbs-up.

It isn't much, but I appreciate it just the same.

The notion to order pizza crosses my mind as I retreat into my massive, vacant house. But then I recall Roman's words.

"All you seem to care about is what you want *to do instead of what you* need *to do."*

And I know he's right.

Leaning my elbows on the kitchen counter with a sigh, I pull up today's meal plan.

Looks like spaghetti squash for one.

8

*T*he next evening, I'm rushing through the foyer, swiping socks off the floor and glancing at dusty tabletops, when I nearly slip and break my neck on a few rogue playing cards.

The second I holler his name, Eli rushes down the stairs, profusely apologizing as he scrambles to clean up his mess.

Up until now, it's been a fairly relaxing Sunday. Yana and I stayed up late last night, watching old episodes of *Dancing with the* Stars, and with no lunatic at my door, I'd had plenty of time to sleep in. I didn't even trip after curling my hair a second time, only for Griffin to stay in the car once again while dropping off the kids. I'd had every intention of stretching across my French living room sofa and indulging in my laziness until I received a text an hour ago: **Headed your way with food.**

It was Roman. Apparently intent on making another house call.

I don't know why I care. He's not even company. But still, the thought of Roman catching me slipping makes my stomach knot.

With a huff, I set a couple of glasses in the sink and make one last attempt at scrubbing some dried syrup off the kitchen counter.

I couldn't be more annoyed with him interrupting the final hours of my freedom like this, but at least he gave me a heads-up this time.

The doorbell rings all too soon, and I rush to open the door.

I had my heart set on giving him the stink-eye the second he arrived, but in his leather jacket and ripped jeans, the setting sun glowing behind him like a halo, it's tough to remember why I was so upset. He cleans up nice.

One side of his mouth pulls into a grin as he flips my hair. "Look at you—all fancy. You got plans?"

"No. Just curled my hair... because." I tuck some strands behind my ear.

Thankfully, he doesn't ask any more questions as he steps inside in his Timberlands, two more bags of groceries under his arm. "Cool. I brought dinner."

Considering the lone thumbs-up he shot over yesterday, I'm shocked that he'd care. "What? No hot date tonight?"

He tosses me a sarcastic smirk as I close the door behind him, and the kids come bounding down the stairs.

"Roman!" Eli runs over, arms stretched wide, but the trainer presses a palm to my son's forehead, stopping him a good two feet short.

"Real men don't hug." Taking a step back, he shakes Eli's hand, being sure to rub the germs on his jeans the second they're done. With the smallest wave to Maddie, he's headed toward the kitchen while I send the kids back upstairs. Hopefully, it won't take long to get rid of our uninvited company.

But my breath hitches when I turn to see Roman eyeing me from the kitchen. Before I can question why, he returns his attention to unloading groceries at the counter.

"What'd you eat last night?" he asks.

I run a hand across my face as I approach him. "Ground turkey with marinara and spaghetti squash. Salad with dressing on the side."

"What kind of dressing?"

I throw back my head with a sigh. "Balsamic Vinaigrette, just like you told me—Roman, why are you here? Isn't this supposed to be my day off or whatever?"

He levels me with a look. "When you're in a fight for your life, you don't take days off."

"Then you must have a terminal disease."

"That supposed to be funny?"

"Of course not." I sense a headache coming on as I dig into a bag and start lining up fish and produce on the counter.

"I figured with the news of your girl getting the lead, you might need a Roman-approved celebration dinner," he says. "So, Roman's here to save you from an extra twenty minutes on the treadmill." He pauses from unloading to flash me a heart-stopping grin. "You're welcome."

As I finish emptying my bag, I glance around at all the uncooked food on the counter. Not a takeout container or heat-and-eat tray in sight. "Where is dinner anyway?"

"You *do* know we're cooking, right?" Roman roars with laughter and slaps me on the back.

We dive into dinner prep—salmon, broccoli, the works—but before long, my back's tight, my calves throb, and I'm questioning my life choices.

The man said I could have a day off. Liar.

At least there's more than enough left over so I won't have to cook tomorrow, but it's looking pretty bland.

Roman crosses his arms as I present my new favorite weapon. "What is that?"

"Low-Sodium Old Bay. I promise, it's bomb."

His fingers brush mine as he snatches the seasoning... and my whole body sparks like he flipped a switch.

Griffin. Griffin, Griffin, Griffin.

The trainer frowns as he reads the label, but I plead with the bat of my lashes. With a critical glare, he runs his tongue across his teeth. "Fine. But not a lot."

I'm quick to give the salmon and veggies a light dusting before we pop it into the oven and push on to the next meal.

Eli skips down the stairs and plants himself at the counter. "Whatcha making?"

Roman gives my son a dry look, then side-eyes me like *I* planned this. But I won't be bailing him out this time. He's not the only one who knows how to torture people.

"Chicken," he says before returning to his prep, as if his answer could satisfy the kid's curiosity.

"Like fried chicken or the nasty kind?"

"*Eli*," I chide, but the little boy ignores me.

"My dad always took the nasty kind to work," says Eli. "Mommy makes the good kind."

Roman glances at me sideways, sending heat up my neck. "The kind covered in blood vessel-popping salt, doused in nutrient-poor flour, and drowned in cancer-causing lard?"

Eli's gap-toothed smile grows two sizes. "What's lard?"

"Eli, honey," I say, still trying to recover from the boy bringing up his father in the past tense, "why don't you go find something else to do?"

The little boy lifts a shoulder. "I don't plan to practice my act again until after dinner." He looks back to Roman. "Will it be done soon? I'm *hungry*."

"You're always hungry," I say.

"Fifteen minutes, kid. Tops," says Roman, expertly spacing his chicken as he places it in the pan.

Seeming somewhat content with his answers, Eli hops off his stool and heads in the direction of my room, where he'll likely pass the time watching TV. But abruptly, he turns back. "Mom, I forgot to ask Dad when we were at his house. Is he coming to the talent show?"

My heart stumbles with embarrassment as Roman takes inventory of me. We've yet to utter a word about the trainer's recent discovery of my husband jumping ship.

"Um, we'll see, honey."

The little boy's gaze is heavy with sadness as he disappears into the master suite.

Roman and I fall silent for the next several minutes of our prep. Once again, I find myself wondering why the man couldn't have just texted the instructions. Surely, he has better things to do than scrutinize my every move... and dig into all the pitiful details of my life. But he's glancing my way as I take the salmon out of the oven and reset the temp.

"So, tell me about this guy."

"Who?"

He bites into a carrot and leans against the counter. "The Baby Daddy. The *Ex*."

What is this? Interrogation: Part Two? As if he didn't have ample opportunity to ask these probing questions at the gym. "He's not my ex... yet."

"Okay." He shrugs. "The *Soon-to-Be Ex*."

"What's there to tell? It's like he took an extended vacation, leaving me to juggle two kids on my own." I break from the trainer's stare to slide the chicken into the oven.

"So, clearly, you're not over him." Amusement plays on Roman's lips as I slam the oven shut and go to wash my hands. "What kind of work does he do?"

"None of your business."

"He must be pretty damn successful if he can afford to leave you in such a"—Roman takes a look around—"comfortable position."

"Maybe *I'm* the success. You ever think of that, hmm?"

Roman munches on his carrot with a patient blink.

"He's the CEO of Blue J's."

"Blue J's?" Roman's face scrunches tight. "Like, the pizza?"

"The whole stinking chain."

"Ah, man!" He throws a fist over his mouth, a high-pitched laugh echoing in his throat. "Their pizza sucks, too!"

"Shut up." I flit water his way as I wring my hands, but he's cracking up.

"It's true. But obviously"—he takes another glance around—"somebody likes it."

And for the millionth time, I feel guilty for wishing that weren't the case.

Roman's still tickled as he checks out his phone, chomping on his stupid carrot. Maybe he's making plans to meet with some chick.

"So, what's your deal?" I ask, moving the sizzling salmon to a platter. "You got a girl?" It'd be nice to know what types of women have had a peek at what's hiding behind the "Roman" persona.

"That's classified," he says, still browsing his phone.

"So, you can ask about *my* love life, but I can't ask about yours?"

"Yep. I'm the teacher." His eyes meet mine. "You're the student."

Unbelievable.

To ensure I don't *overindulge*, Roman sticks around for dinner. It isn't lost on me when he polishes off his properly seasoned salmon and reaches across the dining table for another fillet.

He's ditched the leather jacket. Just him in that fitted black tee… sleeves cuffed and veins flexing beneath skin like carved intention. *Goodness.* The man's got the kind of arms that make women rethink their standards. Not that I'm staring or anything.

"Ballet Girl," he says, cutting his salmon with a fork, "I hear congrats are in order."

Maddie tucks away a humble grin as she digs into her broccoli, springy curls falling in her face. "Thanks. I can't wait."

Roman nods, munching on a floret like it's candy. "If you need pointers or anything, have your mom hit me up. I'm sure I could help you out."

Maddie's beaming. But I'm still trying to read him.

"What's your background anyway?" I ask.

His perfectly arched brow twitches at me. "My *background?*"

"In dance?" I incline my head as he chews. He hasn't exactly been open to sharing what he knows. "What school did you go to?"

Roman continues watching me as he swallows his food but turns to Eli without answering. "What's up, Little One? You don't like broccoli?"

Eli pinches his nose, scrunching his lips. "Broccoli's nasty."

Roman chuckles as he returns to his own. "You should eat it. It's good for you." He may as well have endorsed the boy's notion with that tired phrase.

Eli stubbornly crosses his arms, shaking his head like he has since he was two.

"Don't push it," I mutter to Roman. "It'll only make it worse."

Roman glares at me as if I've posed some sort of challenge, then turns back to my son. "You know, uh, David Copperfield got his magic skills from broccoli."

"No, he didn't." Eli frowns. "I saw it on YouTube. He just practiced and stuff, like me."

Roman leans in slightly, lowering his voice like he's sharing a secret. "But without the broccoli, he wouldn't have had the strength to keep trying."

Eli shoots the man a frosty glare before popping the tiniest green floret in his mouth. My jaw drops as Roman grins at me. But within two seconds, my son spits it out.

Everyone helps clean up after dinner, but I'm left with plenty of pots and pans to wash by hand. When I ask for help, the kids take off in separate directions—Eli to prepare for his talent show, Maddie to practice for the recital. I guess that leaves me and the trainer. But I know asking the guy to grab a towel will only lead to fifty pushups tomorrow, so I get to work on my own.

Why is he still here, anyway? I'm sure there's some hot chick or fitness convention that would gladly welcome his company.

Roman returns to his perch against the counter as he browses his phone, smirking in the direction of the rec room as Maddie stops and restarts her music. "She's got her heart set on this, huh?"

I nod as I scrub. "She's been passionate about that sort of thing for a minute."

He side-eyes me with a hint of curiosity. "How about you?"

A wistful smile curves my lips as I recall the endless turns I'd practice in the studio long after rehearsal was done, the tears that touched my lashes as I packed up my dance shoes for a consignment shop. "For a long time, I was. After a while, I wasn't."

His gaze is warm as he studies me. "And now?"

My body goes still under his stare, like he's just whispered a silent prayer and won't blink until I answer. But I don't know what to say. So I return to my scrubbing.

Tucking his phone away, Roman joins me at the sink. We fall into a quiet rhythm—me scrubbing, him drying—while Maddie starts and pauses her music again. I'll probably have to stop her soon—I can feel the girl's anxiety from here.

Then, without looking at me, he says, "Five years ago, I strained my thigh. Was stuck on my ass for six weeks straight."

"*Six weeks?*" The sarcasm slips out before I can stop it. "That must've been brutal."

He nudges my shoulder as I giggle. "For a guy like me, it was. Couldn't work. Couldn't dance. Felt like everything was meaningless, ya know?"

I do know.

I know what it feels like to watch your passion collect dust while the rest of your life runs on autopilot. To lose the one thing that makes you... you.

I love my family. And I love the life I've made with Griffin. Mostly. There's just always been something... "It's like you're headed out, and you know you're forgetting something—"

"—but you can't quite remember what?" he says, eyes steady on mine.

It's not just about the dancing. It's the slow fade. The way dreams slip out of reach when no one's looking. And how easy it is to stop reaching.

Our smiles meet in the quiet, like maybe we both understand.

Then, a loud thump echoes from the recreation room, and both of us make a dash to see what's going on. Maddie's in a daze as she sits up from the floor.

"Oh no—Maddie!" I rush to my little girl's side as Roman switches off the music. "Maddie, are you okay?"

She grunts as she rubs her forehead, and Roman kneels in front of her.

"How many fingers am I holding up?" he asks.

"Two..." she whispers. "Four?"

"She needs more water," says Roman. He checks her pulse as I rush to grab a glass. "Tell me what happened."

"I was... practicing my pirouettes, and I just couldn't get it right. I..." Maddie wearily blinks my way as I hurry back with water.

"Drink," I say, and she obediently gulps it down.

"Looks like you overexerted yourself," says Roman.

I press a hand to her burning forehead, brushing damp curls from her face. "Maddie, what did I tell you? You've gotta take it—"

"I know, Mom. I'm trying!" Against our wishes, the little girl stumbles to her feet. "You don't understand. It... It's gotta be perfect!"

Her voice shatters something in me.

Because I do understand. I've lived with that pressure my entire life.

Before I can speak, she takes off for the stairs, leaving me speechless.

"I don't know when she got so stubborn."

But Roman's lips quirk at me. "Seems like it runs in the family."

* * * * * *

"A banana and a good night's rest, and she should be good," says Roman, pulling on his jacket as I walk him to the front door.

"I'll get right on it," I say with a sarcastic salute.

He grins, and I catch myself holding the moment a little longer than I should.

Maybe I didn't completely hate his company.

"And *no* stress eating," says Roman, pressing a finger to the center of my forehead. "Just chill out. Take a bubble bath or something."

I have to hold my breath to resist giggling at the serious look on Roman's face as his raspy voice says *bubble bath*. "Yes, sir." I'm about to open the door when I turn back to him. "You still haven't told me about your dance background."

Crossing his arms, he steps closer, specks of light dancing in his eyes as they travel over my face. "So what? You gonna hold me hostage until I do?"

The heat in his eyes could melt gold.

My voice lodges in my throat as he leans in, the seductive arch of his brow paralyzing me.

He grabs my hand and yanks me out of the way.

"Ow."

With a rumbly chuckle, he pulls open the door, then turns back with a soft grin. "For ten years, I was a choreographer in Hollywood. If you'd done your research, you would've known that." He narrows his gaze on mine but doesn't seem quite as pissed as before.

Maybe he's not as much of an asshole as I thought.

"Nine-thirty, sharp!" he shouts and slams the door as he goes.

9

The kids' school auditorium is packed on Wednesday night, parents and siblings crowding the aisles while theater students test and reposition theatrical spotlights at the foot of the stage.

Maddie and I whisper polite pardons as we squeeze down the aisle of the auditorium, sidestepping tripods and outstretched limbs to a half-empty row near the center. I take the aisle seat. As Maddie waves hello to a couple of friends, it crosses my mind to film the performance for my little man to check out later, not to mention anyone who couldn't make it.

To my surprise, Eli didn't seem too nervous when I dropped him off backstage. Not that I'd blame him. I was much too shy to perform by myself at his age.

A text from Yana is waiting when I pull out my phone. *Wish I could be there. Send Eli my love!* She just got a callback for that audition in Ohio. I encourage her to break a leg and put my phone on silent.

It's too bad she couldn't come along. It'd be much less awkward, silently sitting here with my daughter while other happy couples set up their cameras and anxiously await the show. I guess this is what single motherhood is about or whatever. *Goodness. I hate this so much.*

Maddie browses on her phone while I take a lengthy swig from my gallon water bottle—wishing it was liquor—and set it next to my feet. Roman insisted I bring the obnoxious thing along when he heard about my plans for tonight so I could *stay hydrated* and be less tempted to grab food afterward. I swear the man doesn't let me have any fun.

So far, this week's been brutal. But definitely not boring. I'm not surprised after googling him. Turns out Roman toured with Andre Price—one of the biggest R&B stars alive—for a decade, even has a handful of credits for choreographing Andre's music videos. With the exception of the time he took off for his thigh injury, he performed in nearly every concert.

I have no idea why he'd settle to come to Michigan and teach a handful of mediocre dancers like me. Maybe he gets off on torturing people.

With all of Roman's flirtatious smirks and unnecessary touches, I've struggled plenty to remain focused this past week. But his deranged methods quickly ground me. Each time things start feeling easier, Roman pushes me harder. And every time I overcome his little obstacles, he's got another five lined up. The man can be incredibly exhausting, but he swears it's the only way I'll keep seeing results—and I *do* like the results. I haven't fit into these jeans in forever. But it would be nice if my legs weren't so sore. *Stupid Roman and his stupid squats.*

Abruptly, Maddie jumps from her seat, scanning the doors at the back of the auditorium. Her entire face brightens as she frantically waves. "Daddy! Over here!"

I turn and spot Griffin headed in our direction, all dressed up in a suit and fine wool coat, looking like he belongs somewhere on the cover of Forbes magazine.

I look to Maddie. "You knew he was coming?"

She shrugs with a crooked grin, tucking her phone away. It feels like I've been set up.

Okay, Laura. Don't panic. I smooth my sweater and adjust my beanie, thanking God I made a little effort and curled my hair. I meet him with my best smile—tight, bright, and barely hanging on. "Hey."

"Sup?" he says. "Can I sit with y'all?"

He's actually going to stay. That's… great! I should move.

Maddie and I shuffle to the next seats over, and Griffin sits—hitting me with hints of that spicy, woodsy cologne I used to bury my face in. Of course he had to show up smelling like memories. And he looks so damn good tonight. Sharp suit. Clean cut. That quiet confidence he wears like a tailored jacket.

His knee brushes mine, and I squeeze my thighs together, pulse tightening with the reminder of what used to be ours. It's been ages since our bodies touched with intention, but I remember the last time.

It was quick. Intense. An impromptu moment before a last-minute meeting. He'd just gotten word that a major vendor finally signed the deal, and he wanted to celebrate before rushing back to the office. The kids were outside playing, so we snatched the sliver of time like it owed us something—barely made it to the bed.

He'd kissed me like he'd waited all day for it. Urgent. Focused. Gripped my hips like I was the reward at the end of a long battle. And for those few minutes, I was.

It didn't matter that he had a meeting in twenty. He made time for me. Reached for me. *Wanted* me.

When it was over, he kissed me slow. Pressed his mouth to mine like a promise. His hands found the fleshy curves of my waist and squeezed tight as he growled, *"I'll be back for more."*

But he never kept that promise.

And now, he's quiet. Too quiet. Eyes everywhere but on me.

Hoping to at least get him to take off his coat, I thank him for coming, like some greeter at Walmart. He nods, pressing his hands into his pockets, gazing around like he's checking for the nearest exits.

I swallow and lean toward him. "You hit traffic?"

"Hmm?"

"Coming from the office, was there a lot of traffic?"

"Yeah." He coughs into his fist. "There usually is."

We shift away from each other at the same time.

Come on, Laura. He's shown up for you and the kids, and you can't get him to hold a basic conversation? I could kick myself for making things so tense with all the divorce talk last weekend.

"Hey, Dad," says Maddie, extending her phone in front of me. "Check out this cute dog park I found. Piper and Penelope would love it."

Right. Can't forget about the potential new siblings. I hold my breath as Griffin takes the phone from Maddie, pretending not to feel his luxury watch brush against my chest. I scratch beneath my cap as he checks out the phone, cross my arms as he passes it back.

"You're right," he says. "You should send it to Vicki."

Vicki? My daughter has that woman's number? How long has she been hanging around my kids? My gaze pings from my husband to my daughter, who's already texting with a grin. It's like I've just arrived at another party I wasn't invited to.

"How is Vicki, by the way?"

Griffin's smile fades as he blinks at me. "Uh, good." He bobs his head at no one in particular and returns to his hobby of locating exits. Guess talking about the new chick is officially off-limits.

The lights dim and the curtains part as I study the floor. *At least he didn't bring her along.*

The show kicks off with tone-deaf Bruno Mars and fourth graders pretending to be Spider-Man. It's sweet... for the first ten minutes. Griffin's somewhere else entirely. Probably thinking about quarterly losses. Or perhaps the last piece of lingerie Vicki modeled for him. The thought lands hard in my stomach.

Hopefully, he can hang around after the performance. Eli will be so happy to see that he came. Despite the thick wall of silence wedged in the sliver of space between us, I know I am.

A little girl is struggling to recite one of Shakespeare's sonnets when Griffin finally loosens his scarf. He leans into my ear as he shrugs off his coat, whispering, "These seats are small, huh?"

And goosebumps prickle my neck at his breath grazing my skin. I quake with a light chuckle. "I know, right?"

But wait. Is it my size that's making him uncomfortable? Maybe he wants me to switch seats with Maddie.

How's anybody supposed to see the show with your big ass in the way?

I'm reaching for my water when Griffin drops his scarf and bends to grab it, and the two of us bump heads.

"Ow."

"Sorry, I—" Griffin wags his head like a dog coming in from the rain. And now, I can't help giggling. An adorable smile ghosts his lips as he leans in. "It's not that funny."

"Yes, it is." A light laugh escapes me.

Maddie shushes us with scrunched eyebrows as we sit up straight, and that makes me giggle more. Griffin rumbles with a chuckle, too. And before we know it, both of us have a case of the giggles.

"Hush!" says Griffin, the laughter whispering through his nose. "You're gonna get us kicked out of here."

The two of us struggle to calm ourselves as a few stuffy parents glance our way, and Griffin raises a finger, softly apologizing for our obnoxious behavior. And just like that, I forget how tense it was. How long it's been since we laughed together like this.

It shouldn't feel this easy. But it does.

Before long, it's Eli's turn. He's in a little white tux and top hat as he pushes a tray with all types of materials across the stage, and one of the teachers sets up a card table.

"He's adorable," Griffin murmurs, wistfully shaking his head. I agree. Our little boy is *all* about presentation. Though, I honestly have no idea what he's got planned.

"Good evening, everyone," says Eli. "Tonight, I'll be showing you a small sample of my wonders and surprises. Some might call them illusions. But I prefer to call them *marvels!*"

Griffin grins. "That's cute."

The audience is peppered with light chuckles, and suddenly, I find myself wishing I'd paid more attention to what our son's been practicing in the mirror each day.

For his first trick, Eli holds up a lengthy piece of silk fabric. "Behold! A yellow scarf..." His eyes grow two sizes behind his glasses. "Or is it?"

Where did he even get that?

Everyone looks on as he tucks the scarf into the top of his fist, but when he attempts to pull it from the bottom, it's still yellow.

"Wait." Eli scrunches his little brows. "That wasn't supposed to..." Everyone chuckles as my son reexamines the scarf, flipping it inside out for everyone to see that it's orange on the reverse side. I rub my temples, cringing inwardly.

Concern is etched in Griffin's brow as he leans my way. "Maybe we should look into getting him in a sport or something."

"He just needs our support." *Come on, Eli. You can do this!* I silently root for our little boy as he calls the principal to the stage.

"Good evening, Mr. Davis. How are you tonight?"

The crowd ripples with a humored chuckle at Eli and all his little formalities.

Mr. Davis—a man of Black and Korean descent with *impeccable* taste in shoes, according to Griffin—offers a polite nod as he takes a seat centerstage. "I'm well, thank you."

"Those are some nice shoes you have there," says Eli as he eyes the principal's feet.

"Thank you." Mr. Davis tosses the audience a smile. "They're Allen Edmonds. My favorite pair."

Ever the shoe enthusiast, my husband bobs his head. "Fancy."

"That sounds lovely," says Eli as he continues his presentation. "Would you mind if I borrow one of those shoes, Mr. Davis?" The principal hesitates but slips one off.

Griffin looks to me. "Do you know what this is about?"

I shake my head, praying the principal is in on the skit as he passes the expensive shoe to my son.

Snatching a bottle of apple juice from his tray, Eli cracks it open. Everyone gasps as the little boy dumps the entire contents into his principal's shoe.

Oh dear.

He raises the shoe high in the air. "Behold! All the juice is completely—" But several droplets trickle over the sides.

I cover my mouth, and Griffin throws a hand to his forehead. Meanwhile, Maddie grips her belly with a crack of laughter, joining much of the crowd in their amusement.

Turning over the shoe with a frown, Eli dumps what's left of the juice on stage. "Well, that wasn't supposed to happen."

Mr. Davis looks heartbroken as my son passes back the mushy Oxford. "I think we're done here."

"No, wait!" shouts Eli. "I have one more trick. Please!"

With a heavy sigh, the principal nods for him to go ahead.

Eli grabs five small posters, drawn to look like giant playing cards, and sets them up on the table. "I'm going to have you select a card— any card—and I promise, I won't look."

"Oh no. Not this one." I close my eyes, too afraid to watch as Griffin elbows me.

"Should we tell them to stop?"

I'm at a loss. Though I'm terrified my son might embarrass himself beyond repair at this point.

"Did you pick your card?" asks Eli, still turned around and covering his eyes.

"Yes," says the principal.

"Okay. Go ahead and show the audience. I won't look!"

Mr. Davis shows us the card: Ace of Hearts.

"Now, *nobody* say it out loud," shouts Eli. "Mr. Davis, let me know when the card is face down again."

When the principal replaces the card, informing him that he's done, Eli turns and grabs his own small deck. Shoulders quake with silent laughter as he sloppily shuffles the cards and separates them into three piles. He asks Mr. Davis to select one, and the principal does so.

Eli flips the card on top with a sly grin. "Is this your card?"

The principal shakes his head, and my eyelids draw shut. *Not again.*

But Eli moves to the next pile. "Is *this* your card?"

Everyone laughs as the principal shakes his head once more. Poor Griffin cringes as Eli flips over the card on the third pile, asking one last time.

"Is... *this* your card?"

The principal shakes his head again with a shrug. "I'm sorry, Eli."

Our son nods, a clear pout on his face. Then he reaches into his pocket and pulls out a tiny, sealed sandwich bag. He holds it up for all to see as he shouts, *"Is this your card?"* To everyone's disbelief, he presents the bag, an Ace of Hearts tucked inside.

The audience explodes in applause as the principal adamantly nods. I honestly can't believe it!

Thoroughly impressed, Griffin jumps from his seat to give our little boy a standing ovation, and I join him. And pretty soon, the whole audience is on their feet.

—————————

After the show, the kids and I wait near the school while Griffin completes a phone call.

"Cool," he says, hanging up. "My assistant will rush over a brand-new pair of Allen Edmonds tomorrow."

He places a hand on Eli's shoulder, giving him a light squeeze.

"Let's just avoid using other people's belongings in the future. Okay, buddy?"

Eli gives a giant nod, still bubbling with excitement after tonight's performance. But I go still when Griffin's eyes meet mine.

"How about I take y'all out for ice cream?" he says.

The kids jump up and down as they shout, *"Yeah!"*

"That would be great," I say. Maddie and Eli lock hands and dance in a circle, laughing. But I pause, thinking about the fury on Roman's face if he were to find out I took a single bite. "It's just... I probably shouldn't be eating this late. I've got an early workout, and—"

"Right." Griffin's warm eyes rake over me. "The kids tell me you've been working with some tough trainer at Perry Rec."

"Unfortunately," I say with a sigh, thinking about the torture the man's going to put me through for the slimmest chance at dancing tomorrow.

"Nah. It's fortunate," he says. His gaze trails over my body, slow and lingering, like it remembers. "Not for my *bank account*, but... seems like it's paying off."

My cheeks grow warm with delight. It's not a blatant compliment, but I'll take it.

Griffin's still watching me as the kids continue spinning, making each other dizzy. "Sure you don't wanna go?" he asks.

I suppose it would be nice to go out as a family again. Maybe get a chance to talk some things over. Besides, I'd hate to burst the kids' bubble when they're already so excited. And it's been forever since he smiled at me like that.

But Griffin raises a finger as his phone rings. Checking out the screen, he steps away. "Hey, Vicki."

My heart throbs with a familiar pang. *Right. Vicki.*

"Yeah." With the briefest glance toward me, he returns to his phone. "We just got out."

"Mom, can I get Superman ice cream?" asks Eli, skipping into my arms. The creamy treat, with its medley of vibrant colors and fruity flavors, has always been my son's favorite.

"I want strawberry," says Maddie, still breathless from spinning.

I'm silent as Griffin returns, scratching at his beard.

"Sorry, guys. I'm gonna have to take a rain check." Both our kids groan as he presses his hands into his pockets. "Piper picked a fight with Penelope and lost. Vicki's too upset to take her to the vet on her own."

Why am I not surprised?

Eli's lower lip quivers, and Maddie's smile wavers.

"Promise I'll make it up to y'all. And you did great, little man."
Griffin lightly tugs on Eli's top hat and hugs Maddie goodbye. But
when he turns to me, his steps falter. I hold my ground, arms folded
like armor. Even if he were to offer me a hug, I wouldn't want it.

Doesn't he see what he's doing right now?

With a lopsided smile, he backs away. "It was good seeing you."

And I hold the kids close as their father heads off without us. Again.

10

"*C*ome on, Laura! Keep up! I'm gonna make you run it again!"

Roman dances in front of me the next morning, pumping his arms and dropping each knee to some reggaeton.

My legs are screaming after yesterday's madness, but I keep pushing. Because part of me needs this. Needs to prove that I can. I blow out some air, trying to pick up the pace, forcing my feet to match his rhythm.

And little by little, something shifts. Not in the pain, but in me.

A warmth bubbles up beneath the exhaustion as I catch a glimpse of myself in the studio mirror. There's a subtle slope taking shape in my waist, and I don't hate the definition of my thighs in these leggings.

"Aw, yeah." Roman gnaws his lip as I dance. "That's it, mama. *Let's work!*"

We slide and twist side by side.

"Okay, hold it here," he says. We're standing with our feet shoulder-width apart, arms stretched wide, as he wiggles his fingers. "Now, take my hand."

For what?

He impatiently wiggles his fingers again, so I do as he says.

"Alright. This is new. It might seem complicated at first, but it'll look *extra* sexy if you do it right." His eyes glint like a pigeon at a cookout.

His excitement is borderline irritating. But there's something about the way he lights up when he's teaching… I don't want to be the only one not having fun.

I follow along as he walks me through the steps.

"First, I'll pull you closer, and you spin in toward my shoulder." I slowly fold into his sculpted arm, and he nods. "Good. Now stay up on your toes. Usually, this would be better in some nice heels or something, ya know?"

My calves are burning from all the leg lifts, but I grin and bear it. His fresh nautical fragrance also makes things less unpleasant, and his cheekbones seem magnified at this angle, a perfect curve to his jaw. Sparks flicker in his gaze as he looks from the mirror to me.

"You're gonna use your left hand to sorta push off," says Roman, tapping his breastbone. "Right here. Middle of the pecs."

I bust out laughing, unable to help it.

He cracks a smile but quickly tucks it away. "Stop being silly and do it."

Rolling my eyes, I obediently shove him in the middle of his solid chest.

Wouldn't Yana love to be in this position?

"Nah, nah!" Roman grabs my wrist, pressing my hand flat against his chest, the firmness of his grasp coaxing my heart into a steady drumming. "Not all flimsy. Sturdy—like a board."

I push back harder, and he actually wavers a little. "You want me to slap you, too?"

His lashes bat once at my cheesy grin. "Come on, Laura." He tightens his arm around me. "You're wasting time."

"Okay." *Stick in the mud.* "What's next?"

We practice him spinning me in and out, again and again, until I'm dizzy.

"How much longer are we going to do this? My legs are killing me."

"It's good for your calves. Suck it up," he says. "You gotta learn to push off right."

I try to keep my hand as sturdy as possible, enjoying the satisfaction of giving Roman a good shove each time. And when he still complains, I imagine Griffin's stupid face and the way I should've shoved him in front of a car last night.

I still can't believe he ditched his kids over a rambunctious mutt.

"Okay, stop."

But I hear Roman a little too late and thump right into his chin. "Oh, shi—sorry!"

He gazes at the ceiling, running his tongue across his teeth. "Are you back with us now?"

I nod, and he takes a step back.

"After the first spin"—he spins me in and back out—"I'm gonna reach up and give you three twirls like this." He raises my hand over my head and spins me, ballroom style. A giggle escapes me as I stumble back. Something about being spun like Cinderella while he looks like he's solving a crime scene cracks me up. But his face is all business.

"Now your job is to hold it. I'm gonna let you go after the twirls, and you're gonna spin three more times. Got that?"

"What am I, a spinning top?" I chuckle at my own joke, but he's not smiling at all.

"You here to work or not?"

Right. Focus, Laura.

We practice all the twirling and spinning together, and I attempt to push what happened with Griffin last night to the far corners of my mind. But when Roman releases me to spin on my own, I struggle to keep up the momentum. I've seen this sort of thing in dance school and on TV but never had a partner to try it with myself. And I'm not all that light on my feet anymore.

Roman shakes his head, unsatisfied. "Again." He restarts the music, and we take it from the top.

As I watch myself step and sway in the mirror, I know I'm looking better. But maybe Griffin isn't convinced I've changed for good. Or what if Vicki is simply so flawless that he doesn't want anything else, no matter how skinny I get? My eyes burn as I blink away tears, and I stumble.

"Pay attention, Laura!" Roman fumes, a vein bulging in his forehead. "You got this. Again!"

But I'm tired. I wouldn't even be putting up with all this if Griffin had stayed. *I would've gotten it together... eventually. I was just having a hard time, and... He said we'd be together forever. That he'd always take care of us.*

Who would ever want you anyway?

Roman releases me to spin, and I stop.

I know he's going to be upset, but I just... can't.

I expel a hot breath, dizzy with confusion. Roman's eyes burn through my reflection, but I can't bring myself to meet them. He goes to turn off the music while I grab some water, praying he won't send me to the treadmill. Though at this point, it feels like I deserve it.

I startle when I turn and find him standing beside me, hands at his waist as he anchors his gaze to mine.

"Look," he says, "I get it. You're tired. It's been a long week."

He's got that right. I stare at myself in the mirror, the round belly that still hasn't flattened out. The belly that Griffin could never love.

Roman steps between me and my reflection and presses a finger to my temple. "Whatever's going on up here, you gotta get it under control *right now*. I mean, *lasso* that thing, for real." His intense brown eyes pin me in place, quiet but searing. "I need you to give it *all* you got. And if you do, I'll let you go."

I glance at the clock. It would be nice to get out of here early. Go home and take a good, long soak in the tub before the kids are out of school. Roman's handsome brows lift in a challenge as he steps back. Setting my water aside, I rejoin him on the dance floor.

It isn't long before the two of us are back at it, rocking to Cardi B's "I Like It" as we bounce side to side. We pop and wind, shutting out every distraction until we're light as air. And this time, I kill the combination.

Roman spins me in; I push off and spin out before he raises my hand.

"And three... two... one!" He releases me, and I spin and spin and...

Oh no! I slip, and my ankle turns. *"Ah!"* I thrust out my hands as I tumble to the ground, nearly smacking my teeth into the hardwood floor. "Oh my gosh! It hurts so much."

Roman curses under his breath as he rushes to my side. A lengthy hiss sucks between his teeth as he pulls back my sock, and I cringe with pain.

"What did I do?"

"I think..." He winces. "You rolled it."

Great. Just what I need. I squeeze my eyes in agony, running a hand down my face.

"Let me help you up," he says.

"No, that's okay—"

"Give me your hand, stubborn-ass."

Reluctantly, I turn it over, doing my best not to lean on him too much as he helps me stand. "Thanks," I mutter. I move to pull away the second I'm on my feet, but he tightens his arm around my waist.

"You shouldn't walk on it."

"It's not broken. I'll be fine." I take a step, and a sharp jolt sends me back to the floor. "Oh, man. That really hurts!"

With a smirk, Roman looms over me. "You gonna let me help now?"

I end up in the hall with my bare foot propped in Roman's lap as he presses an ice pack against my ankle. His touch is feather-light, but the chill of the ice keeps my hormones in check.

Folding back the hem of my legging, he applies more pressure. "It's really too bad," he says softly. "You've got cute feet."

Feeling a bit ticklish, I snatch back my foot with amusement. "What are you? Some sorta foot kinkster?"

It takes him a moment to register I'm pulling away. He yanks my bruised ankle back into his lap like it came from his own rib. "I just—I mean... they're small, and... Never mind."

I swallow my grin, wondering if the guy is trying to give a compliment or crack a joke. "I can't believe I did this to myself," I mutter, resting my temple against my hand.

"I can," he says.

"What do you mean?"

"I saw that gleam in your eye when you were spinning. If your ankle hadn't slowed you down, you would've gone for at least two more."

"And what's wrong with that?"

"You wouldn't have been following my instructions—that's what. And then I'd have to get you back on that treadmill and whip your ass into shape." The smallest grin ghosts his lips as I laugh.

"You enjoy making me miserable. Something's wrong with you."

Roman lifts a shoulder, and both of us chuckle.

Up the hall, a couple of girls—with perfect bodies and lots of midriff—stroll by, examining my pitiful situation. "Hey, Roman," says one.

He throws them a heart-stopping smile, and they head on their way, giggling like it's prom night.

I purse my lips, cheeks growing hot. "I need to get out of here."

"I don't know how," says Roman. "You can't drive on this ankle."

"Right. No matter how *adorable* it is."

He shoots daggers when I stick out my tongue. Glares like he wants to bite back but doesn't. Instead, he strokes his chin, eyes locked on the floor like he's making a decision he already knows he'll regret. When his gaze lifts again, something's shifted.

"Let me get my jacket."

✦✦✦✦✦✦

Roman stays in a high-rise apartment at the edge of Southfield, a busy area with lots of heavy traffic and shops. The elevator is questionable, and fluorescent lights flicker as he assists in my hobble toward his place. Someone dribbles a basketball upstairs while a large dog barks for them to knock it off. He plans to take me home, but he wanted to swing by here first.

"I've got this amazing natural healing ointment," says Roman, unlocking the door. "The sooner we can get it on, the better."

I take in the space as he helps me inside. The place kinda looks like a bar. Exposed brick walls, neon lighting, and a hardwood floor running front to back. One of the walls is covered with full-length mirrors—perfect for daily shirtless affirmations.

As he lowers me into a seat on the ratty green sofa, I can't ignore the dripping faucet in his tiny open kitchen, the neighbors' TV blaring behind a wall—a far cry from the Porsche we rode over in.

"This is kinda humble digs for a world-renowned choreographer, don't ya think?"

He shrugs, gently propping my foot on a giant, square ottoman. "I'm not home much. Besides, no one bugs me when I'm going over my routines."

I'm sure he blasts his music loud enough for the entire building to hear.

"Look, I *never* do this for my clients, so..." He grabs a couple of deflated pillows and tucks them around my back. "Keep it to yourself that you were here." Gathering a few dishes and abandoned towels, he heads into the kitchen.

"Yes, sir." Pulling out my phone, I shoot Griffin a text. If he can't pick up the kids, maybe one of his sisters can. I'm tempted to snap a picture of this place and send it to Yana while I'm at it, but I won't.

Speaking of pictures, there's a framed photo on the end table beside the sofa. It's a younger-looking version of Roman in a Pistons baseball cap, standing beside a guy who could be his teenage twin if he weren't a shade darker and rocking cornrows.

Wow. Roman is a person with a family and a life. "This your brother?"

His face is scrunched in concentration as he hurries back with a bottle of something green and flips the picture face down. "Yeah. Drink this."

He passes it into my hand, and I dutifully take a swig before spitting it back into the bottle. "It's dirt. Why would you give me dirt?"

His grin tilts just enough to be dangerous as he heads for the bathroom.

Jerk. I set the bottle of poison—that I won't be drinking—to my side as I take another look around. Towering shelves lined with books. A dinky TV on a cart. The only thing that screams Roman is the bench press in the corner. With his nonfraternization policy, how many girls from the rec have even seen this place?

His jacket is gone when he returns with his precious ointment and an ice pack in hand. Taking a seat on the ottoman, he pulls my foot back in his lap. His fingers are cooler now, skin glowing with less perspiration. With his sculpted pecs tensing beneath his loose tank, he kinda looks like one of those hot firemen in a calendar. Puppies optional.

He actually seems kinda... nice? Just as attentive with me as he was with my little girl.

His brows are heavy as he massages the cool cream into my ankle. "Keep it elevated. Plenty of ice. It should be back to normal in a week or so."

"Guess I won't be able to work out now," I say, forcing a pout.

He levels me with a look, one corner of his mouth lifting. "I'm sure we'll figure something out."

Of course we will. I drop my head, smiling to myself. As much as I hate the guy's grueling tactics, it's been nice having his overzealous support. And the dance routines aren't half-bad. Noticing his heavy gaze, I sit up straight and fix my face.

"I think you'll be fine," he says. But instead of releasing my foot, he moves to applying the new ice pack. "Seems like you're in a... better mood."

I twist my lips as all the heavy thoughts come flooding back and try to push them away. Roman's still watching me.

"What happened?" he asks.

"What do you mean?"

"In the studio," he says. "What was going on that had you so worked up?"

I glance away.

He lets the question sit between us for a beat, then nods slowly. "He was there last night, wasn't he?"

"Hmm?"

"Baby Daddy. He was at the talent show last night." He's not even asking, just assuming he's read my mind.

With a huff, I try to focus on the warm sensation of his hands on my skin. I don't want to talk about this right now or ever. But with my injured ankle in his lap, the man is holding me hostage.

"He was there," I say.

"With his chick?"

I frown. "How'd you—?"

"Google."

Of course. I managed to google him. Why wouldn't he google my husband? It wasn't until a couple nights ago that I stumbled across a photo of Griffin and Vicki at a red-carpet event. With the way Griffin totes that girl around, I'm honestly not surprised Roman could put two and two together.

"No. She wasn't there. Not that she couldn't ruin things with a simple phone call."

"*Ruin things?*"

I don't bother answering. I've yet to say a word about why I truly want to lose weight.

Roman nods. "So, how long you been like this?"

"Like what?"

"All lonely and pathetic. Waiting for him to come back."

I scoff, barely managing to smack his unfairly perfect bicep. "I'm not pathetic!"

He chokes back a chuckle as he checks out my ankle, and I fall back on the sofa in defeat.

"Seven months, five days, and... three hours." A spark of concern ignites in Roman's eyes as I release a heavy breath. "He just recently filed for divorce, but I'm contesting it."

"Wow." Roman doesn't even lift his head. Just keeps staring at my ankle.

Suddenly, it's as if I'm his faucet, leaking one sad detail at a time, drip by pitiful drip. "We've been together since my freshman year of college. Nearly a decade, and... he never told me why. He just left. Said it was best for all of us or whatever. Next thing I know, he's dating some new chick and picking up the kids on the weekend. Barely looks me in the eye."

Roman's sober gaze meets mine. It's almost as if he's the one sustaining an injury. But now that I've started, I can't stop. My eyes mist over as I study my hands in my lap.

"Life hadn't always been easy, and... he saw me when no one else saw me. Made me feel like I was actually worth something. Sure, we had our ups and downs, but we always had each other." I brush away a tear I didn't think I had left. "At least, until now."

Roman is staring when I lift my head, but he quickly refocuses on my foot. "That sucks."

My grin is dry as he softly punches my arm.

"Hey. 'Hearts will never be practical until they are made unbreakable.' That's from *The Wizard of Oz*."

I can't help laughing, and so does he. "You seriously memorized that?"

"One of my favorite quotes." He shrugs. "The studio I was at a couple years ago performed it for their recital."

The idea of this tough-as-nails trainer having anything to do with a recital is completely ridiculous. "Roman, *you* are full of surprises."

"You have no idea, sweetheart."

A flutter rises in my chest as we exchange a warm smile.

"Anyway." He pulls his gaze away, as if staring at my ankle will make the swelling go down. "What happened to you sucks, right?"

"Definitely."

"And so does this injury. But are you gonna let it keep you cooped up in bed—never dance again?"

I haven't really thought about it. Roman's face brightens when I shake my head.

"Then don't let that idiot keep you from dancing either."

He's got a point. Dance was always my first love... Then Griffin came along.

Roman and I sit in silence, examining my swollen ankle. I really appreciate him doing this for me. And the therapy is a nice bonus.

But the weight of everything I just said sits awkwardly between us, so I reach for something—anything—to lift it.

I slap his arm again, simply because I can. "I saw you worked with Andre Price for a bit. Those music videos are *hot*."

A soft grin passes over his face as he gives a surprisingly humble nod. "I did what I could. The dude can't keep time for shit."

Both of us laugh. Another lengthy silence passes between us as I study him, praying that maybe he'll share more.

Finally, he says, "Fifteen years ago, he came to the D, holding auditions for backup dancers. And there I was—some poor kid, raised by a single mom, on the brink of enrolling in the military—and the only thing I wanted to do was dance. So, on a whim, I went."

A poor kid, a single mom. Sounds like dancing might've been his ticket out, too.

"Honestly, I wasn't gonna go," he says. "But my little brother—Robert—insisted. Said at least one of us could do better than our mom's TV dinners and game show marathons. We were always that *one number* away from our big break. I couldn't count the number of times she flipped on us for supposedly stealing one of her lottery tickets."

Reminds me of my stepdad. Though I hope their upbringing was much less stressful.

"To this day, my bro is the only one I can talk to about anything," says Roman. "The only one who's not gonna feed me a bunch of bull about myself. So, I wasn't gonna go. Told him I'd wait until he graduated from high school, and we'd head to L.A. together. But he swore it was the opportunity of a lifetime. And as usual, he was right."

There's a familiar sadness in Roman's eyes. One that I know all too well.

He manages to break out of his trance and compose himself. "Anyway. I only danced backup for a month before Andre asked me to be his choreographer. Must've trained a hundred dancers in Hollywood."

His tone shifts, lighter now. Like he's trying to make pain sound professional.

But now that I've had a peek behind the curtain, I can't exactly look away.

"Why'd you come back?" If I achieved half the measure of success he has, I doubt I ever would. Then again, I never thought I'd stop dancing either.

Roman sets aside the ice pack to survey the damage more closely. "The Hollywood life got old fast—lots of shallow people. Even *more* shallow relationships. I wanted real connections again."

That's understandable.

"But"—he adjusts my foot in his lap, lightly applying his thumb to my injury with titillating circles—"by the time I got back, things were different. My dance crew from high school wasn't the same. Everybody changes once you got money, ya know?"

"Definitely understand that one." I exhale, my skin tingling under the slow drag of his fingers.

"And Robert got locked up for stealing cars."

"That really *does* suck." But I can't hold the frown. Not with his eyes on mine and barely an inch between my toes and... *everything* he's packing.

Dear God, why does that feel so good? The guy's got magic hands.

"I think I've spoken to my mom on the phone maybe a handful of times since."

He lets me go, and the warmth fades instantly. A crooked grin masks his face, but the words hit sharp and cold, like ice water down my spine. I blink, body still buzzing, but now my chest feels hollow.

"Better?" he asks.

"Much." I sit up straighter, throat dry, trying not to think about how amazing that felt... or how quickly it shifted. He locates the cap to his ointment and twists it back on. The sadness has already crept back into his face.

"Why don't you and your mother speak anymore?"

He focuses on the tube in his hands. "She promised she'd keep Robert out of trouble, and like an idiot, I believed her." My scoff draws a lengthy stare from him. "I take it you and your mom get along great?"

"Actually, mine passed away."

Roman shifts in his seat, then slowly exhales through his nose. "I'm sorry—"

"It was a long time ago," I say, waving him off. "In high school."

He silently examines me. "An accident or something?"

"Nah. Just... stress."

Officially, they cited a widowmaker heart attack.

"So my stepdad raised me." *Us.* He raised *us.* But I can't bring myself to say it out loud. "The last thing I said to her was, 'I don't feel like cooking tonight.' She'd called, sounding tired, and asked me to cook dinner. She'd do that sometimes. When she asked again, I scoffed and hung up. Only one of the most selfish decisions I've ever made. So yeah, if she were still around, I'd probably be the type to call every day."

I stare at the floor, heart thudding a little too loud in the quiet.

It's surprisingly refreshing to talk about her. I usually keep it inside. I hate crying all over Yana, and with Griffin, I never felt like I could.

But Roman hasn't interrupted. Just listened. It means more than I want to admit.

I just hope it isn't too much. Maybe I should've kept it lighter.

Goodness, why did I make this about me?

Roman nods, eyes on his hands.

"So, is that why you prefer the convenience of chicken nuggets and fish sticks?"

He softly laughs as I grab a pillow and chuck it at him.

"Shut up! You know my salmon was bomb!"

That intoxicating smile curves his mouth as he stands. "Let me grab some aspirin and get you home."

11

The next evening at the rec, Roman's right back in my face. "*Is that all you got?*" he shouts, throat corded with rage.

With a heavy breath, I throw another punch, cursing myself for getting carried away in the studio.

Technically, I'm supposed to be boxing, but the only one receiving blows is me. With Maddie's new rehearsal schedule, Roman and I agreed to work out during her extra classes. But I'm tired, and I'm not a fan of trying to throw punches while balancing on one foot.

Gym members stroll by with amused glances as my leather gloves slap against his mitts.

"Uh-uh. That's weak." Roman scowls. "That's *pathetic*. You wanna be pathetic?"

If it weren't for Maddie, I never would've strapped my kids into an Uber and come back for this. I glower at him as I punch. He's clearly just trying to amp me up.

"That's what you want, huh?" A wicked grin curls on his lips. "To be lonely and *pathetic* for the rest of your life?"

I throw another punch. Then another. *I'm not pathetic. I'm not.*

His eyes flash with cruel amusement. "Why you mad? You're not even trying. You aren't trying now, and you weren't trying back then." His sinister smirk grows wider as he leans in my face. "You know that's why he left."

I punch with the force of a meteorite. That was below the belt, and Roman knows it. But there's no way my family stands a chance if I don't keep going. And I'd give anything to dance again, even if it means continuing to work with this jerk.

"*Aw.* Did Roman hurt your feelings?"

"Shut up," I mutter.

"That's okay. You can quit *whenever* you want, sweetheart." He puckers his lips, brows dancing, as heat blazes in my chest. "Just remember, while you're sitting all alone, bingeing on cupcakes in front of the TV, your husband will be headed home to a sexy, *flawless* piece of—"

I slam my fist into his face.

Roman stands frozen—his big, dumb mouth hanging open—but I don't care. I rip off my punching gloves, throw them to the ground, and limp away.

Asshole.

— ♦♦♦♦♦ —

I find myself on the opposite end of the rec, waiting for Maddie's class to get out while Eli sleeps in my lap. As grown as he pretends to be, the little guy passed out the second I picked him up from childcare. Guess it was a long day at school.

I curl and flex my fingers, wondering if I've just severed my contract with Roman. The nerve of that guy, talking to me like that. After everything we shared yesterday.

Unfortunately, when I lift my eyes, I spot the jerk strolling toward me. He better be headed to another studio 'cause I don't have a single thing to say to him. But he sits beside me anyway.

"You've got a mean hook there," he says, gingerly rubbing his jaw.

I let out a dry laugh, glancing down the hall. If Eli weren't so heavy, I'd move to another bench.

"I guess I deserved that," says Roman.

"Ya think?" He's just lucky my ankle is messed up. Otherwise, I would've given him a swift kick to the crotch.

The sigh through Roman's nose is obnoxiously long. "I suppose that maybe I... pushed you a little too hard."

Is that his weak excuse for an apology? I settle my eyes on Maddie's class as they practice their spins. My heart sinks as I recall all the fun I had spinning yesterday before I fell—and that split second after I hurt myself when I feared never being able to dance with Roman again. Now, I don't even know that I'd want to. But his gaze burns the side of my face.

"Tell me what's going through your head right now."

I huff a humored breath. "Like I would ever tell you anything again."

"Look, you're clearly in your feelings about it. And if you don't get it out, you're just gonna eat 'em later." My glare is harsh, but he looks sincere. "So, let me have it."

It's as if a baby elephant is sitting on my chest. "It wasn't easy to share all that yesterday. I trusted you, Roman, and you just threw it back in my face."

He nods once, almost like he hears me. "Look..." He picks at a loose thread at the hem of his shorts, seeming almost as vulnerable as he did yesterday. "I know what it's like to... be let down. And in the past, I used it to fuel me. I thought maybe it would fuel you too.

I was just itching to see you back on that dance floor, and... Anyway, I messed up."

Up the hall, a dad is playing Hot Hands with his son, another's attempting to buckle his daughter's tap shoes. I can forgive Roman, but I'm not too sure I'm ready to.

"From now on, I'll keep personal things outside the gym," he says.

But I turn to him. "Roman, I don't want that."

The guy I chilled with yesterday was patient. Encouraging. Kind. It's been forever since I truly opened up like that.

Roman crosses his arms, gaze soft and curious.

"I like talking to you, and... I want to be able to. Whenever. Kinda like a friend."

A grin blooms on his lips like a moonflower at night.

"But one thing you're not going to do is talk to me any kinda way," I say. "I've been dealt enough of that to last me a lifetime, and..."

He leans in, intrigue etched in his brow. And that's when I know I need to shut it down. What's in the past needs to stay there.

"Just watch it, okay?" I threaten him with my fist, and he falls back in mock surrender.

Rehearsal has ended, and a flurry of kids rush out to collect things from their parents as Ms. Alyssa's almond-brown face and cropped black hair peek out at the door.

"Hi, Roman," she says with a warm smile. The two exchange cordial waves before she turns her attention to me. "Ms. Phillips, may I speak with you for a moment?"

My throat goes dry as if I'm being called to the principal's office. I glance at my son slumbering in my lap and give her a nod. "Sure." Thankfully, Roman's gaze is still soft when I turn to him. "Can you do me a favor?"

Roman's wide eyes rest on Eli, and he shakes his head.

"Come on. *Please?*" I put a finger in his face. "You *owe* me."

His scowl seems permanent as I lift Eli's little head so that he can take my place.

"It shouldn't be long," I say. He doesn't have another client for at least an hour anyway.

"This kid is potty-trained, right?"

"Please tell me you're kidding."

The man looks about ready to vomit as I shuffle inside.

Maddie's classroom has a different feel from Roman's. Smaller. More intimate and bright. Not all that different from the kind I trained in as a student: scarves and floral props in a corner, a massive decal of a leaping ballerina across the back wall.

"Thanks for coming in," says Ms. Alyssa, eyeing Maddie practicing pirouettes with an assistant at the front of the room. "I've been meaning to chat with you. I just wish it were under better circumstances."

With her petite frame and elegant poise, Ms. Alyssa seems to be a fairly relaxed woman—almost a younger version of Debbie Allen, really. But as graceful as she is, I can still see the quiet concern in her eyes. If she's changed her mind about Maddie getting this part, my little girl will be crushed to pieces. I cross my arms, praying everything's okay.

"Madison had a bit of a breakdown today," she says.

I glance at my little girl. "A breakdown?" She seems fine now, but Ms. Alyssa nods.

"We were reviewing one of her solos, and she forgot a step. And then she sort of went into this compulsive practice, repeating it again and again."

It's just like what happened last weekend.

"And when she made another mistake," says Ms. Alyssa, "she plopped down in the middle of rehearsal and started crying. I had to step out with her so she could get some air. But when we came back, she was fine."

I should've seen this coming. She's been obsessing lately. She's been practicing way too much. "I'm really sorry. This part just means a lot to her."

"I understand. And we don't want to take this special moment away from her. But I think it's vital that we stress the importance of taking lots of breaks and getting plenty of rest." Ms. Alyssa's eyes meet mine. "I'd hate for something like this to happen again before the show."

The woman is much too kind to say it, but I've been in the arts long enough to know what that means. Maddie has to get it together, or an understudy will steal her spotlight.

How did this happen? Does it have something to do with Griffin moving out?

Ms. Alyssa glances back at my daughter, watching as she twirls and twirls, graceful and effortless. "Madison is amazing," she says. "She just needs to believe in herself."

My daughter is full of giggles when we find Roman browsing his phone in the hall with Eli dozing in his lap. I can't help smiling myself.

"See? That wasn't so hard now, was it?"

His glower is worthy of a snapshot. "Can you just take this kid before he leaks or something?"

My little boy is still knocked out, so I go to lift him. But Roman completely flips.

"*Whoa, whoa, whoa!*" The man throws out his hands. "What are you doing?"

"I have to get him to the car, so..."

Roman shakes his head with a huff and tosses Eli over his shoulder. "I don't want you off your ankle for another week. Let's go."

Grabbing our jackets from the coat rack, we make our way toward the front. My smile never fades as the smoldering trainer lugs my sleepy boy through a lobby of astonished onlookers and out to the parking lot.

As Maddie dances ahead of us, practicing her piqués, Roman casts a glance my way.

"Is everything, ya know, *okay* with Ballet Girl?" he whispers.

"Mmhmm. Maybe I can text you about it later," I say with a wink.

"*That* would be great." He gives me the softest punch in the arm. "Old buddy, old... pal."

"It's been a long time since you've done this, huh?"

"You have no idea."

The man is as gentle as a swan with his young as he buckles Eli in the SUV. How the little boy is still passed out is beyond me.

As he shuts the door, Roman rolls his eyes. "What are you smiling about?"

"Just thinking you'd make a great babysitter. That's all." I chuckle at his glare and pass over his jacket. "Thanks. I really appreciate it."

He gives me a light shove on the shoulder, and it isn't so awkward this time. "You sure you'll be alright?" he asks, shrugging into his coat.

"Yeah. I practiced flexing my ankle on the Uber ride over. I should be good."

He crosses his arms, the rays of the setting sun catching in his eyes. "We both know that's not what I'm talking about."

I glance back at my daughter in the car. She's already got her earphones in, probably listening to the recital music. "It's just... Ms. Alyssa said Maddie had some sort of breakdown today. Apparently, she's a little stressed."

"Uh-huh. Well, I hate to tell you this, Ms. Phillips, but more is caught than taught." His hand nudges mine. "Perhaps a good role model would help." The man's smile is his superpower.

"Well, it'd be a lot easier to relax if I weren't so stressed about this divorce. I contested before the deadline, but it looks like the court will be taking its sweet time."

Roman watches me in quiet concern, brow furrowed.

"Seems like things will be moving forward, whether I like it or not." I tuck my hands into my jacket sleeves as I study the pavement, the October breeze scraping my cheeks.

Not a single call since the talent show. If it weren't for the kids needing a ride yesterday, I doubt I'd have received a text.

"To make matters worse, Maddie's tenth birthday is in a few weeks, and she wants a party." My little girl was so impressed with the small festival her abuela threw for Eli that she insisted on having one at our house. "After what happened at the talent show, I'm not ready to see her dad—or any of his family. Especially the woman that could one day replace me—"

But Roman explodes with an abrupt laugh. "Ah, man! I'm there! I am *so* there!"

I'm frozen by his completely inappropriate response to my heartfelt confession. "What?"

Roman's grin is a mile wide. "I've gotta meet this loser in person."

"Excuse me? How are you going to invite yourself to *my* daughter's birthday party?"

"*Of course* you want me there, mama. Somebody's gotta have your back. Besides, who else is gonna keep you from stress eating?"

I smack his stupid bicep, but I think the leather blunts my blow. "Thanks," I mutter.

The man's still struggling to calm himself down. "For what?"

"Yesterday. Today. Everything." It's probably mushier than he's used to, but I mean it.

He silently nods, gazing off to some random destination across the lot. He's glancing at his watch when I stretch out my arms.

Immediately, the man's face curls into a knot. "You know Roman's not a hugger."

I laugh, dropping my hands. It was worth a shot.

But he pulls me in for a hug anyway. And it's just as warm and firm as I'd imagined.

My eyelids drift shut as I indulgently press into his solid trunk and squeeze the sculpted curves of his back, the softest whisper tickling my belly. We may have our differences—and we both have *plenty* of growing to do... But it's nice to have a new friend.

12

I startle when I spot the woman gazing back at me in my dresser's mirror.

"What the...?" I push aside my freshly curled bangs and take a closer look. Between the auburn highlights Yana convinced me to get at the salon last week and the twenty pounds I've dropped since my husband walked out, I barely recognize myself. Waist smaller. Cheekbones higher. Somehow, I don't completely hate what I see. Though I was thoroughly disappointed to step on the scale and only see a one-pound difference this morning. Hopefully, Griffin will notice my efforts anyway.

Scratch that. I grab the portrait of our family at the beach and shove it into my underwear drawer. Then I yank off my wedding ring before I can think twice. Our connection at the talent show meant nothing to him; it shouldn't mean a thing to me, either. But my movement is slow as I place the ring beside the thinner image of me in the frame. This might be the hardest thing I ever do in my life. But despite pissing me off when we were boxing, Roman had a point: If Griffin chooses to settle down with Vicki, where does that leave me? I can't spend the rest of my life bingeing on junk food and Netflix. For the sake of my kids, I've gotta pull it together. Whatever that means.

Three knocks sound at the door, and Yana pops her curly head inside, chomping on a chicken wing. "Girl, this food is bomb. I ain't know you had enough coin for butlers and all that. Let me hold a few hundred." Since learning she didn't get the part in Ohio a couple of weeks back, my cousin hasn't been to another audition. And she claims budgeting is discriminatory. *Why am I forced to restrict my spending when Carol in the next subdivision over can buy whatever the hell she wants?*

My gray eyes catch a gleam of light as they roll in the mirror, and I shove the drawer closed. "I'll have to ask Griffin first if that's okay with you."

Yana's face curls tight as she studies the wing suspiciously. "Ew."

"He didn't plan the menu, just... funded the party," I say with a sigh. "Speaking of which, the pizza should've arrived an hour ago." I cross my arms, a chill rushing over my shoulders. *And that's not the only thing.*

Stepping inside, Yana softly shuts the bedroom door behind her. "You good?"

I nod once. *I just thought he'd be here by now.* Out in the great room, music's bumping, conversation's flowing, and... *Roman's not here.* "Of course it would've been nice if Griffin informed me that his mother and sisters couldn't make it *before* this morning." Guess our party wasn't worth their time. "But they're sending gifts with their love."

"Good riddance," Yana mutters. Setting her greasy wing on my dresser, she moves to my side and dusts her hands before placing one on my back. "Listen, don't let that jerk stress you. You've been good without him."

I suppose it has been a good three weeks since I contested the divorce. The court has acknowledged my claim and assigned a case number, but nothing else so far. And somehow, I'm still standing.

But there's no way I'd survive the uncomfortable silence Griffin's been serving—and the briefest of waves from his car when he picks up the kids—if it weren't for my support system. And at the moment, I'm missing half my team.

"I just want to be smart tonight, ya know? I can't get caught up again like I did at that talent show." I told Yana all about it as we vented over our latest woes while splitting a salad downtown.

She searches the ceiling wearily. "I just wish you understood that you deserve so much better. I mean, look at you." She directs my attention to the mirror. "You're *bad*, girl. Don't let anyone take that away from you."

My mouth slides into a grin as I check out my hair and slimmer frame. "Thanks, Yana."

She smacks my behind as the doorbell rings. "Speak of the devil! I bet that's him now."

With a deep breath, I march out to the hall.

Bouncing bouquets of pink and silver balloons fill every corner, Maddie and her friends—from school and ballet—running around in crowns and tutus. Even the parents are enjoying themselves, sipping on pricey champagne and snacking on hors d'oeuvres. I give one of the moms a friendly smile before making my way to the door with quivering knees. But I'm pleasantly surprised when I open it.

"Hey, beautiful."

"About time!" I shout with crossed arms. "I should make you drop and give me twenty."

Roman's eyes shine with amusement. "Can't I be fashionably late?"

I check him out in his red *Thriller*-reminiscent leather jacket and designer jeans. I suppose I'll excuse him for now.

"Speaking of fashion"—he steps inside, taking a lengthy inventory of me—"you looking *good*!"

"Thank you." My cheeks grow warm as he gives me a twirl, taking full view of my cozy off-the-shoulder sweater and leather skirt.

I've been in lighter spirits since my ankle healed up, and Roman's got me doing so many spins these days that I could practically do them in my sleep. He holds up a birthday card, waving it like some sort of admission ticket, and I gladly receive it.

"You're sweet."

But my cousin's arm shoots out between us as she extends her hand, a beauty pageant smile on her face. "Hey, Roman. Remember me?"

His expression is vacant as they shake hands. "Did you... take one of my classes?"

"Of course, silly!" Yana releases a cackle as she shoves the trainer's shoulder, being sure to give his bicep the briefest squeeze before taking a step back. She's only been waiting to shoot her shot for six weeks. "How's he gonna act like he doesn't—? Roman, you don't remember me? First day of class, front and center?"

He slowly bobs his head. "Shiny, hot-pink pants?"

Yana wiggles her brows at me and bats her lengthy lashes. "Mmhmm."

"Weren't you the one who kept stepping on toes every five minutes and running back for water like you might die of thirst?" Her smile slips as he tilts his head. "Didn't you drop out?"

"Well, uh..." Suddenly, the poor girl has forgotten her line.

"Roman, Yana's my cousin," I interject. "She got me to sign up for your class." And the grin he gives me is as gentle as one of his hugs.

"Come on," says Yana, finally recovering from stage fright. "I'll show you the rest of the house." Grabbing Roman's hand, she pulls him toward the stairs.

"But I've already been here," he says.

"That's okay." Yana casts him a seductive smile. "You seen the bedrooms upstairs?"

Roman tosses me an imploring gaze as they take off, but I lift a shoulder, the same way he does me when I'm about to pass out on the treadmill. *Vengeance is sweet.* I set his card on the gift table, thankful to finally settle my nerves, but I jump when the doorbell rings again. *Griffin.*

Checking my hair in the mirror, I swing open the door. But it's just the pizza delivery guys. I direct them to the rec room and take a breath.

He's late. Again. I don't even know why I care. This is so like him to do this.

Apart from Griffin, pretty much everyone's here. Maybe he changed his mind. Perhaps he has better things to do... like Vicki. I prickle with irritation as I send off the delivery guys with a lucrative tip and head for the rec room, praying Maddie hasn't noticed her father's tardiness.

For the most part, everything seems to be going well. The kids are congregating at a craft station I set up where they can decorate their own ballet shoes; parents snap photos as they chuckle and chat about the festivities. Warmth fills my heart when I spot the bright smile on my little girl's face. With the party planning, she hasn't been too stressed in rehearsals, and Ms. Alyssa says she's doing much better. I just hope to keep things that way.

I pass the kitchen island, and the fairy castle birthday cake at its center catches my eye—a little ballerina at its top. It might not be the massive presentation Daphne presented to Eli, but I did my best.

It comes as no surprise when I enter the rec room and find a little thief peeking in a pizza box. "What are you—a rat?" Eli bolts upright, his hands behind his back, and I point toward the door. "Get out of here. We'll eat soon." But I can't hide my smile as the little boy skitters past me and out of the room. I better make sure he hasn't gobbled down a slice already.

All of it smells delicious. Cheese pizza, pepperoni, too. But the box I open holds my weakness: pineapple and ham. My tummy growls eagerly as I lick my lips. Maybe I wouldn't be so worked up if I weren't so frickin' hungry.

"Are you *trying* to torture yourself?" Roman leans in the doorway, arms crossed, a lazy grin on his lips.

"Oh. I wasn't—"

"You drink your water?"

I nod as he crosses toward me.

"Eat a salad?"

"Mmhmm." And I reported to his class this morning—nine-thirty sharp, like always.

He soberly looks me over. "You gotta relax, alright? Just be cool."

"I'll try."

Glancing at the open box of pineapple and ham, he lifts an index finger. "*One* slice of pizza. *One* sliver of cake. No more than *one* glass of champagne. Got it?"

"Yes, sir."

Then he grabs two slices and takes a massive chomp. My mouth drops open as he chews.

"What?" He shrugs, his mouth full of *my* pineapple and ham. "I get more calories."

Yana's near the cake in the kitchen, tossing back champagne when we return.

"Somebody's thirsty tonight," I say, giving her a nudge. But my cousin focuses on the door with a tense jaw.

"I think I'm gonna need it, too," she says.

My heart stills when I follow her eye line and find Griffin hugging the kids in the foyer. I didn't even hear the doorbell.

Of course Vicki's at his side, sporting another one of her amazing, camera-ready dresses—putting my little ensemble to shame. My stomach curdles as she passes Maddie's gift to Griffin and bends to hug my daughter tight, Penelope and Piper anxiously wrapping their leashes around them.

Yana bitterly shakes her head. "I can't believe he brought that chick."

I might need a drink myself.

Roman rubs my shoulders, his steady gaze meeting mine. "You got this."

I nod. Yana sets her glass aside and joins us as we approach.

Vicki is the first to spot the three of us headed their way. I offer a polite wave as her gaze snags on my new figure. *Golden.*

To my delight, Griffin does a double-take and stands upright. "Hey... Laura."

"Hey." But my voice is small as he closes the distance between us. For the first time in ages, he presses a kiss to my cheek, and my knees go weak.

Dear Lord, when will I ever get over this man's smell?

My cousin sucks her teeth, and Roman gives me a lengthy stare. But Griffin's eye is on him as we part.

Before I can compose a coherent sentence and make proper introductions, Vicki untangles from her dog leashes, extending a hand. "Hi, Yana. We must've missed each other at Eli's party—"

"That wasn't a mistake," my cousin says, arms still crossed.

"Really, Yana?" Griffin squints. "You gonna do this at my daughter's birthday party?"

"*Are you?*" Yana barks.

"I'm happy to have *everyone* here," says Maddie, pinning them both with an anxious gaze.

My chest tightens at my children having to witness the tense exchange at all. And I can't feel my toes.

"Um, Maddie's right. It's good to see you. Both of you." Ignoring my aching heart, I smile at Griffin and his date. Quickly, I turn to Roman. "Can I speak with you for a moment?"

"No," says Roman as soon as I shut my bedroom door. "Absolutely not."

"I didn't even ask you anything."

"You want me to play footsie with you to make Baby Daddy jealous. You think I didn't catch the way you nearly fainted when he greeted you just now?" He crosses his arms like a stubborn toddler. "Nah. Roman hates lying. Roman hates *liars*."

I flop on my bed with a pout. "Then what the hell am I supposed to do? You see how gorgeous that woman is?"

"Eh. That's subjective."

"Didn't you refer to her as *flawless* or whatever when I socked you?"

"I wanted to get you fired up. And, obviously"—he rubs his jaw with a frown—"my strategies are very effective."

"Roman. Every time I'm around them, it's like I'm some random nanny. A surrogate who was invited just to be polite. I'm sick of playing the loser."

Roman assesses me in silence. "The loser?"

I nod, barely. "Every chance he gets, he's bringing that chick around. Letting her bond with our kids, acting like she's already a part of the family. It's like he's hoping it'll make me accept it all somehow."

"*Have* you accepted it?" Roman's critical gaze links with mine, and I look away.

"I'm getting there. But what I don't want is him thinking I can't function without him anymore. He clearly wants me to think he's fine without me. I want him to know I'll be fine without him, too." *Then maybe he'll care about what we've lost.*

Roman's jaw tenses, and he grumbles, "Fine."

"Really?"

He runs his tongue across his teeth. "But only for tonight and absolutely *no* kissing. Also, don't squeeze my ass. I hate when chicks do that."

"Thank you! Thank you! Thank you!" Throwing my arms around his neck, I kiss his cheek, drawing a harsh glare. "Okay. Rules start now."

◆◆◆◆◆

We return to enjoying the festivities hand-in-hand, and I can't deny the tender warmth of his fingers embracing mine as we move through the crowd, chatting and greeting everyone. Roman's hand rests low on my back as we maneuver through the kitchen and rec room, prepping our plates. And his affectionate hands seem glued to my shoulders as we sing Maddie "Happy Birthday" and take one photo after another.

I don't have to look twice to notice Griffin staring at us from across the room as he tosses back his champagne, pretending to have the faintest interest in Vicki and her pups. Yana pulls me aside to ask what she's missed, but I tell her I'll fill her in later. She retreats to hosting the games and drinking out of boredom.

It isn't until the third dance mom asks Roman for a selfie that Vicki finally pulls up something on her phone and shares it with Griffin. Both of their gazes shift between the phone's screen and Roman as they seem to register the broad reach of his fame. They're googling. I bet they wonder why he'd be here with a chick like me. And as he steals bites of my food and wraps his arms around my waist for another photo, I've kinda gotta wonder myself.

Roman and I are huddled close on the living room sofa, checking out a video of a couple dancing the rumba on his phone, when Griffin approaches, extending a hand.

"Sup, man? I don't think we've been formally introduced."

The plan was to express our little "showmance" with nonverbal PDA in order to avoid "as much fibbing as possible," as Roman put it. Up until now, we've managed to keep our distance, but it seems we've been cornered. A wave of anxiety ripples through me as I pray Roman will keep up the act.

He tosses me a hesitant glance. "L, you didn't... you didn't tell him?"

Griffin's lip curls. "*L?*"

Roman stands and slaps fives—instead of giving Griffin the professional handshake we all expected. "Roman Graham," he bellows at ear-piercing decibels. "Nice to finally meet you, man! The kids told me all about you."

Suddenly, I see why Roman was reluctant to take on this role. He's not the best actor.

Griffin's eyes bounce between Roman and me as he and Vicki take a seat across from us, her little mutts sniffing and attempting to climb all over my canapé sofa. "You've talked to my kids about me?"

"Of course," says Roman, tossing a casual arm around my shoulders as he settles back beside me. "When we're chilling at the rec or over Sunday dinner. Of course, L and me appreciate you keeping them overnight every now and then." He wiggles his brows, and I smack his chest, eyeing him to reign it in *fast*. Roman clears his throat and props a Gucci high-top on his knee as Griffin gives him a long stare.

"So, you've been to my house before?"

"*Your* house?" asks Roman, as if reading my mind. "Rumor has it that this fine lady became queen of the castle *months* ago."

"I'm not sure she can hold that title if I'm paying the bills." Griffin swirls champagne in his glass, stone-faced as he leans on his knees. "From what I hear, I might be paying yours, too."

I cross my arms, face on fire. This is getting tense fast. Piper punctuates a low growl with a bark, and Vicki tugs her chain.

"Looks like the girls are ready to go outside," she says, looking to Griffin. "Care to join me, hon?" Her grin falters as he shakes his head, and the pups yank her toward the door. "Be back shortly!"

Roman snorts. "The *girls?*" I elbow him, and he returns to his phone with a low chuckle.

Griffin isn't easily swayed.

"So, *Roman.*" He says his name as if it's something one of the kids made up. "Are you for real, or is that a stage name?"

The men stare each other down as Roman's shoulders go tense. "It's the name my mom gave me."

Griffin smirks, throwing up a hand in defense. "I get it, I get it. A lot of Black folks give their kids eccentric names. Usually out of fear that they'll turn out mediocre."

Roman turns to me, the sexiest grin etched into his cheek. "Do I seem *mediocre* to you?"

"Not at all." And I can say that with one hundred percent honesty.

Griffin's bristling when we look his way. "And you and Laura *dance* together?" His gaze is almost accusing as he glances at me.

Roman releases a rumble of a chuckle just to piss the man off. "I mean, I wouldn't say dancing is *all* we do."

I rub my temples with a sour belly. This is getting out of hand, and with the way Griffin's watching me, he almost seems a little hurt by that one. Before Roman can get carried away, I say, "We spend a lot of time in the gym. The calisthenics are brutal."

"I thought you loved doing squats with me," says Roman, not bothering to whisper as he leans in my ear. I smack his chest again.

Griffin's gaze pings between the two of us like an investigator on a case. "So, what is this? Some form of accountability?"

As if I'm too lame to have a friend?

Roman has already returned to checking out the talented couple on his phone, but I tap his arm, directing his attention back to Griffin.

"I'm sorry, what?"

"Just wondering, what's the deal?" says Griffin. "I'm kinda surprised you have time to come out to a birthday party for your client's daughter."

Seems he's surprised anyone showed up at all.

A grin plays on Roman's lips as he pulls me closer. "Well, she might be a little *more* than my client. Right, L?"

I stare at Roman in shock. I suppose that, technically, he isn't lying. But he doesn't break character for a moment. He leans a little closer, his enchanting lips mere inches from mine, as his fiery gaze puts me in a trance. And my heart flutters like the wings of a hummingbird.

He's screwing with me. He's doing everything in his power to ensure I never ask him to do this again. But as his mesmerizing eyes rest on my lips, I can't help wondering if he really wants to do this. Right here? In front of Griffin?

I playfully turn his cheek away.

———————— ✦✦✦✦✦ ————————

Before I know it, the party's over, and the last few stragglers are headed out. It's technically Griffin's weekend with the kids, so they're spending the night at his place. Despite everything, I still find myself wishing he could've spent the night here.

Maddie received tons of gifts: a makeup kit from Yana, more designer dresses than she'd ever wear from her abuela and aunties, I got the ballet shoes she asked for, and Roman gave her two tickets to see *The Nutcracker*. When everyone turned to Roman, eyes wide, he simply shrugged. "They were on sale."

But no gift could've topped Griffin's: a scraggly white mouse in a cage. Yana choked on her champagne, and Roman suppressed a laugh as kids took off running and shrieking in opposite directions, their parents recoiling in horror. But not Maddie. Glowing with speckles of glitter in her party dress and curls, she set the cage down on my *expensive* French coffee table and went to hug her father tight.

I didn't work up the courage to confront him until he was headed out the door. "Really, Griffin? A mouse?"

His eyes shined bright as he slipped on his coat. Vicki was already out in the car with the pups.

"I'm just trying to do what you said." He grinned, like he expected a gold star. "I asked the girl what she wanted. She said a pet mouse. So, try not to trip... *L*." I pursed my lips as he pressed another light kiss to my cheek and stepped toward the door. Then, with a lingering gaze over my breasts and hips, he said, "You look good, by the way." And just like that, he was gone. I've been anxious to find a quiet moment to collect my thoughts ever since.

My poor cousin staggers as she approaches the foyer, and I rest a hand on her shoulder.

"I don't know if you should drive, Yana. You're looking a little tipsy."

"Please. I put stronger alcohol in my cereal most mornings." Yana cackles as she fishes for her keys for what seems like a good five minutes. She presents them with a lopsided smile, and Roman plucks them from her hand.

"Your Uber will be here any second," he says.

A flirtatious chuckle rumbles in her chest. "You wanna *ride* with me, Roman?"

I softly tug my cousin out of the man's face. "I'm sure Roman has other plans for the evening."

"*Pssh!* You can't keep him all to yourself, girl! Let me get some. I *need* some." Yana turns to him with a devastated pout. "Roman, baby, she don't even have to know. Just *you* and *me*, one night—maybe two... or three. As much as you want, really—"

"Oh, look! There's your Uber." I quickly direct my cousin toward the door and escort her down the stairs. Her palms are still pressed longingly against the window as the car pulls off.

"Guess our little act was a success," says Roman, rubbing his neck as I return.

"Yeah. Maybe a little too successful." I press a hand to my eyes, humiliated for my cousin. Hopefully she'll forget any of this happened.

I'm still watching the Uber pull out of the drive when Roman grabs my shoulders and spins me around. "You did it. You survived!"

"All with the help of my fake boyfriend."

"If it means watching more steam shoot out of that stiff's ears, I'll be your fake boyfriend anytime."

"I'll hold you to it!" I say with a point. "But don't call me L. That was weird."

He nods, stepping closer as a chuckle dies between us. "How about..." He bites his lip, examining my face. "Diamond Eyes?"

I roll my eyes, but the corners of my mouth betray me.

"I don't hate it."

Roman holds my gaze, as if waiting for me to elaborate. But after all the evening's events, I wouldn't know where to start.

"Thanks for coming tonight," I finally say. "And participating, too." It was the highlight of my day, watching him get his face painted with Eli. Though he washed it all off within minutes.

"The sacrifices we trainers make. And the gift-wrapped rodent? That was some creepy shit." He turns for the door, tossing me another glance. "You good?"

"Mmhmm."

We slap fives like boys, and he disappears into the night like it's no big deal.

But it was. He didn't have to come.

Shutting the door behind me, I look around at my quiet, empty house. "And then there was one." With a tense breath, I begin turning off the lights as thoughts about the night's rollercoaster ride creep over my shoulder. Yana and Vicki and Griffin and...

Why didn't his family come? Is it all because of me? Did I make things worse by inviting Roman? My heart pinches at the thought of nearly kissing a man who has absolutely *no* romantic interest in me in front of my husband.

Can't you get anything right?

What was with Griffin's little curveball at the door anyway? It's like he's just cut open a wound that's barely begun to heal. Maybe he was just being nice?

I make my way into the kitchen, where the giant castle cake has hardly been touched. The tiny bite Roman left me was *so* good, too. Vanilla buttercream icing with chocolate cake. So rich and divine.

With the briefest glance toward the door, I scoop some frosting on my finger and pop it in my mouth. *Oh my gosh. That is amazing.*

✦✦✦✦✦✦

I'm halfway through my second secret slice when the doorbell rings. *Oh no.*

I grab a napkin and wipe my hands. But then, the pounding starts. *No. No. No.* I rush to the door, heat rising up the sides of my neck.

"You're back."

"Yeah, I think I left my—" But Roman narrows his eyes.

With his thumb, he smudges something away from the edge of my lips and studies it quietly. My stomach bottoms out.

"Frosting. You kidding me, Laura?"

I scratch the back of my head as he storms toward the kitchen.

"Roman, don't!"

Glaring back at me, he snatches up the plate with the half-eaten slice. "Is this what you're doing now? *Sabotaging* yourself?" He tosses it in the trash. Then he grabs what's left of my expensive, towering cake and hurls that, too. The cake stand violently crashes into the wall as pink and white icing splatters across the fridge.

"Roman! Do you even know what you're doing?"

"*Do you?*" He's heaving with rage as I stare at him.

Collapsing at a stool, I throw my face in my hands. *He's right. I have no idea what I'm doing. What the hell is wrong with me?*

When I look up, Roman's standing over me, his hands firmly planted on the counter as he attempts to steady himself. "I thought you were good," he mutters between clenched teeth.

"I was! I... I think." My gaze rests on the counter as the room spins. Why can't I figure this out?

But Roman doesn't let up. "What happened when he left tonight?"

I shake my head. "Nothing."

"*You wanna drop and give me fifty?*"

"Okay. Okay!" I glower at his fuming face. "He... told me I look good."

Roman's cynical laugh is cruel. "And you fell for that shit, didn't you?"

"You think he was lying?"

Roman drags a hand down his face. "Laura, you've *always* looked good." He stares me in the eye as a scoff escapes me. I thought he hated liars.

"The problem is you just keep waiting for that prick to tell you so," he says. "He was clearly jealous when he saw us together and was trying to get under your skin."

So, he only tossed me a compliment to screw with me? I shake my head as I stand. "That's not true." I head into the living room, stomach queasy. *I don't need this right now.*

Roman follows me anyway. "This is *exactly* your problem, Laura. You're not doing this for you. You're doing all this for *him*! And as long as he's your motivation, you're not gonna stick it out."

"Just... shut up," I say, beginning to pace. "You don't know anything."

"I know one thing. *This* is exactly why you're struggling. You *obviously* lost yourself in that asshole years ago!"

I stop and cross my arms. "He's not the asshole. You are!"

Roman lifts a shoulder with a nod. "Maybe so. But I'll tell you this much—I wouldn't dare drag you through half the shit he has."

I'm not sure if it's his intense gaze holding me captive or the other way around. And my heart twists as tears sting my eyes. I plop my face in my hands, feeling like a complete idiot.

I just love him so much. How the hell am I supposed to go on without him?

But Roman yanks me into his arms, and I crumple into a blubbering mess.

Ten years of laughs, kisses, and tears disintegrating in my grasp. Griffin's affectionate gaze and charming smile vanishing into a dense fog, deserting me.

And as Roman holds me in the silence, the heavy knot of frustration and heartbreak in my chest finally begins to unravel. I weep into the blanket of his arms, thinking about everything I've been through. Everything I've lost.

"Listen, I don't know who convinced you that you don't deserve better. But you do, Laura. *You do.*" Roman's unwavering voice resonates against my hair, his chest heaving with determination. "And I refuse to let you go on doubting it."

13

I'm greeted with a text from Roman when I wake the next morning. *To love oneself is the beginning of a lifelong romance – Oscar Wilde.*

My insides launch into an Argentine tango as a smile tugs my lips. *Thanks. That means a lot,* I text back.

No problem, he responds. *Now LET'S WORK!!!*

I burst out laughing as I picture him screaming at his phone like I skipped a rep. *He's such a sweet asshole.* I toss my phone and fall back on my pillow, thankful for a quiet Sunday morning.

Last night, Roman let me ugly cry all over his bougie leather jacket, then stuck around to clean up the cake disaster and toss any leftovers that might trip me up. I was shocked when he didn't trip over my confession that I'd still been weighing in against his wishes. When I explained my frustration over this week's pathetic one-pound weight loss, he barely batted an eye. Then he gently reminded me to ignore the numbers and focus on how strong and energized I feel instead, how much easier it is to jump and twirl. He then proceeded to deliver thorough instructions on water intake for the next twenty-four hours, which I promised to follow completely.

As he was headed out, he stopped to lift my chin. "You're gonna be alright," he said. "Believe that." And at that moment, looking into his steadfast gaze, I almost felt that I could.

I've barely pulled myself out of bed when he sends the new meal plan.

This is less calories than last week! I shoot over the message with a red-hot-faced emoji. But my pouts rarely affect him in person, let alone by phone.

After what you did last night? You're lucky you got that, he says. *No pain, no gain, sweetheart!*

⁘

"Don't you got any real ranch?" asks Yana, falling across the living room sofa, my Greek yogurt alternative in hand.

I shrug as Jessica Alba slumps before a mirror on the TV screen. "Sorry. Roman tossed it all."

Yana raspberries, squirting the condiment all over her bowl of baby carrots. "At this rate, y'all gon' have me losing weight by osmosis."

I toss back some water as Jessica Alba directs her attention toward the stage, preparing to unveil her awe-inspiring dance moves to the world.

With the grocery shopping out of the way, we've spent most of the day catching up on movie classics: *Save the Last Dance, Step Up One* and *Two.* Then, once we got over the surprise of Vicki, unexpectedly, dropping off the kids this evening, we selected my favorite, *Honey.*

"Girl, I'm glad you got him as a trainer and not me," says Yana, smacking on a carrot like Bugs Bunny. "'Cause I would've lost my damn mind if he chucked *my* birthday cake across the room."

"*Shhh!*" I frown, glancing toward the railing upstairs. The kids are supposed to be taking showers, but their ears are always open. "Maddie and Eli don't need all the dirty details," I whisper. As far as they know, we sent everything home with guests.

"Please," says Yana with a dismissive wave. "They know that man crazy."

"You didn't seem to think so last night," I mutter.

She sits up, pointing a carrot at me. "Hurtful."

The poor thing laughed until she cried when I informed her of her parting words with Roman last night. Then I filled her in on the ruse we created to make Griffin jealous... and all the drama that ensued. I conveniently left out the part where Roman clutched me while I wailed like a walrus for a good five minutes.

Yana falls back on the sofa with a sigh, throwing an arm over her face. "Ugh. It's like I'm cursed."

I go ahead and pause the movie. She's been happily texting all afternoon. But suddenly, she's in gloomy mode. "What do you mean?"

"With men. My acting career." She releases another dramatic sigh that seems to go on forever. "Nobody takes me seriously except you. Sometimes. When you're not laughing."

I snort, and she shoots me a glare that bowls me over. I wave my hand in front of my face, trying to calm down. "I'm sorry. I don't mean to! You're just... *you*. Amazing, hilarious you," I say. "You were always meant to be somebody, ya know?"

Unlike me. My eyes settle on the floor as I think about how I've always been a reject.

"Uh-uh." Yana flings a carrot at me before I can duck. "I see you over there, playing that record in your head. Stop it!"

I wince, rubbing my arm where the carrot hit me. "What record?"

"The *Nobody Loves Me, Everybody Hates Me* record. Girl, you been doing that since we were kids, ever since your momma married that jerk—" But she swallows when I look at her.

We rarely talk about him, and I'm not looking to start now.

Yana sets her bowl aside and moves next to me. "Listen, I know with everything that's gone down with Griffin, it's bringing up a lot of crap. But none of this is on you, Laura."

"I wish that were true."

"It is! Griffin is a jerk, and he'll always be a jerk after dragging y'all through this." I shush her again, and she flippantly flicks her wrist. "Listen, heartbreak is my full-time job. Day after day, I'm falling all over myself, praying for a sliver of spotlight. Ninety-nine percent of the time, it's just another door slammed in my face. But do you know why I put myself through all that hell?"

I give the slightest shake of my head, and she smiles.

"I do it for the one." My cousin's eyes burn with a determination I rarely see outside of my own—when my lungs are burning, and I hate myself for not having more self-control.

"That *one* handsome guy or director who's gonna recognize my shimmer and set me on a hill where I can shine, baby."

Ever since we were little, she's always been a trailblazer—with big dreams and an even bigger heart. Not once have I seen my cousin shed a tear over a no, though she's told me it's happened on more than one occasion. A girl like her should be in the spotlight.

"You deserve that, Yana."

"And so do you," she says. "There's one out there for you, Laura. Hell, there may be seventy-two. But don't *ever* let some dummy who doesn't appreciate how fabulous you are dull your shine."

That's the thing about Yana. She always believes. No matter how many doors are slammed in my cousin's face, she never gives up. Thinking about the missed opportunities and how aimless I've felt over the past decade, I know I never should've given up on myself either.

I take a glance at my phone as my cousin scoops her carrot off the nasty floor and tosses it in her mouth. Not a text from Roman since this morning. I'm shocked he didn't pop up at my door for an impromptu workout. Not that I'd have completely hated getting in a few moves today.

Then, the doorbell rings.

My cousin, who's already returned to her end of the sofa, happily munches on a fresh carrot, grinning my way.

And now it all makes sense.

Rubbing my temples, I head for the door.

"Roman," I say flatly. "What a surprise."

"Good evening, madam." He flashes a slow, wicked smile and presses a kiss to the back of my hand. Soft, lingering. Like he knows exactly what he's doing. "The pleasure's all mine," he says, his voice seductive and low. My knees damn near buckle.

I smooth the frazzled edges of my hair as he struts inside, a giant gift box under his arm. "What's going on?"

"I'm here to take you out, mama!" He turns on his heels and extends the box to me. "And *this* is for you."

I shut the door, checking him out in his slim blazer and jeans, his hair freshly cut. "This a joke?"

Yana ripples with a hearty chuckle as she eyes us from the sofa. "Of course not." Exchanging glances with Roman as if they're in on some big secret, she waves impatiently. "Girl, open it!"

Somehow, these two are texting now. I snatch the ridiculous box from the man's hands and rip off the top. And I haven't seen a more breathtaking dress since the day of my wedding: ivory with sequins and layers of fringe all over. Roman grins with pride as I run my fingers across the remarkable fabric.

"Thanks. But where am I going in this?"

"You and I"—Roman pulls me in for a brief salsa twist and spins me back out—"are hitting the club tonight."

"*The club?* Roman, I haven't been to a club since... since..."

"Since Maddie was two!" shouts Yana. "And I had to beg you to come out then."

I'm not exactly the clubbing type.

"All the more reason for me to take you out tonight," says Roman, pinching my cheek.

I wince at the dress in my arms, doubting Yana gave him the right size. "Roman, I don't know."

"Girl, what's the holdup?" says Yana. "Don't worry about the kids. I can watch 'em. Y'all go have fun!"

I glower at my cousin. She's supposed to have my back! But judging by the saucy smirk on her face, I know I've already lost this battle.

Standing in my bathroom a little while later, I find myself in complete awe of the girl in the mirror. Because even now, after all the progress, I still don't fully recognize her.

I'm actually kinda... hot.

I turn left, then right, checking out the shimmery tassels of the ivory party dress, hugging all the right places. It's shorter than I'm used to, but my legs look sexy and strong.

Whoa. When did my ass start curving like that?

I grab some makeup and start fixing my hair. And lucky for me, I've got some old heels that'll match perfectly.

Technically, it's past bedtime. But Eli and Maddie are in full PJ mode, perched on the upstairs landing like Roman's the main event below. All the commotion of his arrival likely stirred them up. But everyone falls silent when I step out of the room.

Eli gasps, glasses sliding down his nose. "*Woah.* Mommy looks so pretty!"

Maddie nods in agreement. "You do, Mom."

Yana breaks into applause, laughing loud enough to wake the neighbors. Roman turns and just... stops. Mouth open. Staring. For the first time since I clocked him, he actually seems speechless.

My cousin shakes her curls as she stands. "Girl, you are *working* that dress, for real!"

"Thanks." A part of me wants to believe she's not lying.

Roman manages to shut his mouth, approaching me. "My goodness." In a thorough assessment of my appearance, he takes hold of my hand and leads me in a slow spin. "This has got to be some of Roman's *best* work." His eyes dance as Yana laughs.

Upstairs, the kids are giggling, too, so I wave them off to bed, and the two of us prepare to head out.

"Don't come back anytime soon," calls Yana as Roman holds open the door. "It's time to shine, baby!"

14

We hop into Roman's Porsche and head downtown to a massive nightclub overlooking the Detroit River. The full October moon casts a spotlight on the club's sleek exterior and expansive windows as vibrant city lights dance on the rippling water below. It takes forty minutes to park and another thirty to get through the lengthy line snaking around the corner, but finally, we make it inside.

The club is a shadowy sea of skimpy dresses and bodies writhing beneath sweeping strobe lights. Flashes of blue, green, and white beckon couples to the dance floor, tempting, teasing, drawing together lips and hips. The DJ calls over his spin of Ludacris' "Stand Up" to ensure everyone's having a good time, and they respond with a round of cheers.

I tug at my dress, regretting checking in my jacket, while female servers with lustrous hair and supermodel legs strut toward VIP, capturing the attention of men with wandering eyes. The shimmer of their barely-there tops and even shorter skirts mirrors the sparklers adorning the pricey champagne bottles on their trays.

"Just relax," Roman says in my ear, pulling me to his side. "You're gonna have fun tonight."

Right. Fun. Relaxation. How else am I supposed to enjoy my brand-new single life?

I follow as he shoulders through the dancing crowd and makes room for us at the bar. Why is this place so crowded anyway? Don't any of these people have to work in the morning?

The bar is sticky as I perch my elbows on the counter, waiting for Roman to place an order. The occasional breeze from a ceiling fan overhead cuts through the balmy air.

Out on the dance floor, Instagram models who look about half my age bend and dip in front of their dance partners, presenting twerks that would put Cardi B to shame. Other women gather at tall tables and the bar, whispering in men's ears and giving flirtatious shoves.

This isn't my thing.

I fold my arms, trying not to compare myself to the blur of glitter and silicone around me. I feel like someone's awkward aunt who wandered into a music video.

Roman slides in beside me, chill and unbothered, sipping his drink like he owns the place. But I don't see one for me.

"Don't I get anything?"

The corner of his mouth lifts, his smoldering gaze dragging over me in that slow, maddening way. A flurry of butterflies ignites in my belly, soft and unwelcome.

"She'll have water!" he calls out.

I grit my teeth as we post at our stations, wondering how long I'll have to stand next to this tease like some mannequin on display.

Roman explained the plan on the drive over. *"The reason Baby Daddy's got your panties in a bunch,"* he said, *"is you're locked up in that little mansion all the time. So, Roman has arrived to rescue you. You're welcome."*

Apparently, this was never meant to be a date after all. Just a chance for him to show me the vast variety of *partners on the dance floor*. Not that I'd be foolish enough to believe he'd seriously consider dating me.

As usual, Roman looks perfect tonight—in his sexy blue blazer, the top buttons of his dress shirt undone to give the tiniest preview of his sculpted chest. There's a certain air of confidence he exudes as he casually rests against the counter, sipping his drink, his expensive-looking watch glowing in the neon green hue of the bar. He steadily scans the dance floor, probably on the hunt for his next prime catch. But for a professional dancer, Roman sure seems to be a wallflower tonight. Then again, with his flawless appearance, he can afford to be picky. A guy like him doesn't chase. He selects. Maybe he's just waiting for the right partner.

I lean in close, straining my voice against the DJ's mix of "Baby Got Back." "What's your type anyway?"

Roman lifts a brow. "My type?"

I nod a thank you to the hot bartender as he passes me what's sure to be a delicious glass of water and take a sip. "Both of us know you've got one."

Roman studies the ceiling. "Hmm... attractive, of course. Confident..." A girl in a sparkly red jumpsuit strolls by, and his eyes are glued. "*Perfect* cheeks."

"So, fairly shallow then?"

Roman laughs as he sips his drink, and I return to perusing the dance floor with a sigh.

"If these men are anything like you, I don't stand a chance."

But he turns to me, brows drawn. "See, that's what you gotta understand. Not every man wants the same thing. And not every man wants the same thing *all* the time."

Seems like most men want the *exact same thing* in a different wrapper to me.

"It's kinda like…" Roman taps my shoulder as a thought strikes him. "Ice cream. You might like chocolate. I might like strawberry. But who's to say I can't have chocolate every now and then?"

"Is chocolate referring to men in this analogy or…?"

He purses his lips. "The point is, I'm sure there's a guy around here looking for a girl with a sweet personality, thick body…" His intense gaze sweeps over me before settling on my face. "And stunning eyes."

Warmth floods my cheeks as his grin captivates me. I whip forward, fanning myself. "Goodness. Don't they have AC in here?"

"What's up, little lady?"

Little?

A guy with golden skin and short braids leans his elbow on the bar beside me, showing off all his teeth as he checks me out.

Oh my gosh. He's actually talking to me. What do I do? What do I say?

The last time a guy hit on me was at a Walgreens just before I found out I was carrying Eli. But the second he noticed the pregnancy test in my hand, he was on his way.

I offer a soft smile. "Hi."

With an appreciative glimpse of my dress, he moistens his lips, making my heart rate kick up a notch. "Can I buy you a drink?"

I begin to answer, but Roman's piercing stare holds my attention.

Right. No liquid calories. I toss the guy a helpless shrug. "Thanks. But I can't."

The guy gives a small nod as he excuses himself, being sure to size Roman up as he goes. How in the world am I supposed to snag a man with frickin' Regé-Jean Page at my side?

The second the guy's out of earshot, Roman slaps my arm. "What was that?"

"You said I couldn't drink!"

"I know! But—"

A second candidate, sporting a low fade and attractive goatee, approaches. And his designer suit isn't half-bad. He presses a delicate kiss to my hand.

"The name's Jerome Patterson. How you doing tonight, miss?"

Realizing his scent is the same as my husband's, my heart falls out of rhythm, and I stumble over my words. "I, uh... Good. Thanks."

The man draws nearer, coaxing a breathless giggle from my lips. "I was standing across the room—wondering if I should stay—when I spotted the most *gorgeous* thing I've ever seen. And I just had to come over and find out her name."

Oh, he's good. I'm still trying to remember who I am when Roman's arm wraps around my waist, pulling me into his side. He stares the charming guy down like an aggravated grizzly bear until he backs away.

"Roman!" I push the trainer off. "He was nice!"

"Yeah. *Too* nice," he says. "You're here to have fun, not get slipped a roofie."

I throw up my hands as he takes another sip of his Whiskey Sour. "I *can't* accept a drink. I *can't* talk to a nice guy. How am I supposed to have fun?"

He silently studies the dance floor. "The next guy that asks, just say you wanna dance."

I lean against the bar, wondering if I should move over. It's been a really long time since I received this much attention, and Roman's messing up my chances.

Thankfully, I get another opportunity: curly hair, caramel skin. Not quite as handsome as the first two, but I bet he knows how to have a good time.

With a charming glance, he steps up beside me, leaning his elbows on the counter. "How's it going?"

He seems friendly enough. "Good. How about yourself?"

He nods, scanning the impressive selection of alcohol behind the bar, showcased in a vibrant rainbow variety of choices. But he doesn't ask me anything.

Maybe he was just being courteous? I glance at Roman, but he looks away as if we're strangers.

"I'm Kevin, by the way," the guy finally says.

Progress. "Nice to meet you, Kevin." I shake his hand. "I'm Laura."

Seeming to notice Roman standing beside me, he quietly returns his attention to the bar, and I blow out some air. The guy must think we're here together—which is a ridiculous notion. After the way Griffin played me last night, I'm pretty sure he saw through the ruse. I impatiently tap my elbow, searching the bustling crowd. *Then again, like my husband, maybe the guy just isn't that interested.*

But the DJ's spinning Cameo's "Candy," one of my favorite songs, and I can only stand in these heels for so long. I sweep aside my bangs, thinking about what Yana would do in this situation. Before I can lose my nerve, I throw my shoulders back and turn to him.

"Want to dance?"

The guy seems pleasantly surprised and maybe a little relieved as he grins my way. I take him by the hand before he can say no.

Come on, Laura. He doesn't know who you are. Raising my arms and swinging my hips, I lead my new partner to the dance floor, pretending not to notice Roman watching from the bar.

The bass strums my veins, and I sway to the melody, eyes drawing shut. *This is your thing, Laura. What you've been waiting for.*

With hands lifted high, I bend and sway, the pulsating music caressing my calves, fearlessly hugging my hips. *I'm here.* The lights catch Kevin's bashful smile as he moves in closer, placing a hand on my waist.

Griffin never took me dancing after we got married, and I stopped dancing altogether after having Eli. But right now, I don't care who's watching.

On stage, the DJ bobs his head, hypnotized by his own beat, as scantily clad girls dance on either side. The vibe is hype, and the feeling is magical as the crowd swells with heat, the lights swirling in anticipation.

Teasing Kevin with a flirty brow, I circle him, shuffling back with a gentle sway. He's breathlessly laughing as he tries to keep up. Looking toward the bar, I bite my lip. Roman would keep up just fine. But I don't see him anywhere. Maybe he found the girl he was looking for.

"You're a good..."

But I can't hear Kevin over the music. I turn, leaning into him. "What?"

He attempts to raise his voice. *"I said, you're a good—"*

But the DJ switches the song.

"Excuse me, bruh." A much taller guy with bulky muscles and a shiny bald head shoulders Kevin out of the way and moves into my space. With a curt nod, Kevin steps aside.

Maybe he wasn't as interested as I thought. But Mr. Muscles grips my waist and starts grinding before I can say goodbye. *Okay, Laura. Just go with it. You know Yana would.*

I do my best to relax as he basically humps me. If I have a type, this guy is *definitely* not it. The man gawks at my chest as he smacks on the gum in his mouth. He hasn't even bothered introducing himself. Thankfully, the song switches again.

Time to make my exit. I pat the brute on the shoulder and back away. "It was fun." But as I turn for the bar, he grabs my hand.

"Where you goin'?"

Great. I smooth some hair behind my ear, wishing I actually were Yana. She'd be giving this guy a piece of her mind by now, but I'm not quite as feisty. I'm still struggling to come up with a kind way to turn him down when a skinny guy with locs steps beside me.

"Excuse me, ma'am? Is this guy bothering you?"

With a weak smile, I stare at the dude's oversized hand, still squeezing mine.

I swear he growls at the good Samaritan. "Hey, man, back off!"

"Why don't *you* back off?" The skinny guy yanks my hand from Mr. Muscles' grasp, only serving to piss him off more. "Maybe she wants to dance with somebody else."

"Oh yeah?" Mr. Muscles' chest swells as he steps into the lanky dude's face. "Like who? Your scrawny ass?"

I take a step back, rubbing my arms as the men circle one another, heaving angry breaths. This is getting to be a bit much.

But a warm hand grips mine and spins me around.

Roman?

I smile with a sigh of relief as he rocks side to side. The trainer's lost in a trance, fixed on the fringe of my dress as he sways to a club mix of Salt n' Pepa's "Push It." I follow along, shaking my hips and mirroring his swag.

As the two guys start shoving, Roman grabs my elbow and guides me to the center of the floor. He's just as talented in the club as in the studio: smooth glides, body rolls, sparks in his eyes. His arm and ribcage isolations synchronize perfectly with the music's beat, making me just a little jealous.

I fall into the rhythm, giving my hips an extra swerve as I turn around. Roman moves closer, his hands molding my curves, rolling with me. Unlike Kevin, Roman's moves are assertive and sure. Every touch says, *I got you.* Every glance says, *You're mine.* He *knows* my body. In his arms, I'm his to command, and he'll do with me whatever he well pleases. I arch into him as if to say, *Have your way*, and he happily indulges. Smiling wickedly, he whips me around and grinds his hips on mine, his fingers splayed against the small of my back. His breath is sweet and his gaze ravenous as he presses his forehead closer, nothing but heat rising between us.

My heart starts pumping a little too fast, so I turn, dropping my hips for a change of pace. But Roman never misses a beat. He yanks me into him, unable to go a second without our bodies touching, even if it means following my lead. His chiseled torso presses against my spine as his firm grip traces down my thighs, enveloping them in a satisfying squeeze.

It doesn't matter the style; Roman is a great partner for any song. And I can't think of anyone I'd rather dance with.

I'm just considering asking him to stay for the next when he leans in my ear, the aroma of his aquatic cologne igniting my senses.

"You ready?" His breath brushes against my cheek, kindling a flicker of desire in me.

"Ready for what?" I ask with a soft exhale.

His powerful hands grip my waist as he spins me back around, locking eyes with me. "Your moment."

My moment? "Roman, what are you—?"

But as he sways his hips with mine, gaze charged with electricity, I already know. I shake my head, and he nods.

"It's time, mama."

I swallow, peering left and right. *There are so many people here. What if I can't?*

But Roman's smirk couldn't be more confident as he counts. "Five... six... five, six, seven..."

And just like that, I'm without a choice—I'll look like even more of a fool if I don't. Step by step, I follow his lead, repeating our reggaeton routine, as we dance in perfect harmony. People step back, giving us the floor, and the swelling rhythm floods my veins. I haven't had this much fun since my early days in college, haven't felt such a connection since the first time Griffin and I made love. But here on this dance floor with Roman, all that pales in comparison, and the rest of the world fades away.

Before long, it's time for the spins. *In, push off, back out...*

My heart races with excitement as Roman twirls me around and around before letting go. And without the tiniest hesitation or flaw, I execute my three spins perfectly. The crowd explodes with gasps and applause, and I've *never* felt more amazing.

Before I can stop, Roman swoops up on one knee, pulling me into his lap. And everything goes still. There's a moment of pleasant surprise as our gazes meet, my hand on his shoulder, the other on his chest, his strong arm girdling my waist, holding me prisoner. Just like our feet moments ago, our hearts are completely in sync. And it's the perfect ending.

The crowd goes wild with approval as our eyes lock in a silent exchange, an indescribable heat encasing us.

What is happening?

Roman seems to be wondering the same as he swallows. "I better get you home."

"I can't believe you put me on the spot like that!" I shove Roman's arm as we pull into my driveway, and he laughs.

"You've gotta admit, it was pretty incredible," he says.

"Yeah, it was." I shake my head, studying the shadowy pine trees as we round the curve. "And I don't know when was the last time I received so many compliments." *Let alone so many guys vying for my attention.* I swallow a lump of emotion at the thought.

"You deserved every single one," says Roman, putting the car in park. His sober gaze snags something deep in me, and I'm forced to swallow again.

I look out at the sprawling grounds, gnawing my lip. "I never told you, but I was an assistant dance instructor for a bit. After having Maddie."

Roman lifts a curious brow, encouraging me to go on.

"It was a small studio with a nice little daycare. After class, I'd steal a few minutes whenever I could, practicing my jumps and twirls. Blow off some steam. Ya know?"

Roman watches me silently, the softest curve on his lips.

"But then we found out Eli was on the way, and Griffin suggested I should probably let it go." My chest aches as a lengthy sigh eases from my nose. "Tonight was the first time in a long time that I really felt like *her* again. The girl I used to be."

Roman's hand inches across his thigh, but he rests it on his knee.

"Anyway." I toss him a crooked smile. "Thanks for showing me an amazing night."

"Fa' sho." The moonlight dances in his eyes as he says, "We should do it again sometime."

And a stillness settles over me. The way he says that almost sounds like... like this actually *was* a date.

But his brow creases with a frown. "Not that I'd expect you'd want to after tonight. Those meatheads nearly killed you."

"You mean my *fearless suitors*? I thought it was adorable."

Honestly, I was terrified, but at least no one had to call security.

Roman doesn't crack a smile. "I'm serious. I shouldn't have left you out there on your own."

And as I take in the genuine concern etched in his face, a comforting warmth fills me.

"I'm glad you were there," I say with a nudge. After the electricity of that dance, I can say that with complete certainty. "Besides, with the way I was killing it tonight, how could these boys resist me?" Still on my high, I toss him a wink.

"You always kill it," he softly responds.

His lengthy gaze gives me goosebumps. "This was your plan all along, wasn't it? That's why you got me this flashy dress."

"You oughta be happy I helped you burn off some of that cake. I could've had you doing laps instead."

Touché. It's been a whole fifteen hours since we've talked calorie counts.

I gasp, pressing my hands together. *"Please* can we start an hour late tomorrow? I'm going to be *so* tired." Roman looks at me like I'm crazy, but I give him my best pout.

To my surprise, he relents with a huff. "You better be there at ten o'clock sharp."

I hop out of the car before the man can change his mind. But he leans down, his gaze fixed on mine.

"Goodnight, Diamond Eyes."

One happy butterfly after another. "Goodnight."

We share a lingering smile as I shut the door, and he doesn't pull off until I head up the stairs.

My hands tremble as I pull out my keys, and I know exactly why. Because I've realized—just tonight—that I'm catching feelings. *Serious* feelings. More than a mere attraction or the occasional naughty thought. But a real, honest-to-goodness, in-over-my-head crush on an amazing dance partner and friend. And it couldn't be clearer. I am so screwed.

15

After receiving Ms. Alyssa's encouragement to help Maddie unwind, I decided to institute "Crafting Time," a tradition my sister April and I started when we wanted to get our minds off things. It's a great way for Maddie and me to bond on Friday nights while decompressing from the week's pressures.

Tonight, we're in her bedroom, making friendship bracelets—something we did plenty of before Griffin left. It always kept the little girl from fixating on when Daddy would or would *not* be home from work. But it's been difficult focusing on my daughter with my cousin hitting me up every five minutes.

This is it, girl, Yana says in her text. *I can feel it!*

Her agent booked her a major audition in Chicago, and she swears if she doesn't get the part, she'll fire him. I'm hopeful as I tell her for the hundredth time to break a leg. The spark I saw in her eye last weekend comes to mind as I hit send. *"I do it for the* one," she'd said. With faith like that, how could anything in the universe resist falling in line?

Just because, I pull up this morning's motivational quote for my own dose of inspiration. *Too many people overvalue what they are not and undervalue what they are – Malcolm S. Forbes.*

Roman has sent me an uplifting text every day since Maddie's birthday, and each one wraps around me like a slow-burning hug.

Yana couldn't stop wiggling her brows when I told her about how we danced on Sunday night. *"Something happened,"* she kept insisting. But I wouldn't confirm or deny. The firmness of his grasp and the warmth of his body against mine were more thrilling than I ever could've imagined. And when I think of all his sweet compliments and soft gazes...

It's funny. The guy puts on this tough *Roman* act when he's up on that platform, but get close enough, and he's just a cuddly teddy bear.

A faint smile is on my lips as I immerse myself in the rhythmic weaving and blending of black and red strands.

"Mom, is Roman your boyfriend?"

My thoughts come to a screeching halt as I stare at my little girl seated across from me on the canopy bed. She eyes me curiously, threading beads onto strings with nimble hands.

I blink, trying to play it cool. But my heart's thudding like I've been caught in the act. Though, I'm not even sure what the act is.

Clearing my throat, I select a bead of my own. "Why would you ask something like that, sweetheart?"

She lifts a shoulder, gathering her legs into a cross-legged position on the lavender blanket. "You guys hang out a lot. And you're always *smiling* at him." She rolls her eyes with a smirk, and a flush of embarrassment washes over me. I had no idea she was paying so much attention. Has Eli noticed, too?

"You've at least got a crush," she adds.

I fling a red bead at her. "What do you know about crushes, young lady?"

Maddie's round cheeks glow as she hops off the bed. "I'm just saying, it kinda seems like you like him." She moves to the vanity, adorned with ballet ribbons and old family photos, and pulls scissors from the drawer.

A storm of panic rages inside me, threatening to break through my calm demeanor. If things are that obvious to Maddie—who's consumed with ballet practice four days a week—how much more obvious could it be to the trainer himself? Ever since our night at the club, I've been acutely aware of the delicate proximity between us as we work together. The way my skin burns at every tender touch.

Then there was today. A carnal hunger surges through my core as I think of the one hundred pulsing squats he required as he counted. Boldy, I'd asked, *"You're staring at my ass, aren't you?"* Not that I would've minded if he were. The smile that danced on his lips was deliciously wicked as he'd said, *"You pay me to stare at your ass."* I started to question why we were doing calisthenics in the studio instead of dancing. Normally, squats were done on the track anyway, but he cut me off. *"Shhh! I'm counting."* Yeah, right.

Maddie's still waiting as she snips the frayed strings of her bracelet, but I don't want her thinking I've completely given up on her father.

"He's just a friend," I rush to say, thankful that, on some level, I'm telling the truth. I know how much Roman *hates liars*. Not that this conversation would be any of his business.

Maddie lifts a skeptical brow as she crosses back to the bed. *Crap.*

"How about you?" I ask. "I saw you waving goodbye to that boy from your dance school. What's his name... Quentin?"

"Ew! Mom! I'm only ten!"

"Sorry!" I laugh as she throws a bead back at me with a gag. "I liked boys at your age. I didn't know it was all *that* crazy."

She casts an uneasy glance toward the hall, likely concerned about eavesdropping ears. But the door is safely shut, her favorite pair of pointe shoes dangling from its knob. Last I checked, Eli was busily working on a new magic trick anyway. But Maddie's pace slows as she ties off her bracelet. If she isn't thinking about dating yet, she will be soon enough.

"I was only eighteen when I fell in love with your dad and had you," I say. *And it changed my life forever.* Not that I would take it back.

"Hey." I give her leg a light swat. "What would you think of Mommy starting a new job?"

Maddie cocks her head in contemplation. "Hmm."

I have no idea what I might do or when, but even if plenty of support comes with me contesting the divorce, the kids are getting older. And if I have to move on from Griffin, I'll need something to keep myself occupied.

Maddie's still considering my question when a blood-curdling scream rips through the silence.

I drop the scissors and bolt. My heart slams against my chest with every step, each beat screaming: *Too late. Too late. Please don't be too late.*

We race across the hall only to find my little boy rolling around on his bedroom floor, bright orange flames engulfing his hand. Snatching the quilt from his bed, I wrap him up, smothering the fire.

"Owww!" His high-pitched cries melt into a lengthy wail as he collapses in my arms.

I'm paralyzed as his tiny hand trembles in mine—jagged red burns streaked across his palm, blistering bubbles emerging by the second. With a breath, I look to Maddie. "Call nine-one-one!"

⁘ ✦✦✦✦ ⁘

Second-degree burns. Overnight observation. How could I let this happen?

I suppose it could be the late hour, but the children's hospital hums with a sleepy kind of stillness. Soft whispers. The occasional elevator ding. Parents fidgeting with magazines. No one really reading.

A steady stream of doctors and nurses bustle in and out of the evaluation room as I pace the lobby, wringing my hands. Each medical expert offers a sympathetic nod as they pass, all likely thinking the same thing.

What an awful mom... She shouldn't have children.

Can't you get anything right?

Maddie's sniffles pull me out of my head, and I quickly move into the chair beside her. We were initially allowed in the room with her brother, but she got so worked up over his wounds that we had to step out.

"Don't worry, sweetheart. Eli's going to be okay." *Please, God, let him be okay.*

It's times like this that I remember just how young she is, so innocent and unscathed. If only I could keep her that way.

My little girl nods with a tear-streaked face but goes still as she lifts her eyes. "Dad? Daddy!"

Maddie bolts from her seat to race up the hall and into her father's arms. He bends on his knee as he embraces her, pulling her into his chest.

My heart doesn't know whether to leap or drop. I left him a voicemail and a text saying where we were headed, but I figured he'd simply call when he had the time. I fix my bangs and cross my arms as I approach, wishing I'd changed out of my slightly singed sweater.

"You gotta have faith, alright?" Griffin brushes back Maddie's curls and dabs the tears from her cheeks. "Eli needs us to be strong right now." Maddie nods, and he looks to me as he pushes to his feet.

If he wants to cuss me out in front of all these parents and children, that'd be completely okay. I should've been more present. I should've paid more attention. My hands tremble at my sides, the edges of my vision blurring.

But in two giant steps, he's pulling me into his arms, his broad chest and strong embrace overwhelming me.

I collapse against him, sobbing, unable to hold it together another second. The guilt is suffocating, clawing up my throat, choking out every word.

"I'm so sorry," I gasp against his neck. "It's all my fault. I never should've—"

"Hey... *Hey*." He shushes me, stroking my back the way he has for years. Grinning softly, he searches my teary eyes. "Don't do that. You were there, and I..." His brow is stern as he swallows. "I know you're doing your best."

He seems to grind his teeth these days, most often when he's tossing aside a thought for a more acceptable one. And when it comes to this, he couldn't be more wrong. I failed Eli. And I've failed Griffin, too. *So many* times.

His shoulders rise and fall with a sigh as he presses his hands to his waist. "Tell me what happened."

I study the floor, trying to recollect all the details that were hurled my way. "Uh, he wanted to attempt this magic trick he saw online— holding fire. And somehow, he snuck off with the lighter we used for Maddie's birthday candles. He thought hand sanitizer would protect his hand, but..."

Griffin sucks air through his teeth. "Ouch."

I nod. "It's pretty bad." And Griffin has every right to be upset.

I don't care what Yana said; this *is* all on me. If I'd pulled it together, none of this would've happened. If I'd pulled it together, he never would've left, and we'd be back to spending our Friday nights as a family, playing card games and baking cookies.

It's completely justified if he blows up at me, demands full custody, and lets Vicki raise his kids.

But being the sweetheart he is, he draws me back into his arms, tucking my head beneath his chin. "It's gonna be alright. Don't worry, okay?"

A sharp ache builds in my chest as I fold into his warmth, breathing in the familiar spice of his cologne. Months without his touch, and now he's blessed me twice on the same day. I've missed him more than I miss my mom.

Griffin dries my face the same way he did Maddie, leveling his eyes with mine. "We're gonna get through this together, alright?"

Together?

He steps back, gazing toward the evaluation room. "Is it cool to go in?"

I nod, brushing away what's left of my tears as I toss Maddie an unsteady smile. "He's in and out, though. They gave him some pretty strong meds."

I tell them I'll be over in a bit. I need to gather my thoughts.

As Griffin heads across the lobby with a much braver Maddie, I release a heavy breath, wishing all the man's promises didn't mean so much to me.

"I'm gonna take care of you, always," he'd said.

"From now on, it's gonna be different," he'd said. *"You'll see."*

But I promised him a lot, too. A final tear slips down my cheek as I gaze up the hall, my chest aching with years of heartbreak.

Roman? I have to blink twice to be sure I'm not imagining the man charging up the hall, rubbing his brow. My stomach twists in knots when he spots me. He's got the slightest urgency in his step as he makes his way forward. And without a word, he wraps me in a hug, rubbing my back.

My pulse steadies as my eyes draw shut, indulging in the warmth of a hold that's somehow become more familiar than my husband's. In Roman's arms, the tension and anxiety melt away, leaving nothing but a quiet peace. But he was supposed to meet up with Theresa—that double-jointed Pilates instructor—for drinks tonight.

My voice is small as I brush away tears. "What are you doing here?"

"What you think I'm doing here? I saw your text and jumped in my car." He softly grins as he taps my arm. "Kinda like a friend and all that."

The sweetest asshole I know.

"How's he doing?" he asks as we take a seat across from the evaluation room. The drapes are drawn back from the room's window, offering a clear view of Griffin and Maddie as they check on my little boy.

I rub my neck and stretch my back. "He's still under evaluation, but... his left hand's gonna be out of commission for a while."

"*Yikes.*" Roman rests his forearms on his thighs as I fill him in on what happened. "*The next Whodunnit.*" He chuckles.

I nod, wishing the boy had any other passion in the world.

Roman nudges my knee, his sincere brown eyes softening something raw inside me. "And how are *you* feeling?"

I look beyond the window at my tiny son dozing in an emergency bed that's twice the size of his own. Griffin holds Maddie close, seeming to offer quiet reassurance, as a nurse checks Eli's vitals. "Like... a horrible mother."

Roman scoffs. "You serious right now?"

"I should've been watching him. I should've kept him occupied. I left out the lighter after lighting Maddie's birthday cake, and... this whole thing is my fault."

Roman shakes his head with a dubious laugh. "Laura, you're spiraling. I'm gonna need you to get a grip."

"You're not a parent. You wouldn't understand."

He gives a half-hearted nod. "Look, you're a fallible human being, just like the rest of us. Nobody could've seen this coming."

I gnaw my lip. "I guess you're right."

"Of course, I'm right!" The man's cackle is loud enough to draw the entire lobby's attention, not to mention Griffin's. He looks over, noticing Roman for the first time, and the two exchange an icy nod.

Sitting upright and throwing an arm across the back of my chair, Roman says, "Look who forgot to bring along his little accessory. No dogs allowed, huh?"

"She'll probably come by later." The words hit like a bruise. Vicki popping up with a giant teddy bear, slipping into my son's world with soft hands and sugary-sweet smiles. Pressing kisses to Griffin's lips like she belongs.

But as the nurse exits Eli's room, my estranged husband seems to be having a staring contest with Roman. And is Griffin... scowling?

Roman leans into my ear, his breath softly brushing against my cheek. "Is it just me, or are homeboy's briefs a little tight right now?"

I drop my head, choking back a chuckle. "He's probably just ticked I'm over here with you. I should join him."

"Nah," says Roman, pulling me back. "I don't think that's it." Tightening his grip around me, he rubs my shoulder.

I glance at his hand and back to him. "Roman, what are you doing?"

His signature grin slithers across his face as he stares back at Griffin. "Just... making him jealous."

I shake my head, knowing this isn't the time or place. But Roman's got a point. I need to relax. I settle into his warm embrace simply because I can.

Roman's crisp, sea breeze scent is a delightful tease as he holds me, just as rich and alluring as it was that night at the club. Just as intoxicating. He turns his face to mine, rekindling memories of the magnetic gaze we shared while grinding on the dance floor, the heat of his thigh between my legs.

"I'm gonna give you a kiss," he says. My lips part in response, only serving to draw his gaze. "Don't freak out," he whispers.

But I'm not sure I can make that promise.

Cradling my head against his shoulder, he presses a delicate kiss to my temple. He concludes the sweet gesture with another small rub of my arm.

I can barely hold back my smile as Griffin quickly turns back to Eli. He's fuming.

Roman dips his face into my hair, chuckling low.

"You see that?" he whispers. "He is *so* pissed!"

Against all odds, I can't help laughing myself.

———————— ‹‹♦♦♦›› ————————

Roman and I are still chuckling when we arrive at the house.

"The kid's a trooper," says Roman, placing the groceries from our late-night run on the kitchen counter. "He'll be just fine."

I figured Roman simply offered to escort me home in hopes of ticking Griffin off, but after witnessing my late-night binge last week, he wasn't taking any chances.

"And yet, I still feel awful for agreeing to come home while my little boy spends a whole night at the hospital for the first time since he was born." I toss my keys on the foyer table and join him in unloading the bags.

"Like I said, just chill," says Roman. "Even Mr. Stiff had to tell you to loosen up."

I cut my eyes at Roman's latest nickname for my kids' father. Griffin practically pushed me out the door, claiming I needed rest and reminding me that, technically, it was supposed to be his weekend with the kids. I don't care if both he and Roman insisted; I never should've left. Even Maddie's skipping ballet tomorrow to comfort her little brother overnight. But a certain idiot assured everyone that attending his cardio class in the morning would be the best way to cope with stress. And for whatever lame reason, Griffin agreed with him.

I still can't shake the gentle curve of my husband's smile as he squeezed my shoulders and told me to head home. After my little performance with Roman in the lobby, I didn't know where his aggravation had gone. All I knew was Griffin seemed close again, less chilly, almost.

Roman eyes me as he sets aside the salmon. "I saw you, by the way."

Saw me what? Grinning? Staring? Gnawing my lip longingly as he bent over his laptop to select the next song? I brush back my edges, turning to him. "Saw me?"

"When I came back from the vending machine," he says. "Huddled close while he whispered in your ear... lightly stroked your back."

My pulse quickens as I head for the sink, thinking about each time Griffin hugged me tonight. How he brushed away my tears, looked at me in a way he hasn't looked at me in a long time. *"We're gonna get through this together,"* he said. And I wanted *so badly* to believe him.

"It was nothing," I say, washing my hands. "He's just as worried about Eli as me. That's all."

"I bet," says Roman, bumping me out of the way.

"Hey!" I jab him with an elbow as he rinses his hands. "I wasn't done, jerk."

"And Roman doesn't care," he says with a haughty chuckle.

I purse my lips, reaching for some paper towel, but my mind goes blank when I turn to find him no more than six inches from my face.

"I bet that drives you crazy, huh?"

"What?"

His hand is sopping wet on my hip as he moves me aside without reason. "Him... being all nice. Trying to make you think he'll be back." His taunting laugh grates on my bones as he dries his hands and tosses the napkin in the trash. "Don't fall for it."

I pass him a baking sheet with foil, and he starts lining the pan.

I suppose Roman's got a point. It isn't all that different from the birthday party or Eli's talent show. But I caught plenty of guys' attention at the club. What's so wrong with believing Griffin could have a change of heart?

I take my station beside Roman, preparing to chop the asparagus. "Maybe he's having second thoughts." Roman stares at me, jaw slack, but I mean it. "He fell for me before. Who's to say he couldn't fall again?"

He releases another insulting laugh as he reaches for the olive oil. "You're trippin'."

I turn with the chef's knife firm against my hip. "Am I?"

"Over some loser that enjoys parading his side chick in your face while scolding you for even looking at another dude? Yeah, Laura, you are."

I press my lips together at his point.

Meanwhile, Roman's muttering as he rubs the salmon with oil. "Lay your heart on the line and get it stomped every time."

For a fleeting moment, his typically confident stance softens, revealing the tiniest chink in his armor. It reminds me of what he said that day when I socked him. *"I know what it's like to... be let down. And in the past, I used it to fuel me."*

Who hurt him? And why?

He tenses when I rest a hand on his shoulder. I wait for him to look me in the eye.

"Is that why Roman's not a hugger?"

A smile curves his lips as he snatches me up by the waist, smearing oil all over my sweater. "He's got no problem hugging *you!*"

I laugh, trying to shove him away. "Roman, you're messing up my shirt!"

"You were planning to salvage this scorched disaster?"

I smack his arm as he tickles me, but he doesn't let me go.

Then something shifts. His gaze falls to his hand on my arm, his thumb tracing the ridges of my sleeve. "I'm just trying to look out for you, alright? People can be cutthroat." His voice is gravelly, as soft as his eyes. "If someone wasted the opportunity when they had it, why give 'em another one, ya know?"

He's right. Griffin is toying with me. Again.

Who would ever want you anyway?

But I'm caught off guard as Roman's gaze rests on my lips... the same way it did earlier tonight when he told me he planned to kiss me. The hesitant breath that escapes me seems to snap him out of his trance, and he quickly returns to his pan.

I get some music streaming to slice through the tension. "Speaking of *cutthroat*, poor Theresa. Did she sound upset when you bailed?"

"Actually..." He winces as I open the oven for him to slide the pan inside. "I shot her a text."

My jaw falls open as I shut the oven door. "Roman *Asshole* Graham." He laughs, and I bump him with my hip—payback for before.

"She'll be fine," he says, unfazed, as he wipes his hands. "From what I hear, homegirl's a certified maneater. I never would've broken my policy otherwise." He wags his tongue as I chuck a piece of asparagus at him.

Right. The nonfraternization policy.

I'll admit, I was a little thrown this afternoon when I overheard the Pilates instructor asking Roman if he'd like to meet for drinks, but I was hoping he was just being friendly by accepting her offer. Roman deserves a social life as much as the next guy. But I'd much rather he ask me out instead.

Oh well. Hopefully, we'll take another trip to the club soon. Even if it's just as friends.

I get my pan of chopped asparagus in the oven, and the two of us start cleaning up. Thankfully, my favorite song—Rihanna's "Only Girl in the World"—pops on to help us pick up the pace. On impulse, I'm swaying to the tempo—grooving just a little as I wipe the counters down.

Roman chuckles behind me, one hand covering his mouth as he props himself against the sink, clearly enjoying the show.

"What's so funny?

"You are! Being all shy and shit." He crosses his arms, thoroughly amused. "What the hell was that?"

I suppose it's easy to slip into mom mode when I'm at home. I shrug in defense. "I can dance however I want." I return to swaying as I clean, refusing to let him destroy my groove. But he turns the music up, brow raised in a challenge.

"If you're gonna do it, do it right."

He dances toward me with the same irresistible allure he had in the club, only ten times sexier. And heat fogs my mind like a fever.

I shake my head, returning to my scrubbing, but he yanks my hips to him, humping like a dog in heat.

I can't help laughing. "What are you doing?"

"Come on. You wanna dance? Let's dance!" He rolls his pelvis seductively, as enthusiastic as a rookie at Chippendales.

Despite the lovely temptation, I push him away. "Nobody wants to dance with you." Both of us know I'm lying. He drifts right back toward me.

"That's okay, Diamond Eyes. You know you can't handle *all* this." His breath is hot against my ear as he whispers, "Just like you couldn't handle it at the club last week."

He's got a lot of nerve. He knows I never turn down a good challenge.

With a hand upon his shoulder, I join him in swaying to the beat, beckoning with a seductive gaze, my hips as mesmerizing as a pendulum. Roman's teeth dig into his bottom lip as he moves in close, his eyes ravenous as they trail my figure along with his hands. I give him my back, and we begin to grind, just like we did at the club. Only this time, nobody's watching, and we can get as loose as we want.

Reaching my hand behind his neck, writhing along his toned torso, I let the melody carry me away, melt into him like a candle's flame. Who cares about his stupid rules? All that matters is that the sex magnet is into me right here, right now. His warm body presses firmly against mine, his heart thumping wildly against my back. We swing and sway, thrust and pop, in a divine symphony. His grip tightens as he pulls my hips closer, his breath panting on my neck. It's as if the rhythm is pulsing through the two of us as one.

He whirls me around, eyes drunk with desire. "It's time to work, mama."

Then he lets go, fluid and fearless. He pops and glides, twisting low, springing back up like a live wire, his footwork slick and electric.

Every time I think he's blown my mind, he surpasses my expectations. Each beat pulses through him like the music was made for his body.

Without a thought, I match him—every turn, every pump, in perfect time. His smile widens as I move with him, clearly impressed that I'm still right here, step for step.

Just like that, we're locked into another routine. Only this time, it isn't planned. We're just vibing—not all that different from my second day in his class. But now that our bodies are intimately acquainted, it's on another level. Something so infinite and deep that there's no language to describe it. It's like we're connected somehow. And when we dance like this, it's as if we're long-lost soulmates.

He pulls me in for our reggaeton spin. *In, out, three twirls, and release...* And I spin and spin, simply waiting for him to come get me.

As if reading my mind, he swoops in and dips me back. And it's even more perfect than last time. A breathless smile breaks across my face as I thank God for the chance to dance with someone so incredibly amazing. Roman's smiling, too, as he lifts me up.

And I have to wonder... *Does he feel it? The electricity? Our hearts beating together in perfect time?*

His thumb strokes the curve of my waist as he gazes at me. Then he lowers his mouth to mine... and I don't dare stop him.

Our lips meet with an insatiable yearning, our bodies racing as if time's running out. His mouth is sweet like chocolate and as warm as foamy champagne bubbles, smooth as silk, yet strong like *him.* With every shared breath and scorching touch, I lose myself in a sea of desire, a fire blazing in my veins that I couldn't contain if I tried. My knees buckle as he parts my lips, seizing control of my tongue. His hands clench my waist as they draw me closer, sparking another flame.

My heart intensely pounds in my chest as our mouths slip into their own unique dance, moving in harmony, an intimate melody only we can hear. A soft moan escapes me as he presses sweltering kisses to my cheeks and jaw, insisting on tasting every visible inch of flesh.

He groans into my neck as he presses me against the island, growls as he runs his hands along the curves of my ass, and hoists me on the counter—no problem. I gasp against his mouth as he returns to my lips, igniting my body with a primal desire.

But suddenly, he stops and blinks—as if waking from hypnosis. "I, uh... I gotta go."

What does he mean he has to go? I don't want him to go!

I'm still in a daze as he grabs his jacket. "What about the salmon?"

"Right." He snatches up his keys. "Um, five more minutes. Plenty of water. Alright?"

He walks away like he didn't just taste every secret I've been hiding in my smile. And I'm left, lips tingling, heart echoing the rhythm of a song that cut off too soon.

16

I'm glancing at my phone for the tenth time as I park at the rec the next morning.

Not a single message. Not even a motivational text.

Like last night didn't happen.

Like I imagined his lips on mine, the heat of his hands, the way he looked at me like I was more than just a project.

I don't know what's worse—the ache of not hearing from him, or the fact that I keep checking like he might care.

Everything about last night—from the light touches to the dancing to the lush, heated kisses—felt like a dream. At least until he took off.

The first man I've kissed since my husband, and suddenly I'm being dodged like a pothole.

Sure, it was impulsive and wild and... *hot*. But we've crossed a line now, and I doubt we can turn back. And what about Griffin?

Blowing out my lips with a huff, I yank down the visor to check my hair. Great. I didn't drink more water like Roman said, and now my face looks bloated. It's no wonder he recoiled when he came to himself.

With a face like that? Who's gonna want you?
I flip the visor shut and hop out of the car.
Pull it together, Laura. You've gotta get through this day.

◆◆◆◆◆

"You're looking good, girl."

One of the taller brunettes in class slaps fives with me as I stretch.

"Thanks." I toss a small smile as she passes, wishing Roman felt the same way.

Where is that guy anyway? It's five minutes past, and he's never late.

Everyone's attention is drawn to the front of the room when Theresa, Roman's hot Pilates instructor, jogs onto the platform, in all her limber glory. She's got a full head of red curls, which she usually rocks in a ponytail, and green eyes that certainly outshine my own. But I can spot the bags beneath them from here.

"Good morning, everyone." Theresa folds her hands together, a manufactured grin on her freckled face. "Unfortunately, Roman won't be joining us this morning."

Everyone groans, throwing up their hands. But no one's as shocked as me.

He's never missed a class. Not once.

Theresa gives a rueful nod. "I know, I know. And on behalf of Roman and everyone here at Perry Rec, I apologize—"

But everyone's got their questions: *Where is he? When will he be back?*

Would he ghost the whole class over me?

"I'm honestly not sure where he is," Theresa says. "But he should be back next week. In the meantime, I'll be holding an extra Pilates class for all who are interested."

And I am definitely not. I head out with over half the class as I check my phone.

Did he have some sort of emergency? I'd give him a call, but with everything that went down last night, I'm not completely sure he'd answer. And after seeing Theresa's eyes just as puffy as my own, I realize it probably isn't uncommon for him to bail. But for me... for *us*, what does that mean? No more hanging out? No more dancing? Did I just technically cheat on my husband with someone who doesn't even want me?

I'm taking a seat in the crowded hall, my thumb still hovering over the phone's screen, when I receive a text from Yana. *How's my little Eli doing?*

My cousin was mortified when I contacted her about my son's incident last night, but she won't be able to make it home until after her callback audition tomorrow.

Griffin said he was still sleeping when I tried to video chat this morning. Update you as soon as I can. It crosses my mind to tell her what's happening with Roman when she shoots me a thumbs-up, but frankly, I'm not too sure what's going on myself.

I push to my feet and trudge toward the lobby, legs heavy with protest as I pass the gym. But the buzz of my phone on my thigh brings me to a halt. It's Roman!

Paying a last-minute visit to my brother in Chicago. Here's a workout plan for today. He shoots over a no-nonsense to-do list. The kind I hate—with crunches, squats, and lots and lots of running on the treadmill. I mean, I appreciate it, but... no *how you doing?* No *what happened last night was amazing, and I can't get you off my mind?*

I stare at the screen, waiting for something more. But it never comes. Just reps and routines... like none of it meant a thing.

I remember he mentioned his brother getting locked up for car theft. Maybe something happened? Or maybe it's the perfect excuse to get away from me.

I just keep replaying it all. The heat of his mouth, the pulse of the music, the way he looked at me like I was the whole damn stage.

And then, nothing.

I suppose I could apologize. But what for? *He* asked *me* to dance, and *he* kissed *me!*

Instead of making things more complicated than they already are, I keep my text neutral. ***Will do. Enjoy your visit!***

Of course he doesn't respond. Then again, why would he bother? I'm just another fat client. I head to the gym to get to work.

<hr />

I'm pretty wiped out by the time I get to the children's hospital, but the buzz from my workout puts some pep in my stride. Without Roman barking in my face, I had to push myself, but the high was completely worth it. Especially after all the pent-up tension I had from last night. My shower was certainly on the chillier side this morning. But the fact of the matter is, I did it without him, and if I had to, I'd do it again.

My fingers dance along the hospital's wall—filled with encouraging quotes and colorful paintings—as I make my way to Eli's room. But when I enter, no one except Griffin is around, dozing in a hospital recliner.

My steps are soft as I quietly take a seat across from him. It's been ages since I've seen him like this. He breathes in gentle rhythm, arms folded across his chest, head resting against the window, the late morning sun casting a warm glow over his face. Peaceful. Angelic. I can't seem to look away.

I used to steal mornings like this. Before he'd wake or after he'd collapse on the old apartment sofa following a late shift. Watching him breathe, brow soft, lashes low. Memorizing the curve of his lips, the peace on his face when the weight of the world let go. Ever since the first time I woke with him beside me in my tiny dorm room bed.

A phone rings at the nurses' station in the hall, and he stirs awake, a soft grin touching his lips when he sees me.

"Hey." He stretches his back and rubs his eyes like Eli. "About time you got here."

"Thanks for waiting." Setting my purse aside, I cross my legs. "Rough night?"

He nods, running a hand over his groggy face. "Those nurses are kinda crazy with those hourly check-ups." But his gaze lingers as he looks me over.

I adjust my hoop earrings, pretending not to notice. At least I'm more composed today—a form-fitting sweater with a little mascara, the tiniest hint of lip gloss. He almost seems to appreciate my efforts.

"How was your workout?" he asks.

I release a heavy breath, rubbing my aching quads. "Intense. But what matters is I got it in, right?"

"Absolutely." He cracks his neck, being sure to flex his muscular chest beneath his cashmere sweater. "I need to get back to the gym myself."

"Hmm." The man hasn't missed a week at the gym in the past five years. I pull out my phone to double-check my messages… and avoid staring at his mouthwatering biceps.

Still rubbing remnants of sleep from his eyes, Griffin clears his throat. "The kids should be back from the cafeteria in a minute. Eli wanted to get lunch, so Maddie wheeled him down. I think he'll be discharged soon."

I bob my head as I pull up Roman's most recent text. It was incredibly impersonal. I wonder if he'll even call. But Griffin's stare causes me to sit up straight. "What is it?"

He raises an inquisitive shoulder, propping one suede Oxford on his knee. "No Roman today?"

Look who's suddenly curious. I mirror his little shrug. "No Vicki?"

He leans back with a conceding grin, and I return to checking my phone. I don't know why I care anyway. After all he's put me through, I certainly don't owe him an explanation, and I'm not interested in playing his little games.

"Ya know, I've been meaning to ask about you and this *guy*." He leans forward on his elbows, a deeply concerned expression on his face.

Wait. Did he actually fall for our little act yesterday?

"I suppose I'll ask like they used to on social media," he says. "Are y'all... *just friends? In a relationship?* Or..."

I bite my tongue to keep from smiling. "It's complicated."

Griffin nods like a delivery driver who's just received a meager tip. "I see."

At least it's the truth.

"Mommy!" Eli throws out his arms as Maddie wheels him inside. Griffin stands as I rush to hug our son tight.

"Hey, little guy. How you been?" I ask, fingers brushing through his curls like a prayer. His hand is wrapped in gauze, and I can barely see his fingernails, but he doesn't seem to care.

"Mommy, this place is *so* cool!" He beams. "They've got a computer room and *all* these dogs. And there was a clown making balloon animals downstairs. Is Roman coming? He's gotta see this!"

My gaze meets Griffin's in a panic, but his smile couldn't be warmer.

"Actually, you're going home in just a bit, buddy," he says. The little boy pouts as Griffin squeezes his shoulder. "But don't worry. I'll keep my promise."

Both of the kids gasp with excitement, Eli celebrating with a little jig in his seat as Maddie giggles.

I'm lost. "What promise?"

"Just the promise to take them out for ice cream." Griffin scratches his beard as he leans my way. "Wanna come?"

Griffin takes us to one of our favorite old-fashioned ice cream shops—a hidden gem near his mom's. With its cozy booths and vintage posters, the place is reminiscent of a classic diner, the sweet scent of freshly churned ice cream and waffle cones permeating the air. The central counter, with swivel stools on either side, boasts every flavor of ice cream imaginable, a lengthy, colorful line of candy canisters stretching across its glass shield.

Eli's eyes double in size as he looks over the rainbow variety of flavors. Before Griffin can even ask, the little boy is demanding his top choice, Superman—with M&M's all over, of course. Maddie wants the same with chocolate sprinkles.

Seeing the kids point out the assortment of options with brilliant smiles only serves to remind me of how things used to be... surprise visits to the toy store, exploring the local aquarium. I'd be lying if I were to say I didn't miss it all.

"And what would you like, Mommy?" asks Griffin, his grin filled with charm.

"Nothing for me, thanks." He hasn't called me that in ages.

He frowns but doesn't argue as he turns to order the selections.

I really should've eaten before I came out, but I had a lot on my mind. My stomach growls impatiently as I request a large cup of water and check out all the diet-busting options. But the strawberry sitting beside the chocolate fudge jogs my memory.

You might like chocolate. I might like strawberry. But who's to say I can't have chocolate every now and then?

Somebody certainly wanted chocolate last night.

In a cruel act of indulgence, Griffin orders a double-scoop of butter pecan—my favorite—for himself, and we huddle into a booth near the front of the shop.

Griffin's elbow brushes mine as he digs in. "You remember that time we came here for Eli's fourth birthday?"

I nod and sip my water through a straw, attempting to pace myself. "We got an ice cream cake for his party at that indoor rollercoaster place. And he was *not* a fan of either one," I say, eyeing our son. Eli tucks away a sheepish grin as Maddie gives him a nudge.

"But that wasn't our first time here," says Griffin, giving the kids a prideful nod. "We came to this shop for our first date."

"Didn't you guys meet in the fall?" asks Maddie, as invested as always. But even Eli seems a little curious this afternoon.

"Yep. One *unseasonably* warm fall. We were playing 'Twenty Questions' on the phone when your momma told me butter pecan was her weakness. First place I brought her was here." Griffin's shoulder bumps mine for no reason. "Ain't that right, Mommy?"

He's toying with me again. I refuse to look his way as he not-so-nonchalantly stretches his arm across the back of my side of the booth and points over Eli's shoulder.

"Grabbed a seat right out there on the sidewalk—the tables were still out. And I swear Mommy had this permanent smile on her face."

The kids' eyes meet with a glimmer of hope as Griffin swirls the ice cream with his spoon, combing golden-brown ribbons into its ivory surface.

"The entire time, all I could think was how *amazing* her eyes looked that day, sparkling in the sun." He looks at me. "They're still amazing."

Why is he doing this to me? Why is he doing this to them?

I gaze out the window as I chug my water, but he offers me a heaping spoonful of ice cream anyway. "Griffin, you know I can't. And I'm not sharing a spoon with you."

"It's just a bite, and it's not like we haven't shared before." He dances the spoon in my face, making the kids giggle. And finally, I open my mouth. The ice cream melts on my tongue as he feeds me, a sweet medley of flavors exploding against my taste buds.

Oh, that is incredible. A wicked smile spreads across Griffin's face as I quickly rinse the delicious flavor from my tongue.

"Man," he says. "Mommy's *strict* about her diet these days. Right, kids?" They both agree as they polish off their scoops. "I mean, no cheat meals or nothing."

Eli's eyeing the gummy bears at the counter, and despite my frown, Griffin gives him the money. Both of the kids take off before he can change his mind. But I won't be changing mine.

Careful, Laura. Don't get your heart stomped all over again.

Griffin's teasing gaze lingers on me as he returns to his ice cream. "Roman don't play, huh?"

"You'd be surprised how often he says that." *Though, he was plenty playful last night.*

Griffin chuckles, licking his spoon. "What type of stuff does he have you do?"

"What *doesn't* he have me do? Crunches, wall sits, endless laps around the track." *Pulsing squats while he watches, make-out sessions on the kitchen counter.* I release an aching sigh as I reach for my cup. "More than anything, we're just dancing."

That jogs Griffin's brow. "At the party, you said y'all are mostly in the gym."

"We are—in the gym, in the studio. It's half and half, really." I sip from my straw to stop rambling, but an apologetic gurgle signals I'm all out.

There's a discerning glimmer in Griffin's eyes. "I bet you're loving that."

"It's a lot of fun," I say, playing with my straw. Of all the times we've danced together, last night was the most fun I've ever had. And now he doesn't want to talk to me.

"Well, I gotta say"—a satisfied smirk dances on Griffin's lips as he once again checks me out—"Whatever you're doing... it's working overtime."

My pulse slows as I return my attention to outside—where we fed each other bites of ice cream for the first time on that gorgeous autumn day.

"Not that you needed it," he adds.

I turn to Griffin, puzzled. For the longest, he wouldn't look at me while exchanging the kids, didn't even glance back on the day that he left. "Griffin, be for real."

"What do you mean 'be for real'? I'm serious. I've *tried* to tell you, but it's like talking to a wall. You were banging before, and you're banging now."

I suck my teeth, staring out the window. "I'm sure that's what you had in mind when you exchanged me for a new model."

"Hey." He cradles my chin, turning me back to him, his gaze as tender as his touch. "First of all, I wasn't talking to Vicki when I left. And your figure was *never* an issue." His gaze lingers, sweet and scorching, like he knows exactly what he's doing.

He's toying with me. He's always toying with me.

Disbelief must be written all over my face because soon he releases me, returning to his food with an affronted huff.

Then why? I want to say. *If it wasn't my weight, then why did you leave?* But the kids are headed back now, and I don't want to make things any more tense than they already are.

Griffin's shoulders relax as the kids happily shuffle into their seats, and he tosses them a warm smile. "I'm just saying," he says to me, "I don't see the point in wasting my hard-earned money on some dude screaming in your face when you're gorgeous as you are."

I'll admit, the trainer's always on my ass. But my mind drifts back to his comforting words after my late-night binge. *Laura, you've* always *looked good.* And the way he clocked my estranged husband getting flustered when another man so much as glanced my way...

Could Griffin be jealous?

Before I can digest what any of it could possibly mean, he jumps up and grabs another spoon, then presents it like some grand romantic gesture. Of course, I hesitate, but he holds it out patiently, waiting for me to give in. Annoyed, I snatch the spoon with a glare, and both of us dig in.

17

I exhale with relief when Roman texts me a new meal plan and tells me to meet him at our usual time.

But when I walk into the rec on Monday morning, he's not in the lobby like always.

I tap my elbows as I glance around, wondering if maybe he changed his mind.

Ugh. I've been dying to dance all weekend long, and I really miss my friend.

I'm just considering checking for him in the studio when he strolls in from outside, a full two minutes late.

I step into his path and point to the floor like a drill sergeant. "Drop and give me twenty, mister!" But he keeps walking.

Somebody woke up on the wrong side of the bed.

Pushing aside my bangs, I follow him toward the gym. "Thanks for that plan you sent on Saturday. I got in a good sweat. But the girls in class were *so* pissed. Theresa offered a Pilates session, and—"

"Look, just—" He turns back and stops with a swallow but refuses to look me in the eye. Instead, he gazes behind me, arms crossed, shoulders tense. It's a look I've grown accustomed to over the past several months. The kind a man gives when he doesn't want to be bothered.

"Just let me put my things down, and we'll get started," he says before heading off.

This might not be as easy as I thought.

———— ✦✦✦✦✦ ————

Roman's all business as he starts me out with crunches, holding my ankles as he counts.

"Twenty-five... twenty-six... That's good. Keep going."

My core burns as I struggle to lift my upper body. I'm wheezing so hard I could pass out. This didn't feel nearly as difficult last week. Meanwhile, I'm itching to talk to him just as much as I'm aching to dance. "How was your weekend? Your brother okay?"

He nods as he continues counting, and frustration rises in my chest.

Are we seriously doing this? After everything that went down on Friday night, he's going to act like things are business as usual?

"Thanks again for the new meal plan," I say with a grunt, perspiration forming at my temples. "It's going to be nice having more calories this week."

But he stops counting, so I stop, too.

"What'd you eat this weekend?" he asks, examining me.

"The usual. Lean protein, lots of veggies." I gaze across the gym. "Maybe a little treat here and there."

Roman's fuming when I risk a glance at him, a ticking timebomb ready to explode.

"Okay, so maybe Griffin took the kids and me out for ice cream." His nostrils flare.

"But I didn't have a lot," I add quickly.

He takes me to the upstairs track.

"Run."

So, I do. One lap. Then another. Then a third. My lungs scream, my legs wobble, and between his temper and my heaviness from this weekend's slip-up, I'm about to collapse.

Okay, so maybe eating my feelings over the past twenty-four hours wasn't the best idea. I certainly didn't think I'd wear out so quickly. But much more disappointing than being forced to confess my little blunder is the fact that it was the only time Roman's been willing to look me in the eye all morning. We've gotta get on the same page, and soon. Otherwise, I'm not sure he'll want to move forward with my training. The thought of never dancing with him again feels like losing part of myself.

I'm gasping for air as I make my way back to him. "Look... can we talk?"

"Keep going," he says, gazing at his watch.

I glower at him before puffing on.

When we finally make it to the studio an hour later, he's still refusing to talk to me. I yawn as he drones on, reviewing some of the most basic moves.

"Cross, kick. Cross, kick. Turn... Jump out and in." Even Roman looks bored to death as we go through the motions. But he restarts Justin Timberlake's "My Love" on the laptop like it's just another day.

It's not until he's taking his place in front of me that he finally notices my tired expression in the mirror.

"You got a problem?" he asks, quirking a brow.

I don't want to lie. "I think both of us know you could do a lot more with this song."

His flawless face curls into a frown. "Excuse me?"

"It's lame, Roman. It's lame as hell."

His stare pierces my reflection in the mirror, but I mean it. Everything—from the kick to the turn to his stupid behavior—is lame. Sure, when things took a turn on Friday night, I was as caught off guard by it as him, but we're grown. We can't bury our heads in the sand and dance at the same time. And so what if I let Griffin get to me again? It's pretty clear at this point that the man's charm is my kryptonite. But... none of my husband's sweet talk or ice cream shop memories could make me forget about Roman. Not after that kiss.

He gives the smallest nod and stalks back to the laptop. The track switches to Usher's "O.M.G." as he raises the volume. "Let's kick it up a notch."

I gnaw my lip in anticipation as he takes his place in front of me. He explodes like a force of nature—kicks and jumps, muscles contracting and releasing in a symphony of pops and locks. He seamlessly flows into some of the most amazing footwork I've ever seen, feet twisting and gliding as if on skates. He defies gravity, sneakers lifting off the floor, his sculpted body tilting midair like a dancer from another world. With an abrupt jolt, he returns to his grind and isolations, finishing off with an epic spin.

I wasn't expecting it to be quite so difficult. And he's definitely been holding out on me.

"Let's work," he says with a loud clap.

I feel like I'm approaching the base of Mt. Everest as he counts me off.

My initial efforts could be worse. Despite my fatigue, the jumps are getting easier, and most of his kicks aren't foreign to me, but I stumble through the glides.

Roman rubs his temple as he watches me struggle through the end. I figure he'll laugh or taunt me like he did on that first day of class. Instead, he simply says, "Again."

When I still come up short, he takes pity on me and repeats the demonstration. Each move seamless, each step a quiet flex. Like he's starring in his own dance movie.

Okay. I think I got it.

He counts me off once more, and I go for it: kicking, gliding with all my heart. The air seems to crackle around me as I focus on my reflection, moving with precision and extending my arms with grace. It isn't nearly as perfect as his, but I feel better about my efforts by the end.

Roman doesn't blink. "Again."

He insists on me repeating the routine so many times that it isn't long before it becomes second nature. With each round, I'm pushing a little harder, making the moves a little more my own. He's waiting for me to give up. I know he is. But I can do this. I'm good enough for this routine. I'm good enough for him.

With an inferno raging in my gut, I go hard, holding his attention captive in the mirror, refusing to break. He crosses his arms as he leans against the back wall, smoldering with intensity, watching my every move. At this point, I'm sure he realizes he's made a mistake. Because now that I know the routine, I'm going to kill it every time.

Roman tilts his head, his ravenous eyes devouring the elegance of my arms, the arch of my back, the swerve of my behind. I add the slightest twerk to my hips and catch him licking his lips, chest rising and falling with desire.

Seeming to catch his breath, he says, "Again." And I'm happy to oblige him.

A fervent gleam ignites in Roman's gaze, only intensifying the rush of adrenaline coursing through me. Ignoring the burn of my lungs, the beads of sweat at my brow, I dance with all my might, faster and faster, harder and harder. Until, finally, he can no longer resist.

Roman jumps on the dance floor, mirroring my passion and intensity, jumping, twirling, swaying in perfect sync. Sure, my reflection's not quite Instagram-ready. But the way I'm owning this routine? You'd think I've been dancing backup for Beyoncé. And I've gotta say, I look pretty damn good. And next to him? I look *amazing*. We rock it out five more times before he finally stops with a breathless smile.

"Man," he says on an exhale. "I needed that."

The track switches to Amerie's "1 Thing," and he steps forward to stop the music. But I'm just getting started.

With electric thrusts and pops, I move his way, passion radiating in my gaze. My body is an instrument of seduction, and I'm begging him to play. Magnetic energy fills the air as I drop my hips, roll my body to the beat. Effortlessly shifting from sharp isolations to fluid movements—reaching back to my training in ballet—I bend and stretch in a picture of sensuality and grace, heart thumping, every inch of me tingling.

Roman watches me, entranced as I snake my arms around him, slithering with charm. He's rendered powerless by the rhythmic sway of my hips, unable to pull his eyes away. He couldn't resist me on that first day of class, and he can't resist me now.

Throwing my hands over his shoulders, I do a saucy twist—the kind reserved for sexy salsa routines and exotic dancers. The only thing that gives me pause is the sight of his delicious mouth. I come to a standstill, my parted lips mere inches from his.

He swallows, looking away. "I think we're done for the day."

Moving around me, he cuts the music, not bothering to look back. Over his shoulder, my flabby reflection mocks me in the mirror.

You're disgusting. Nobody wants you.

I turn to get my things, then head for the door.

If Roman wants to live the rest of his life as an asshole, that's fine by me. He can go dance on his own, and I can go dance on mine. But the very thought stops me in my tracks.

I clench my fists and turn back. "Why are you doing this?"

He doesn't even glance up, his focus steady on the computer. "Doing what?"

"This! Acting like a jerk, not being my friend... Treating me like I deserve to be punished for a whole lot more than a scoop of ice cream."

He reluctantly lifts his eyes to meet mine, and I stubbornly hold his gaze.

"Did it *ever* occur to you that between Eli and Griffin and everything else that happened this weekend, I might've been just a little stressed without my support system?"

His attention shifts to the floor, his hands curling into fists. But just as he turns, there's a knock at the doorway.

Theresa. She shifts her emerald eyes between us, wringing her hands. "Hey, Roman. Can I talk to you for a minute?"

My heart constricts when he glances my way. It's the one thing I've been asking for all morning. Attention. Conversation. Realness.

But with her, he doesn't hesitate. Just nods.

I blink, trying to swallow the lump in my throat. Without another word, I make my way out, each step heavier than the last.

<hr />

By the evening, I've still yet to figure out where I went wrong. I'm too ticked to confirm our session for tomorrow, and I doubt Roman will call. For all I know, he's worked things out with the Pilates instructor, and I'm the furthest thing from his mind. I cringe, thinking about how desperate I must've looked, throwing myself at him today.

In the rec room, Maddie stops and restarts her recital music while Eli holds me hostage on the living room sofa. His tongue dangles from the corner of his mouth as he attempts to shuffle a half-deck of cards with one hand. He makes it through a good amount before they tumble to the floor, and he races to pick them up.

"Keep trying," I say with a smile. At least he's optimistic.

My heart leaps when my phone chimes, but I'm surprisingly disappointed when I see it's my husband. *You remember that time we took the kids to the splash pad, and I pushed you under that giant tipping bucket of water?*

The warm memory eases my nerves. I didn't want to wear a swimsuit, and he was clowning me for being uptight.

The softest grin touches my lips as I reply, *I still haven't forgiven you for that.*

He shoots back a picture of me standing under that giant bucket, drenched from head to toe, and I can't help laughing.

How'd you get this? My hair was a mess!

May have snapped it while you were freaking out, he says. *Always been one of my favorites.*

My stomach twists with discomfort as I stare at his message.

He's been hitting me up like this ever since we went to the ice cream parlor. A couple of times yesterday before dropping off the kids, this morning to joke about his aching back. We haven't been in this much contact since before he took over his father's company.

I didn't care about your hair, btw, he adds. *I thought you looked cute.*

Cute. I hate how fast my stomach flips. Like a teenage girl getting her first compliment. I was bigger in that photo than I am now. I shoot back an *LOL*, but I'm not laughing at all.

I gnaw my tongue, unable to shake the memory of his hungry gaze at the ice cream shop. *"Your figure was never an issue,"* he'd said. So why did he leave?

I'm thinking about giving him a call for a much-needed talk when Eli waves his little gauzed hand, shouting, "Okay, Mommy, here we go! Here we go!" He cuts the cards perfectly and goes for bridging them together. But it's a fail.

The doorbell rings, and I stand. "Sorry, buddy. Keep practicing, okay?"

Poor guy. He's so determined.

But I freeze when I open the door.

"Sup?" says Roman. "Can I come in for a minute?"

Yana said she'd swing by after her last coaching session. She got the part in Chicago and wanted to celebrate with wine. But I never expected... I step aside to let him in.

Roman's hands are pressed into the pockets of his leather jacket as he strolls inside and glances around as if it's his first time here.

"Hey, Roman," says Eli, darting into the foyer. "Look what I can do!" The little boy takes another crack at bridging the cards, and several pop out of his hand.

I've gotta find my son another hobby.

But Roman takes what's left of the stack. "Look, if you keep your thumb just a little bent like this and slowly release your other fingers, it'll work better." He demonstrates for my son, and the cards collapse perfectly in the palm of his hand.

"That's so cool!" shouts Eli, eyes nearly falling out of his head. He eagerly snatches back the cards with a thank you and takes off to keep trying.

My lips part in surprise. "How did you even—?"

Roman shrugs, shoving his hands back in his pockets. "You'd be surprised what you'll pick up when you're stuck on the road for twelve hours."

Always full of surprises.

Roman looks toward the rec room as Maddie stops and restarts the music and turns back to me. "Can I speak to you in private?"

He's pacing near my nightstand when I shut the doors and take a seat on the side of my bed. I've never seen him like this: eyes darting, rhythmically pounding his fists.

"You want to sit?"

He stops and shakes his head. Then he takes a seat but, after a moment, stands again.

I'd laugh, but his anxiety is contagious. Why is he here? Did he come to tell me he wants to quit in person? And if so, what does that mean? No more talking? No more dancing?

Finally, he plants his hands on his waist and says, "I'm... sorry about the other night. I told myself I wouldn't go there with you, but I—I think I crossed the line. And I *never* cross the line with a client."

Of course he's sorry. I scratch my head as he continues.

"Look, I really like working with you," he says. "More than I should, probably. And... I don't wanna make this harder for you—"

I raise my hand. "Roman, please look at me." I deserve at least that much.

To my relief, he lifts his gaze to meet mine, and it seems like it's painful for him to do so.

I don't know why I ever thought he would be into me. But I could've sworn something was there. 'Cause *he* kissed *me*. He kissed me over and over again.

"So, I'm just another client to you?"

Roman opens his mouth but closes it again. He looks to the ceiling with a heavy sigh. "Nah. You're... You're real cool."

Something flickers behind his eyes, and I catch it before it disappears.

I study his clenched jaw, the subtle shift in his shoulders, trying to read between the pauses, the hesitation.

"Then why are you treating me like one?"

He blinks, but I'm not letting this go. Too much has been left unsaid, and I need to know if I made it all up in my head. I stare at him, waiting for an answer.

Running his hands over his face, Roman throws back his head before finally taking a seat beside me. "You're right," he says. "You're much more than a client to me."

"Okay. So, exactly what am I... to you?"

He shrugs. "You're fun, beautiful, a tenacious thorn in my side..." I laugh as he looks me over. "And you're an amazing dancer."

Beautiful? Amazing?

My pulse slows as he searches my face, the same way he did before he pressed that sweet kiss to my lips. And I swear I'd give anything for him to do it again. Instead, he looks away.

"That's exactly why I don't think we should work together anymore."

"What?" I try to get him to look me in the eye, but he refuses this time.

He came back. Finally. Said everything I've been aching to hear... everything I once begged Griffin to notice.

He sees me. *Gets* me. So how is this where we land?

"Roman, for *years*, I let go of the one thing I loved more than anything in the world. That girl who was so passionate—full of hopes and dreams—I left her in the past. And ever since, I've felt empty inside."

Roman's gaze is sober when he turns back to me, but at least he's looking.

"I tried to fill that void with everything I could—TV, junk food, online shopping—and nothing worked. But when I'm with you, I find that girl again. And dancing with you today... and at the club on Friday night, I felt a connection that I've *never* felt with anyone in my entire life." *Not even my husband.* "You going to tell me you didn't feel it, too?"

His shoulders rise and fall with a sigh, but he nods.

So, it's not just me. Cautiously, I place a hand on his knee, which isn't much, but it makes him smile just a little.

He drops his head with a humored breath. "Uh, I went to Chicago to get my brother's advice... about you."

"Me?"

He nods, resting a hand on top of mine. "'Cause I've been... confused about you. I've been pretty confused for a while."

Confused? "So, what was his advice?" I say with a chuckle. "Ditch me?"

His gaze sweeps over my face, and he swallows hard. "Not exactly." Holding my breath, I wait for him to go on, but again, he looks away. "You remember how I told you I was let down in the past, and I let it fuel me?"

How could I forget?

"Let's just say I can relate to what you've been through with Baby Daddy more than I care to admit."

"You divorced?"

"Nah. But what happened wasn't all that different."

Somebody dumped him? Seriously?

Roman rolls his eyes. "There was this girl. One of my backup dancers in Hollywood—Jennifer. This Afro-Latina firecracker with ruby-red hair. Passionate, could pick up steps on a whim, loved to go rogue and do her own thing." He softly looks at me. "Not all that different from someone I know."

The two of us exchange a warm smile, and something soft and familiar pulls at me.

"She had me hooked, then broke my heart," he says. "It was pretty serious. So, ever since, I don't really *do* serious."

So he didn't bolt because of my size?

The subtle curve of his back as he bows his head reminds me of when he told me to guard my heart. How long has he been guarding his?

"I mean, don't get me wrong, Roman has had *plenty* of relations in the past. But nothing... real." He stares at my hand in his, running a thumb across my knuckles. "There's just something about you that I can't shake. I mean, I've *tried*. But you're like this song I can't stop playing. And—"

Before he can say another word, I close the distance. My mouth crashes into his, hungry and sure. The kiss is deeper this time, hotter. His lips part like he's been waiting, needing me just as badly. And I pour it all into him—the confusion, the longing, the slow ache I've carried for days—tasting him, testing him, daring him not to feel it too.

When I pull back, his chest rises fast, like I knocked the breath from his lungs. He stares at me, dazed and undone. "Damn, Laura..."

And before I can catch my breath, he leans back in, desperate for more.

For all his brute behavior, the man's kisses are as tender as his touch. He delicately traces the spine of my back, gently folds me into his warm embrace. His hands explore the curves of my body as if he hadn't memorized every contour weeks ago.

The kiss is slower this time. No rush, no panic. Just heat simmering beneath every brush of lips. It's as if we're picking up where we left off, but deeper now, more deliberate. My fingers slide into the soft coils at the nape of his neck, anchoring him to me, and he groans into my mouth, like the taste of me is something he's craved for far too long. He eases me back onto the pillows, his body molding to mine as his palm glides down the slope of my thigh, then curls possessively around the curve of my behind. Cupping the back of my neck, he draws me in with reverence, while his grip at my waist tightens like he's barely holding himself together. I gasp against his mouth, heat unraveling in my core, and he deepens the kiss, drinking from me like I'm the only thing that's ever satisfied him.

"Mommy, I got it—*Ahhhh!*"

Roman springs off me as Eli shoots his tiny, gauzed hand over his eyes.

"Eli!" I bolt upright. "It's okay, honey. We were just hugging."

"You really think he's that dumb?" asks Roman, and I glare at him.

"I don't know," says Eli. "That looked like more than hugging."

"Okay, maybe Mommy kissed Roman, just a little."

"Yeah, Mommy needs locks on her doors," says Roman. I smack him in the chest as concern travels across my little boy's face.

"Is this where babies come from?"

"Wow." Roman jumps to his feet as my mouth drops open. "I think that's my cue to head out."

That probably isn't the worst idea. Though I'm sure we have so much more to talk about.

With a gentle grin, Roman turns back to me. "See you tomorrow?"

I nod. "Nine-thirty sharp."

He runs a thumb across my lips, and in the softest voice, he says, "Can't wait."

18

*I*n just a few days, it's like we never missed a beat.

I follow Roman's every kick and glide, captivated by the ease between us. It's more than just chemistry. It's trust. Rhythm. The rare kind of sync that makes me feel like I was always meant to dance beside him. Like we were choreographed long before we ever met. Our bodies glide and twist in tandem, like muscle memory and magic wrapped in music.

For the first time in a long time, I feel something dangerously close to joy. I used to believe happiness couldn't exist without Griffin. But here I am, laughing, sweating, dancing... with someone who watches me dance like it's a privilege.

The song comes to an end, and Roman's smile wraps around me like a tender embrace. "That was perfect."

"It helps that it was fun, too," I add.

"Ha-ha. You always got jokes."

I stick out my tongue, heading to the back of the studio for some water, but I can feel his eyes on my behind.

He's watching. He's always watching lately.

I smile to myself as I take a drink.

"We'll review it again tomorrow night," he says, reaching for his towel. "I think I can make it a little more challenging."

I look back at him. *"More* challenging?"

"I can't keep taking it easy on you," he says. "What kind of trainer would that make me?"

"A sweet one."

There's a bashful grin on his face as he dries off.

"That reminds me…" I pull my phone from my bag and start typing. "I need to send you a payment before I forget."

He steps over, signaling for me to stop. "Nah. I can't take that anymore."

"Roman, it's fine. Griffin just deposited the money this morning."

"Just… put that away. We got more dancing to do." He turns and heads for the computer as I reluctantly do as he says. Hopefully, he'll come around tomorrow. I couldn't live with the idea of him helping me like he does for free.

I don't even try to hide my smile when Rihanna's "Only Girl in the World" starts playing. He knows exactly what this song does to me. And based on the wicked gleam in his eye, he's counting on it.

A tingle runs down my back as I glance toward the hall. Does he really want to get into it? Right here in the studio? 'Cause last time, things got *pretty* heated.

He grabs my hand and pulls me toward the center of the room. Suddenly, he's twirling me, spinning me in and out, in some sort of ballroom routine. And checking out our reflection in the mirror, it actually doesn't look half-bad.

"What are you up to?" I ask with a giggle.

Roman steps to my side, that electric fire in his gaze. "Follow me."

I match his rhythm, feet chasing his every move as he rolls and pops like liquid lightning—isolating, tilting, and sliding like it's nothing.

"Now, do that sexy swerve of yours," he murmurs behind me, one hand guiding my waist.

I roll my hips, just enough to brush against him. "This one?"

He nods as he rolls along with me, eyes blazing in the mirror like he's drunk on the sight of us. "That's perfect."

I've gotta admit, we *do* look pretty good together.

"Now, you're gonna pop in that direction while I go the opposite way... Yep, just like that. Left, right. *Tease* me."

This routine is fire. Intimate. Dripping with heat. I should've known he was saving something like this. Waiting for the moment. Maybe even waiting for me.

"It's your turn," he says. "Throw me a few of them moves you pulled on Monday. The sexy ones."

Holding his gaze in the mirror, I let my body answer—bending, twisting, extending my leg high. His teeth sink into his bottom lip as he watches, and heat swells between my thighs.

Snatching my hand, Roman yanks me back to him, kicking off our reggaeton spin. But this time, after the three twirls, he doesn't release me. Instead, he snatches me in by the waist and tosses my head back, staring me down like a man seconds from devouring me.

We stay locked in place, my breath hitching as his hand lingers at the soft bend of my knee, his eyes burning through me while my fingers tighten in the fabric of his shirt

Man, that's hot.

His wicked grin wrecks me. "Dance with me."

"Weren't we dancing just now?"

"I wanna dance with you at the Christmas recital," he says. "Somebody's gotta see this."

"*What?*" I tap for him to pull me upright, and mercifully, he does so. "Roman, what are you talking about? This dance isn't even Christmas-themed."

"There's a whole section with random people going on about what they want for Christmas." He shrugs. "We could slip it in there."

In front of all those people? I can't help laughing. "And exactly what would my *random* character want to ask Santa for?"

He throws out his arms as if it couldn't be any more obvious.

I laugh, giving him a good push back. "You swear you're God's gift!"

But he reels me back in, arms slipping around my waist. "Come on," he says, voice low and full of promise. "It'll be *perfect.*"

"Roman, my daughter's a huge part of the show. I'm not trying to steal her moment! And I'm certainly not about to make a fool of myself in front of hundreds of people."

"Ain't nothing foolish about it, mama. What we've got is something *amazing.* And your girl will be ecstatic to see you kill it on that stage. Besides, you handled rocking it out at the club just fine."

"That was different. It was dark and crowded and..."

Incredible. Especially that buzz I got from all the applause and compliments. I haven't felt anything like it in... *years.*

I honestly can't believe I'm actually considering the idea, but when I look into Roman's handsome brown eyes, I can see just how much he believes in me.

I shove a finger in his face. "You better not embarrass me, Roman."

He tightens his grip. "*Please.* Roman embarrasses *no one!*"

"Except maybe himself, right?"

I'm cracking up as he tickles my waist, but he's not laughing at all. He stops and searches my face, a soft grin dancing on his lips.

He could kiss me right here if he wanted to. But there's chatter in the hall.

Roman's gaze drifts over my shoulder, and he takes a step back.

Noticing the curious members glancing our way as they pass the studio, I straighten my clothes and brush at my edges.

Best to keep things professional, I guess.

Roman returns to the computer, scratching his head. "Let's run it one more time before you head out. Okay?"

+ + + + + +

When our session has ended, Roman walks me out to my car as he's been doing ever since we made up. And for the third day in a row, we find ourselves awkwardly standing beside the Lincoln, neither of us in a hurry to say goodbye as the crisp November breeze rushes over us.

On Tuesday, he was all over me—couldn't get enough of my lips. But yesterday evening, with the kids here, he gave me nothing but a hug and a peck on the cheek. And that was so light I couldn't be sure he'd kissed me at all. I honestly have no idea what to expect today.

I linger, playing with my keys, hoping for a slightly better sendoff.

Roman lightly taps my elbow. "You think you'll find time to practice tonight?"

"Sure. Whatever I can remember."

A soft chuckle dies between us as we exchange a quiet grin.

Part of me wonders if this thing between us exists in a bubble. Only safe behind the studio doors. Maybe he's scared of what people will say. Or maybe... he's scared of what it means.

Truth is, I am too.

It's getting chilly, so I better go. "See you tomorrow?"

He nods and opens the door for me.

I blink at him one last time before turning to get in the car.

But grabbing my hand, he spins me into him. Then presses a kiss to my lips that's so tender and so sweet, I forget what I was nervous about.

And it's not a question.

It's a promise.

– 211 –

19

*T*wo weeks later, despite the temperature dropping along with a light dusting of late autumn snow, we're still tangled in heat like we're on borrowed time. The two of us fall against the side of the Lincoln like a teenage cliché, going at it again. Roman groans against my lips, pressing into me, and I sigh as I indulge in the slow burn of his tongue.

All of it, from the laughter to the dancing to his affectionate kisses, has been wonderful. But outside of this and the occasional impromptu meal at my house, we haven't done much else. It wouldn't hurt if the man would bother taking me to dinner once in a while.

Speaking of dinner... I gently pull away from Roman's syrupy lips, gazing into his eyes.

He leans his shoulder against the Lincoln with a soft, knowing smile. "What's up?"

Though he's clearly in a good mood after our lengthy dance and make-out sessions, I don't want to throw a wet blanket on things. I gaze into the cloudy sky, fiddling with my keys. "So... Thanksgiving's coming up."

"Is that this month?"

"Mmhmm."

He chuckles. "What is it? You want an extra day off for Black Friday or something?"

"Actually..." I gnaw my lip. "I was just thinking, if you don't have plans, maybe you'd like to join the kids and me for Thanksgiving dinner." The holidays have been difficult for most of my adult life, and with the loss of my husband quickly approaching, it's probably not the best idea for me and the kids to be on our own.

I'm prepared for Roman to laugh in my face, but instead, he lifts a brow. "Join you for Thanksgiving dinner?"

"That's... if you don't already have plans, and... if you want."

It feels like an hour passes before he clears his throat. "Well, *maybe*—if I don't have plans—*maybe* I'll drop by."

My heart leaps for joy. *But he did say maybe.* "Look, if you can't, I understand—"

But he cuts me off with a sweet kiss and whispers, "I'd love to."

+ +++++ +

Roman arrives at four o'clock sharp on Thanksgiving, a bottle of Chardonnay in his hand. "Hey, beautif—*oh.* Yana's here."

"Hey, Roman!" My cousin struts up the foyer in a leopard mini-dress and thigh-high boots that scream holiday thirst trap. Roman gives her a wave, but his eyes dart to me the moment she yanks him into a hug.

I shrug. "She got a break from rehearsals for the holiday and didn't feel like cooking, so I said, 'Hey! The more, the merrier!'"

Roman tosses me a death stare as Yana steps back and snatches the bottle from his hand.

"Chardonnay? Roman, you sure know how to treat a girl." She playfully shoves him on the shoulder before giving his bicep another unnecessary squeeze. "Ooh, *girl.* He's even *beefier* than the last time I saw him. You been doing extra workouts, baby?"

Roman hits me with a naughty grin as my cousin sashays toward the kitchen. *"If only,"* he mutters, squeezing my behind. I smack him in the chest with a giggle.

Despite her constant teasing since Roman and I hit the club, I've yet to fill my cousin in on our new relationship status. I suppose I've just been waiting for the green light from him.

"You know what? Let me get that for you, sweetheart." Roman jogs into the kitchen, giving Yana a charming smile as he slips the bottle from her hands. "Laura, could you help me with the glasses?"

Thankfully, the kids are begging my cousin to join them in a game of *Go Fish,* so she doesn't question him before heading into the living room.

With Yana out of earshot, Roman leans my way, unwrapping foil from the bottle. "So, exactly when did you plan to tell me your thirsty cousin would be here?"

"Thirsty? Didn't you slip her your number?"

"I was trying to be nice," he grumbles, uncorking his bottle of wine. "Do you know how many drunken texts she sent me after the party? If it weren't for you, I seriously would've considered blocking her."

I stare at him as he pours. "If it weren't for *me?*"

He turns his attention to the glasses, attempting to mask a sheepish smile. "Well, we had to collaborate to get you out of the house. And she knew what size you wore."

I study him, thinking about what a gentleman he was that night—the dress, the dance floor, the way his eyes found mine as he pulled up to the house.

Diamond Eyes, he'd whispered, like it meant something.

I still can't believe he did all that. Just for me.

Across the room, Yana gives Roman a flirty wave, and he tosses her a kind smile.

"Is she still hitting you up?" I ask.

"Not since the club," he says.

Of course not. But for whatever reason, my shoulders relax a bit. "Well, it's not like I have in-laws to invite or anything—and I've got a lot of food."

Roman's gaze turns sober as he passes me a glass. Recently, while we were jogging the track, I shared that this would be my tenth Thanksgiving without my little sister. She passed away just before the holiday during my freshman year of college. I didn't get into the details, but Roman knows that ever since, Griffin's all I've consistently had.

Roman x-rays my soul with his penetrating gaze. "You good?"

"I'll be fine." Though I'm disappointed when I raise the glass to my lips to see that he's barely filled it halfway. He shrugs at my frown.

"Pace yourself."

With pursed lips, I take a sip as he glances toward my cousin again.

"Laura, did you, uh… tell her about us?" I shake my head, and he releases a breath he probably doesn't want me to hear. "Okay. Don't."

I nod as he pours a tall glass for himself. He's about to take a sip when he notices me staring.

"What is it?" he asks.

"Nothing… I'm just kinda wondering why this whole thing is such a big secret."

His eyes dart between Yana and me as he sets his glass aside. "Come on, Laura. You know it's not like that."

I nod. "It's not like what?"

"I—" He stops and subtly brushes a finger against my hand, careful to ensure nobody's watching. "Look. Just for tonight, let's keep this between us, okay?"

Despite the less-than-satisfying response, I agree.

Roman takes a slow sip of wine, eyes dragging over my plain sweater and jeans like I'm draped in satin. "You look gorgeous, by the way." I toss him a lopsided grin, still trying to shake off my nerves as he nudges me. "And you'll never guess what I did today."

My curiosity holds my dejection at bay. "What?"

"I called my mom. We actually talked for more than two minutes."

I gasp, pinching his cheek. "Roman Asshole Graham, maybe there's hope for you after all."

He rolls his eyes, batting me away. "Baby steps."

Presenting a plate of low-fat cookies I made just for him, I say, "I think your efforts are worthy of a reward. Want a taste?"

Roman curls his nose as I hold one up to his mouth. "Before dinner?"

"Live a little."

The man looks doubtful but ventures to take a bite. "Wow. That is *amazing*." He takes another nibble as I bounce on my toes. "What'd you add to make it so sweet?"

"Just a little honey." As he frowns, I add, "It's still fat-free."

He chews pensively. "I'm gonna need another one."

· ✦ ✦ ✦ ·

After a few rounds of *Crazy Eights* and magic attempts from Eli, we all gather in the dining room to give thanks and dig into our meal. I've got all our favorite dishes prepared, along with some minor healthy substitutes: turkey, mustard greens, cauliflower "mashed potatoes." And Griffin or no Griffin, I'm determined to give my family a very happy Thanksgiving.

Though Roman has yet to begin harping about my eating choices, I know he's keeping an eye out. So, I focus on lean turkey and veggies, with tiny helpings of stuffing and cranberry sauce. With a soft grin, he takes notice of my choice to cut a small sliver of sweet potato pie. Meanwhile, he's piling up his plate beside me, and I bet he won't put on a single pound.

Yana leans her elbows on the table with a roll in hand, a not-so-subtle smirk on her face. "So, Roman, rumor has it that you and my cousin might be performing at Maddie's recital."

I freeze mid-sip, pulse spiking.

The last thing I want is for Roman to think I'm out here broadcasting our every move. Especially when I just promised I wouldn't.

"So what if it's true?" he asks, splitting a glance with me. But I haven't breathed a word.

I shift my attention to Maddie, who manages to shovel three spoonfuls of mashed cauliflower into her mouth in four seconds flat. I may have given Roman my word to keep things private, but there's no guarantee my kids will cooperate.

Yana rips off a chunk of her roll, eyes narrowing as they bounce between us. "I just wanna know what kind of dancing it is. The *Dancing with the Stars* kind or the *Dirty Dancing* kind?"

My Chardonnay slips down the wrong pipe, and I cough, pounding my chest.

Roman chuckles, unmoved. "Well, I wish I could share, but that information is classified. You'll have to come to the performance and see like everyone else."

Yana hums, but the way her eyes drift back and forth says she's clocking everything. Roman and I exchange confrontational glares the moment she returns to her meal.

"I can't wait," says Eli. "Mommy and Roman practice *all* the time. This one time, I walked in on them practicing in Mommy's—"

"*Eli!*" I pin the little boy with a harsh glare, and Roman throws up his hands.

"Don't go spreading all our business, man!"

Yana cocks her head, and my heart stutters. I force a breath, then roll my eyes dismissively. At least, I hope it looks that way.

Though I'm not the biggest fan of all this secrecy, I'm not in a rush to share every dirty detail with my cousin. Just the same, Roman isn't doing a great job of hiding our latest developments. He quickly turns back to my son.

"I mean... Cousin Yana doesn't need to know all our top-secret rehearsal spots. We wouldn't want her stealing a peek at our number ahead of the show."

Eli tilts his head with a frown, but Yana's blinking between all of us.

"True," I add. "But... my rec room isn't all *that* secret, Roman."

The two of us exchange an awkward nod and return to our meals. I don't even know why I'm bothering to assist with this nonsense.

I'm grateful when my phone chimes, releasing me from the inter-rogation. It's Griffin. *Happy Thanksgiving!!!*

He told me he and Vicki were headed to his mother's for dinner, then to some charity event later. Still, I appreciate him taking the time to shoot us a message.

I'll call you and the kids later tonight, he says.

That would be nice.

Since Eli's accident, Griffin's been... present. For the kids. For me. He's been showing up more. Texting to check in. Taking the kids out. Even invited me to a Lions game when he was gifted four tickets. Apparently, Vicki had other plans.

I told him I had practice with Roman that weekend, which was true... but also easier than saying what I was really thinking:

I don't believe you. Not anymore.

If he truly wanted me back, he'd say so. Plain and simple. But he never does. He just floats back into my life when it's convenient for him—smiling like nothing happened, stirring up old feelings, acting like we're one nostalgic memory away from working again.

I don't know if he's trying to soothe his ego or simply mess with my head, but I can't go there with him anymore.

So I turned him down. Because I can't keep mistaking hope for a sign.

I'm still contesting the divorce, if for no other reason than to ensure our kids never have to ask him for a dime. Besides, after the way he abruptly decided to uproot our lives, it wouldn't hurt for him to bear a little of the burden. But if it's bothering him, he doesn't show it.

Even with the hearing finally scheduled, Griffin calls regularly. Sends breezy check-ins. Took off work for Eli's last appointment. It's more attention now than we ever got before he moved out. But at least he's finally making an appearance. And that matters more than my feelings.

I take a breath and keep it light: *I'll let them know. Happy Thanksgiving to you, too.*

I'm really glad we can get along like this now. After he filed the papers, I wasn't too sure we ever would. Guess we'll see what happens after the hearing.

I'm taking a sip of my Chardonnay and appreciating Roman's knee pressed to mine under the table when Griffin responds. *It's times like this that I really miss you.*

My pulse stutters, and I set down my glass with trembling hands. I read it three times.

Once as sarcasm. Once as guilt. Once as the lie I want to believe.

Before I can decipher the meaning behind his cryptic text, he sends another to clarify. *I miss all of you. But especially you.*

What? Why would he even...?

I toss back my head, preparing to chug what's left of my Chardonnay, but Roman pulls back my glass. "Slow down there." He frowns as I grab a napkin and dab my lips. "You alright?"

"Yeah, I'm fine. I'm completely fine." I snatch a roll and start munching.

How dare he? He misses us? How the hell could he miss us? He wasn't even here last Thanksgiving. He was too busy feeding pizza to the homeless or whatever. That jerk!

"How about we ease off the carbs, huh?" says Roman, yanking the roll from my hands.

I glower at him as I grab my phone. ***I'm not sure what you want me to say.***

Tossing my phone back on the table, I turn to piling a generous serving of greens on my plate. Everyone's curious eyes are fixed on me. Even Yana lifts a brow.

"You okay, girl?"

"Can't I enjoy free calories?"

No one says a word.

I stuff the greens in my mouth and chew like it's therapy.

Why is he doing this to me? It's shady. It's shady and confusing and cruel. Just another one of his sick pranks.

When the phone finally chimes again, Roman snatches it up before I can.

"Hey!" I reach for the phone as he slides it into his pocket. "Roman! Give me my phone!"

"*Laura!*" Roman brings his face closer to mine, his gaze burning with intensity. "Be. Present."

I'm still trying to catch my breath as my eyes fall on his shoulders, watching them rise and fall as gently as ripples on a lake. And just like in every dance, I fall in perfect time, breathing in and out... in and out.

Despite my stress and anxiety, with Roman's covert requests and Griffin's random texts pushed to the far corners of my mind, I manage to enjoy the rest of our evening. Everyone teams up in knocking out the dishes, and we play charades. It isn't long before Yana's heading out, but she stops in the foyer as I'm walking her to the door.

"Mmhmm. Don't think I don't see what you're up to."

"What do you mean?"

She gives me a once-over that feels like a full-body side-eye. "I saw you with Roman tonight."

I nearly swallow my tongue as I shoot a glance toward the rec room where Roman's teaching the kids a new dance number. Thankfully, the music is loud enough that he can't hear us. "I don't know what you're—"

"Oh, please!" Yana taps me with her plate of food. "You told me nothing happened at that club, but I see you making googly eyes at him."

I rub the back of my neck, my heart still struggling to find its normal rhythm. "Is it that obvious?"

Yana nods in my face, grinning ear to ear. "It is!" She laughs. "I bet he likes you too."

I raise my brows, feigning surprise. "You think so?"

"Mmhmm." There's a glimmer of acceptance in her gaze. "But I tell you one thing, one of y'all better make a move before I do."

I force a chuckle as she tosses back her curls and stomps out the door, my heart aching to share every detail.

"I'll call you later about that little meltdown you had over dinner," she says. "I know that was Griffin hitting you up."

I drum my fingers against the door as she hops in her car. *Yeah. Unfortunately.*

We wrap up the evening with our favorite Thanksgiving tradition: watching *Home Alone*. More recently, with Griffin's schedule, it's become more of a thing for just me and the kids. But I suppose traditions can change.

Macaulay Culkin's just setting up his toy cars when I look over and find my little boy passed out against Roman's chest, the trainer's arm casually resting across the back of the living room sofa.

Roman meets my stunned gaze with a smirk. "He's leaking, isn't he?"

I chuckle into my hand, noting Maddie yawning on the opposite sofa. With a familiar warmth in my belly, I pause the movie. "Why don't we call it a night for now? It's been a long day for all of us."

Completely unprompted, Roman scoops Eli in his arms and carries him upstairs, with me and Maddie not far behind. I've just kissed my daughter goodnight when I turn to see Roman tucking Eli into bed. A soft grin is on his lips as he pulls the blankets over Eli's little scarred hand with care and awkwardly pats his head. Despite the knot of emotions that have been turning in my gut all evening, I'm breathless as he whispers, "Goodnight, Eli."

It comes as no surprise when, only moments later, we're in my bedroom, the doors firmly shut behind us. His kiss lands like a spark to dry leaves. Fast, consuming, dangerous. I melt into him, fingers buried in his curls, hips pressing forward like my body's already made the decision for me.

His kiss deepens, grows hungrier, as his hands trace the line of my back, lower still, coaxing a sigh from my lips.

It would be so easy to let go. To stop overthinking.

To let him feel what I've been aching to give.

And in this moment—warm skin, tangled breath, his heartbeat thrumming beneath my palms—I'm not sure I want to stop.

"Will you stay?" I breathe, savoring the sweet notes of his tongue.

"I can't." He caresses the curves of my hips as he smiles against my mouth. "Class in the morning. Who knew it'd take so long for them kids to tucker out, huh?"

My body stiffens as his lips trail slow, sweltering kisses along my neck. I should be lost in it. In the way his mouth lingers, the way his hands know exactly where to land. But my thoughts spiral.

If he doesn't want more... what does he want? Does he truly want me at all?

Because he's amazing. He's hot. And so damn sweet when he wants to be. And I'd be lying if I said I didn't want him too.

Of course, this is the closest we've felt all day.

Can't you get anything right?

I break from Roman's kiss in a daze, and he groans with disapproval.

"Hey, I been craving this all night—"

"And whose fault is that?" I ask.

Roman's grin falters as he reaches for my hand. But I pull away.

"Laura, I... What's up?"

My first notion is to tell him it's nothing. I always want to say it's nothing. Mom was the same way, and April... Then again, how long did I do this song and dance with Griffin? Not to mention our latest hit: *Good Enough to Miss, Not Good Enough to Stay.*

My gaze drifts over Roman's shoulder, and he moves into my vision. "Why are you trippin'? I thought we were on the same page."

Maybe the secrecy isn't just about Yana. Perhaps he doesn't want to get Eli and Maddie's hopes up. Or mine.

"Look, it's been a long night, and... if you're *that* terrified of people seeing us together, then maybe you should just go. At least that way, you can keep your little secret."

With an irritated breath, he presses his hands to his waist. "Laura, what's this about, really?"

Maybe he got the wrong idea. And maybe I should've spoken up sooner. But between his sneaking around, and Griffin, and all it takes to deliver a "happy holiday" despite my grief, I think I've had enough. "This is my home. The one place I shouldn't have to walk on eggshells. The one place I should be able to express how I feel. If you can't understand that, if you're *that* embarrassed about us, then maybe there shouldn't be an *us* at all." I hold open the door, averting my gaze.

Maybe it wouldn't be the worst thing for me to be alone for a while. I'm stressed enough as it is.

Of course, Roman doesn't have a word to say. It's not like any of this meant a thing to him. Maybe I was just having fun too. My heart still sinks as he moves toward the door.

But he pushes it shut.

The next thing I know, he's got me firmly pressed against it, his tender lips brushing over mine, enticing me with citrusy hints of Chardonnay. His hand slips under my sweater, intensely caressing my waist, and a moan echoes in my throat.

I shouldn't be doing this. I'm confused and upset... There's no way it can end well.

But before I can pull away, he stops and whispers in my ear, "You're right, I'm sorry."

And a symphony of butterflies releases in my stomach. *He's sorry.* Judging by his soft expression as he looks me in the eye, he couldn't be more sincere. So why can't I let this go?

"Especially with you so stressed after dinner." His gaze lingers on mine as I lean against the door. "You gonna tell me what's really going on?"

Where would I even start? Griffin? April? It's all so much. "You first."

Thankfully, that's distraction enough. He steps back with a sigh and takes a seat on the bed. "Look, Laura, I'm just... not quite ready to let this get out around the rec, ya know? I mean, I can't be sure how much your cousin likes to talk, but it hadn't been twenty-four hours since I took you to the club before the entire rec knew about it. People been looking at us sideways ever since."

I suppose some of the girls at the rec have been a little less chummy lately. Someone stepped on my hand when I was sitting against the back wall at the end of class but swore it was an accident.

"Theresa asked about it when I told her I'd rather be friends," he says. "The guys are giving me hell... and I just—"

"Feel embarrassed?"

"No." He frowns as he pulls me into his lap, linking his arms around my waist. "I'm not embarrassed, Laura. I just don't know how to navigate all this for my brand. I mean, you'd be surprised how much of this business is about selling the dream. Roman's the type of guy to have a different girl in his bed every night."

"A different girl *every* night?"

"Well, obviously, I don't, but... that's what I let them believe. If Roman's a hot commodity, all the girls wanna train with him, and all the dudes wanna be him. Without that..." He exhales through his nose. "The ladies are gonna give me a *really* hard time. They're gonna give *both* of us a hard time once they know how I feel about you."

How he feels about me?

He runs a hand up and down my arm and presses a kiss to my shoulder. "Especially as strict as I've been with the whole nonfraternization thing—they'll see it as preferential treatment or something. And after you *kill it* in this recital, I'm probably gonna take a lot of heat."

Griffin was always about his brand, especially on the red carpet. There were plenty of times he'd ask me to step aside while he took photos by himself or alone with the kids. The optics always mattered to him.

But I'd never want to come between Roman and his life's work. I'm intimately familiar with the heartache it can bring.

I'm studying the floor when Roman lifts my chin. "But hey, you got a point. Maybe we don't have to hide *everything* from your kids." A mischievous grin touches his lips as I nod. "Should we get in a little practice now?"

I take his jaw in my hand and kiss him gently. "You actually called him Eli for once."

Roman's lip curls. "Did I?"

After a bit more kissing, Roman and I reluctantly agree that he should head out. I may have my reservations when it comes to all this sneaking around, but I'd kinda like to see where this goes.

I'd hoped my lips were distraction enough, but he still pauses at the threshold. "When you're ready—I mean really ready—to talk, I'm here."

We both know what he means, but I won't be sharing any of my dramatic past or present anytime soon if I can help it. I nod anyway.

Roman's grin is soft as he heads for the porch. "Thanks for the invite. It's been a long time since I did something like this."

"I'm just glad you liked the food."

"The food was *absolutely* amazing," he says, making his way down the stairs.

"Hey!" I call, waving him back. "Come here!"

He's quick to jog back up the stairs. "What's up?"

I flit my eyes, playing with the zipper of his leather jacket. "You still... have my phone."

With a snort, he hands it over before pressing one last kiss to my temple. And I gotta say, despite plenty of bumps and bruises, it's turned out to be a decent Thanksgiving after all.

I don't dare check my phone until Roman pulls out to the road. But my heart sinks as I read Griffin's message. *I'm just hoping that maybe you miss me too.*

20

I turn up the music and step in front of the rec room mirror, counting myself off as I let the rhythm take over.

With Maddie practicing so often, it's rare that I get time to myself back here. So, I relish every second—relaxing into the melody, letting it lift me as I go into the new routine.

Roman's taking me out for our first real date tonight, and the last thing I want to do is spiral like I did on Thursday. Maybe he'll treat me to a nice steak dinner or something. May as well burn the extra calories now.

I roll my hips in the mirror like we reviewed before, step out and in, swaying to the beat. A faint smile curves my lips as I recall Roman's words: *"You're like this song I can't stop playing."* I know exactly how he feels.

Not that the ladies at Perry Rec would be thrilled about it. I definitely caught a few side-eyes and whispers in class this morning. Just to play it safe, I slipped out with the rest of the crowd, but not before tossing Roman a meaningful glance. He shot me a text before I even picked up Maddie, telling me to keep my evening open. Apparently, he still feels guilty about the drama on Thanksgiving and couldn't imagine a better way to spend his Saturday night than making it up to me.

But what could that mean? Dinner? Champagne? Seeing me naked?

Goosebumps skitter down my spine at the thought and I miss a step.

Focus, Laura. Be present.

I come up on one of the spins and imagine holding Roman's hand as I step out and twirl, and twirl, and... *Griffin?*

I stumble, blinking at the sight of my husband leaning against the doorframe, arms crossed, a wistful grin on his lips.

"Hey, Laura."

"Hey." I try to catch my breath. "Where'd you come from?"

He's wearing an expensive-looking bomber jacket and jeans, as casual as he was when he took the kids to the Lions game. "Maddie let me in," he says, pointing back with his thumb.

"Oh." I almost forgot he was supposed to pick up the kids this afternoon.

His gaze travels down to my sports bra and yoga pants. "Sorry if I scared you."

I go to turn off the music, my heart still racing. I've been avoiding him since he sent his little forward texts on Thanksgiving, and thanks to Roman confiscating my phone, I conveniently missed his promised call. But Maddie said he reached her just fine. Now that he's here, I'm going to need a better strategy.

He's already approached by the time I turn around. Slipping his hands around my waist, he hugs me close and kisses my cheek. My eyes flutter shut at the scratch of his beard, my senses betraying me with every inhale of that familiar spicy scent... No. I can't do this again. He says we're done. But every chance he gets, it's like I'm his puppet, and he knows exactly which strings to pull to get me falling all over myself. I quickly move out of his grasp.

"Damn, girl!" He shakes his head, eyes roaming every inch of me. "What you doing with that trainer? You lookin' *hot!*"

"Thanks." I grab a towel off the sofa and dab my brow. No matter what he says, I know he means nothing by it. He never does lately. "I was just going over this dance Roman and I made up for Maddie's recital."

"Y'all are dancing together in the recital?"

"Yeah. A duet."

Griffin's not even looking me in the eye. He's too busy ogling my behind.

I cross my arms. "You think you'll be there?"

"Hmm?"

I lean against the foosball table. "The Christmas recital. Are you coming?"

"Oh—of course. Wouldn't miss it for the world." He's got this adorable lopsided grin on his face—the same one he wore the night he snuck into my hospital room with balloons and a strawberry milkshake after Maddie was born. "You need anything or...?"

"Nah. We're good. But if anything changes, I'll let you know at the hearing."

He offers a small nod. "Um, I'm taking the kids to the movies this evening if you wanna come along." I haven't seen him look this hopeful in a long time.

Before my nerves can get the best of me, I force a polite smile. "I have a date."

The words leave my mouth smoother than I expected, but my heart's still racing. It still feels strange, saying no to the man I once said yes to for life. Even stranger that it doesn't break me. At least, not this time.

He tucks his hands in his pockets. "So... things are getting kinda serious with this Roman guy, huh?"

With a shrug, I reach for my water. "Maybe. We'll see."

His eyes hold mine. And for a moment, I'm back to that text on Thanksgiving.

I miss all of you. But especially you.

For months, I longed to hear those words. If only it were real.

"Laura, listen. About that text—"

"Yeah, I get it. We're all a little sentimental around the holidays." *Besides, wouldn't want you thinking it got my hopes up.*

There's a quiet concern in his eyes as they connect with mine. "Were you okay?"

"Mmhmm. Roman was here, Yana, too. We had a great time." His gaze remains fixed on me as I take another drink. "How about you and Vicki? Did the charity event go well?"

A lengthy moment passes before he clears his throat. "Yeah, we..." He scratches his nose. "We had a nice time."

"She isn't joining you all for the movie?"

"Nah. She's out of town."

I bet he misses her, too. But he takes a step closer.

"Laura, why don't we—?"

"*We're ready!*" the kids sing as they come skipping down the stairs. Music to my ears.

I press kisses to each of their angelic faces and usher them to the door, being sure to give Griffin the smallest of waves as they pull him outside. I can't be too sure what their father was going to say, but I can't afford to give it another thought. Besides, I've got a hot date to get ready for.

✦✦✦✦✦✦

I answer the door in the evening with my makeup flawless, my hair freshly curled, and my ruby-red dress snatched in all the right places. As expected, Roman's jaw drops when he sees me, but I pout at his jogging pants and Adidas.

"Yeah," he says with a wince. "You might wanna bring a pair of sneakers."

An hour later, I'm at a rec center in Grosse Point, clinging to a rock-climbing wall for dear life. *"Roman! I don't think this was the best idea!"*

"You can do this, Laura!" he calls from far below. "Just push off with your toes!"

My legs are trembling, palms sweaty. Any minute now, I'm going to fall. I squeeze my eyes tight. *"I need to come down!"*

"Nah! Nah! We're not quitters!" he says. "Since when do you quit, Diamond Eyes?"

"It wouldn't be the first time!"

He has the nerve to laugh. I'd glare at him, but I'm too terrified to look down.

"Wow," he says. "I didn't know you were afraid of heights."

"I didn't either... until now."

But he's not responding.

Why did I ever agree to this? They're going to have to call the fire department to get me down. My stomach churns, heart drumming. This is *definitely not* my idea of a good time.

I startle when Roman climbs up beside me. "How'd you do that so fast?"

He flashes a captivating smile, as charming as a superhero. "I'm here, and I got your back, okay? Now, let's do this."

My elbows feel like jelly, my jittery fingers willing to slip from the wall's tiny knobs at any moment. "I... I can't, Roman. It's just too hard!" Pushing through a sprint is one thing; this is another. I'm on the brink of tears, thinking about how foolish I was to try and impress him.

But Roman levels his gaze with mine. "Look, whatever you're hearing in your head right now, you gotta shut that garbage off. Don't ever let anybody tell you that you can't do something—especially you. Alright?"

I nod. But I'm not moving.

"Right now, you gotta bottle all that up," says Roman. "Push through that fear. If anybody can do this, it's you." And looking into his sweet brown eyes, I know he truly believes that. So, for now, I'll do my best to believe him.

I push off on my toes and climb to the next grip.

"There you go! There you go! Try again."

I grab the next rung... and then another.

Roman explodes with a shout. "*Whoo! Let's work!*"

A breathless laugh escapes me as we move together, step by shaky step. By the time I realize I've done it, we're already at the top.

"There's my Diamond Eyes!" Roman winks. "I knew you could do it."

A breathless smile escapes me. I didn't think I could. But, like always, he believed in me when I didn't believe in myself. "Okay. Now, how do we get down from this crazy thing?"

"Well, that's easy," says Roman. "You just let go."

I lose what's left of my breath as he releases his rope and glides down like he was never afraid to fall.

"Uh... Roman? Can you come back? *Please!*"

After about ten minutes of arguing, I finally make my way down. Shaking and muttering every prayer I know, I collapse into his arms. He's still cracking up as he lowers me onto the mat.

"Roman!" I swat his chest. "Don't you *ever* ask me to do something that crazy again!"

He's still laughing as he pulls me in for another embrace. "Aw! You know it was fun, and you were *amazing.*"

I'm still a little shaken and in disbelief that I did it myself, but the sweet kiss he presses to my lips despite the onlookers is reward enough.

"Come on," he says, eyes blazing. "I've got an idea."

—————— ·♦♦♦♦·· ——————

Not so surprisingly, he takes me back to his studio at Perry Rec. "Seriously, Roman?"

He wiggles his brows at my reflection as he takes off his jacket.

The guy is *always* thinking about dancing. I'm just wondering how long we're going to be here 'cause I'm getting pretty hungry.

Roman waves me over, that electric spark in his gaze. "You ready?" Though I'd much rather be anywhere else, I relent with a nod. "Okay. So, you remember that spot in the dance where I had you spinning circles around me? I'm changing it."

He's seriously trying to work right now.

"Look, I know it sounds crazy," he says, acknowledging my lengthy stare. "But you gotta trust me. It's perfect."

I release a heavy breath, knowing we won't be getting out of here anytime soon if I don't go with it. "What do you need me to do?"

With an eager smile, he has me get into position at his side. "So, instead of going into the spin, you're gonna throw your arm around my shoulders. Kinda drape it around me." I do so, and he wraps his arm around my waist. "Then fall into me with your hip and cross over with your left foot… Yep. Just like that. Let's try again."

After a few more attempts, he says, "Now, don't panic, alright?"

"What do you mean?"

"Just trust me. It's gonna be great." He's unmoved by my curious stare. "Come on. We gotta try this!"

I get into position as he counts us off. But just as we're wrapping up the sequence, Roman tightens his grip and tries to lift me off the floor! I yelp, tumbling out of his grasp.

"Roman, what are you doing?"

"I was *trying* to lift you, mama. At least until you stopped me."

"Wha—? Are you crazy?"

"No, I—I thought it might be worth a shot." He looks completely sincere as I step back.

"Roman, there's no way. I'm too big."

"No, you're not. We can do this."

This is crazy, and he knows it. What if one of us gets hurt?

"Come on, Diamond Eyes." Roman takes me by the hand. "You mean to tell me you're not even gonna try?"

I glower at his incredibly handsome, optimistic face. "You better pray that one of us doesn't end up in the hospital tonight." He chuckles as we start over.

"Arm drape, hip in, cross, step. Point your toes!" He struggles to lift me again, and both of us stumble back.

This is so embarrassing. I must be as heavy as a log. "Can we just stick with the spin?"

Roman's staring at my thick waist, wagging his head like a toddler refusing to nap. And here I thought *I* was stubborn.

He whips out his phone and pulls up a video of some couple nailing the move like it's nothing. That girl probably weighs half of what I do.

Roman isn't swayed. "You see how she kinda lifts up with her torso? I need you to engage your *full* core, alright? Let's make all them crunches count!"

Got it. Suck in my gut. Which shouldn't be hard since I'm in dire need of a milkshake.

An hour later, we've barely gotten anywhere, and I'm so tired and humiliated that I could cry. Why is he insisting on doing this? The man is about ready to sprain his wrist.

He's still requesting we try again when one of the security guards knocks at the doorframe. "Hey, Roman. We're about to close for the night."

Roman blows out some air, his hands on his waist. "Thanks, man. We'll head out now."

Finally! With a sigh of relief, I throw on my jacket. First, the Wall of Terror, and now this. It hasn't been a very romantic evening at all. "So, what's up? You taking me home?"

But I turn to find a wicked grin on Roman's face.

———————— ✦✦✦✦✦ ————————

Before long, we're back at his place, practicing barefoot. And I have just about reached my limit. This isn't a real date... And I'm *hungry.* To top it off, Roman has barely figured out how to get me off the ground, repeating this humiliating exercise over and over.

"Come on, Roman." With a frustrated breath, I throw my hands on my knees. "Maybe it's just not meant to be."

"Laura, I told you, we're not quitters!"

"I know, but... *physics!*"

Roman shakes his head, pondering as he stares at the floor. My stomach growls in protest.

"I think I got it." He claps. "Let's go again!"

He's not listening to me, the same way Griffin refused to listen when I'd tell him something was off again and again.

"No." I shake my head.

"Come on, Laura. We got this—"

"Roman, I said *no!*"

He blinks at me in a daze, but I am beyond spent.

I plant my hands on my hips, taking a step back. "You told me you were going to show me a good time tonight. And right now, I am *miserable.* Do you even know what my idea of a good time is? Hmm? How about a movie? Maybe even champagne? Do you have the *slightest* clue when I last ate or drank *anything?*"

The man drops his eyes as if the thought never even occurred to him.

"Roman, this is *nothing like* a date. And if I didn't know any better, I'd say you were just trying to put me back to work." He's frozen as I release another hot breath. *I can't believe my incredibly bad luck.*

Slowly, he pads over and laces his fingers with mine. "You know what, you're right. And I'm sorry. I just got a little caught up. That's all."

What an understatement.

He lowers his head, searching my eyes. "What do ya say I take you out to dinner—wherever you want?"

"In this?" I look over my tank top and yoga pants. "I doubt we're going anywhere special."

"Okay." He laughs. "You wanna order Chinese or something?"

I guess that would be nice. I haven't had it in *months.*

He slips into the kitchen, grabs a bottle of water from the fridge, and hands it to me like it's flowers wrapped in plastic. "A peace offering."

I glare at him as I crack it open. *He's lucky he's cute.* I'm taking a lengthy swig when I spot that hint of electricity sparking in his gaze. "You are unbelievable!"

"Just… one last time! *Please?*" He flashes an imploring smile. "One last time, and I'll let it go. I swear."

"If I end up in the hospital, you're paying my medical bills." I set the bottle aside with a shake of my head.

"Okay," he says as I join him in front of the mirrors. "This time, wait until I grab around your waist. Then press off before you point your toes. Kinda like you did while rock climbing."

I rub my temples as he counts us off.

When he wraps his arm around me, I push and point my toes as instructed. And suddenly, I'm off the floor. Lifting me by my waist, Roman swings me in a circle and sets me back down as gently as he would a figurine.

I blink at his smiling face. "We did it?"

"We did it, Laura. *We did it!*"

He grabs my face in both hands and presses his lips to mine like he's trying to rewrite every kiss that came before this one.

"That was incredible," he murmurs against my mouth, his voice low and reverent. "I *knew* you could do it, Diamond Eyes."

His breath fans my cheek, warm and uneven. And for a second, I forget how hungry I am. My chest lifts just a little, like something inside me cracked open and let the light in.

He believed I could do it. And now I have.

I meet his gaze, lips still tingling, heart settling where the frustration used to be.

He didn't let me give up.

Griffin never looked at me like this. Never made me *feel* like this.

Roman brushes his thumbs along my cheeks, his eyes burning into mine like they already know the answer to a question he hasn't asked.

Then he kisses me again. Deeper this time, slower, like he's tracing a map he never wants to forget. His lips move with purpose, and when I sigh into his mouth, he groans like he feels it everywhere.

My hands slide up his chest, around his neck, pulling him closer until there's no space left between us. His body is warm, solid, and pressed so tight against mine I can feel every breath, every beat.

And suddenly, I'm not so tired anymore.

We tease and taste, lips grazing, mouths open just enough to make it dangerous. He backs me toward the sofa, one slow step at a time, his kisses growing hungrier, like *he's* the one who's been starving all night. And I'm the only thing on the menu.

Are we doing this right here? Right now? Besides Griffin, no man's ever seen me naked.

With a huff, Roman tugs at my shirt, and I swallow what I can of my nerves.

Griffin saw my belly all stretched out, witnessed me in my full glory when I gave birth to our kids. He said my stretchmarks were the sexiest battle scars he'd ever seen—though I never believed him. I'm sure the type of women Roman typically brings home are tiny, toned, and perfect. Here's hoping what's under my bra is enough to keep him from noticing everything else I'm trying to hide.

I barely lift my arms before he stops me, pressing his forehead against mine. Chest rising like he's fighting something bigger than both of us.

"Um... we need to talk."

21

very second of my time with Roman is on my mind the next day. Yana and I are grabbing a bite at the local deli, cherishing the hours we have left before she heads back to Chicago.

But all I can think about is him.

"You ain't hungry?" asks Yana, glancing between her sandwich and my full salad.

"Not really." I reach for my water, thinking about the egg rolls I split with Roman while binge-watching old episodes of *So You Think You Can Dance*. "I ate pretty late last night."

"*Ooob.*" Yana's eyes grow two sizes, crumbs falling from her lips. "Roman's gonna get you."

"Actually," I say with a sigh, "it was kinda his idea."

Yana freezes mid-chew. "I'm sorry, what?"

I guess now's as good a time as any. "We were sorta hanging out..." I drown my confession with a gulp of my drink, but it's too late. The sandwich falls from Yana's hands as she blinks in slow motion.

"Laura, please tell me you're not saying what I think you're saying."

I didn't *plan* to say anything. But the mess in my chest won't untangle itself, and if I keep holding it in, I'll explode. I scratch my head, praying I'll choose the right words.

"Okay, um, Roman and I have kinda been hanging out for a while. Last night was sorta our first official date."

The gape in Yana's mouth expands with every word I say. She shoots out of her chair with a jolt. "Wha—? *What?*" Her curls sway with agitation as she glances around as though looking for something to hurl. "*When did this happen? Girl, why didn't you tell me?*"

I shush her repeatedly, desperately waving for her to sit down. We've drawn plenty of stares already.

"I can't believe this." Yana scowls with her hands on her hips. "Laura, how could you?"

Up until now, it hadn't occurred to me that she'd be so upset. "I thought you gave me the green light—"

"Of course I did!" Yana gives a half-hearted apology to a few nearby customers before taking a seat, but her eyes are wild with fury as she turns back to me. "Girl, how could you keep me in the dark on this? I'm your cousin."

"I know. And I'm sorry. I just wasn't sure—"

But the weight of her affronted gaze is more than I can handle. I shift my eyes, taking another sip from my straw.

"Laura!" She slaps the table, and all the silverware jumps. "*You hit that?*"

I nearly choke on my tongue as I shush her again. "Would you *stop?*" I hiss. Honestly, if anyone should be disappointed, it's me. Because I didn't *hit* anything.

Looking me over in astonishment, she sits back, arms crossed. "Girl, I don't know what you're doing in them workout sessions, but you must be *hella* good at it." She throws up a hand for a high-five, and with a sigh of relief I indulge her.

For a second there, I didn't know where this was headed. But she seems to be getting over it pretty fast.

"You *have* to tell me everything," she says. "And I mean *everything*. Let's take it from the top. Where was it? How long did it last? Is he just as good horizontally as he is on the dance floor?"

Not that it's any of her business, but I've got nothing to report. Because last night, Roman informed me that he's celibate. And he plans to keep it that way for a while.

"Yana, I—" I lower my voice, glancing around. "I'm really not comfortable talking about all this right now."

"Then why the hell would you bring it up?" Yana snatches her drink from the table and takes an irritated sip.

A heavy sigh eases from my chest. "'Cause I need your advice."

"My advice?" She leans in, whispering, "Like tips or something?"

"No!" I run my hands down my face. "I'm just... confused."

Roman didn't get into the details, but he's been celibate for *years* now. He seemed sincere when he asked me to stay for dinner and kissed me goodnight like he meant it. But I can't shake the thought.

What if he saw me, *really* saw me, and decided he wasn't interested after all?

I know he likes me. I feel it when he looks at me like I'm something to be unwrapped slow. Maybe he's into the woman he thinks I'm becoming, not the girl who's stitching herself back together. Maybe it's safer to admire me from across the room than up close in the light.

What if my curves, my stretchmarks, my not-there-yet body turned him off—and he just needed a convenient excuse to shut things down?

I wasn't asking for a label. I just needed to know if he sees me as something more than a distraction. More than a warm body with a past written across her skin.

"Last night," I finally say, quieter now, "I mentioned that Griffin asked if Roman and I were getting serious. And I... sorta wanted to know too."

Yana flings a hand to her chest, inhaling all the air around her. "Laura! You did not!"

"I did," I say with a wince. "But he kinda shot it down. Said, 'It is what it is.' Whatever that's supposed to mean."

I know it seemed foolish and hasty, but after the ice-cold bucket of water he'd thrown on our entire evening, I didn't know what to think. What am I exactly? Some chubby plaything that will hopefully help him go viral?

"How long y'all been hooking up?" asks Yana.

"A little over a month now."

"*A month?*"

"Just... kissing. It didn't get more serious until last night, which is why I'm confused."

"I can't believe you two," she says with a scoff. "I should've known better. All the goo-goo eyes y'all were making. The way you were feeding him that *nasty* cookie on Thanksgiving."

"*Nasty?*"

"The point is, you can't go bringing up something that heavy when y'all are so new. Girl, you gonna mess it up for the both of us."

"*The both of us?*"

"Yes. The both of us!" She swirls her drink, leaning back in her seat with a smirk. "Honey, I need you to enjoy that ride for as *long* as you can, mmkay? And if you break his heart, I'll certainly be there to pick up all the juicy little pieces."

Before she heads back to Chicago, Yana encourages me to chill out and simply take this Roman thing one day at a time. That's much easier said than done when I haven't heard from him all day. Then again, it *was* a late night. Maybe he's napping?

Later in the afternoon, Griffin drops off the kids but doesn't bother coming to the door. I suppose that's for the best. I certainly don't need any more awkward exchanges right now. I can barely give the kids a kiss before they take off for the stairs, and when I check my phone, still nothing. Not even my daily motivational text.

What if he slept on it and came to his senses? What if last night was enough for him to realize I'm too much? Too complicated. Too curvy.

You're disgusting. Nobody's ever gonna want you.

I'm thinking too much, and my head is pounding. I could use some sleep, but I'd much rather dance. I've got a boatload of calories to burn off anyway.

After thirty minutes of going over the new routine, I'm a lot more chill. I'm just getting out of the shower when I remember my children need food.

"Hey, kids!" I call to them as I step into the hall. "What do you want for dinner? Chicken or—?" But Maddie and Eli are sitting at the kitchen counter, their dad standing right across from them. And his grin is agony.

"Hey, Laura."

"Hey." *But I could've sworn he left.*

His gaze slips down to the sliver of cleavage my robe won't stop offering. I cross my arms and pull it tight.

"Griffin, what are you doing here?"

"Daddy's making dinner," says Eli, his face alight with excitement.

The man's got quite the project set up: a pot of boiling water, a few cans of Vienna sausages, packs and packs of open ramen noodles…

"Ramen Noodle Casserole?"

"You got it." Griffin grabs the pot and starts draining noodles. "We were just talking about how this was Maddie's *favorite* back in the old apartment." He tosses me a wistful smile. "You remember that?"

How could I forget? He came up with the absurd recipe one night when we had nothing to eat and only five bucks in our bank account. But the dish was such a hit with Maddie that it became a regular staple.

Griffin's still eyeing me as he pours the ramen into a baking dish. "The kids didn't tell you I'd be back after I ran to the store?"

I give the kids a pointed look as they exchange a giggle.

"So, is this your thing now?" I ask. "Showing up at my house whenever you feel like it?"

His gaze momentarily meets mine before he glances at the kids. He pops open a can of Vienna sausages, the slightest grin playing on his lips. "Technically, it's my house. Besides, I wanted to make it up to you guys since I missed Thanksgiving and all that."

Please. It would take a good two years for him to make up for all the lost time he owes us.

With a butter knife, he presses through the tiny sausages, sweater sleeves rolled up to his elbows, forearms flexing with each slice.

There's no way I can kick him out in front of the kids. At a loss, I take a seat.

"You see, kids, Mommy and Daddy know what it's like to have *very humble* beginnings." He side-eyes me as he mixes the dish. "Ain't that right, Mommy?"

Why is he doing this? He has to know how difficult this is for me.

"See, your grandpa," he says, continuing, "Grandpa Jay, was *all* about working your way up in the world. He wasn't trying to give *nobody* a handout—but *especially* Daddy."

"Didn't Grandpa love you?" asks Maddie, her little eyebrows scrunched.

"Of course he did." Griffin chuckles, ripping up slices of pasteurized cheese and layering it over his casserole. "He just had a funny way of showing it." The smile he gives is soft, almost shy. Like we're holding onto a secret that no one else in the room would understand.

He's right. It was hard. It was *really* hard. Scraping pennies. Sharing tears. Surviving. But we got through it together.

"How long will it take?" asks Eli as his dad pops the dish in the oven.

"Five minutes, maybe," says Griffin, wiping his hands with a towel.

Eli leaps off his stool, breaking into a jig, ecstatic about something he's never even tasted.

"Why don't you two run upstairs while you wait?" I say. "Let me talk to Daddy for a minute." The two obey my wishes and take off for their rooms while I battle their dad in a lengthy stare.

"Ya know, if you want to drop by, I'm just a text away."

His smirk is evident as he takes a fork and twirls it inside what's left in his pot. "Maybe I wanted to surprise you."

Why do I suddenly feel like it was a secret between him and the kids that he'd be back after all? He pierces a small slice of sausage and a scrap of cheese. Blowing on the noodles, he presents it to my lips, but I jerk away.

"Griffin, you know I can't eat that."

"Why not? Hot or cold, it's still bomb." His eyes flick to my mouth, then linger.

I purse my lips, and he chuckles low.

"Oh, I see. The trainer will be all *mad*, right?"

"The last time I ate with you, I ended up doing an extra five laps around the track."

He dangles the pasta in my face anyway, like he knows I'm about to fold. And I hate how good it smells—creamy, garlicky, buttery as sin. The kind of comfort you don't realize you've been craving until it's too close to resist.

With a sigh, I take a nibble. And *man*, that is good. Gooey, rich, and full of regret.

Griffin awaits my verdict with an expectant smile.

"It's aiight." I stick out my tongue as I head to the fridge for some water. Between this and my last-minute lunch with Yana—not to mention our heavy meal last night—Roman's going to kill me.

"You know you like it," says Griffin with a chuckle. "You've *always* liked it."

"You're going to be grateful for whatever you can get when you have no other choice." His father made sure of that from the day we decided to get married. Withholding money, along with his love, was the man's ultimate way to get his children to do as he pleased.

But Griffin was stubborn for much too long.

He nods, seeming to reminisce, as I fill my glass. "My dad's been on my mind all day, actually."

Something tightens in my chest as his expression grows sober. It happened often after he lost his dad, only to be quickly tucked away. Less than a month after he took over the company, he was all business.

"Not now, kids. I've gotta get to work." Neckties and stuffy overcoats. He expected me to do the same when it came to my mom and sister. *"Just stay focused. Keep your head up."* He always excelled at sweeping feelings under the rug. Nothing like me.

"I had the most *vivid* dream about him last night," he says. "I mean, in full color and everything. It was like he was *right there*."

"Oh yeah?" I take a seat with my drink. "What happened?"

"I was… at the office," he says. "And out of nowhere, he walked in, this huge smile on his face." He doesn't look at me when he says it.

And for once, there's no edge in his voice. No performance. Something shifts.

It's in the way his shoulders lower. The way his voice softens, like he's scared he'll break if he breathes too hard.

I can't remember the last time I saw him this unguarded. This... present.

And damn if it doesn't ache a little.

He rests his elbows on the counter, eyes distant. "And then, he gave me the most *amazing* hug—like nothing I've felt before. Not in real life."

Hugs from a father. Neither of us had much of that growing up. It's something the two of us bonded over when we met.

I'll never forget the way I hugged him tight when he got the call about his dad. He sagged to the floor as the phone tumbled from his hands, and all I could do was hold him as he cried, squeeze him close.

That grief bound us tighter than vows. We were two broken kids trying to build something whole. But pain was never meant to be the foundation.

His fingers tap the counter now, slow and rhythmic, like he's trying to find a beat that used to belong to him.

"I just wish I could hug him like that now."

And for a moment, I see it. Just beneath the surface.

Not the charm. Not the games. Just... heartbreak.

I tuck my hands as I cross my arms, a familiar knot tightening in my gut. Regardless of how I feel, I can't hold him anymore. It's just too much.

Eventually, he recovers. "What's that Janet Jackson song say? 'You don't know what you've got 'til it's gone.'" He shoots me a lopsided grin like he's just dropped wisdom.

There's a familiar crinkle at the corners of his eyes as he silently holds my gaze, as sweet and warm as he did at our wedding, during the births of our children, and after each funeral.

I rise to my feet before the tears give way. "I'll go get changed."

—————— ⁺⁺⁺⁺⁺⁺⁺ ——————

Griffin stays for dinner with me and the kids—they devour the casserole while I have leftover chicken and veggies. And somehow, a while later, we find ourselves putting up the Christmas tree.

Maddie and I enjoy fresh-popped popcorn while Griffin lifts Eli to put the star on top. And when I wasn't looking, somebody got our old holiday favorites streaming on the speaker.

I know the visit was unexpected, but Griffin's clearly in a sentimental mood. He said it himself, he misses us, *all* of us. And he lost so much precious time with his dad. Who am I to hinder him from creating more memories with his own kids? Besides, bonding with my family is the perfect way to get Roman off my mind.

"There we go," Griffin grunts as he sets Eli down. "Man, I don't know what I was thinking, letting you eat that second helping. You getting heavy, boy!" Our son beams his brightest smile before taking off to scarf down more popcorn, and Griffin rubs his palms together, eyeing our little girl.

"Princess, how you feeling about that big solo you got coming up?"

My chest fills with warmth as Maddie giggles.

"It's more than a solo, Dad. I got the lead."

"Which is full of solos, last I checked." Griffin casually slings an arm behind my shoulders as he drops onto the sofa, wrapping me in a blanket of tantalizing spice. And making my entire body go still.

That grin—smooth and shameless—has me caught.

"Ain't that right, Mommy?"

I bob my head with a swallow as Eli happily climbs into his lap. Despite the hint of discomfort in my gut, it all feels so familiar.

With a few nudges from her dad, Maddie agrees to run upstairs and get her ballet shoes so she can perform a number for us. My heart swells as she bends with elegance, extends on her toes, and spins the perfect pirouette at the center of the living room. And seeing the glimmer in Griffin's eye as we watch our little girl dance with precision and grace makes all the commutes to Perry Rec worth it. The three of us applaud as she completes the number with a perfect bow.

"That's my girl!" Griffin takes her into his arms and presses a kiss to her temple.

Overwhelmed with emotion, I excuse myself to the kitchen. I need to drink more water anyway.

Cursing myself for being so ridiculously fragile, I quickly brush away a tear as I pour. I'm startled to find Griffin standing behind me when I turn.

His smile fades as he searches my eyes. "You cool?"

"Mmhmm." Leaning against the fridge, I take a sip of my drink, praying it'll soothe the lump lodged in my throat. A holiday classic from Stevie Wonder begins to play, and the kids dance in circles, laughing with jingle bells in hand.

Griffin sighs as he settles beside me, watching them. "Seems like she's better since I got the mouse."

I start to elbow him as he chuckles but pause with a frown. "The mouse?"

"For her anxiety," he says. "She told me what happened at her dance class, and I read somewhere that a pet might help."

All this time, I thought he'd bought it just to spite me. I had no idea he was even aware.

"Today's been cool," he says, gently pinching my arm. "Just like old times, huh?"

In some ways.

The two of us silently watch our babies play like they haven't a care in the world. Curly hair bouncing, big brown eyes shining. So much like him. Like me. Like *us*.

And for a second, it almost feels like I'm back inside the dream— the one where we kept adding to the noise. Where I still believed he'd love me through every stretchmark, every breakdown, every child we never had.

But that's the thing about Griffin. He doesn't just stage a scene. He sells the fantasy. The one where we grow old together and love each other through every storm. He wrote it with me, whispered it into my skin. And now, every time he shows up unannounced, all charm and spice, it feels like he's trying to reenact a scene from the life he walked away from. Like I'm supposed to forget who ended the story.

"Does Vicki know you're here?" I ask.

Griffin doesn't even look at me as he softly shakes his head. His finger grazes my thigh, and I quickly shift away.

"Laura, don't—" But he has the decency to stop as I raise my hand.

I don't know what he had in mind, but I'm not interested in playing side chick today.

Glancing toward the kids, he rubs his neck. "Ya know, switching Maddie to that new dance school was a great idea. She's gonna shine in that recital."

Shine. "If only you'd felt the same way about me."

"Hold up, Laura. You know full well that dropping that stuff after having Eli was your choice."

"And who came up with that idea?"

The night I packed away my dance shoes, I'd cried for over an hour in bed. I don't know how many times I must've insisted I was just being hormonal when he cuddled up behind me. And when I finally confessed my fear of never dancing again, instead of encouraging me or denying that fact, he'd said, *"Sometimes we gotta make sacrifices, ya know?"*

It was as if another loved one had died.

Griffin huffs as he moves in closer, lowering his voice. "You really gonna bring up old shit after the incredible day we've had?"

"It's always old shit to you."

Mercifully, my phone chimes, slicing through the tension. Griffin plants his hands on his waist as I step aside to check the message.

About those moves last night... says Roman. *Magic.*

Typing my reply brings a smile to my lips. *Glad to see you're still under my spell.*

Sure, things didn't go as far as I would've liked. But it means something that I'm still on his mind. I push my phone back into my pocket as Griffin's eyes take on a darker shade.

"That your dude?"

I shrug. I suppose I hadn't really thought of him that way until now. But if Griffin can screw the weather girl across town, why not?

Griffin's gaze settles on the kids in the living room as they take a break from dancing to snack on what's left of the popcorn. "I take it y'all had a nice... date last night?"

He looks like he swallowed a mouthful of bleach.

I smile to myself, thinking about the way Roman kissed me, caressed me, how close he came to making me feel like the *only girl in the world.* "Yeah, it was fun."

Griffin frowns at me. "*Fun?*"

"Yeah." Crossing my arms with my glass, I clear my throat. "We went, uh, rock climbing."

"*You* went rock climbing?" Griffin lifts a skeptical brow. "Ain't no way. You can barely climb bleachers without getting lightheaded."

"Sure. I was nervous, but... Roman helped me through it." *He always helps me.*

"Well, damn," says Griffin. "Here I thought you could never be happy when, *obviously,* you was just waiting for my ass to leave."

"Griffin, what do you mean? I was happy."

His discerning gaze bores into me. "Both of us were there, Laura. There's no sense in lying to yourself."

My pulse kicks up as I study the glass in my hands. Between the bills, the drama with his family, and... everything else, I suppose I didn't know how to feel. There was just so much going on.

Griffin moves closer, his fingers brushing mine. "Look—"

"Please, stop." I turn away and set my glass in the sink. The last thing I want is to confuse the kids any more than we already have. Both of us know all this is a game to him. He wouldn't still be with her otherwise. And for once, I'm seeing that I can be perfectly fine without him.

Thankfully, Griffin respects my wishes and gives me space, but his gaze is heavy on me as my phone chimes with another message from Roman.

With a body like that? How could I not be enchanted?

22

"Almost there," says Roman, his firm hand ushering me in from the cold. "Don't be scared. I got you." The door shuts behind us, sealing us inside with warmth.

After our somewhat disastrous first date last week, Roman wanted to give it another shot this weekend. But I didn't think that would involve me getting all dressed up in heels, only to be blindfolded for an entire car ride and a lengthy walk.

Water softly trickles and gurgles in the distance, evening birds tweeting overhead.

"Roman, where are we?"

"Just a few more steps." He moves me a couple of inches to the right, then adjusts my shoulders toward the left.

I laugh. "Can I take this stupid thing off already?"

With one more adjustment to my shoulders, he seems to settle with a sigh. "Alright. Here we go." Stepping behind me, Roman removes the blindfold, and a sweeping gallery unfurls around us.

We're encompassed by what looks like two circular platforms of art collections and exhibits, Poinsettias, and glowing Christmas lights adorning every pillar. A glass dome extends over our heads, high into the nighttime sky. It's breathtaking.

Roman steps before me in his handsome black suit, arms wide. "You said I owe you dinner." Behind him, a little table decorated with a fine green tablecloth—a gorgeous vase of roses at its center—awaits us at the heart of the lobby. The seating is just for two.

My hands fly to my mouth as my heart stutters. "Roman, how did you—?"

"You'd be surprised what a little money can do." Ushering me over, he pulls out a chair. "Welcome to the Wildlife Interpretive Gallery."

"We're at the zoo?" I take a seat, looking around. I can't believe I've never brought the kids into this building before.

Roman ensures I'm comfortable before joining me at the table. "I know you've been complaining about missing red meat, so I ordered the top sirloin."

Oh, he is *definitely* making up for turning our last date into a boot camp.

Right on cue, a couple of servers appear with salads and Chardonnay, welcoming us to the venue and complimenting my red dress as they pour.

Once our glasses are filled, Roman raises a toast with a charming grin. "To a relaxing, work-free, and *very* romantic evening."

"Agreed."

It isn't long before we've polished off the delicious steak and potatoes and are working on our second glasses of wine. I honestly have no idea why I'm surprised that Roman would be capable of something so sweet. But looking around this vast gallery, I know he must've spent a fortune on this date, which is quite the investment for someone he's casually dating.

"How you feeling?" There's a gleam in his eye as he lowers his head to examine my face.

I drop my fork, throwing a hand over my belly. "Full!" A chuckle bounces between us.

"That's alright," he says with a soft grin. "We can run it off on Monday. Together."

Together. I dab my mouth with a napkin. "I have something to tell you."

Roman nods, leaning back with his glass. "Sure."

With a gentle drumming of my nails, I press on. "Griffin has been... friendlier lately." Roman doesn't say a word. I know the timing could be better, but if I ever hope for anything serious to develop between us, that starts with me being honest. "It's kinda been this way since Eli's accident."

"He make a move or something?"

"Not really. He just... kinda drops compliments here and there. He sent me a text saying he missed me on Thanksgiving." I take a lengthy sip of my drink, too jittery to get into all the flirting and light touches he attempted last Sunday—not to mention our little confrontation.

Roman bobs his head. "So *that's* what was behind that meltdown you had at the dinner table."

At the time, I figured Griffin was just screwing with me. Same script, same charm. But after Sunday, I hate that a small part of me started wondering if maybe he meant it. I still don't believe him. Not really. But if Roman's going to keep showing up like this, he deserves to know what's up. Even the messy parts I haven't sorted out yet.

The servers return to take our plates, and each of us thanks them. When they disappear, Roman meets my gaze again.

"I appreciate you sharing that with me," he says, tossing back his Chardonnay.

I wait for him to go on, but he doesn't. "So, that's it?"

"Hmm?"

"That's all you're going to say? You're not jealous or anything?"

"*Jealous?*" He scoffs. "Roman doesn't get jealous!" His boisterous laughter echoes into the air, but when I don't join him, he clears his throat. "What is it?"

"I just don't get why you do that sometimes."

He sits up straight, adjusting his suit jacket. "Wh... What is it you think I'm doing, exactly?"

I part my lips in search of the right words. "It kinda feels like... sometimes you throw up this wall. This *Roman* persona. Why do you get to pick my brain when I can't pick yours?"

He tilts his head with an affronted snort. "You know my darkest secret, Laura. Of course you can pick my brain."

"Oh yeah? Tell me. What are your dreams? Do you even *have* fears?"

His scoff is lighter this time as he gazes across the gallery, but my eyes remain on him.

"I just want you to be real with me, ya know?" I extend a hand across the table, and with the slightest hesitancy, he accepts my invitation.

His chest rises and falls with a sigh as he studies our interlocked fingers. "Well, there's definitely one thing that terrifies me."

"And what's that?"

He assesses me as if deliberating whether I can be trusted with any more of his dirty little secrets. "Being real? Being on my own."

Seems he's kinda been a loner for a while now. And according to him, he's not a huge fan of commitment.

Noticing my puzzled expression, he lifts a shoulder. "Obviously, I can only be a sex magnet for so long, so I been thinking about my next game plan. I've always wanted to open my own dance studio. One for adults—not kids." His thumb delicately traces my palm. "Maybe I can help a few of them find what we have on the dance floor."

"Roman, that's a great idea."

"I think so too. But I don't have a partner to help me get it off the ground, and... honestly, the thought of doing something like that *on my own* kinda freaks me out. I'm not sure I'd be able to keep it afloat." His focus returns to my hand as his fingers lightly dance over mine.

He seems so anxious about it. But a flicker of excitement sparks within me, imagining him opening the doors to his own place, challenging and inspiring students on his own time. And maybe with a passionate assistant...

But before I can ask more questions, he stands.

"Let me show you something."

With my hand still in his, Roman leads me across the lobby, where an attendant awaits, prepared to usher us into the butterfly garden. And the place is truly incredible. The sweet fragrance of exotic flowers laces the air as an assortment of orange, white, and yellow butterflies flutter around us. Towering into the glass ceiling, lush green trees and bushes create a mesmerizing scene, accompanied by the soft babble of a water fountain nearby. I struggle to catch my breath at the fascinating sight as Roman watches me take in the view.

"Ya know, each species of butterfly has their own dance," he says. "It's how they know whether they'll vibe or not when they meet."

"Like a first date or something?"

He nods as I look around in awe.

"Roman, this place is—" I gasp as a stunning black butterfly with neon blue wings rests on a branch overhead. I've never seen anything so magnificent in my entire life.

"Ah, the Blue Morpho," says Roman. "My favorite."

"*You* have a favorite butterfly?"

"You kidding? Those vibrant colors. That *amazing* wingspan... I also may have asked the curator about it when I dropped off my deposit last week." His gaze grows soft as he watches me laugh. "How could you not fall in love with something so beautiful?"

My senses spark with wonder as I lift my eyes, captivated by the awe-inspiring creature and all its majestic features. "I swear, they're like these lovely, little flying flowers."

Roman nods, observing with me. "All the stages it goes through before it's officially considered beautiful."

"And I bet it's worth every single one."

With the tug of my hand, Roman leads me to the fountain, peacefully gurgling at the center of the atrium. The water is a brilliant blue—almost as marvelous as the butterfly we left behind. He points to a small caterpillar near the middle, inching its way up a giant plant leaf. At first glance, the little thing is almost frightening—it's black and white with yellow splotches all over. But it's furry and kind of adorable as it wiggles its tiny head around, seeking its next nibble.

"Cute." I chuckle softly.

"A month or so, and this one will be just as gorgeous as her momma back there," says Roman.

I glance back at the electric blue wings fluttering nearby. "This is going to be a Blue Morpho?"

"It already is," he says with a hint of a smile.

I blink from him to the furry creature in front of us, wondering how anything could transform so miraculously in such a short period of time. "I wonder if she already knows her destiny."

"Does it really matter?" Roman holds my gaze, slowing my pulse. "She's living it anyway."

This is even better than his daily motivational texts.

"Thanks," I say, "for making me feel beautiful tonight."

But he shakes his head. "You've always been beautiful, Laura." He reaches up and runs a thumb across my cheek. "The only one who couldn't see it was you." He kisses me just as gently and softly as the butterflies dancing around us. I can't remember the last time I felt this way.

Roman cradles me like I'm something rare and wild, tucked away deep in a place only he could find. There's reverence in his hold. A kind of awe. And for the first time, I don't feel watched or studied. I feel seen. Held by someone who's not trying to fix me... just feel me.

Reaching into his pocket, he pulls up a playlist on his phone. A mischievous grin tugs at his lips as Donny Hathaway's rendition of "A Song for You" fills the air, the piano soft and achingly intimate.

"I should've known," I say, dropping my head with a laugh. "Roman can't go a day without dancing."

"I don't think he can," he says. "But right now, I just wanna show off the most beautiful one in this room." My cheeks warm as he takes me by the hand, his gaze drinking me in like a slow pour of wine. "That alright?"

I nod.

Twirling me around, he draws me into his arms. And the two of us sway among the butterflies beneath a starry sky.

• • ✦✦✦✦ • •

It feels like time has passed much too quickly as Roman walks me to my door.

"Thanks for an unforgettable date," I say, lacing our hands. "Everything about tonight was perfect, from beginning to end."

"Well, almost," he says. The two of us eye the lovely little gifts a couple of birds chose to leave on Roman's shoulder as we walked through the atrium.

A soft chuckle escapes me. "I could wash it while you wait. If you want."

His eyes drift over my shoulder, and my cousin's curls duck behind the drapes.

I almost forgot Yana decided to swing by for the weekend. She was a little homesick but made for a convenient babysitter.

On our way to the zoo, I ended up confessing that I'd told her the truth about us, but Roman said the handful of winks she tossed when he'd picked me up gave it away. Still blindfolded, I sat in silence, fearful that he might flip. But instead, he calmly took me by the hand and kissed it.

It's been a night of sweet surprises.

The two of us share a lengthy silence as we stand on the porch, each of us a little reluctant to say goodbye.

"Nah. I should probably head home," he says, his gaze shifting toward the moonlit grounds beyond the drive, and a pang of disappointment hits my chest.

I don't know why I keep trying.

"Hey…" Roman lifts my chin, studying my face. "Don't be like that. I just need time."

"Of course," I whisper, forcing my best smile. *Or maybe he needs someone else.*

"Laura, how many times I gotta tell you? You're *sexy.*" He slips his hands around my waist and squeezes my behind. "Besides, after all this? How am I supposed to dance without you?"

It's as if every butterfly we met tonight is dancing in my belly.

With a silent prayer, I press a tender kiss to his lips—slow, deep, and lingering. The same way I'd make love to him if given the chance. When I finally break away, his eyes stay closed for a beat, like he's chasing the echo of it.

He stares toward the house as I turn to head inside, but he doesn't let go of my hand.

"Get rid of her within an hour?"

23

I'm flipping pancakes the next morning when Roman emerges from the master suite, bleary-eyed and barefoot.

"What time is it? I *never* sleep..." But he freezes when he spots the kids giggling at the island. Abruptly standing up straight, Roman pulls his navy bathrobe closed.

"Wait"—Maddie tilts her head—"isn't that Daddy's robe?"

Roman's eyes ping to mine.

I force a smile, tucking away the wince I feel in my chest. I know exactly how it looks—Griffin's robe, Roman staying over, the kids watching—but the truth is, last night was nothing but warm conversation and quiet comfort. And for the first time in a long time, I didn't feel alone. The two of us curled up in bed, chatting until we fell asleep. But Roman's suit is still air drying, and the man didn't exactly bring along a change of clothes. Besides, I was kinda hoping he'd stay for breakfast, which required him to strut around in a little more than his boxers.

Thankfully, Roman quickly recovers, donning his best smile. "Good morning, guys." He takes a seat beside Eli at the counter, exchanging a warm glance with me. "You sleep good?"

"Out like a light," I say with a wink.

His grin is unexpectedly sheepish as I return to mixing the batter. When he curled up behind me in bed and asked to stay the night, my heart soared.

Eli squints at him, his mouth full of pancakes. "Are you my new daddy now?"

My spoon belly flops into the pancake batter as Roman's eyes do their best Looney Tunes impression.

"Eli, don't ask questions like that," I chide, praying the man won't take off for the nearest exit. "It's rude."

Maddie wags her head in quiet amusement as my son lifts a casual shoulder. Roman softly drums his fingers as they return to munching on their breakfast.

Before the kids can scare him away, I make his plate and slide it across the counter.

His brow lifts. "Pancakes?"

"Protein Pancakes," I say. "And plenty of eggs with *no* salt—just the way you like 'em."

Not even giving the sugar-free syrup a second glance, he grabs his fork and digs in. The man is going to town like he hasn't eaten in days, scarfing down enormous mouthfuls at a time.

"Does that mean you like it?" I ask, spatula on my hip. He barely lifts his head as he offers an enthusiastic thumbs-up. *Somebody's got a healthy appetite.* I turn to ladle more batter on the griddle for the second helpings that are sure to be requested.

"Mommy, can I have more orange juice?" Eli grins with all his remaining teeth. "*Please?*"

"Sure." Swiftly, I refill the kids' glasses and pour Roman some water before wiping down the counter and returning to my pancakes.

Roman stares as he chews a little more slowly. "You're, like, a pro at this."

"I *do* have ten years of experience," I say with a laugh.

He's still watching me when my son sets his fork aside and gives him a nudge, pointing at the top hat and magic tools on the counter.

"I'm practicing my latest trick. Wanna see?"

With a brief glance at me, Roman nods for him to go ahead.

Grabbing his little wand, Eli waves it over the hat, putting on his best illusionist voice. "And now, for my next trick, I'm going to pull a mouse out of my..." But Eli stops when he flips over the hat. "Uh-oh."

Roman straightens his back. "*Uh-oh? *What do you mean, *uh-oh?*"

The second my son starts scratching his head, I know we're in trouble.

"Eli, *no.*"

Maddie springs out of her seat. "Eli, did you lose Mr. Nibbles?"

"I didn't mean to!"

"Oh no. No, no, no." I drop the spatula and hop on the counter, clutching my arms around my waist. My wary gaze falls on Roman, and he shakes his head.

"You're kidding, right?"

I offer a weak smile. "Please?"

Fifteen minutes later, Roman's crawling around the kitchen in his borrowed robe—a spatula in one hand, a mouse cage in the other.

"Roman, please don't hurt him," says Maddie, wringing her napkin in her hands. "He's just a baby."

"Right, of course not." Roman creeps across the floor, peering left and right. "I'm just gonna... use this spatula to steer him along. That's all."

I shush everyone. "You hear those squeaks? It sounds like they're coming from the dining room." Roman nods, inching in that direction.

"*Roman, be careful!*" shouts Eli, and all of us shush him harshly.

So much for a relaxing morning with me and the kids. At this rate, the trainer will be hitting the door before he zips his pants.

Roman's just peeking into the dining room when the white rodent bolts between his legs.

"*Ahhhh!*" The spatula and cage go flying as Roman leaps like he's been electrocuted, somehow teleporting to the counter beside me. Hugging his knees to his chest, he frantically scans the floor with wild eyes. "Where'd he go? *Where'd he go?*"

Maddie rushes to the corner and kneels down. "Mr. Nibbles," she beckons in a hushed tone, making a gentle kissing noise.

By some miracle, the tiny mouse scrambles back into her hands, and she tenderly scoops him up. Roman and I are a couple of statues as we watch my daughter slip the mouse back into its cage without so much as a flinch.

"Roman screams like a girl," says Eli with a giggle.

"Do not!"

I'm chuckling myself as I hop down. "It *was* a little high-pitched."

"Whatever." Roman scoffs, finally setting his feet back on the floor. "Maybe that was just my strategy. I wanted to startle him into submission."

Maddie chuckles. "Sure, Roman."

<hr />

In all our amusement, the day rushes by, and it isn't long before the sun is setting again. Surprisingly, after deciding to rock his undershirt and slacks, Roman hung around all day. Together with the kids, we enjoyed each other's company and got in a little meal prep for the week. Every chance he got, Roman would twirl me through the kitchen or press a kiss to my cheek like he belonged here. Like this—*us*—was something he didn't want to miss out on. I kept waiting for him to pull back. But he didn't. Not once. I even got him to hang a few Christmas lights on the front bushes—in exchange for my healthiest version of hot chocolate, of course.

We're gathered in the living room when Roman throws down his final card. "Uno. *Out!*"

"Aw, man." Maddie slaps her last two cards on the table, and Eli stands with a pout.

"I want a rematch," the little boy demands. But Roman shakes his head, gathering up the remaining cards like poker chips.

"Sorry, kid. No rematches." He laughs wickedly as I jab him with an elbow.

"It's time for you all to get ready for bed anyway," I say, checking my watch. "It's a school night." The kids only whine a bit before hugging me goodnight, and with the briefest of waves to Roman, they head for the stairs.

Maddie and Eli haven't hit the second-floor landing before Roman scoots over and tosses an arm behind me. "Have I told you how pretty you look today?" He ogles me shamelessly.

"Who knew all it took was them leaving for you to be so bold," I say, sorting the cards back in their box.

"Well, I didn't want the little one thinking I was gonna propose or anything."

I give him a shove, and he steals a kiss... soft, smug, and way too satisfying.

Spending time with him like this has been really nice. And despite his poor sportsmanship, the kids seemed to have fun. Our lips part, and I swallow my smile. "I'm surprised they didn't run you off."

He settles back, brows pinched. "Why would you say that?"

"Well, you've never seemed like the hugest fan of kids. You weren't exactly in a rush to warm up to Eli." I toss the box of cards on the coffee table with a forced laugh, but Roman's still watching me.

"Actually..." He takes me by the hand, tugging me around to face him. "You know what you said yesterday about being real and all that?"

"Of course." Witnessing such a genuine side of him in the butterfly garden meant the world to me.

His gaze falls on the floor. "I haven't exactly been as... *real* with you as I could be."

I sit up straight, mind racing with all the possible thoughts he could be holding back. He's already shared so much with me. But I still have my doubts. Is this when he tells me it's been nice, but he's gotta run?

"I never finished telling you my story," he says. "About Jennifer. My ex."

"Okay." My heart thumps softly as he takes my other hand in his.

"It was one of them whirlwind romances," he says. "The way she'd smile, the way we'd dance. We fell in love practically overnight."

The gentle glimmer in his eye pinches my heart, but I know our own relationship hasn't been all that different. Given, no one's professed their feelings or anything.

He runs a thumb over my knuckles, voice barely above a whisper. "Wasn't long before she said she was pregnant."

My heart cracks in two. "Pregnant?"

"A boy." He gazes off behind me. "I wanted to name him Jaxon— with an X—but she hated the idea. Thought something lame like Brian or Sam would be better."

I let out a gentle chuckle, but it isn't enough to break up the tension that's formed in my chest. I couldn't count how many times Griffin and I must've tried for a third child. After dozens of negative pregnancy tests, we eventually stopped making love altogether. I've never forgiven myself for it.

I squeeze Roman's hand, fearing the worst, but he pulls away, absentmindedly picking at the seam of my sleeve.

"Anyway, I was down for whatever. Moved her into my place, started looking at rings. Pretty soon, it was time for another ultrasound—six-month checkup. And *man*, I couldn't have been more excited, was already buying toy cars and shit. But… he was measuring a little big for six months, and we hadn't been together quite that long."

The words hit like a gut punch. I picture Roman pacing the toy aisle, full of hope, not knowing what was waiting for him on the other side of that appointment. A man like him, soft beneath the muscle and mischief, already dreaming up bedtime routines and baby names. It's no wonder he's so cautious with his heart.

His jaw tenses as he presses on. "She broke down right there in the doctor's office…"

Roman's voice grows quiet, rough with something he's not saying. "Said the baby was her ex-boyfriend's… Suddenly, I knew exactly how it felt to be gutted like a fish."

My chest goes tight. The betrayal in his eyes louder than any scream. It's an awful tragedy. I rest a hand on his knee.

"Is that when you left?"

"Wish I could say it was." His attention returns to the floor as I stare at him. "I wanted to stay—told her I'd raise him as my own. But then, she told her ex-boyfriend the truth, and they decided to try and work things out. So, I packed my shit and bounced."

"Roman, I am so sorry." After all that? Of course he'd have reservations about getting serious with me. Especially with the father of my children looming in the background.

He softly scoffs. "I feel like such a loser right now."

I press a hand to his cheek, wondering how anyone could be so cruel to such a kind soul. "You're not the loser in this story. She is."

"You're sweet." Embracing my hand, he kisses my wrist. "After that, I was done. Racked up a body count that I'd rather not brag about. Meanwhile, my little brother found Jesus behind bars and started spitting all this wisdom. Kept going on about it when I swung by for a visit... And had no problem telling me how lame I was for becoming the most *debased* form of myself." He releases a bitter chuckle.

I'm not sure my sibling and I would be so close if she'd said something like that to me. But Roman seems unfazed.

"I'm no pew-warmer," he says. "But some of the principles made a lot of sense. So, I decided to chill out until I'm sure I've found something legit, ya know?"

My heart drops, tangled in weeds I thought I'd already cleared. "Legit?"

"Mmhmm." He pulls me close, tucking my head under his chin. "So, between all that and Jennifer, you can see why the mere thought of a long-term relationship with most chicks gives me hives."

Talk about an understatement.

But it hits me, hard and fast, that maybe I've misread everything. The way he's held back. The careful distance. The abrupt goodnights.

Maybe it wasn't restraint. Maybe it was reluctance.

Because even after everything we've shared—after opening my home, my heart, letting him this close—he still talks like he's on the fence. Like he's waiting for someone better. Someone whole.

And I get it. He's been scarred. Was betrayed in the *worst* way.

But I'm not *that* woman. Not to him. I'm not the woman he can trust with his heart. That's something I'm too broken to carry.

And I hate how easily that thought takes root. How fast it unearths all the old fears I thought I'd buried.

I'm too complicated. Too damaged. Too late to be the one a man like him actually *chooses*.

So I swallow my nerves and ask the inevitable question. "Is that how you feel about me?"

"Hmm?"

I shrug as his eyes return to mine. "Does being with me give you... *hives*?"

He searches the ceiling, sending my heart into a panic. Its beat falters as his gaze slips back to mine. Then sweetly, quietly, he kisses me.

And for a moment, I let myself believe.

24

mid the snowy drizzle, I hustle my son up the front steps, shielding us from the cold.

"Take off your boots as soon as we get inside. Okay, Eli?"

He agrees as I fumble through my keys with a huff.

With the Christmas recital only eight days away, I should've been at the rec practicing with Roman. Instead, I found myself spending my entire Friday afternoon in traffic, trying to return from a follow-up appointment for Eli downtown. I'd dropped Maddie off for an early rehearsal before we left, but judging by the accident that was blocking the freeway, I knew I wouldn't be picking her up on time.

With my back against the wall and my cousin out of town, I clenched my fists and made the call. Fortunately, Roman didn't trip about my predicament. When I asked if maybe he could check on Maddie and confirm she was working on her homework in the hall, he'd scoffed.

"Laura, I'm not gonna stand by while your little girl sits out there by herself. Just head home. We'll meet you there."

A grin crossed my lips as warmth bloomed in my chest. Maddie *did* have a key to let herself in, after all. With many thanks, I promised to pay him back.

"Can't wait," he rumbled seductively.

His Porsche is still out front as I step into the house, smiling at the thought of getting in some late-night practice.

"Hey," I say, setting my things aside. Roman's standing in the foyer in his leather jacket. But he's tense as I press a kiss to his jaw. He's staring at my estranged husband, who's looming over the island in the kitchen.

The air is charged—tight and unspoken. Like they both just stepped out of a boxing ring.

"Daddy!" Eli dashes into his arms as I look on at a loss.

"Griffin?"

"'Sup?" He hugs Eli tight and looks to me as he sets him down. "Where y'all been?"

"We were just..." I start to point over my shoulder, then stop. "Griffin, what are you doing here? I didn't see your car out front."

"I parked around back. Had to pick up a few things in the garage." I blink at him as he presses his hands into the pockets of his trim wool jacket. "You forget about that Christmas party I'm throwing tonight?"

I shut my eyes. "Right. How could I forget?" He told me a couple weeks ago that he and Vicki were having a party at his house, even had the gall to invite me along. I respectfully declined, of course, but agreed that the kids could go—so long as he'd be willing to drop Maddie off at her dance class tomorrow. Outside of a couple texts I ignored, I've barely heard from him over the last two weeks. Roman's still staring him down.

Did I miss something?

"Eli, why don't you run upstairs and grab your stuff? You guys don't want to be late."

The men are locked in a silent staring contest as my son scurries off.

I glance between them. "Is everything okay?"

Griffin steps from behind the counter, strolling our way. "Yeah. I was just reminding your... trainer here that I'd prefer he not step foot in my house without me or my wife present."

Wife?

He stops inches away from Roman's personal space, neither of them blinking.

"Griffin, what are you talking about?" I say. "Roman volunteered to bring Maddie home. It's fine."

Griffin fixes me with an intense gaze. "Is it?"

He's got some nerve. Have I ever called him out for sending his little weather girl along to drop off the kids?

Before I can steady myself to address Griffin calmly, Roman closes what's left of the space between them. "If the lady of the house *says* it's a problem, I'll respect that. But she didn't."

Griffin drops his head. "Laura, you got about five seconds to get this tired mother—"

"*We're ready!*" the kids sing, trotting down the stairs.

Thank God.

Roman and Griffin glower at each other one last time before putting on happy faces.

"Wow!" says Griffin, clapping. "That's gotta be a new record for you guys."

Suddenly, he's father of the year again.

Maddie and Eli are beaming as I hug and kiss them goodbye. Then, without warning, Eli wraps himself around Roman's trunk. The man is frozen, holding out his arms as if someone just doused him with an entire cooler of Gatorade. Tossing us a panicked glance, Roman cautiously lowers his hand to pat Eli's back with a nervous chuckle. "Take care there... little guy." Clearing his throat, he shoves his hands in his pockets while my son trots water all the way through the house to the garage.

Griffin's face tightens, that signature glare loading like a warning shot just for me. "I'll call you, Laura," he says, following Eli out.

As they shut the door behind them, Roman's jaw ticks, sharp and deliberate.

"Okay," I say, "can you tell me why it was so tense in here just now?"

With a shake of his head, Roman studies the floor. "Don't worry. It was dumb."

But all I need is five minutes. Linking my arms around his neck, I press a soft kiss to his lips. "Ready to practice?" But he barely touches me as he heaves a sigh.

"Maybe we should take a raincheck. I filled in for the cycling class today, and I'm kinda wiped out." I pout, and he throws back his head. "I know you're excited for the recital, and we've only got so much time, but I could seriously use a shower. How about we get in some extra practice tomorrow after class?"

"I suppose that isn't the worst idea." Lifting on my toes, I offer him another kiss, slower, deeper. "You know what else isn't a bad idea?" I murmur, lips grazing his. "You showering here."

A lazy grin plays on his mouth as his gaze darkens. "You did say you owed me, huh?"

"Mmhmm."

But he takes a step back. "Nice try. See you tomorrow, mama."

My heart sinks as he heads for his car.

Ugh. Why did I have to catch feelings for *the most disciplined* thirst trap in all the Midwest? I may as well take a cold shower myself.

What did Griffin say to him anyway? And why is Roman so thrown by it?

Shaking off the tension, I head for the bedroom in silence. But I find a voicemail from the court waiting for me when I set aside my phone. It's an automated message informing me that the planned hearing has been canceled, citing a scheduling conflict involving one or both parties. It goes on to advise me or my attorney to file a formal request to reschedule.

Tapping my fingers impatiently, I listen to the message again. *What the hell, Griffin?* With the meeting set for Tuesday, I'd already resolved to grant him the divorce and simply sort out the financial matters. I don't want to drag all this drama into the new year.

Ticked by Griffin's obnoxious last-minute meetings, I shoot him a heated text. *First, you pop up at the house, throwing your weight around. Now you're postponing my hearing? Griffin, what is going on??*

Within seconds, he responds. *We need to talk.*

What is this about? And why won't anyone tell me anything? Meanwhile, it's going to take weeks to get all this sorted out with the court. For what? Some minor inconvenience to Griffin's business schedule?

I shoot him three more question marks. But his only response is, *After the party.*

25

I rush from the bathroom, yank on a tank top, and jam my feet into pre-tied sneakers.

I was thoroughly disappointed when Roman chose not to stay last night, and I dozed off after my shower, forgetting to set my alarm. Of course, without Maddie around to nudge me, I woke up late. Roman's going to have me doing wall sits if I'm the last one to class, and after missing yesterday's session, I do not want to waste time on calisthenics. I've gotta get back on that dance floor. I shove the absence of my daily motivational text aside and scrape my hair into a ponytail.

Look at you, that raspy voice whispers. *You're pathetic. And you're always gonna be pathetic.*

I grab my keys and sling my gym bag over my shoulder, heading for the hall. But the sharp click of the front lock turning from the outside makes me jump.

The door eases open.

And in steps my soon-to-be ex-husband.

"Griffin?"

"Hey." He offers a lopsided smile as he shuts the door. "Glad I caught you."

"Where are the kids?"

His hands disappear into his pockets as he inches toward me. "Vicki's dropping Maddie off at practice, and she's gonna hang with Eli for a bit."

Vicki's driving my kids around. Again. "How'd you get in here?"

"My key."

I nod. "I'm going to need that from you."

"What?"

"You heard me." Blood rises like lava in my gut. "You don't get to pop up whenever you feel like it, Griffin. You don't *live here* anymore!"

He blinks hard, like my words short-circuited something.

But between all his little games, the mysterious back-and-forth between him and my boyfriend, and not even being sure I'll *have* a boyfriend at the end of the day, I am done.

He steps closer, jaw tight, but I'm already moving back.

"Laura, just—" His voice cracks, and he searches my eyes. "Let me talk to you first. Please?"

He gives me that look again. The same one he wore beside Eli's hospital bed. But I'd be a fool to trust it. He never called after the party last night.

With a glance at my watch, I plop my bag aside. "Fine. Let's start with that little confrontation yesterday. You going to tell me what that was about?"

"You know what that was about," he says.

"Do I?"

"Of course you do! Laura, why was that man walking up in my house with our daughter?"

"This isn't your house! And she's *ten*, Griffin. He wasn't going to leave her alone."

"But I was right here!"

"How were we supposed to know that?"

Griffin shoves his hands on his waist with a huff. "You know, you got a million and one excuses for some dude you practically met last week."

"Says the man who hooked up with the weather girl within months of walking out of my life."

The two of us lock eyes in a fiery standoff. My chest ignites with rage at his continual attempts to blow up my life like this, always lighting another match just as I'm starting to pick up the pieces.

But he's not backing down. "Laura, how well do you even know this guy?"

I fix my gaze on the door. He shouldn't even be here. But he edges into my view anyway.

"Do you have *any idea* what kind of danger you could've put our little girl in yesterday?"

"Griffin, it's not like that, and you know it."

"Look, I don't know what's going on," he says. "But you need to break this thing off with this guy—and *right* now. You know as well as I do, he's just using you."

I stare at him. "What?"

"Really, Laura?" He presses his hands back into his pockets with a shrug. "A guy like that? He's had at least five chicks in a hotel room at one time. What makes you think he'd even give you a second glance?"

The ache comes fast, curling tight in my chest. "That *guy* saw me when you were too busy with your mistress to notice."

Griffin scoffs out a laugh. "Or maybe he saw an easy lay."

The room spins on a tilt as I turn away, a hand pressed to my forehead.

I can't do this. I don't need this!

"Laura, you *know* you don't belong with him," says Griffin. "'Cause you belong with me."

I blink, mouth parting. *He can't be serious.*

I turn to find him staring at me with glassy eyes. "Griffin, what are you talking about?"

He lifts a shoulder, a tear skipping down his cheek. "We belong together, Laura. We always have."

He can't possibly mean... "Griffin, we're in the middle of a divorce. If it weren't for your schedule, the hearing—"

"It wasn't my schedule," he says. "I called off the divorce weeks ago."

What?

My knees go soft beneath me. I reach for the island, gripping the edge until my knuckles burn.

This isn't happening. This can't be happening.

But Griffin steps closer. "Seeing our son in that hospital bed changed everything for me. It made me wanna be a better dad. And a *much* better husband. I mean, we struggled for so long, trying for another kid, and to come so close to losing the baby we already had?" He soberly shakes his head. "Quitting on you... quitting on *us*, would just feel like another failure."

"And what else was a failure, hmm?"

His brow creases as he stares at me.

"How about knocking me up just after we met?" I ask. "Disappointing your father? Humiliating your family? You've been trying to make up for all your little 'failures' ever since."

I expect that maybe he'll try to deny it, but he takes another step toward me. "You're right. The way they shut me out, all those disapproving looks, I couldn't stand it. And when he passed, I just didn't know how..."

I press hard against the counter as he takes my trembling hands in his.

"I was scared, babe. I was... confused. My dad left *everything* to me. And I didn't know how to handle it, who to please or how. And Vicki seemed like—"

"The smarter option," I say.

He wags his head. "No."

"We both know that's what you mean. *She's* the one your family would approve of. *She* fit the picture."

He keeps shaking his head like denial might rewrite history. But we both know better.

"Look, Laura, I was bitter, alright? You fell into that depression after you quit dancing, and I thought more kids might make you happy, but nothing came of it. And the bigger you got, the more it felt like..." He drops his head with a swallow. "Like you were punishing me."

The tears begin to fall as I attempt to pull from his grasp, but he won't let me go.

"And then, and then, no matter how much I tried to move on, you wouldn't give up. Refusing to sign the papers, loving me so damn hard. I thought I could be happy with Vicki, but... Laura, ever since I left, I been lost. Nothing's the same," he says. "I never should've put all that on you, babe. I *never* should've left you alone. Especially after what happened with your mom... and April."

My eyes lock on the floor, silent tears slipping free before I even feel them.

We've been intertwined for so long. It only makes sense that we'd lose our way in the shuffle. For years, I struggled to become who he needed, and I suppose he tried to do the same. But deep down, I always felt he had a right to leave me. I'm broken, and I always have been.

Griffin tightens his grip, capturing my gaze. "I want my family back, Laura. I want *you* back." His voice cracks like a prayer. And I hate that some part of me still aches to answer it.

I shouldn't even consider it. He broke my heart, and what I've found with Roman is amazing. But this is my husband, the father of my children. All those months ago, he gave up on me—on us as a *family*. Could I really do the same?

Griffin's gaze lingers on my mouth like a memory he can't shake, and he leans in, dredging up memories of our first kiss, our wedding day... and every single time we made love.

But how many times has he kissed her?

Before he can lower his mouth to mine, I turn away. "I need time to think."

His breath is hot against my neck as he gazes at the side of my face. Finally, releasing me, he steps back with a nod. He clears his throat as he faces the master suite, brushing at his cheeks. "Yeah. I get it."

Nine months. For nine months, I prayed he'd come back to me, and now, he's here. But... "What about Vicki?"

He turns back to me, eyes red. "I was planning to break it off after the holidays. But if you want, I'll end it now."

"*If I want?*"

He lets out a light chuckle. "I mean, it's what I want, too."

"You sure about that?"

A scoff escapes him. "Listen, I know all this is a lot to process, so I'm gonna give you a minute. But you need to know..." He takes my chin in hand, leveling his gaze with mine. "I love you, Laura. I *never* stopped loving you." He studies my face, as if waiting for me to reciprocate. But I need time to sort this out.

So, with a gentle nod, I direct him toward the door.

He turns back to me as we reach the porch. "I meant what I said, okay? I'm gonna end it. Today." A grin creeps into his beard as he extends his arms for a hug, and I let him squeeze me in an embrace. "Man. I don't remember the last time you was this *little*."

I release half a chuckle as an unnerving feeling eats at my gut.

But a Porsche is pulling into the driveway. And this isn't the best look. Tugging away, I scratch my head as Roman parks behind Griffin's car and hops out, examining us.

With a hand on my back, Griffin presses an unnecessary kiss to my temple. "Hit me up when you're ready to talk." He heads down the stairs before I can respond, leaving both Roman and me to look on as he pulls off in his car.

Damn him.

Slamming his car door, Roman heads my way—a tall cup of coffee in hand.

"Hey." I manage a feeble smile. "What's that?"

"One of those ridiculous Cinnamon Dolce Lattes," he says, jogging up the stairs and passing it along. "I thought I'd surprise you and take you to class, but thanks to those obnoxious lines at Starbucks, it looks like we're gonna be late."

He came all this way to surprise me? "You're sweet." I take a sip and gag. "Ugh. And *that* is much sweeter than I remember."

Roman's still gazing over his shoulder. With scrunched eyebrows, he turns back to me. "Laura, what's going on?"

I shake my head, heart pounding. "Why don't you come inside for a minute?"

His hands are on his waist the second I close the door behind us. "Laura, that didn't look like nothing."

"I know, but—"

"If you know, then you'll tell me what that was I just pulled up on."

I refuse to look at him, but the man's gaze has heat vision today. Taking a moment to collect myself, I make my way over to the kitchen counter and set aside my drink. "He, uh… he came to talk to me."

"Talk to you?" Roman takes a few steps in my direction but stops short. "Talk to you about what?"

"Just... things. About you. About yesterday."

Roman sucks his teeth. "Why am I not surprised?"

I can't seem to breathe right. I have to grip my hands to keep them steady. "I just don't get why you wouldn't tell me. You said it was... dumb."

"It *was* dumb."

You're dumb. You're an idiot. Why would anyone want an idiot like you?

Roman shrugs as if I'm wasting his time. "Look, are you gonna tell me why he was all hugged up on you just now?" I don't say a word. "Laura, you can't keep putting up with this nonsense. Both of us know what he's after."

You know as well as I do, he's just using you.

My stomach lurches as I press against the counter, and whisper, "And what are *you* after?"

Roman stares like I just smacked him across the face. "You serious?"

I lift a shoulder, waiting for him to prove me wrong. But I doubt he will.

Maybe he was just trying to throw me, but Griffin's got a point. I've seen the heart-stopping grins Roman tosses those chicks at the rec, the way he makes each one feel they might be the next lucky girl he takes home. No matter what I swing his way, he's not interested in seeing me naked. Maybe he's finding relief elsewhere. Maybe he's just passing time.

"Laura, have I *ever* lied to you?" One look, and I'm staring at the floor like it's got answers.

Thinking about his sweet words over the past several weeks, the way he's held me, kissed me, I would hope not. But... could he ever commit to someone like me? A single mom, with a messy life... and *so* much baggage?

Roman's nostrils flare with impatience. "Laura, I told you, you *can't* let that jerk get to you. He's just trying to—"

"He wants me back."

Roman goes still. And despite his lack of response, I know he needs me to clarify.

"He wants me to take him back," I say. "He wants to be a family again." *Up until now, I thought maybe it was all a game. I never thought he'd actually...*

Roman's lip curls. "And what did you tell him?"

Rubbing my temples, I take a breath, my mind still reeling with his rational arguments, his attempt to kiss me, and all of his... promises.

Roman starts pacing like a lion. "Laura, what did you *tell* him?"

"I'm just a little confused right now, Roman. I... I need time to think—"

"Time to *think*?" He turns for the door but stops and looks back at me. "You know what? I *honestly* can't believe you. After everything we've been through—after *everything* he's dragged you through— you're gonna do this shit *now*?"

"I... I don't know."

"*How the hell do you not know, Laura?*" The sharp escalation of his voice is magnified as it pierces through the vacant house. But I can't bring myself to answer.

He said he loves me. He said he messed up. He wants me back.

Roman stands at the front door, staring at me like I'm crazy. "Can't you see how shallow he is? He didn't give a damn about you three months ago."

I sniff, cheeks burning. "Neither did you."

With a blink, his expression grows dark. "What?"

"You're the one who wanted to turn me into your little... project or whatever."

Roman scoffs, a tear rolling down his cheek. "I just wanted you to see what I saw inside of you all along."

I don't know what to think. I don't know who to trust.

You're a waste of space, and everybody knows it.

"You know what?" Roman reaches for the door. "This is *just* like you, Laura."

"What's that supposed to mean?"

"It's just like you," he says, louder now, more fire than filter. "All this nonsense you talk about being real, and you can't even be real with your damn self. After the birthday party and on Thanksgiving—the second something feels too good, you gotta burn it down. 'Cause Heaven forbid you'd actually believe you deserve something better." He yanks open the door and gives me one last look—sharp, disappointed, and done. "And I'd be a fool to sit here and watch you do it." He steps outside, and something in me moves before my mind can catch up.

"Roman, wait!" He keeps walking, and I heave my shoulders. "What about the dance?"

He throws up the peace sign, not bothering to look back. And my heart shatters all over again as he takes off in his car.

⸱⸱✦✦✦⸱⸱

I'm torn between the familiar steps of the charming slow dance I know or embracing the allure of an exciting, unexplored routine. No matter what I do, it seems I'm bound for heartbreak. If that's even my decision to make.

I seek refuge in my rec room, where the music holds me close, guiding me in a gentle sway. I need to clear my head. Roman might be upset, and Griffin might be on the fence, but at the end of the day, I can be certain of one thing—dance will forever be my first love.

I spin and jump, my body moving to the rhythm as the music envelops me, the weight of my worries rolling off my shoulders. Dancing has always been my lifeline. My escape. The one place I still recognize myself. As much as I loved Griffin, as much as I wanted to make everyone happy, I don't know how I ever let anyone convince me to let this go.

Watching my balance, I curl and extend my leg in perfect form. I glide and roll across the floor, as graceful as a rose petal on the breeze. With exhilaration, I leap into the air and execute a flawless pirouette. A smile plays on my lips, reflecting the joy that surges in my chest with each and every twirl.

In the mirror, my newly flattened belly peeks out below my tank top, stretch marks racing against the sides like little tattoos of lightning.

You're disgusting. And you're always gonna be disgusting. Why even try?

Gasping for air, I throw my hands on my knees, choking back tears. "No. I'm not disgusting." Standing up straight, I extend my hands overhead, turn and turn, refusing to look at myself. But it won't go away.

Look at you. You're fat, you're lazy... Nothing but a waste of space.

"Don't think about it. Forget about it." Brushing away the tears, I return to my combination, jump out with my feet, and roll my hips like Roman taught me.

Why don't you just disappear? It's not like anyone would miss you anyway.

I stumble to a halt, screaming at the top of my lungs. *"Shut up! That's not true! It's not!* It's not..." I collapse to the floor in tears.

I bury my face in my hands, sobbing until my throat burns. Weeping over every memory. Every broken smile, every hug that begged me to hold on.

"*I couldn't take it,*" her letter said. "*I'm sorry for being so weak.*"

They found the letter on April's bedside table, nestled beside the empty pill bottle—the note delicately sealed in an envelope labeled just for me. Mom must've told us a hundred times how charming he was when they first met, how he never got into his moods before his back injury. The meds just made him a little "testy" at times. Mom couldn't have trusted him more when the widowmaker struck. But it never got any better.

April begged me not to go. *"Don't leave me with him, Laura. I won't make it."* But after losing our mom, I needed to get away, and my scholarship to Michigan was the perfect escape.

"It's only two years," I'd said. *"I promise, time will fly by, and I'll be back every holiday."*

She didn't make it to Thanksgiving.

The words in her letter were a regurgitation of everything he'd said over the years:

I can't get it right... Nobody wants me around... I'm just a waste of space.

We'd heard it so much that it was hard to believe he hadn't written the letter himself.

The last time I saw him was on Thanksgiving Day. He stood on the lawn, casually puffing on a cigarette, as apathetic as a random spectator as they wheeled her body out. I swear, I would've killed him if Griffin hadn't held me back. Suddenly, I was an orphan. Suddenly, I'd lost what family I had left. Who would've known that less than a decade later, Griffin would abandon our family, too? My heart pricks with the memory of his words as he slipped from my grasp. *"This isn't healthy anymore. It's toxic."*

But Roman's voice echoes in my mind:

Look, whatever you're hearing in your head right now, you gotta shut that garbage off. Don't ever let anybody tell you that you can't do something—especially you. Alright?

Grabbing my phone, I pull up the quotes.

Beauty begins the moment you decide to be yourself. – Coco Chanel

Too many people overvalue what they are not and undervalue what they are – Malcolm S. Forbes

To love oneself is the beginning of a lifelong romance – Oscar Wilde

Something soft flickers in my chest as I recall his handsome face at the butterfly garden. *"You've always been beautiful, Laura. The only one who couldn't see it was you."*

A final tear escapes me as I lift my gaze to the mirror. And I gasp at the sight of my smooth caramel skin, the auburn highlights in my hair, my shimmering, diamond eyes.

I'm beautiful. Just as gorgeous and breathtaking as that Blue Morpho butterfly, and he saw it all along.

Without hesitation, I start typing. *I think—*

But I jump as my phone rings. It isn't him. It's Griffin's sister.

"Gabriela?" But all I hear is sniffling on the other end. "Gabriela? Everything okay?"

"Laura," she whispers. "It's… It's Griffin."

Panic grips my chest. "What about Griffin?"

"Griffin. He…" She sniffs again as someone sobs in the back. *"Mijo… Mijo… ¡Ay, Dios mío!"*

Is that Daphne? "Gabriela, what's going on? You're scaring me."

She releases a shaky breath. "He was in an accident, Laura. A car accident."

I've suffered so many losses. My mom in high school, my sister during my first year of college. I don't even recall my biological dad. Yet, it never gets easier. Griffin was in such shock at the news of his father's passing that he lost grip of the phone. His knees went limp, and he slumped in the middle of the floor. And until this moment, I never imagined the exact same thing could happen to me.

26

*I*t must've taken me hours to pull myself together because the sun is already setting by the time I arrive at the hospital. I just couldn't bear to face what could happen.

The waiting area is packed with people concerned about Griffin, several of whom I recognize—like his family and colleagues—and plenty I don't. A messy mixture of his past and present, all converging to see what the future may or may not hold.

"Mom!" Maddie rushes into my arms with tear-streaked cheeks. She trembles as I hug her tight. "Mom, I don't know what happened. Vicki wouldn't tell me. She said… She said Daddy got hurt and—"

Gently calming her, I draw my daughter into my chest, welling up with tears I didn't think I had left. "Where is she?" Though Vicki isn't my favorite person, the least I could do is thank her for bringing the kids to the hospital. But glancing around, I don't see her anywhere. Maddie shakes her head as if my guess is as good as hers. Thankfully, Eli is a little ways away in the seating area, peacefully napping in Daphne's lap.

Sitting beside their mother, you would never know Griffin's sisters were in the midst of a tragedy. The three of them look like a group of triplets in their flawless designer dresses—the girls' raw honey skin glowing like rays of sunshine on a cloudy day. Rising from their seats, Bianca and Gabriela approach, the slightest hint of puffiness forming under their eyes.

"Laura." Gabriela pulls me into a hug with quivering lips, a soft sob escaping her as she looks me over. "You look *gorgeous*."

"Amazing," Bianca agrees, her eyes glistening with tears.

For so long, I thought it would mean everything to hear those words from them. Now, it means nothing at all. "Thank you," I whisper, rubbing Maddie's back. "Any news?"

Gabriela soberly shakes her head. "He's still unconscious. They won't say..." Her voice cracks, and she presses her palm to her eyes. Bianca moves in to soothe her sister, barely holding it together herself.

They filled me in earlier by text. It was a rollover accident on a secluded, unpaved road. If Vicki hadn't been on the phone, who knows how long it would've been before somebody found him.

"The doctor should be around with an update before long," says Bianca.

With a terse nod, I follow them to the seating area, exchanging a tearful acknowledgment with Daphne as I sit.

It still feels unreal. For all the pain he caused, he was still mine once. My husband. The father of my children. The boy I used to dream with. How does a love like that end like this?

Maddie's nestling against my chest when my phone rings. With apologies to everyone, I answer the video call. Yana's face pulls up with an uncharacteristic frown.

"Hey," she says softly. "I'm at the train station. I'm catching the next one out."

"Thanks, girl." She was at rehearsal when I called but dropped everything when she saw my text. "I hope this won't put your role in jeopardy."

She waves a hand. "If it's not meant to be, it's not meant to be. Now, where's my Maddie?"

I turn the phone to my daughter, and Yana offers gentle encouragement, vowing to take her and Eli out for milkshakes the second she gets back. As I look to Griffin's mother and sisters sniffling to my left, his assistant having a complete breakdown to my right, I know that everyone fears the worst just as much as I do. The man hasn't been perfect, but he's done what he could to be a decent father and son. And for a long time, a really decent husband.

Eli groggily stretches as he wakes, slowly seeming to recall the circumstances of where he is. I brace myself for the onslaught of questions he's bound to hurl at me. But he sits up straight, adjusting his glasses.

"Roman?"

I look up the hall, and standing near the nurses' station, I see him—in his jeans and favorite leather jacket, hands stuffed into his pockets.

Springing out of Daphne's lap, Eli takes off for him, and Maddie isn't far behind.

"How'd he even know we were here?" I'm talking to myself, but a soft smile inches across Yana's lips.

Despite being a blubbering mess earlier today, I managed to fill her in on the horrific confrontations I had this morning and how this was the worst way it could end. But I didn't contact Roman. I couldn't.

"He picks up the phone every now and then," says Yana. "I'll see you all in a bit."

Hanging up, I head across the lobby with weak knees, but Roman's already got Eli in his arms by the time I reach him. After embracing my son for what seems like forever, he turns to Maddie and offers the same as I look on in astonishment.

I can't believe it.

Pulling away, Roman kneels, staring each of them in the eye. "How y'all been? You taking it easy?" The kids nod, and he squints at Maddie. "You sure?"

She releases a teary giggle. "I'm sure."

"Alright," he says. "We don't need you passing out before that recital."

The kids' laughter cuts through the tension like sunlight. I didn't realize how much I missed that sound.

I link eyes with Roman as he stands. "Thanks for coming."

He nods. But instead of offering me a hug, he shoves his hands back in his pockets, his jaw as tight as it was this morning, the same ache behind his eyes. No matter how he feels about Griffin, I know all this must be hard on him, too.

Clearing his throat, Roman glances in the direction of the over-crowded lobby. "How's he doing?"

"We're waiting on an update now," I say, voice trembling.

Roman just studies me, his eyes tracing every inch of my face.

"And you?" he asks softly.

"As best as could be expected," I murmur, swallowing the lump of emotion in my throat. I'm terrified that if I blink, he might disappear.

As he stares toward the hospital room, all I can think is how much I long for his touch, to have him hold me again. It hasn't been twenty-four hours, and it feels like it's been an eternity. His distance is agony.

Across the lobby, Griffin's mom and sisters are watching us. With all our ups and downs, I have no clue how much Griffin's shared about this little love affair of mine. Let alone what the kids might've said. But at this point, I'm not sure I care.

I turn back to Roman with an unsettled heart. "After everything, I wasn't sure you'd want to hear from me."

"I know."

But he doesn't say anything else. Which basically confirms the worst. He wouldn't have answered.

Not because I stayed silent. But because when he showed up, open, honest, choosing me...

I blinked.

I let fear speak louder than what we had. Let doubt crack the door wide enough for Griffin to slide back in.

And the worst part? I turned into the very thing Roman spent years trying to heal from.

Another Jennifer.

My throat constricts as everything goes blurry. Before I can work up the strength to restrain the tears, he pulls me into his arms and holds me tight. And finally, I allow myself to exhale, the heavy breaths transforming into sobs within seconds.

With his gentle touch, the fresh scent of his cologne, the simple rise and fall of his chest, I get exactly what he meant. *How am I supposed to dance without you?*

A whisper escapes my lips. "I just... I just don't know how to—"

But before I can get out the words, the doctor arrives, and everyone gathers around.

Roman's hand is warm on my back, but his gaze is no less wounded. "You should go."

"But Roman—"

He shakes his head, encouraging each of the kids to lead me across the lobby. My eye is still on him as he stands back, watching them usher me into the crowd.

To our relief, the doctor explains that Griffin is stable but appears to have suffered a concussion. She suggests that his closest loved ones take turns talking to him, sharing memories, and offering support in an effort to wake him. Everyone looks to one another, trying to decide who should go first.

"Where's Vicki?" asks Bianca. "She's our best bet."

"Don't be stupid," says Gabriela, slapping her sister's arm. "It only makes sense for Mamí to see him first."

"Actually..." Daphne looks at me. "Laura?"

Pointing at myself, I frown. *"Me?"*

Daphne nods. "My son has loved you dearly since the day you met. If anyone stood a chance of bringing him back to us, it's you. *El amor todo lo puede.*"

In the midst of the soap opera our marriage has become, I doubt it. But every head turns in my direction, each face mirroring a desperate plea.

＋＋◆◆◆＋＋

From the bare walls to the bright overhead lights, the entire hospital room is bathed in stark white, like a waiting room at Heaven's gates. The rhythmic beeping and humming of the medical equipment are something out of a telenovela, pumping a steady soundtrack of tension in the air.

My footsteps seem silent as I cross the polished linoleum floor to Griffin's bedside, the door softly shutting us in. Though scarred, his face maintains its angelic expression as he rests at the heart of the bed. Lying here, he reminds me of a wounded soldier, heavy strips of gauze wrapped just beneath his wavy hair, his sculpted arms and chest ensnared by a swarm of tubes and wires.

Pulling up a chair, my shoulders sag. Looking at his sweet, bruised face, his words from this morning come to mind.

"I love you, Laura. I never stopped loving you."

Do I still love him?

I loved the handsome, young delivery boy who forgot my total because he was too busy staring. I loved the man who promised me forever in our tiny apartment, broke and barefoot. The sophisticated father and businessman who worked endless hours, all in hopes of giving us a better life and making his daddy proud.

All he wanted was one kiss. One final reassurance that I cared about him just as much as he cared about me. I'm not sure I'll forgive myself if he doesn't wake up.

Looking over the monitors and blinking lights surrounding him, I know my time is short. So, taking his hand in mine, I begin.

"The words you said this morning meant everything to me. For so long, all I've wanted..." But it doesn't feel right. Clearing my throat, I start over. "You gotta wake up, okay? Maddie's recital is next week, and—"

I stop again, gritting my teeth. None of this feels real.

But maybe that's the problem.

Tears touch my lashes as I squeeze his hand tight.

"You... *asshole*. All this time, I waited and waited. And finally, when I'm ready to move on, you declare you want me back? All this song and dance—at the talent show, and the birthday parties, and the ice cream shop—and you wait until the day of a deadly car accident to see the light? Asshole!"

I throw a hand to my mouth, restraining a sob.

"You broke my heart, Griffin. You broke it on the day you left. And the kids? How the hell were we supposed to go on like nothing had changed? I don't care how *scared* or *confused* you were. The day you married me, you made a promise—a commitment to be there for me, for *us*, no matter what. But you broke that promise... and so many more."

A fragile breath stirs his ribs. I don't know if any of this is working, but I've gotta get this out.

"I get it. You made an incredibly *stupid* mistake," I say. "The pressure from your family and all the publicity got to you, and you just...

caved. And I can forgive that. But if you don't wake up and, instead, leave your kids' lives the way my mother left April and me... I will never forgive you. Maddie and Eli deserve better than that, Griffin. Me and the kids deserve better."

A soft groan rumbles from his chest. His fingers twitch, curling around mine. And miraculously, his eyes flutter open.

"You're awake!" I throw my hands to my mouth with a gasp and dash to swing open the door. "He's awake! He's awake!"

Elated, everyone gathers in the doorway, but the nurses hold them back.

Having me step aside, the doctor and nurses check his vitals, questioning if he's aware of what happened and if he remembers his name. He patiently answers their questions, but his unwavering gaze is locked on me.

The doctor is just clearing him to see everyone else when he raises a hand. "Can I have a moment with my wife, please?"

With reluctance, the doctor and nurses step out, insisting they'll return shortly. I'm still frozen in the corner as they shut the door. It's as if I'm confronting a ghost.

To my surprise, Griffin extends a hand, and I slowly accept his invitation, returning to my seat beside him.

A soft grin curves his lips. "That was quite the speech you gave me."

Heat rising in my cheeks, I drop my head, wondering if I could summon the courage to say it all again or if I was simply emboldened because he couldn't talk back.

"I'm sorry," he whispers, caressing my hand. "For leaving, for giving up... scaring you just now. You're right, Laura. You deserve so much better."

The words hit soft and heavy, like a lullaby I used to believe in. I've imagined this moment a thousand different ways. But none of them hurt quite like this.

"That's why I told her."

I stare at him, confused. "Who?"

"Vicki. I called her the second I turned out of the driveway. She got all worked up, and I suggested we talk later, but..." He studies my hand in his. "We got into an argument, and I was so distracted I swerved into a ditch."

An argument? Over me? It's no wonder she didn't hang around for an update.

With a swallow, I sit up straight. "What'd you tell her?"

"Exactly what I told you. I screwed up, and I want you back. Coaching, counseling, whatever it takes, I'm here." He presses my hand to his chest, just over his heart. "I won't give up again, Laura. I promise."

One more promise.

"It's all my fault," he says, studying my face. "I knew exactly how dancing made you feel. I could see it in your eyes at those performances, every time you'd twirl around the kitchen, do that little swerve of your hips."

I release a teary chuckle, but there's sadness behind his smile.

"After you had Eli, I never encouraged you to go back to it. You were this lovely accessory in my life—my lady on the red carpet, the mother of my kids. I couldn't handle the thought of you loving anything more than you loved me."

His voice cracks. But it's the guilt in his eyes that guts me.

Maybe it was the roll of his jaw or simply his refusal to talk about what I'd left behind, but deep down, I always knew.

"I get it now," he says. "This is who you are. And I'm willing to follow you in whatever you wanna do. You wanna go to Vegas? See your name in lights? I'm here for it, babe."

With a bitter laugh, I break free of his grasp. "Both of us know that isn't true. You're not abandoning your father's legacy. And as long as your momma's around, you're not leaving the state."

"I don't care, Laura—"

"Yes, you do, Griffin. From your dad's first frown to the day you walked out of our home, you've *always* cared about you and what they *think* of you. Why are you the only one who gets to decide? Why don't I ever have a say?"

He reaches for me, but instead, I place the wedding rings that have been burning a hole in my pocket in his hand.

I didn't know whether I'd be lying them on his chest or in a casket, but no matter the circumstance, I've decided to let him go. It's the only way I'll truly embrace joy again.

His eyes gloss over as he stares at them. "Laura, l-let me fix this," he chokes out, voice trembling. "I can make it right—"

"No, you can't, Griffin." His shoulders sag at the firmness of my gaze. "I get pregnant? *'Let's get married.'* I don't fit the picture? *'Let's divorce.'* You can't slap a Band-Aid on this one and act like it never happened. You failed the one person that was in your corner from day one, and you don't get to bounce back from that. Not this time."

Griffin shakes his head before I've even finished speaking. "Laura, what about our family? What about our kids?"

"Our kids deserve a home built on truth, not fear. I gave everything to make ours a happy one. Poured love into every corner of it. But I need to be happy, too."

His fist curls around the wedding rings as I stand, his tearful gaze locked on me. "But what if you're what makes *me* happy? What if *you're* what I love?"

I brush my fingers over his beard, memorizing him like a photo I'll never frame. "I'll always love you. But you were right. This is what's best. For all of us."

Even if I have to dance alone.

He's still watching me as I head for the door, and the family rushes in.

But when I push through the crowd, something cracks deep in my chest. Roman is gone.

27

*T*he news outlets are still talking about Griffin's dramatic car accident when I arrive at the rec on Monday afternoon. Combined with his status, his "miraculous" survival made for great ratings this weekend.

As I move through the lobby, the image of him with the kids and me at Virginia Beach is splattered across every TV screen.

Of all the photos they could've used.

Maybe his mother had a copy.

I finally reached my attorney, and she's working on filing new papers. In the meantime, I'm on a mission. Waving hello to the staff at the front desk, I head for the classrooms.

After paying Griffin a surprisingly cordial visit and treating the kids to those milkshakes she promised, Yana came back to the house and stayed the night, consoling me. I spent most of our Sunday recounting the remaining details of what happened with Griffin and Roman, including the dramatic conclusion at the hospital. As I wrapped up the lengthy tale, Yana shook her head in adoration. *"And finally, she sees the light,"* she'd said, throwing an arm around me. *"Now that you know your worth, it's time to go get what's yours!"*

Not that I was so easily convinced. When I stepped out of that hospital room and saw Roman was nowhere around, I spiraled. He's a sweetheart. Of course he came to check on the kids and me. Even if I was the last person he wanted to comfort at that moment. It didn't mean he wanted to continue dancing with me... or anything else. The fact that he didn't even bother to call was all the confirmation I needed.

Yana told me to pull my head out of my ass and go after him. It may have taken her all day to push me out the door, but I'm here.

One of Roman's hip-hop classes is held around this time. If I hurry, I should make it.

He's just completing the warm-up on the platform when I arrive. "Alright, y'all. We're gonna start out nice and easy. And then—" He stops as I rush inside and toss my bag to the back before taking my place front and center, like always.

These aren't the same ladies from my usual Saturday class, but with the news about Griffin—along with that silly Virginia Beach photo—being blasted across local media outlets, it's likely most of them are fairly acquainted with my face. I've caught some of them eyeing Roman and me sideways during our evening sessions. News travels quickly around this gym, and surely the rumors about him escorting me to the club haven't helped. Add the fact that, up until this point, I was technically still married, and it's no wonder ladies are rolling their eyes and sucking their teeth as I get in position. But I'm not here for them. I'm here for him.

Roman clears his throat, gaze falling on the platform. "We're gonna start out slow. And then, we'll pick up the pace. I want y'all to give it all you got. Alright?"

Joining in as the other ladies whoop and clap, I shout, "That's right!"

But he barely looks my way as he starts the music.

The first song selection is "Caught Up" by Usher—one of my favorites. And I'm not the only one. All around me, hips are winding and arms are flowing, and I fall right into step. I've missed being on this dance floor, the collective energy of bodies in motion, the pulsating beat beneath my toes.

The music flows through my veins like water, and I soak it up like a sponge. Like always, the fire that ignites in Roman's eyes as he falls into his element—twisting his legs and hips—is infectious. He looks so incredible. He *always* looks incredible.

But my foot catches on something slick, and I damn near faceplant into next week.

"Oops!" A girl snatches up the rogue towel before resting a hand on my arm, a little smirk on her face. "My bad." But she doesn't look sorry at all.

Whatever. I turn my attention back to Roman. *I didn't come this far to hold back. I'm not going to let anyone stop me.*

Roman starts us off with a gentle routine. Basic steps, soft sways to the beat.

It's nice to move alongside him again, to feel the rhythm between us. But he's obviously going easy on us. We run the combo a few times, and I'm barely breaking a sweat. Roman, on the other hand, won't give me so much as a glance.

After a couple rounds, he stops, hands on his waist, chest rising with breath he hasn't spent.

"Let's take a two-minute break," he says, voice low. "Grab some water."

I frown as he goes to grab a bottle himself and gulps it down like he hasn't had a sip in days. With reluctance, I head to the back with the other ladies, plenty of them leering my way.

"Can you believe her?" whispers one.

"This is *so* sad," says another.

"She's ruining it for *all* of us."

But I keep my eyes fixed on him. *Whatever it takes, I'm not giving up.* I'm the first to jog back out to the dance floor.

Roman's returned to practicing his moves in the mirror, clearly trying to ignore me. But he's fooling himself if he thinks I'll let him get away with it.

Once everyone gets back on the floor, Roman picks up the pace. And with some sweet isolations and a sexy spin, we're vibing again, the synchronization of our steps echoing like a steady heartbeat. A smile finally creeps back to his lips as we wrap up another section.

Ladies toss each other high-fives, and despite not receiving any, I'm feeling the high.

"Y'all ready to get sexy?" asks Roman, lifting his brow in a challenge. Ladies shout in return, and he bobs his head. "Alright, this is where we separate the cute from the committed. Y'all ready to leave it all on the floor or what?"

The entire class explodes with cheers and applause as a familiar electric current charges behind his gaze.

From the turn, we go into knee punches and jump side to side, right into footwork I can handle and arms I absolutely cannot. It's tough, but I love it.

I've missed this. I've missed *him.*

With each move, I keep in perfect time—like a shadow, mirroring his every motion. But someone steps on the back of my shoe, and I stumble. It's the same chick from before.

"Sorry," she says with a snort.

I glower at her as I bend to slip my shoe back on. *These girls are extra catty today.*

The trainer throws out his arms as he shouts, *"Now, who's ready to give it to Roman?"*

The girls scream like they're at a boy band concert.

"I'll give it to you, Roman!"

He wags his tongue at the thirsty vulture behind me, and a fiery ember burns in my core. If I don't fix this quick, I'm sure there's a lengthy line of ladies waiting to mend his broken heart.

Standing up straight, I brush my hair from my face. No matter what, I'm doing this.

With the intensity of a roaring engine, Roman counts us off. "Five... six... five, six, seven—*let's work!*"

Taking it from the top with the class, I give it my all, doing everything I can to keep up. My heart may be racing, and my legs may be sore—I *definitely* should've done more squats over the weekend—but I'm not backing down. And neither is he.

"Keep it going!" he hollers as we come up on the end. "Five, six, seven—*let's work!*"

With a deep breath, I push through. *I have to do this. I refuse to give up on him. I refuse to give up on myself!* Throwing my punches as hard as I can, jumping in perfect time, I sync my feet with Roman's, following him as closely as his own reflection.

And for just a hint of a second, he glances my way.

"That was good," he says as we fall into a breathless march. "But y'all can do better."

Despite my shortness of breath and the sweat beading my brow, I nod.

"Again!" he shouts.

C+C Music Factory's "Gonna Make You Sweat" kicks on as we launch into the next round, and I dig up all the pain and heartache and passion—every ounce of strength I can muster. Jumping even higher, turning even faster. And *finally*, I'm feeling my groove.

My pulse surges, a wave of adrenaline rushing through my veins. The pounding of my heart and the searing of my lungs is addictive. A high I couldn't find anywhere else.

Suddenly, I don't give a damn about anyone or anything else around. It's just me and him, dancing in seamless harmony.

Turn, punch… side to side.

Roman explodes as we come to the end of the routine. "Whoo! Y'all wanna do it again?" The ladies clap and holler. "I said, *do y'all wanna do it again?*"

"*Let's go, Roman!*" My voice carries over them all. And finally, I've got his attention.

I smile at him in the mirror, and he nods at my reflection. Then we're going for it.

Summoning every source of energy I've got, I surrender myself to the rhythm, allowing its gentle embrace to lead my body in whatever direction it wants to go. And before I know it, my eyes are no longer on Roman.

They're on that sexy woman in the mirror instead. And she is *tearing it up.*

She spins with incredible grace and jumps with the ease of a grasshopper. Her feet are like lightning, and her arms are *mind-blowing.*

That woman is *amazing.* And that woman is me.

In perfect time, I kick out with Roman and execute the epic spin… And it's flawless!

My heart explodes with joy. I've never been happier in my life!

I used to think I needed someone to see me.

But now I do.

And that's enough.

Everyone's clapping and congratulating each other. Even Roman smiles my way as he catches his breath.

But I can't catch mine… The room tilts.

And everything goes dark.

Roman's leaning over me when I wake. "Laura? Laura! You alright?"

I blink a few times as I stare at the ceiling overhead. I must've fainted. I'm lying on the floor. But from what I can tell, the rest of the class has cleared out. "I'm not sure what I was thinking..."

"Yeah, me neither," he mutters.

Shaking my pounding head, I prop up on my elbows. "I think I got carried away—"

"Yeah. What else is new?" He calls over his shoulder, *"Can somebody get in here with some oxygen, please?"* As I sit up, he grabs my arm. "Hold up! You shouldn't—"

"Roman, I'm fine. I just—I just need to talk to you."

"People don't pass out when they're fine, Laura. Did you sleep last night?"

"Yes, but—"

"You drink water?"

"Yes! Now, can we just—"

"Laura, I *need* to know what's going on! Did you eat today?"

"I may have forgotten breakfast," I say. "And maybe lunch."

"Theresa! I need some juice in here ASAP!"

"Roman, please. Just... Look, I was being an idiot—"

But the on-site medical staff rushes in with a stretcher and supplies.

Roman pushes to his feet and informs them of my situation. "I think she went too hard. She hasn't eaten since yesterday—*Theresa! Has anybody seen Theresa?"*

Pursing my lips, I allow the paramedics to strap an oxygen mask over my face. Meanwhile, out in the hall, ladies from class are peeking inside, whispering and shaking their heads. I bet they really hate me now. As expected, the second I pull off the stupid mask, the paramedics freak out. But I can't hold this in.

"Roman, you were right."

He turns to me with a frown. "What?"

"You were right!"

In a frenzy, the paramedics strap the mask back over my face. "You need more oxygen." But I snatch it off again.

"Ma'am, we need you to—"

"I was burning it down, just like you said."

When the paramedics try once more, I push the mask away, my eyes locked on him.

"On Thanksgiving, Maddie's birthday." I shrug. "Being real? I was ready to end everything with you simply because I was afraid things wouldn't work out."

Roman studies my face in silence as the medical staff turns to him.

"Roman, we're going to need you to give us a moment while we do our job."

He takes a step back as they check my vitals, his uncertain gaze shifting to the floor. It isn't until they remove the blood pressure cuff that his handsome brown eyes return to mine.

"Being real?" I say. "I thought I'd never be good enough for you. But Griffin, he already knew what I was about."

Roman doesn't seem to have a word to say as Theresa rushes in with juice. She hands it to one of the paramedics, and they insist that I drink. But I'm still watching him.

"Roman, please say something."

The paramedics groan. "Ma'am, we're going to need you to drink."

"Roman?" I stand, and the paramedics nearly lose their minds.

"Ma'am, we need you to stay seated!"

"Miss, *please* drink the juice!"

"I came to talk to you, Roman. And that's exactly what I'm going to do."

He throws a half-hearted shrug, eyes hard. "Laura, why would I give a damn what you have to say right now when you don't give a damn about yourself?"

"Fine." I grab the stupid cup and toss back the juice. Shoving it into the paramedic's hand, I throw out my arms. "Now, will you hear me out? 'Cause I'm in love with you!"

The entire room is frozen. The paramedics exchange concerned glances with Theresa and each other. Roman looks as if he's forgotten how to breathe. But I've gotta tell him everything that's on my mind. I may as well start with the most important part.

Looking to Theresa and the paramedics, Roman says, "Um, thanks, guys, but I think we're good for now." Of course, the paramedics argue, but he shakes his head. "If you can just give us a minute, I'll let you know if we need any more help."

With a reluctant nod, the three head out, a glum Theresa shutting the door behind them.

And finally, it's just the two of us.

Roman turns to the mirror, his hands pressed to his waist. "You think I don't know what *El amor todo lo puede* means? Jennifer used to say that crap all the time."

My heart deflates as it dawns on me that he must've heard what Daphne said at the hospital:

"Love conquers all."

It's no wonder he didn't stick around.

"You don't understand. I—I gave Griffin the rings. It's over—"

"So, what does that make me?" he asks. "Runner-up?"

"Roman..." I take a few steps his way. "You were the winner all along. I just never told you."

His eyes are watery as they lock on my reflection. "I saw y'all in front of the house on Saturday. It certainly didn't look that way."

"I know. And maybe I was a little mixed up at the time."

He rolls his eyes, brushing away a tear, and a weight settles on my shoulders.

"Speaking of being real, there's something I've gotta tell you."

He shrugs, studying the floor. But I know he's listening.

In through the nose, Laura... Out through the mouth.

"Look, my mom married this *really* awful man who made it his job to torture me when I was a teenager. Verbal abuse," I add, as Roman's startled gaze pings back to mine. "But it may as well have been physical. He told me every single day how ugly he thought I was and how nobody would ever love me."

Roman turns to me, and suddenly, I can't look him in the eye.

"For my mom and my sister April... it wasn't all that different. Eventually, Mom's heart couldn't take it anymore, and... Well, you know what happened. Two years later, my sister decided she couldn't take it either. Griffin was there when I learned about April's suicide and... for a long time, he always was." I finally manage to raise my head, and the pain staring back at me nearly undoes me. It's like he's holding every word like it matters.

With a shuddered breath, he says, "Shit, Laura."

I nod. "Thankfully, the man I called my stepdad is no longer a part of my life, but his words stuck with me. For years, his cruel insults played back in my head over and over. And once I began blaming myself for my sister's death, it became nearly impossible to determine which of the voices were his or my own."

The crease in Roman's brow deepens as he takes a step toward me.

"Roman, I didn't grow up hearing that I was beautiful *ever.*" Tears cling to my lashes as I meet him halfway. "And Griffin, he was the first man to tell me he thought so."

Roman takes another tiny step, and I mirror his grace.

"So, being real? Maybe it was a little hard to believe another man could genuinely care about me 'cause I never believed I was worth caring about. At least until now."

He studies me like he's seeing me for the first time.

"Flaws and all, even if I've been burned before, I still deserve to be loved. And that starts with me." With a few steps, I close what's left of the space between us. "Thanks to you, for the first time in my life, I truly believe that."

Roman's stare seems eternal, but I don't dare blink. I hold my breath along with what's left of my tears, praying he won't turn and leave.

Instead, he snatches me into his arms and hugs me to his chest.

A collective gasp echoes from the crowd in the hall.

And it's so incredibly nice to feel his arms around me again.

But it's not just the warmth of his arms. It's the way he holds me like he sees every scar... and still chooses to stay. Roman exhales against my hair and sinks into the hug like he's trying to pour every unspoken word into this moment... so I'll never question it again.

"Really cool bonus?" I whisper into his chest. "I hit my goal weight on Friday."

He jolts back in shock.

"I know, you told me to ignore the numbers. I was just curious, and—"

"You're incredible," he says, and I nudge him with a grin.

"I know."

"You're phenomenal," he says. I nod at that, too.

His lips find mine like it's the most natural thing in the world. Like he's done waiting, done hiding, done pretending he doesn't feel this.

Whispers rise in the hall. But we don't give a damn.

He rests his forehead against mine, breath warm, eyes steady.

"And I swear, I've never been in love with a more amazing woman."

The butterflies in my tummy take flight as he pulls me in for another kiss. Softer, deeper, and laced with everything we couldn't say until now.

Then he grabs my hand and tugs me toward the swarm in the hall. "Come on."

"Where are we going?"

"Over to my studio. You know Roman. *Can't go a day without dancing.*"

I laugh as he opens the door to a sea of wide-eyed onlookers. "Okay, but… can we get a sandwich first?"

28

*M*y hand trembles as I apply the finishing touches to Maddie's lipstick, trying not to smudge the edges with my nerves. "You sure about this, honey? After everything with your dad, I'd understand if—"

"Of course I'm sure, Mom." Her brilliant smile could calm a group of anxious mothers watching their babies take their first steps. "After all this practice, it feels like I was born for this role. Besides, Ms. Alyssa would have a heart attack if I backed out now!"

My daughter stands, running her hands over her glittery dress, delicately brushing at the slicked-back edges of her hair. Definitely on the brink of turning twenty-two.

With several wardrobe changes, Maddie gets her own dressing room for the recital—a small classroom not too far from the auditorium. Tri-fold mirrors with a compact vanity table for every hair accessory, a rack of meticulously organized costumes standing nearby.

The stage director knocks at the door and pops her head inside, announcing that we'll be gathering with Ms. Alyssa for a huddle before the show begins. We agree to be right out, and she heads to the next classroom. I tuck away my makeup supplies along with my smile, a familiar buzz of energy in the air.

"Honestly, without Dad, I might've quit ballet this year."

I look back at Maddie. "Really?"

She lifts a shoulder, pushing in her chair. "I've got a lot more homework these days, and I don't wanna pass out again." Both of us chuckle. "But I didn't wanna sit around being sad about him leaving, so I danced. It's what makes me feel the most like me."

When I was in high school, I felt the same way. Whenever I needed to get away from my stepdad and his relentless insults—whether it'd be in my room or at school—dance is where I found solace, where I found joy. Refusing to ruin my makeup, I hold back the tears as I squeeze her delicate shoulders. "I suppose you're a little more like me than I thought."

Maddie beams as we head for the hall. "You know what's so cool about playing Susan? We always wanted the same thing."

I stop with a squint. "You mean a family?"

She shakes her head. "For our moms to be happy. And nowadays, you always are."

A warm smile bounces between us as I escort her out the door.

⟡⟡⟡⟡⟡

In no time, I'm backstage, watching my little girl perform her favorite solo. A moving rendition of "My Grown-Up Christmas List."

Her Saturday class joins her mid-song, backing her up like they've rehearsed this moment a thousand times.

I've heard Maddie start and stop this song all year, replaying verses until they stuck. But the lyrics still prick something soft in me. And paired with her seamless jumps and radiant smile—each pirouette turned with a flawless grace—the melody wraps my heart like a bow.

As I watch her leap and turn, gliding in her flowing silver coat and matching winter cap, the spotlight catching every shimmer, a lump rises in my throat. She's so at home on that stage. I can see it clear as day—this is something she could love for the rest of her life.

And I get it. I really do.

A squeeze at my shoulders startles me. I turn, ready to react, but quickly cover my mouth to stifle a laugh. Roman's eyes twinkle as he hushes me with a grin. Sound travels backstage.

He's dressed head to toe in a ridiculous red and green elf costume, complete with curly-toed shoes and a jingling jester hat.

"You didn't tell me you'd be wearing that," I hiss.

Maddie had some wardrobe trouble at the dress rehearsal yesterday, so I unfortunately missed this whacky number.

"An elf's gotta do what an elf's gotta do," he whispers.

Oh, Roman. Always full of surprises.

Spotlights dance over his hungry gaze. "And you… are *smoking hot.*"

I laugh softly, smoothing my hand over the bodice of my red dress. "Thank you."

Neither of us wore our costumes at the dress rehearsal. Mine was being altered, and he forgot his altogether.

He's still checking me out when a group of boys and girls, not much older than Maddie, line up behind him, all dressed up as tiny elves in sneakers and festive hats.

"Wish us luck," Roman whispers, pulling me in for a hug.

I kiss the air beside his cheek and murmur, "Don't break a leg."

I bite my lip to keep from laughing as he jogs onstage and launches straight into a whirlwind of flips and breakdance spins with the kids.

The crowd erupts in applause, whooping and hollering as he moves like a pro.

He's really been holding out on me!

With the end of the first act creeping closer, something shifts in my chest. My sequined red dress with its flared skirt still makes me feel like a star. But my shoulders are cold, and my mouth's gone dry. I keep picking at the hem like the fabric might calm the nerves churning in my stomach.

This moment isn't just about hitting the steps. It's about showing up. For *me*. For the girl who thought she'd lost her rhythm for good.

As I compose myself, I'm acutely aware of Griffin's mother and sisters sitting in the third row with Yana and Eli, awaiting my performance. Griffin's still in the hospital, but thanks to Gabriela, he's watching the show by video call.

Only a few more minutes until we go on. But I haven't seen Roman since he and the other elves went flipping offstage at the opposite end. My palms are clammy as Maddie delivers her lines.

"Your beard doesn't have one of those things that goes over your ears." She reaches up, pretending to inspect Santa's snowy, voluminous whiskers, and charmed chuckles ripple through the audience.

I suppose the girl is right. Seems she was born for this role.

Something brushes my waist, and I nearly leap out of my skin. Roman wheezes with soft laughter as I swat him.

"Are you trying to ruin this recital?" I hiss.

But my nerves quickly subside as I take him in—open collar, suspenders, sleeves rolled to reveal those toned, corded arms. The whole look gives Frank Sinatra-era swagger.

If Sinatra had arms like that.

"How's this look?" he asks, tilting his chin like he doesn't already know he's fine.

I nod, letting my gaze linger on his sculpted behind in slacks. *"Much* better. And sexier."

Lord knows I should be focused on the performance... but the way those pants hug him? Got me praying for a wardrobe malfunction.

With a wink, he flips a fedora on his head and tilts it just right. "You're gonna knock 'em dead." He kisses me quick, spins me toward the stage, and gives my shoulders a squeeze. "This is your moment, mama."

The audience is already screaming as I strut on stage, hips swaying, sequins catching the light like camera flashes on a red carpet.

After Roman came clean about his feelings at the gym, I figured folks might keep their distance. But they came. My people. Cheering, hugging, hyping me up like they knew I needed it. Like they weren't just here for the recital, but for me.

I sink into Santa's lap with a playful pout, fluttering my lashes as he delivers his line.

"And what is it you want for Christmas this year?"

"Oh, Santa..." I lift my gaze to the ceiling with an exaggerated sigh, riding the crowd's anticipation. "There's only one thing I *really, really* want."

He leans in, playing along. "And what's that?"

I spring to my feet, fanning my arms out with the drama of a Broadway diva.

"To feel like the *only girl in the world*!"

It's extra. It's absurd. And I love it.

The crowd roars, the music hits, and Roman takes the stage like the showman he is—spinning into view, smile first. It comes as no surprise that the audience is falling all over themselves. We all know who the *true* star is here.

He twirls me in and out, each step a promise, each glance a spark. My skirt flares with every turn, sequins catching the spotlight like they know this moment is ours.

This is it. My time to shine. My chance to just be me.

My body hums with joy as we move in sync, a perfect collision of ballroom grace and hip-hop heat. And for the first time in a long time, I don't just feel seen. I feel unstoppable.

Whatever is left of my nerves quickly fades away. Tilting, spinning, popping side to side. There's not a doubt in my mind: We're perfect.

The crowd hollers as Roman drops to his knees, and I press the heel of my glittering dance shoe to his chest. He looks on in awe as I deliver my lyrical solo flawlessly. Everyone's out of their seats as Roman jumps back up, joining me in a body roll so hot it could melt glass. And when his hands slide to my hips for my infamous sexy swirl, audience members scream so loud it seems they might faint.

As the chorus plays, Roman and I go into our combination, perfectly in sync. I kick when he kicks. He glides when I glide. The two of us flow like a pair of butterflies in perfect harmony.

The crowd goes wild. And I *love* this. I love *him*!

He gave his word that he would get me to my goal by Christmas, and he did. But better than that, he got me up on this stage, and I couldn't be more grateful for his unwavering support.

The music breaks. Roman hits me with that electric gaze. And we circle each other like a fuse meeting flame, daring the room to watch us burn.

He nods—barely—but I feel it. The question in his eyes: *You ready?*
I lift my chin. *Watch me.*

The music swells, we close the distance. I drape my arm, press off with my toes, and... he lifts me—like I've always belonged in his arms. Everyone screams as we go back into the chorus routine, and the rush I feel is better than all the pizza and ice cream in the world.

We conclude the dance with our dazzling reggaeton spin.

In, press out, three twirls, and he lets me go...

And I spin, and spin, and spin until he catches me in his arms and lays a kiss on me that's much too hot for this family production!

My heart is pounding in perfect time with his. And the crowd completely explodes.

⁺⁺✦✦✦⁺⁺

"Maddie, that was amazing, girl!" says Griffin as we line up in the hall to thank family and friends for attending the show.

Her whole face glows. "Thanks, Dad."

Griffin's attention shifts to me on the video call. "And Laura…" But he stops as Roman slips an arm around my shoulder, being sure to give Griffin a pointed look. Clearing his throat, Griffin says, "Y'all were really good. I've never seen you happier."

His eyes search mine, unflinching. But when I say nothing, he lowers his gaze.

It hasn't been a week since I left the rings in Griffin's hand, but I appreciate him respecting my decision. Regardless of how reluctant he may be.

"Congratulations, Maddie."

All of us look on as Quentin—one of Roman's breakdancing students—presses a giant bouquet of carnations into my daughter's hand.

"Thanks," she says, the blush on her cheeks seeming to expand.

"Who is that?" asks Griffin as the boy heads off.

"Where did he even get…" says Roman, looking on.

And here I thought the girl would be plenty guarded by one father figure in her life. Now it seems she might be blessed with two.

"Gotta go, Dad. More people to greet." Maddie hangs up before Griffin can object.

"Maddie! Laura!" Daphne rushes over, kissing both of our cheeks, Gabriela and Bianca in tow. "Stunning. *Simply* stunning!" We humbly thank them for their compliments.

"And that *kiss*..." Bianca pings a suggestive glance between Roman and me. *"Muy caliente."*

"Yeah. We didn't exactly practice that." I swat Roman's chest with a laugh.

"Sure we did," he says, licking his lips.

Yana drifts over with Eli not long after Griffin's family has left. "Maddie, you were *fabulous*, girl! Who's your acting coach?" My cousin tosses her a wink, and Maddie giggles as she hugs her tight. "And *you two*." Yana throws a hand on her hip, staring down Roman and me. "I needed a drink of water just to get through that performance."

I'm still laughing when Eli tugs at my hand. "Mommy? Can we go for ice cream?"

"Well..." I wince, glancing at the clock.

"Of course we can," says Roman, plucking a rose from a nearby florist's bucket and passing it into my hand. "We all worked hard tonight. Might as well celebrate."

I cradle his cheek and kiss him.

"Actually," says Yana, slinking up beside me, "you see that fine man over by the water fountain?" I look over and nod. "Successful casting director from New York. That little girl in the tutu? His niece. He offered to take me for a drink."

I lift a brow, intrigued. With Yana's abrupt return to Michigan, the part in Chicago fell through. But in true Yana fashion, she's already scouting her next big thing. Girl doesn't waste a minute when it comes to networking.

"Well, don't let me hold you up," I say with a playful shove.

"Oh, I won't!" Then, gazing back at the dark chocolate man with his designer glasses and an irresistible smile, she says, "Feels like destiny."

I grin as she struts toward him like it's fate.

My cousin's off to chase a new dream, and for once, I think she might just catch it.

EPILOGUE

The sky extends in a boundless blue, and a cool breeze tickles my chin as I angle my phone and smile for the camera.

A few stray hairs, but I'll take it. The deal with my therapist? Three shots max. No filters, no picking myself apart. Just me, exactly as I am. But that does give me an idea.

Settling into my beach chair, I type: *Taking a moment to relax, recharge, and just be me. Don't be afraid to appreciate yourself and let your inner light shine. #MiamiBeach #EmbraceYourself*

My cousin Yana hits the like button before I can turn off my phone. Even with her busy life in New York, we talk more now than we did when she lived in Michigan.

Tucking my phone away before more likes and comments can roll in, I slip my Ray-Bans back on. I'm supposed to be wrapping up my vacation. But the gurgle of my youngest son's voice catches my ear as my husband treads across the sand with Baby Kyngston in his arms.

"Look," Roman says, passing me the baby and plopping the world's girliest diaper bag in the sand, "if I'm gonna be doing diaper changes in public, I at least want something that doesn't scream Target clearance."

I stick out my tongue as I tickle Kyng's belly, getting him to giggle and coo. In his little sun hat and swim trunks, the three-month-old is the spitting image of his dad, with the same smile and zeal in his gaze. At least he got *something* from me—those signature gray eyes.

I thought it would be harder on my body, having another baby after more than seven years. But surprisingly, I've had more energy since having Kyngston than I had with my first two kids. Therapy and dancing helped me bounce back stronger than ever.

Though Roman loves seeing me on the curvier side these days.

He glances over his shoulder as he returns to the seat beside me. "Nobody hit on you while I was away, right?"

The concern etched across his forehead makes me smile. "Maybe two or three."

Roman shakes his head as he checks me out in my bikini, a playful grin on his face. "You haven't even been my wife a full year. Don't tell me you're thinking about leaving."

"I'm not going anywhere, babe."

The two of us share a sweet kiss as our son gurgles between us.

"What do you think, Kyng?" asks Roman, looking down at him. "Will Mommy and Daddy stay together?" Kyng laughs, swatting at Roman's face, and he kisses the baby's forehead. After all my worries, getting pregnant so soon after the wedding felt like a miracle. Roman couldn't love being a dad more.

We're still laughing when Maddie and Eli come running back from the shore.

"Mommy! Mommy! Look what I can do!" Squeezing his hands together, Eli makes obnoxious fart noises with his palms, and Maddie frowns.

"Mom, will you tell Eli to stop being gross?"

I look to Roman for help as Eli cracks up laughing, but my husband's got a hand over his mouth as he chokes back chuckles himself. I sigh. "Eli, don't you have another trick for us?"

In a flash, the boy runs over to the blanket and grabs his cards. He returns, showing off his one-handed shuffle. Separating the deck, he presents it to us. "Okay, Kyng. Pick a pile."

The baby stares at the top of the cards with all their fancy designs until Roman reaches over, helping his little hand select one.

Eli slides the card out with his thumb and turns to Roman. "Go ahead and take a look." Roman does so while Eli turns around and lets him show everyone else. It's a Five of Clubs. After having him add the card back to the top of the deck, Eli stacks both of the piles together before shuffling again and cutting the deck one last time.

I glance at Roman, thoroughly impressed. He helps Eli practice most nights.

Flicking the surface of the deck with his finger, Eli flips over the card on top and holds it out to Kyng. "Is... this your card?"

Kyngston flashes a gummy smile, and my mouth falls open. It's the Five of Clubs.

"Whoa!" Maddie shouts. "How'd you do that, Eli?"

With a sly grin, the little boy returns to shuffling his deck. Even Roman seems thrown as he shrugs back at me.

I look on as my son goes to put his cards away, seeming nearly a foot taller. "You're getting better at this every day, little man."

"Just wait till I show Dad," says Eli, beaming with pride.

For the millionth time, I thank God that his father survived that car accident with no major injuries. Despite his flaws, his children still need him in their lives.

Griffin and I settled on reducing his custody of the kids to one weekend a month. It fits his schedule better, and honestly, keeps my stress low. He can still plan outings whenever he wants, but the kids know where home is. We even have him over for dinner occasionally. He and Roman might not be best buds, but they get along fine these days. Last time Griffin stopped by, I caught them comparing notes on custom fitness apps. Baby steps.

"Hey, Mom, can we take Kyng to the edge of the water?" asks Maddie. "I promise not to let him go." I look to Roman, and we agree it'll be alright. The girl *is* eleven, after all. Passing the baby her way, I relax in my chair, and Maddie carries him out to the shore with Eli at her side.

"She's amazing with him, huh?" says Roman, lounging in his own seat.

I smile, watching Maddie twirl at the edge of the water with Kyng in her arms. "She's got that performer sparkle. I still can't believe how she shined in *The Nutcracker.*"

Roman takes my hand. "They're already talking about her helping with the younger kids. It's only a matter of time before she gets a scholarship to that new performing arts school downtown."

He's right. Not that my daughter would need a scholarship. Money's never been tight for us. Plus, Griffin's working day and night to keep up with child support. But Griffin says it's the least he could do. Our family will always be his top priority. I figured he might float back to Vicki after the divorce went through, but so far, the kids haven't seen her around.

"My mom called, by the way," says Roman with a soft grin. "Said she can't wait to see the kids again. She's hoping we can drop by for New Year's dinner."

A fond smile touches my lips as I run a thumb across his knuckles. "I'd love that."

Roman's mom was the first to say sorry. She didn't want to lose another son. Not after everything.

And Roman gets her now. After seeing what I carried as a single mom—and getting some therapy of his own—he finally understood. Once she got to meet me and the kids in person, she was thrilled to welcome us to the family. She really is a lovely woman, and it's nice having someone to swap diaper-change horror stories with.

"And then, maybe we can get back to work," says Roman, eyeing me. "You ready?"

I peer into the clear blue sky. "Almost... I'm loving this winter sun." Both of us laugh.

After the success of last year's Christmas recital, Roman requested my help, insisting I'd love teaching hip-hop ballroom dancing with him. And, of course, he was right. So many questions came in, I ended up launching a social media account with weekly tips and tricks. Just in time too. By summer, I was waddling through life with a belly that had its own zip code. Little Kyng has pulled much of my focus since the fall semester, but my husband's great at watching him while I nap and sharing nighttime feedings. And though he makes it a point to twirl me every day, I love nothing more than standing next to Roman in front of a full-length mirror, dancing side by side. And I'll get to do so even more when we open our studio next fall.

"Seems I'm getting questions after *every* cardio hip-hop class," I say. "All the wives can't wait to get back to dancing with their husbands."

Roman gives me that sly grin I'll never stop falling for, and we watch the kids splashing in the waves. Their laughter bubbles through the air. And for once, I don't just smile. I feel it.

All the way through.

Springing out of his seat, Roman pulls me from the comfort of my chair.

"Hey!" I pout. "What are you doing?"

"Come on. Let's go enjoy this water!" He gives me a twirl and pulls me along, and I laugh as we join the kids at the shore.

Eli splashes around while Maddie encourages Kyng to stamp in the sand. And pulling me close, Roman leads me in a slow dance at the water's edge.

"Merry Christmas, Diamond Eyes," he whispers, like it's our secret.

"Merry Christmas to you, too."

He kisses me slow, like time owes us this. And when he pulls me close, we sway—just us, our babies, and a love I never thought I'd get to keep—as the waves curl around our feet and carry the past out to sea.

ACKNOWLEDGMENTS

First and always, to my Heavenly Father. My faithful, loving Savior, Jesus Christ. The *literal* Author and Finisher of my faith. Thank You for staying beside me through every storm—the tears, the doubts, the silence, even Argentina. With You, I always bounce back. You saved me in every way imaginable.

The Dance was born out of a moment on social media. A plus-sized woman dancing with so much joy and freedom that it stopped me in my tracks. It reminded me of my own days in dance school and college, when people were somehow surprised that a girl like me could move like that. Even after losing and maintaining a 100-pound weight loss, I still struggled to see myself the way others did. That tension? That ache to feel worthy in your own skin? It became Laura's story. And it became mine.

Writing this book cracked me open in ways I didn't expect. I started out thinking I was writing a love story about a woman trying to win back her ex. But somewhere along the way, it became something far more honest: a story about falling in love with yourself. Laura forced me to confront my own self-doubt, the negative talk in my head, the fear that maybe I couldn't actually do the thing I dreamed of. But chapter by chapter, I found healing. I found hope. And I hope you do, too.

To Jaime, my amazing husband, my real-life book boyfriend: thank you for being my cheerleader, partner, alpha reader, and the steady presence I didn't know I needed. *Te necesito en mi vida.* Always. I love you.

To my beautiful children, Jonathan and Isabella: you gave me space to dream. Thank you for your patience, your jokes, your artwork, and your hugs when I needed them most. Bella, your promo ideas and cover sketches lit up my world. Jonathan, your joy is contagious. I hope both of you chase your dreams fiercely.

Mom, thank you for watching the kids, encouraging me, and reading this book in its earliest stages. And of course, for giving me life.

To my big sister, Latrice: thank you for the ways you've shown up over the years. Your thoughtful feedback on my early manuscripts stayed with me, and I truly appreciate the support you offered when I was just starting to find my voice.

To my street team and homegirls, y'all hyped this book like I was already on a bestseller list. You made me feel like a star when nobody knew my name. To all my Black Girl Bookworms who had my back during the query trenches, when I walked away to pursue indie publishing, and beyond—thank you for riding with me.

Jemiscoe Chambers-Black, thank you for believing in this story back when I was chasing traditional publishing and for supporting me when I stepped out on faith to go indie.

Raquel Brown, thank you for sticking with me through draft after draft, career pivots, and everything in between. You're not just an editor. You're a rock.

Katharine Bost, thank you for being a brilliant editor and passionate partner in this work. Your "hahahahaha" comments and book-club-style reflections made me laugh, cry, and feel seen. I can't wait for all the books we'll bring into the world together.

Gowtham Thangaraj, thank you for capturing Laura's story in such stunning visual form. Jose Pepito Jr., thank you for laying out every word with precision and care. Abby Hale, thank you for your eagle-eyed proofreading and precision.

To my beta readers, early critique partners, and loyal readers at Substack and Threads, your encouragement carried me through every rewrite and 2AM editing session. You remind me why I do this.

To every woman who's ever been told she had to shrink to be seen: this book is for you.

Thank you for reading. Thank you for feeling. Thank you for dancing.

And to the girl I used to be, thank you for not giving up.

With love,
Kimberly R. Vargas

LAURA AND ROMAN'S DANCE PLAYLIST

1. **"The Way You Move"** – Outkast (feat. Sleepy Brown)
2. **"Move Your Feet"** – Junior Senior
3. **"Lose Control"** – Missy Elliott (feat. Ciara & Fat Man Scoop)
4. **"Swalla"** – Jason Derulo (feat. Nicki Minaj & Ty Dolla $ign)
5. **"I Like It"** – Cardi B, Bad Bunny & J Balvin
6. **"Push It"** (Club Mix) – Salt-N-Pepa
7. **"1, 2 Step"** – Ciara (feat. Missy Elliott)
8. **"Electricity"** – Silk City & Dua Lipa (feat. Diplo & Marc Ronson)
9. **"A Song for You"** – Donny Hathaway
10. **"Caught Up"** – Usher
11. **"Gonna Make You Sweat (Everybody Dance Now)"** – C+C Music Factory

THE DANCE BOOK CLUB DISCUSSION GUIDE

General Discussion Questions

1. What were your first impressions of Laura? How did your perception of her change over time?
2. Roman challenges Laura in ways that are both uncomfortable and healing. How did you feel about their dynamic?
3. Laura's journey focuses on self-worth and rediscovery. Which moments in her growth felt most relatable to you?
4. There is a difference between someone seeing your potential and someone loving you as you are. How does *The Dance* explore that difference?
5. Griffin is not the stereotypical villain. What are your thoughts on him by the end of the book?
6. The dance class becomes a place of healing. How do movement and community help Laura reclaim herself?

Healing Circle Reflection Questions

1. Have you ever struggled to believe you were worthy of love or good things? What shaped those beliefs?

2. What parts of your identity have you had to reclaim after being overlooked or silenced?

3. How do you speak to yourself on hard days? What words or truth do you need instead?

4. What would it look like to choose yourself in this season of your life?

Reflective Prompts for Deeper Conversation

1. When was the last time you did something just for you?

2. Have you ever gone through a "separation season" in your life? Not just in marriage, but in friendship, purpose, or identity?

3. What role does movement, dance, or creative expression play in how you process emotions or rebuild confidence?

Bonus Fun

- **Dream Cast:** Who would you cast as Laura and Roman in a screen adaptation?

- **Character Pairings:** Which character in the book reminded you of someone in your own life?

- **Post-Book Ritual:** Try doing something joyful and embodied—like dancing around your kitchen, lighting a candle, or journaling what you're reclaiming right now.

CONNECT WITH KIM

Thank you so much for reading *The Dance*! I hope Laura and Roman's journey touched your heart and reminded you that healing doesn't make you soft. It makes you unstoppable.

If you'd like to stay connected and keep up with my latest stories, behind-the-scenes reflections, and upcoming releases, here's where to find me:

Join my newsletter:
Get exclusive updates, bonus content, and new chapter drops from my serialized fiction
Subscribe at: kvargasauthor.substack.com

Read more of my work:
Check out *Fallin' for the Fame*—a flirty, messy, Hollywood romcom with all the heart and heat.
Available now on Substack.

Follow my weekly Fiction Threads and reflections
I share love notes, healing-centered advice, and serial short fiction about rediscovery and the kind of love that sees you clearly.
Find me on Threads: @kvargasauthor

Follow me online:

Instagram + Threads + TikTok + Substack: @kvargasauthor

Website: www.kimberlyrvargas.com

I love hearing from readers. If this story moved you, feel free to tag me, message me, or just say hi.

ABOUT THE AUTHOR

Kimberly R. Vargas is a contemporary romance and women's fiction author who writes soulful stories about love, heartbreak, and second chances. She's the creator and voice of *The Next Chapter*, an audio newsletter devoted to healing and hope through storytelling. Her work centers captivating women of color who find joy against all odds and the tender romances that help them along the way.

When she's not homeschooling, editing, or chatting with the characters in her head, she can be found struggling to hit a Mariah Carey octave or dancing in her basement. She lives in Michigan with her husband and two children.